THE KING
A GENTLEMEN ROGUES NOVEL

NANA MALONE

COPYRIGHT

This is a work of fiction. Names, characters, places, and incidents either are the product of the author's imagination or are used fictitiously, and any resemblance to actual persons living or dead, business establishments, events, or locales, is entirely coincidental.

The King, Book 1 in the Gentlemen Rogues Series

COPYRIGHT © 2022 by Nana Malone

Cover Art by Najla Qambar

Edited by Angie Ramey, Michele Fight, and Regina Kaye

Published in the United States of America

1

SAFFRON

IT WASN'T LIKE I was sneaking out.

I was a grown adult, and I could do what I wanted.

Except it was midnight, and I was sneaking around the back of the property. The moon hung low in the sky, brightening up the whole side of the gardens and expansive rolling hills, bathing the grounds, and subsequently me, in bright light.

Shit.

When I told Tabs I would handle the midnight run down to the shops three kilometers away to get ice cream, I hadn't wanted to risk going out the front in the likelihood that my brother would see me, stop me, and ask me a whole slew of questions I didn't feel like answering.

Big brother Gabe had all kinds of rules about my presence on the compound. Which was bullshit, because dammit, I was a grown ass adult.

So really, he was forcing my hand.

You could just move out.

I could, but that would be surrender. Besides, the enormous

compound that was the Gentlemen Rogues headquarters was my home. So for now, I'd stay subversive.

Dressed in all black, I kept to the shadows along the edges of the trees heading toward Tabatha's car on the north lot. She'd left it parked at the bottom of that hill, and her keys jingled in my pocket as I headed that direction.

She liked to see if she could find a way to sneak onto the property. Every time she managed it without someone stopping her, she gave herself a high five and then properly closed up that security gap. We all had our oddities. I wasn't going to begrudge Tabatha hers.

When I passed the training lodgings, I crouched under a window by one of the hydrangea shrubs. God, this was ridiculous. I should be able to take my own car and come and go as I pleased.

As if your brother is going to allow that.

Ever since my birthday three months ago, he'd been a little *extra* about security. Almost as if he'd known what I was up to. I vanished off the security cameras for a whole four hours, and he'd gone mad when I came home. I'd gotten a lecture, and he'd gone on and on about responsibility. But I'd explained that I'd left the club early and gone to Tabatha's, giving our guys the slip. Needless to say, he didn't buy that for a minute.

I was twenty-two years old. I hardly needed a security detail. Hell, I was my own bodyguard. I was well-trained, almost always well-armed, and...

A rustle behind me made me hold perfectly still in the shadows. What the hell was that? Had someone snuck past the perimeter?

It was one thing to get out; it was a whole other thing to get in. I reached for my phone, ready to make an SOS call if needed. And just as I turned my attention back to my original target, a hand clamped over my mouth and a hard body jerked me up. My body went ice cold and burning hot all at once.

I struggled against the hold, and a very male voice behind me whispered in my ear. "Hold tight. I don't want to hurt you."

Hurt me? The fuck? I was going to hurt him.

I slapped my hand back toward the easy target, his groin. But he blocked it, which left me few other avenues. I clamped both hands on the hand that was covering mine, peeled it down just enough to get my teeth free, and then bit him with every ounce of pressure in my mouth. With a muffled curse, he groaned and released me, pitching me forward.

I stumbled, but then I caught my balance and whipped around.

I couldn't see him well in the dark, but he was big. Taller than my five-foot-eight frame at least. Was he familiar?

"You don't want to do this," I warned.

"Are you sure? Seems like I'm about to enjoy dragging you in."

His voice was low and smooth. It sounded like whiskey pouring over rocks, and I could almost see that sort of amberish smoke coming off a solitary ice cube in a glass. Holy hell. Why did he feel familiar?

"Dixon, is that you?" Ryan Dixon had been a recruit a year ago, and he'd flirted relentlessly, despite the Rogues no-dating rule. He'd been kicked out of training for making unwanted advances toward a female recruit.

"I don't know who the fuck Dixon is, but I know *you're* in trouble."

"Oh, you think so?"

He lunged for me, and I turned out of the way, sending a strike straight to his throat that sent him sprawling. I was on him in a flash, trying to get him in a headlock. Unfortunately, I didn't have any purchase, so he stood easily, lifting me with him and backing me up against the wall of one of the training facilities. Since no one came running out, I assumed it was empty.

Fuck. Fuck. Fuck. Fuck.

He tried to dislodge me, but I had my arms locked around him. My legs as well. With a grunt, he crashed me back against the wall, and I gnashed my teeth, feeling my spine rattle.

Who the fuck was he?

He smelled good.

Sandalwood and male. Familiar. Like a song that was just on the tip of my tongue but I couldn't grasp.

Luckily for me, he started to sag from the lack of oxygen. He sank to the ground and then pitched forward. I held on for another second. I didn't want to kill him. I just wanted him to pass the fuck out.

I released my arms, unlocked my legs, and climbed off him. But not quickly enough. His arm snatched out, grabbed me by the ankle, and tugged me down. He rolled on top of me, and we struggled.

"What the fuck?"

Again, a hand clamped over my mouth. The moonlight gave me little to go on in terms of his identity. His hair was inky dark, slightly curly, with a lock falling on his brow as he loomed over me. Suddenly, a tingle of awareness skipped my spine.

I *knew* him.

No. God, no.

He was still for a second, and then he laughed.

Out loud. Head thrown back. And even though I couldn't see his face, I knew his laugh would be rich and warm, which turned my insides into a pooling puddle of need. I *knew* that laugh.

He eased his weight off me a little while clamping both my hands above my head as his hands roamed over me.

"Just what the fuck do you think you're doing? I will scream, and so help me God, if you touch me—"

"Sweetheart, I like my women *willing*. And while you are stunning, I generally like women who *want* to climb into my bed. I'm just checking you for weapons. Who are you? What did you take?"

Who the fuck did he think I was? He knew me. "I didn't *take* anything," I muttered.

"Lay still."

"I'm sure you've asked many girls to lay still, but I won't be one of them." I lifted my hips and rolled him over. His eyes widened in surprise just before I delivered an elbow to his jaw, wrenching my wrist from his hold. He growled, but by then I'd already adjusted my legs and pinned down his arms.

"Who are you?"

Why was he asking who I was? Did he just assume I was undercover?

I pulled the small knife that I always had strapped to my lower back and held it at his jugular. "You first."

"My name is Lachlan King."

What. The. Actual. Fuck.

He said it without hesitation. What the hell was he doing here? Was he an agent? Had he always been an agent? Had he played me?

Of course he played you.

Three months ago when I'd met him and slept with him, I was nothing more than his mark.

Lachlan

WHO THE HELL was this woman?

She was tall. Five-eight maybe? And she was strong. A couple of hits she'd gotten on me were going to leave bruises. And she was wily, staying in the shadows.

She snapped out a kick and I grabbed her foot. I was probably more surprised than she was because I lost focus for just a moment thinking about how delicate she was. And then my world rotated. My feet were kicked out from under me, and all I saw was night sky and stars as I whooshed out, "Motherfucker."

"You kiss your mother with that mouth?"

What the fuck? Was she taunting me?

The hum of electricity under my skin made me smile. What the hell was wrong with me? Had I been so long without a woman that now any contact was getting me hard? "Nope. But I kissed *your* mother with it."

Oh yeah, mature. Real fucking mature.

She laughed. "Oh God, you're into necrophilia? My mum's dead."

The way she said it, the hollowness in her voice, made me realize I'd hit a nerve. A painful one. And the guilt ate at me, even as I quickly rolled. I tucked my right leg under my left, placed my hands down to lift myself, and sprang back up into a defensive position.

What the hell was going on here? I'd heard her outside my fucking window.

The residences, as they called them, were guest houses dotted along the property. Each one with three bedrooms. Mine was on the north side of the property. I shared it with Saint, my flatmate for the duration of this adventure. There was also an empty room, and if she'd been on that side of the guest residence, I wouldn't have heard her. But she'd been right under my fucking window, so I'd gone looking.

When I arrived three months ago, I'd made my escape

attempts. More than once. But I lacked the skill set to actually escape. It was after my third attempt that Gabriel Webb dragged me into his office. I wasn't a fan of his. Everything about him screamed SAS.

Okay fine, *prick* was what it really screamed. He was overbearing. Domineering. Reminded me of my grandfather and my father. Thought his shit didn't stink. He stared me down and gave me some speech about how I was never getting out of there. It was unnerving. He talked to me about Charlie, about how this place was something Charlie had wanted and had trained for.

I had to admit, it was a good tactic. It made me listen. He talked about how Charlie had wanted to do something bigger than him, greater than him. And I'd known all of that already. My brother and I were born with the proverbial silver spoons, but Charlie was always looking for some greater meaning. And I... Well, I'd been looking for some greater party. Charlie was the serious one. The one people expected to do great things. I was the one people expected to fuck up.

And you did fuck up, didn't you?

I tried to shake off the heat of shame, but I was doused in it. I was here because I had fucked up. And Charlie wouldn't have.

After my little heart to heart with Gabe, he'd called in the big guns. My grandfather. While I loathed my father with the strength of a thousand suns, I actually respected my grandfather. Not that he was warm or cuddly like most grandfathers. No, he wasn't. But he *had* actually taken time to get to know me, unlike my father. Some of my earliest adventures were with my grandfather. He didn't say much. He believed in leading by example, and seeing him walk into my prison hadn't sat right.

And then he'd given me the spiel. Most of it unimportant except for the fact that I would be here for a fucking year. One year to become a better man than I was. One year to get the training my brother was supposed to have received. One year to prove that I could be something more. Whatever the fuck that was, I didn't know. If I chose to leave again, I would be completely cut off. No money, no nothing. Those dreams that Charlie and I had together, all his foundation ideas and things he wanted to do, the things I planned to do, were over. I was in jail for a year.

And now, this woman was sneaking in here? Why? Was it a jailbreak? I hadn't seen other women trainees. There were some trainers who were women, working on staff, training us, but I hadn't seen any female trainees. Or maybe they were being kept somewhere else.

Maybe we didn't need the distraction.

"I don't want to hurt you."

She stepped forward then, and I felt like I'd been poleaxed right in the solar plexus. Jesus Christ. As the moon shone down on her ebony skin, I could see her amazing bone structure. The delicate line of her jaw to the point of her chin, the almost too full lips, the wide dark eyes framed by thick lashes, and her skin appeared so soft like satin. Dear God, something about her froze me, which was a problem, because when she actually physically came at me, I wasn't ready.

I was more in the shadows than she was, but she still managed to land a hit to my sternum that had me gasping for air, and then another sweeping kick which put me on the ground.

"Stay down."

"Why the hell should I stay down?" I pushed myself back to my feet.

She came for me again, and this time I was quick enough to shift my feet slightly to the left and turn, grabbing her by the waist with my arm around her neck. I didn't actually close the gap to tighten my hold, but I did plant my hand on her shoulder, so there was no wiggling.

Her scent washed over me, and I felt like I couldn't breathe. One inhale, and everything in my body went tight. I could feel the blood rushing to my cock and fucking hell...

I'd never been into this kind of thing before, but Jesus, fighting her was sure as hell doing it for me.

She wiggled in my hold, and her arse ground right on my cock as I cursed low. "For Christ's sake, just relax. I'm not going to hurt you."

She laughed then. Laughed like a crazy person. "Said the lion to the lamb."

Then she ground on me again, and this time I groaned. "What the fuck are you doing?"

"Making sure I have my target."

Her next blow was a direct hit right into my dick. She'd shoved her hips back, creating space between us, and then landed an open-palm smack right in the center of my balls. I had no choice but to release her, coughing as I went down to my knees. I glowered up at her. "What the fuck?"

I fell forward, too dizzy to think. The bile tried to rise up from the depths of my soul as I tried desperately to keep it down. "Fucking hell. *Fucking hell.*"

"I told you to stay down."

I'd fallen forward but then rolled over as I kept a hand over my balls. I figured it was better if I could see her coming than her landing a blow on the back of my head. But no blow came. When I peeled my eyes open, she was standing over me, a look of shock on her face. Lips parted, eyes wide. "It's you."

Her expression indicated she knew me.

"Yeah, it's me. It was my dick you might have just severed."

She stepped forward and almost looked like she was reaching for me.

I rolled away automatically, forcing myself to my knees. "Who are you? What are you doing on the property? Or are you making an escape?"

"Who am I? Are you serious?" She searched my face, and her confusion had given way to what looked like annoyance. Why was she annoyed?

"Yeah, who the fuck are you? Why did you attack me?"

"Me? Attack you? You're insane."

"Honey, I'm the one on the ground."

Her eyes scanned my face, and I locked gazes with her. Her eyes were dark. Soul seers. That's what my grandfather would have called them, soul seers. The kind of eyes that could suck you straight in, peer into your soul, and see things that you didn't want them to see. And I felt like I knew her, like I understood her, and I couldn't look away. Despite the pain in my balls, despite being on the ground with her standing over me about to do whatever the hell she wanted to do on the property, I couldn't look away.

My gaze dropped to her lips, and I had to swallow hard as a hit of blood to my groin caused another roll of pain. Fuck me. What the fuck was it with this woman?

All of our rolling around must have caused some kind of ruckus, because I could see the flashlights up ahead, and I nodded that direction. "Oi."

She darted a quick look over her shoulder and then back down at me, careful to stay just out of range of my arms. She was smart. Knew how to stay out of reach. She was well-trained.

As evidenced by her kicking your bloody arse.

She had to be a trainee. But who was she? I needed to find out.

She just completely bollocksed you, and you want to fuck her?

No. Well, yes, because she was absolutely stunning to look

at and she smelled incredible. Something with roses in it? But beyond that, I felt like I knew her. Which was ridiculous because all we'd done was fight.

My grandfather had always talked about how he'd met my grandmother and known her in an instant. This felt like that. Like I needed to know every secret she held.

Fuck, my balls hurt. The more I looked at her, the more I thought about her, the more blood rushed to my groin, and the more I regretted that. Fuck.

The guards were quickly approaching, and she stepped back.

One of them sighed once they pointed the flashlight on her face. "Jesus Christ, Saff. What the fuck are you doing?"

She put a hand up to shield her gaze from the flashlight. "Oi, Jason, can you take the light out of my eyes, please? What are the chances you're not going to tell Gabe about this?"

Jason shook his head. "Sorry, Saff, your little fight was caught on camera."

She cursed under her breath.

Fuck me.

She glowered at me then. "This is all your fault."

I had to laugh. "My fault? You should be apologizing to me. Or rather to my balls."

Jason laughed and then the other guard... What was his name? Hector? I'd only seen him a few times. He smirked at me. "Oh yeah, she put you on your arse, huh?"

"I almost had her."

They both glanced at each other and chuckled. Jason shook his head. "I promise you, King, you didn't almost have her."

I pushed to my feet and glanced at her.

She smirked. "I was taking it easy on you."

"You wish."

"No, you wish. How are your balls right now?"

I narrowed my eyes at her. How could she be so beautiful *and* so irritating? She was staring at me too. I couldn't explain it. Something about her face transformed from lively and heated to cold disdain.

"Next time, stay out of my way." Then she turned to Hector. "You might as well lead the way. If you're going to tell him, I'd rather get it over with tonight, so at least the yelling can only last so long."

Hector shrugged. "Can you put King back where he belongs?"

Jason nodded. And just like that, without a second glance back toward me, she was being led away by Hector. And my gaze, moron that I was, immediately dropped to her arse, noting it was just enough to overflow in my hands. Fucking hell. Why couldn't I do anything easy?

Why the fuck did I want the one woman I'd seen here who was intent on killing me?

2

SAFFRON

I WAS NUMB. Certainly too numb to speak or to understand what the hell was going on.

He. Didn't. Remember. Me.

How could he not remember? It was three months ago, a stupid one-night stand.

No, it wasn't stupid. It was reckless, yes, but it was hot.

No, I refused to think about how hot it was because he was currently in one of the Rogues bungalows. Which meant he was a Rogue. I didn't have a lot of rules about my personal life, just one or two. But they were necessary. Top of that list, no Rogues.

Also dating a Rogue was forbidden so agents could plug in to any scenario with no entanglements.

I loved my brother. God, I really did. But with mum and dad gone, he'd taken the whole *I'm your big brother* thing to heart. Adopted or not, Gabe saw himself as my only remaining family, and he was determined to see me protected. *Over* protected, actually.

When Hector led me into the hallway to Gabe's office, he slid me a glance. "You okay?"

"Yeah, I'm fine. Totally fine. A hundred percent."

He laughed. "If you weren't fine, what would you say?"

I wrinkled my nose up at him. Hector Alvarez. I like to call him the Mountain Man. He looked like he belonged on a mountain with his beard and muscles that looked like they were really ideal for chopping wood. He'd been one of the Rogues guards since right before mum and dad died, so at least two years now.

Like most of the Rogues, he was ex-military. He wanted to do something more. He'd been injured fighting for Queen and country.

But now he worked here. His specialty was security tech. They'd installed new cameras I didn't know about. Which meant sneaking out was going to become even more difficult.

We paused at Gabe's door, and Hector gave me a warm smile. "He loves you. He's just looking out for you."

"By being my prison warden?"

Hector smiled grimly. "After what happened to your parents, you know he's going to keep a tighter watch."

"Right."

I wanted to scream. I understood why he was like this. I understood all the reasons why Gabe thought he had to protect me. I understood that he felt responsible for not being there. I understood that to him my parents had saved his life. It just felt like I was suffocating.

And there was no making him see sense.

I didn't bother knocking. I just opened the door because it was nearly midnight and I wanted to get this over with as quickly as humanly possible.

I found Gabe sitting on the corner of his desk, scowling at Tabs.

She was scowling right back. I was surprised there was no furniture overturned. No blood anywhere. "Everyone okay?"

Tabs glanced up at me. "Oh my God, you're okay."

"Yeah, of course I'm okay. Why wouldn't I be?"

Tabs snorted. "According to your brother, your life was in danger."

I laughed. "From the trainee? I put him down easily."

Gabe winced at that. "No, your life was at risk because you tried to sneak out."

I winced at that. "Gabe, why is Tabs here?"

"Because whenever you break a rule, it's either her doing or as a direct result of something she did."

I gave Tabs an apologetic wince.

She shook her head. "Don't worry. If you're living a little, I'm happy to take credit for that, even though it's all you. Busting out? I'm impressed. Please tell me it was to go somewhere fun."

I winced. "I was going for ice cream at the corner shoppe."

She laughed. "Well, I hope it was worth it."

"I didn't make it far. Stupid idiot bloke caught me."

She laughed. "Someone caught you? Are you slipping?"

"He *surprised* me. I didn't expect anyone to come out of the residences."

Gabe tsked. "You know you're supposed to always be ready."

"Yes, I know. Can we get this lecture over with?"

Gabe scowled at me. "You're being cavalier? There are rules in place for a reason. They're to keep you safe. You think you can just go off gallivanting and nobody is going to notice? No one is going to miss you? You know better."

"For fuck's sake, Gabe."

Tabs clapped. "Yeah, for fuck's sake, Gabe."

He scowled and pointed at her. "You. You are the reason she's doing this. My sister was never like this. Never rebellious."

"Don't you think it's about fucking time she was?" Tabs

stood just as I sat, and she started to pace. "You want to blame everyone else for Saff attempting to have a life when you're the one to blame. You keep her in a chokehold, Gabe."

"Oh, we're on a first name basis now?"

Tabs just laughed. She was the only one I knew who could actually give Gabe a run for his money. I wondered how long it was going to take before the two of them realized that they belonged together. Or that they at least needed to shag it out. I didn't care which. Tabs was the kind of beautiful you read about in books. A face to launch a thousand ships. Due to her South African mum, her Italian and Ethiopian dad, and a British grandparent or two, she was 'ethnically ambiguous.' It made it easy to be a spy.

She could be white. Or she could be Spanish. She could be biracial. She could be anything. And then there was her body. As an agent, it served her well because men were so focused on what she looked like that they couldn't focus on what she was doing. I lacked finesse and guile when it came to men, but I made up for it in cunningness, hand-to-hand, and general caution. I'd been so shy as a kid, so when I started training, I made it a habit to just try everything. The more terrified I was of it, the more I volunteered to do it first.

I cleared my throat as Tabs and Gabe went after each other. Pointing fingers, pushing off the blame. "I love that you two think you have anything to do with my decisions, but honestly, I just wanted ice cream. And I didn't want to go out the front door because I didn't want to go with an armed escort, Gabe."

My brother glowered at me. "The escorts are there for your safety."

"Yes, I know. You remind me all the time. You remind me that Mum and Dad are dead. You remind me that I was right there, powerless to do anything but watch that plane go up in flames. You remind me I couldn't do anything about it. It's been two years since we lost them, and I don't want a guard everywhere I go because I feel like I'm dying. Jesus Christ, Gabe, I understand why you are doing it, because you love me or something, but you're choking me out. I need to figure out my own grief and how to heal. Keeping me prisoner here is not going to do it."

"I'm not keeping you prisoner."

"It feels that way. Do you understand that? It just feels like you are. And I know you don't mean for it to, but it does. I just want a little freedom. I mean, I could have taken out your agent tonight. You were nearly down one Rogue."

"I don't know if he's staying."

"I don't care. He's not bad. He's brash though. He thinks he knows everything."

My brother chuckled. "Sounds like someone else I know."

"I don't think I know everything."

"No, but you think you know what is best when it comes to safety. And I don't know how to hammer home the danger to you more than I already have. Drake Webster, right hand man to arms dealer Antonio Igno, bombed our parents' plane and killed them. And his son, Massimo Igno, is still out there, too. So until we have them, we have to follow security protocols."

"Fucking hell, Gabe. What if I just left?"

He pulled back as if I'd slapped him. "That's enough, Saff. I'm done. I'm glad you thought so highly of our trainee, because you'll be training him moving forward."

My stomach dropped. No. There was no fucking way I was going to train the guy I'd shagged who didn't even remember me. The world could not be that cruel. "No, I'm not."

Gabe laughed, and Tabs glanced between the two of us. "What's going on?"

Gabe glowered at her. "What's going on is the two of you roam around as if the rules don't apply to you. I counted on you. You're her best friend, so fucking act like it. You're supposed to take care of her. You're supposed to look out for her. She deserves better."

Tabs pressed her lips together and honest to God, I thought she was going to strike him right across the face. I stepped in. "Tabs is what I need. She's my friend, and she doesn't choke the life out of me. For fuck's sake, Gabe."

He scowled. "Effective immediately, Tabs, you are off active duty, and you are training. We have a new recruit for you, too."

Tabs glowered at him. "You're not serious."

"Oh, but I am. And Saff, your trainee, like I said, is going to be Lachlan King."

Tabs frowned for a moment, and I could tell she was trying to remember where she'd heard that name from. I hoped to Christ she was able to hold it in until we were out of there. I shook my head. "No, I'm not. Find another punishment."

"Sorry, but this is the one that's going to stick. Because I've tried everything else. If you won't listen, I'm going to put you to work. That way, you won't have time to not listen."

"I hate you."

He gave a sharp chuckle. "Excellent. I love you. See you for dinner in two days."

I ground my teeth. Tabs grabbed my elbow and started tugging me out because she knew I was going to launch myself at Gabe. And ever since we were kids, it didn't matter how many times I tried to go at my brother, I always lost. Why the fuck was I being punished now? I hadn't done anything wrong except try to leave to get fucking ice cream.

Tabs pulled me. "Come on. You can talk when you're both more rational. It's late."

When I reached the door, Gabe called out, "Don't forget. Training tomorrow, six a.m. And baby sis, you may be the heir, but I am running the show right now. The sooner you fall into line, the easier things will be for you. Lachlan King is your trainee. Make him good and make sure he does not die, because then it'll be my arse in a sling, and I will be very cross about that."

I turned to glower at my brother. "I love you. I always have. But this is bullshit, and you know it. Mum and dad would not want you treating me like this. I'll train him. But when I'm done, I'm leaving. You won't give me a mission, you won't actually make me a full-fledged Rogue, and you're keeping me in prison. Sure, it's a gilded tower, but it's still a prison tower."

One way or another, I was going to get out from under Gabe's thumb.

———

Lachlan

I HAD KNOWN I was going to be called in. There was no avoiding it. I'd expected it last night, so I'd lain in bed tossing and turning, waiting for Hector or Jason to come, but neither one of them did. No one showed up to get me until I was in the training hall grabbing breakfast. I had my croissant half way to my mouth when Jason nodded at me and angled his head. I grabbed my pastry and a bunch of grapes before running and pouring my coffee into a to-go cup. "I assume this means I'm being summoned?"

Jason nodded. "Yeah. You're being summoned."

I groaned. "Right. How much trouble am I in?"

Jason shrugged. "I don't think you're in trouble."

"Sure."

On the way, I caught my flatmate, Saint, working out in the gym. Our gazes met, and he gave me a nod. When he saw we were headed toward the main house, he leaned out the window, "Oi, mate, where are you going? We're training in ten."

I grinned and lobbed a grape at his head, which he caught effortlessly with his mouth. "I've been summoned."

Saint raised a brow. "Right. For last night?"

I shrugged. "I'll fill you in and give you all the gossipy details your teenage heart needs later."

Saint smirked. "You know you're dying to tell me."

Surprisingly, he'd become an actual mate. The first couple of months in here had been rough. I'd been lost and confused and shocked that I was even in a place like this. And fair enough, it was like a country resort where I got to live out all my boyhood fantasies. I got to learn to fight, and knife throwing was a particular favorite of mine. I learned hacking skills and how to shoot. It was like summer camp, except I couldn't leave when I wanted.

You just have to survive it here.

A whole fucking year though. How was I supposed to survive that? I was three months into what seemed like a life sentence.

I caught sight of two women further along the path. One was short and curvy. When she turned and started jogging backward while talking to her mate, I realized she had the kind of face that sculptors probably loved. Beautiful. Excellent bone structure. Her skin was tan, her auburn hair sleek and bouncing in a long ponytail. She was beautiful.

But my gaze was focused on the arse of her friend. Tight. Clearly in shape. Long, lean frame. I knew what her face would look like if it was sculpted by the masters themselves. Wide eyes that could bore into my soul. Full lush lips that looked like they were born for sucking—

Nope. Stop it.

The rush of heat to my dick was instantaneous. What the fuck was wrong with me? I didn't know her, but as far as I knew, she was trouble. So best to stay the fuck away because something about her was unsettling. I couldn't pinpoint it or explain it. I just knew that she was trouble for me. Besides, she carried clear back-off signals. And let's not forget what she'd said. 'You don't recognize me?' I'd been too focused on the pain in my nuts last night to really think about it, but did she think I *should* recognize her? I didn't remember seeing her before, and I would remember someone like her. Mostly because I hadn't been able to think about anything other than her when I got to bed.

They veered off the path before we even reached them, and I pretended like I wasn't watching, but out of the corner of my eye, I was absolutely fucking watching. It was impossible not to. Her movements were lithe, easy. What was she talking about? Was she telling her mate that she'd kicked my arse?

Probably. She'd seemed to enjoy it last night. Hopefully, Jason didn't notice, but I let my gaze flicker to watch her walk away. And it turned out Jason was stupid observant. "How are you feeling after Saff ran you through?"

"She did not run me through. I feel fine."

Jason chuckled. "Right. Saff is one of the best."

"Yeah, she's not bad."

Another laugh. Jason was like one of those blokes you saw in the SAS. Except, while he had the look, his countenance was relaxed, though I didn't doubt if some shit popped right then, he'd spring into action. Every bloke I'd ever met who was in Her Majesty's Service was exactly the same type, buttoned-up to the hilt. Hell, even Saint was that way. Although, Saint had a mercurial, playful side about him.

"I feel fine. She just happens to be good at hand-to-hand, that's all."

He laughed. "And make sure that's exactly what you say to Gabe."

I frowned at that. "What do you mean?"

"He feels, uh, *protective* of Saff, so when he asks how it went, what happened exactly, you tell him she's great at hand-to-hand, bested you summarily and then shut your mouth."

I frowned at that. "Is there something I should know about Gabe and Saff?"

Jason eyed me. "No. Just know that he's protective of her and speak about her accordingly."

I was led further up the path to the side door, and then we took the stairs up to the main level and down the hall to Gabe's office. I'd only been here once and never really desired to return again. Gabriel Webb wasn't a man I saw often. He didn't handle the trainees. He *did* handle mission specs, but I hadn't been on a mission yet.

Jason knocked on the door, and Gabe's voice was a low murmur when he said, "Come in."

Jason gave me a smile and said, "Good luck, bro," and then he made a quick escape.

When I walked in, Gabe stood and nodded at me with what he probably meant to be a half smile, but I could read the tension around him.

"Mr. King."

"You might as well call me Lock."

Webb's smile widened a bit then. "Fair enough. How is your training going?"

"Why don't you tell me?"

Why was I making this difficult? I was stuck there for another nine months with him. It would probably go better if I could just get along.

I took a seat and leaned my elbows forward on my knees. "What can I help you with?"

Gabe did smile then. And when he did, I marveled at how much younger it made him look, like he wasn't that much older than me. Maybe because he was serious all the time that's what made him look foreboding or like he should be in charge. "I just want to know how your training is going."

"I'm sure you get reports, right?"

"Yes, but last night you had a change in routine."

I ground my teeth just thinking about the woman with the braids.

"She was well-trained sir, but yeah, I'm not going to lie. She had me."

Gabe laughed then, and I wasn't quite sure what the fuck he was laughing at. "You took on Saffron Abott and you lived to tell the tale?"

"You know her?"

Gabe frowned. "Yes, of course, I know her."

"I thought she was trying to sneak around the place to break in, so I went out to see what the fuck was going on. It's not a big deal."

Gabe shrugged then. "I beg to differ. I think it is a big deal. It's the first time that you've fully committed yourself to being here. It's the first time since you arrived that this wasn't a chore, something to be finished so you could leave. You heard something and voluntarily went looking. Or am I to believe that you were trying to make another escape?"

"Look, I heard something. I went to investigate. It's not a big deal."

"If you say so. How did she bust you?"

"A strike to the balls. Not particularly fair, but as I've been taught, all is fair in survival."

"How did she get to your balls, King?" He held up his hands as I began to correct him. "Okay, fine, Lock."

"I had her in a choke hold. And then... Well, then I didn't."

He grinned. "She is very good."

"Tell me about it. Why haven't I ever seen her with the other trainees before?"

"Because she's not a trainee."

"Is she an agent?"

He shook his head. "Not quite."

"Okay, she's clearly exceptionally trained. Is she a trainer?"

Gabe nodded. "Of sorts. You're going to find out exactly how good she is."

"What do you mean?"

"King... Lock, I mean, last night you took a leap. You defended this place like it was your own. Like you are choosing to be here, not like you're forced to be here."

"You can look at it however you want."

"Okay, I will. I'm just inviting you to be more open. You're ready for your next phase of training, which will be real-life scenarios. Out in the field."

I lifted a brow. "You're letting me out?"

He chuckled. "Supervised, of course. You know the drill. If you make an escape, your grandfather laid out the consequences for you, I believe."

I ground my teeth. "What is the assignment?"

"Well, I'm going to leave that to your new trainer to explain. You'll start tomorrow at noon."

"I have a new trainer?" So far, we'd worked with several different trainers in special fields.

"Your new trainer is more comprehensive and will guide you through real-world scenarios."

"Okay, who is it?"

He grinned then. "Saffron Abott."

I groaned. "Is there a reason for that sir?"

"None except that I think you two can learn something from each other. That'll be all, Lock."

I ground my teeth. I wasn't sure why, but it felt like I was being punished. For what though, I wasn't sure. All I knew was that Gabriel Webb had a weird hard-on for Saffron Abott. The question was, why?

3
LACHLAN

I SHOULD HAVE KNOWN it wouldn't take Saint long to find me. I had just finished Operations and Strategy class when he came bursting around a corner and plowed right into me.

"Mate, there you are. Tell me everything." Saint bounded around me like a giant Labrador puppy.

"You are much too excited. Nothing happened. I need a refill on my sports drinks. Come with."

Saint shrugged and followed me, chattering all the while. "Well, I see you're still alive."

"Why wouldn't I be alive?"

His brows lifted. "How can you not know about Webb? He's a little protective and territorial over Saff Abott."

"You know, you're not the first one to say that to me today. What's their deal?"

"I don't know. But what I do know is that he's always watching her. Forever watchful, paying attention, zeroed in on her."

Their relationship was none of my goddamn business. And I liked it that way. Except, I couldn't help but ask, "Is she zeroed in on him?"

Saint thought about it. "When you say it like that, no."

That made me uneasy. "So she's not into whatever obsession he has?"

"Look, I don't know them well. But he is very protective. Barely lets her off campus. Unless she's with Tabs or one of the other Rogues, it doesn't happen."

But he wanted her to train me. So what was the angle there?

Saint had no idea what was happening in my reverie. "So, are you going to tell me what happened last night or what?"

"Mate, nothing really. I heard a sound, and I went to look. And there she was, all in black. Skulking about the place."

"So you tried to challenge her?" Humor laced his words.

"How was I supposed to know she was a ninja?"

"Mate," he spread his arms wide. "This is Rogues Division. Assume everyone is a ninja. Moreover, assume everyone will kill you in your sleep."

"Good to know. Anyway, we fought. She is..." I struggled to find the right words. "You've seen her . You know what she looks like. She's fucking gorgeous."

Saint nodded. "Proper stunner. That body?" He kissed his fingers making a chef's kiss motion in the air. "And just to note, I've been here the last six months, and there hasn't been a single trainee who can put her down."

"Why have I never seen her before?"

"Don't know. She primarily works in assessment, ops readiness, that sort of thing. You probably just haven't come across her yet." He shrugged. "And then there's her mate, Tabatha. That rack on her. She looks like one of those dolls my bloody niece used to love. Too full lips, the kind of eyes you picture staring at you when you're getting a blowjob. She's fucking well fit. The two of them on campus are one hell of a combination."

I didn't care how Saint talked about Tabatha. But I did care what the fuck he said about Saffron.

Why?

I had no fucking clue. The woman made me itchy and on edge. And now she was my new training officer. Shit was already complicated enough. I didn't need someone with an axe to grind determining whether or not I could make it into the field. She'd seemed irritated about something last night. Sure, I'd thwarted whatever plan she had...

It was more than that.

It was a feeling I couldn't shake. It felt like there was something under the surface. But what? I didn't know her, so how had I already irritated her?

Saint was no help, slipping his hair back and tying it with that tiny ponytail holder. "You look like you're thinking about dipping your wick, mate."

I flipped him off. "I'm not that stupid."

Saint grinned at me. "Sure, you're not."

At one of the replenishment kiosks set up all over the compound, I grabbed two six packs of vitamin waters. Saint grabbed a case of water and energy bars. We were just rounding the kiosk when I heard a familiar voice and I forced him to halt.

"What's the plan?" one woman asked.

"There is no plan. Gabe thinks he can control me, but he can't. He can't make me train him. The last thing I want is anything to do with Lachlan King." That was Saffron. I would know her husky voice anywhere. She sounded like she was always on the verge of saying something dirty.

The quick flash of heat that rose at the sound of her voice was quickly extinguished with a splash of ice water to the nerves. Saffron Abott. Of course. All the time I'd been here, I'd never once seen her before. And now I was seeing and hearing her everywhere.

Let's not forget that she's talking about you. She has no intention of training you. If she doesn't train you, you don't get out of here any faster.

Once Saffron and her mate continued straight up toward the main manor house, Saint and I continued on our way. My mate slid a glance toward me. "Speak of the devil and she shall appear... looking well fit I might add."

"And she clearly isn't a fan of mine."

He lifted a brow as if he didn't believe me. "What's with all the questions about her? Because it sounds like you're eager for her to touch your balls again."

My balls ached as I remembered the previous night. "Fuck off."

"Can't say I blame you. She's gorgeous. But I'm no fool. I see the enormous *Keep Out* sign hanging around her neck. Besides," he shrugged, "I like my balls... unlike you."

I clearly was a fool because every nerve ending in my body craved Saffron Abott. What the hell was I going to do about her?

4

SAFFRON

"OKAY, what gives? You're mad and justifiably so. But you're mad for more reasons than I can pinpoint. What's going on?"

I was marching down the hallway toward the elevator that would take me to my residence. My grandfather's house was one of those massive country estates like you saw on *Downton Abbey* or other period dramas.

To the outside world, that's what it looked like. Of course, it had been modernized over the years. There were several guest bungalows dotting the property, each with three bedrooms. They weren't overly big, but they were comfortable, and they housed our max number of trainees. Once trainees made it to full agents, some stayed here on property, moving into the main house, ten agents at a time if they chose to stay there. Most chose to go back to their lives until they were called in for missions.

Tabs was a hybrid. She liked to stay on the property the night before missions. She said it helped her get her mind in the game. The trainers also stayed on the property. There were ten trainers, each with their specialties. I had assisted all of them at one time or another, but I'd never had to train on my own. I usually helped out with evaluations, assessments for mission readiness, etc., but all I'd ever wanted was to be a Rogues agent. Just like my parents, my grandfather, and my great-grandfather before him. Gabe knew that, but he always said no, stating that I wasn't ready. While we were Rogues Division, there were other black site organizations that handled the weightier things that diplomacy and politics couldn't solve. We all answered to Oversight. My great-grandfather had been one of the founders of Oversight, eventually leaving to start Rogues Division. It was in my blood. After all, I was what everyone like to call *the heir*, but Gabe handled the day-to-day management of Rogues Division.

Hell, I was only twenty-two. And I knew he was trying to groom me and prep me to follow through with my legacy. Except no one bothered to stop and ask me how I felt about my legacy or what I wanted from it. No one asked if I wanted to be seen as me, Saffron Abott, more than just the heir. No one ever saw me as that. Every one either looked at me as Gabe's little sister, Saff, the heir, or the not-quite agent.

I was pretty sure some of the trainers thought I didn't have what it took to cut it. Which was bullshit. I'd been stuck in my own head for so long I didn't realize that Tabs wasn't following me. When I realized her usual chattering next to me was dead silent, I stopped and turned to find her back closer to Gabe's office with her arms crossed. "What are you doing?"

"I'm not taking another step until you tell me what the fuck is going on."

I sighed. "I'm sorry. Gabe had no right to tear into you last night."

Her brows furrowed and she rolled her eyes. "Are you kidding me? I don't give a fuck about Gabe. He can feel free to kiss my barely brown arse."

"It's not brown right now."

She laughed. "Okay, I haven't had any sun today. Besides, I had to pale out for the last assignment. He was a notorious racist, and I needed to get close, so I played it very Italian." She rolled her eyes. "Arsewipe. I hated that assignment."

"You got them though, right?"

She grinned. "Oh yeah, we got them. Weapons charges, the whole thing. We shut down his operation. It was so satisfying."

"God, I want that level of satisfaction."

"Well, you can have it. It's called sex."

I frowned and then turned on my heel and started back toward the elevator.

"Hey, I was joking," she called out. "What's wrong with you?"

"Sorry, I can't think about sex right now."

"You're still lusting after that bloke in the club?"

A flush crept up my neck. I was certain she couldn't see it, but I could feel it as I started to sweat right under my bra strap.

"Yeah, about that... funny story."

Tabs was all ears as she grabbed my arm. "Oh my God, did he find you? Did he text you?"

"How is he going to find me? I left him nothing."

"I don't know. The way that guy was obsessed over you, maybe he asked the bartender for your credit card information and tracked you from there. It's very hot."

"Um, that's very stalkery."

She waved a hand. "You aren't reading enough romance novels. That's how it works."

"That's not what I'm dealing with."

"So what's up?"

"That guy, he's here."

Tabs laughed. "No, he's not."

"Yes, yes he is. He's a trainee. That's who I fought last night."

The elevator dinged and the doors opened, and Tabs remained perfectly still, staring at me.

The doors of the elevator closed and I charged at her in frustration. "Say something."

"Sorry, computing. It can't be him. You would have known if he was a trainee."

I shook my head. "I don't know all the trainees by sight. He took me to his flat, so there's no way a trainee would even be off property. Even if he had permission. This place was real. It was a lived-in place. He had photos of him and his brother, and family, and other stuff. It was a real place."

Tabs swallowed hard. "Oh God, do you think it was a test from Gabe?"

Heat flushed my whole body in a rush, sending the bead of sweat rolling down my back. "No. He's not that diabolical. Him, willing to send someone to seduce his sister? That's... That's gross."

"No, not like that. Do you think he's testing letting out the trainees? We should find out more about him."

"We should, I agree. But, Tabs, that's not the problem."

"What's the problem?"

"The problem is, he didn't fucking remember me."

Tabs laughed. "What?"

"He didn't remember me."

"Wait, from what you told me, how could he not remember you?"

"I don't know. It was three months ago."

"How much sex do you have to have for someone to not remember you?"

"I don't know, but he doesn't remember."

"I refuse to believe that. He's fucking with you."

"No, Tabs. I saw his face, he was genuinely confused. He had no idea who I was. When I stepped into the moonlight, he looked at me like he'd never seen me before."

"Look, I saw him that night. I will go and assess. But I promise, it's not the same guy."

"Tabs, I had sex with this guy." I slid my gaze around because I was terrified that Gabe was going to hear or there were prying ears nearby. I stepped into the elevator and shook my head when she tried to talk to me, reminding her that the elevator was tapped. When we made it upstairs to the kitchen, I grabbed a couple of mugs for hot chocolate. And as I was preparing it, pouring the milk, she was still staring at me, slack-jawed. "No, this is... That isn't cool."

"I don't know why he doesn't remember me or what the fuck happened, and I don't know why he's here. It doesn't make sense that he was a recruit. I was in his house. Unless it's... Oh my God, unless he was a trainee."

Tabs started to pull back on her initial thoughts. "Wait, hold on... Except he couldn't have been a trainee. That was three months ago, and Gabe wants you to keep training him. If Gabe wants you to train him, it means he's not a full-fledged trainee, which means that he was cooped up sometime *after* that night."

"I don't know, Tabs. It's one hell of a coincidence."

"Maybe it's not a coincidence. Maybe Gabe does know about you guys and that's why he picked him up."

"But why pick him up and then not tell me, you know?"

"Your brother is a dick. I'm sure he didn't see any reason to explain it."

"Fuck, Tabs, I don't know what he's doing here. But now I have to *train him*, the man that I shagged once. Okay, several times. Point is, I have to train him every day and pretend I don't know him."

Tabs ran her hands through her hair as I started to pace.

"Hey, we'll figure this out. You and me, we will come up with a plan."

"What's the plan? Because I don't know what to do."

"Well, we have to find out why he doesn't remember you."

"Um, yeah, I want to just ask him, 'Hey, so we shagged that one time. You don't remember me. You made me feel like you saw straight into my soul, but somehow you forgot me?' It was a game, Tabs. Had to be. You know guys like this. I was a game."

Tabs squared her shoulders then. "I'm going to kill him."

"Don't bother. We can't have a trainee dying on our watch."

"Fine. I'm going to kill him quietly."

"I appreciate the sentiment, but Gabe apparently wants him alive."

She shot me a bothered look then. Every bit my bestie. "Well, we're going to leave him alive, but we're going to make him rue the day. I still think maybe it's a misunderstanding and not the same guy. But in case it's *not* a misunderstanding, I'm going to help you torture him."

"I appreciate it, but right now the problem is me, because I have to completely forget everything that happened. Or at least shove it down."

"You know, I still really have that conceal-don't-feel notion on lockdown."

I had to laugh at that as I pushed over her mug of hot cocoa. "I love you."

"Yeah, I know you do. As for your brother, I intend to make him pay for punishing us because you wanted a little freedom. I have to figure out a way to make Gabe realize that's not the right course."

"Good luck, because as you already know, Gabe listens to no one but himself."

"You let me worry about Gabe. You worry about your trainee."

It felt so unfair that I was being punished for a small indiscretion, and the punishment hardly fit the crime. I was being forced to train my one-night stand from three months ago. It really couldn't get much worse than that.

———

Lachlan

NOTHING SAYS *I hate you* quite like an arm bar around the neck.

I attempted to remove my would-be assailant. Sidestep, strike to the groin, another sidestep, twisting and angling the body, pulling the arm right where I needed it. Left arm up over my head, finger under the chin, push up with the hips, and assailant down. Strike to the chest.

Except when it came to the strike to the chest portion, I was slightly distracted by the chest I was about to strike. Saffron Abott, the most stunningly beautiful assailant I had ever seen in my life. So I hesitated. Which was my bad, because Saffron Abott was also one of the most skilled fighters here. And for such a little thing.

Okay fine, she wasn't little. She was tall. Lithe. Athletic. But still curved in all the right places plenty enough to distract. When she swiped out and twisted her body on my own, hooking my leg, I missed it. And then I was careening face-first toward the ground.

She wasted no time. She lunged on my back, using one of our plastic sparring knives and placing it against my neck so that the plastic would leave some of the ink that was on the edge to show that it was a strike.

And then she was off. Probably because mounting me for her last strike was too much touching for her. With a grunt, I shoved myself to my feet and frowned. In our training room there were mirrors everywhere, so I could see the clean slice across my neck. I was dead.

Motherfucker. What are you going to do in the field, asshole?

I'd like to think that in the field I wouldn't be distracted, but fuck, if I couldn't manage this, knowing it was a test and that I was being evaluated, that wasn't a good sign.

I'd arrived at Rogues Division three months ago, my life completely turned upside down. One moment I was living a carefree lifestyle. Sure, there had been some scandals. But then the next thing I knew, I'd been black-bagged in my flat and turned up here. And I was given the Rogues rundown.

The Rogues started a hundred years ago to do the work governments were too strung up to perform, blah, blah. Training would be six months, blah, blah. If I had the skill set, I'd become a Rogues agent, blah, blah. If I didn't, I'd be spat back out into my life exactly where I'd been taken from it.

That was what I wanted. At least it was what I *thought* I wanted, to return to normal. I'd gone through the motions, done the training, learned to fight, learned strategy, learned tactical maneuvers. I'd been in decent shape before I got here, but the kind of shape I was in now didn't come from the gym and a trainer shouting at you five times a week. These muscles were survival muscles.

The problem was that the life I'd had before seemed so far away. Another whistle dragged me out of my reverie, and I knew what that meant. It meant Saffron Abott had taken another victim. I studied her across the way as she stood with her arms behind her back, gaze on her next victim. We called him *Rookie*, Westin Rourke, and he *was* a kid. At twenty-five, I was young, but he looked barely nineteen, maybe twenty.

He'd only been here two weeks, but he'd already progressed so quickly that he was training with me now. His hand-to-hand wasn't as smooth or as good, but he was scrappy. He knew how to fight, and he was a survivor. He'd made his way through a three- year study course at Cambridge in a year and a half and only missed graduation by two weeks because someone had finally caught on to his con.

He was a grade hacker with a photographic memory, sharp wit, and the kind of smile that made people, especially women, want to take care of him. But the Rogues had busted him and brought him here because they were in need of a hacker, a good one, and Rookie was thriving.

Then there was Saint. He was affable. A real mate to me. Former SAS. But there was something about him that was hidden away, a part of himself he never showed.

Saffron was standing in front of Rookie with her head cocked, braid sliding over one shoulder as she tilted her head, studying her next victim.

Saint leaned over. "You keep looking at her like you want to eat her, and Gabe will have your head."

I shook my head. "I don't want to eat her. I want to know why she hates me. She's just a trainer, that's it."

Saint chuckled. "Yeah, if you say so."

I slid my gaze over to him and saw that he wore several of Saffron Abott's strike marks too. Across his shirt, through his arms. She'd given him the essence of a Columbian necktie, slashed from ear to ear and down under his chin to his sternum. Fucking hell.

Saint lifted his chin. "Yeah, she's savage. Why do you reckon she's not in the field?"

I shook my head. "She's certainly good enough, deadly enough, probably. And somebody told me she wanted to be a field agent, but she's always held back in some kind of way. There is a restraint in her."

"Eyes off her arse, mate, if you like your balls where they are. Webb will castrate you."

I scowled over at Gabriel Webb. He was in charge of the Rogues Division and gave the final word on which of us were graduating to field status, which of us didn't make the cut and were headed home, and which of us were getting retraining. He was the man in charge.

The whistle blew again, and I was surprised to see Rookie mostly on his feet. He looked at Saffron and grinned. "I'm alive."

She angled her head and shook it. "Not quite. You might want to check your back."

He groaned and turned his back to me. "Mate, tell me it's not so bad."

There was a slash mark from the back of his neck all the way down along his spine. I winced. "Aw mate, you might live, but you won't be able to walk."

He cursed.

Saffron shrugged. "Each of you made a mistake with me. Especially you, King."

I liked her calling me King. She could be my queen. And we could—

I slammed those mental images down, because shit, they were too vivid. Ever since I'd met her, I kept having these mental flashbacks. Vivid dreams of me and her in my flat and combusting in the damn sheets, over and over. And obviously it wasn't real. Because, well, she hated me. Besides, I'd never met her before coming here, so I knew my overactive imagination was going wild and getting in the way.

"What do you mean, especially me?"

"You hesitated. Your gaze was on my tits."

I heard Saint chuckle. Rookie just laughed out loud. And Gabe scowled. Of course, he scowled.

"I was just looking for the best angle to strike at."

She rolled her eyes and turned to Saint. "You pulled your punches."

He frowned. "You're smaller than I am. I'm happy to spar, but I just don't want to hurt you."

"Yeah, and you died for it. As for you," she turned her attention to Rookie, "You played it well. You played dirty. You're inventive, but you underestimated me."

He grunted and nodded.

"The three of you need to realize that out in the field the enemy could look like a twelve-year-old girl. You don't know the scenarios you're walking into. You've had accelerated training, and some of you will need more. Some of you will become field agents, but if we put you out in the field, you can't do what you did today.

I ground my teeth, glancing at Gabe as he jotted notes down. He gave us all a sharp nod and then dismissed us. Across the room, I watched our other evaluator, the curvy redhead, Tabatha Smith. The lads on that side of the room were having an even more difficult time. There was one female trainee though, and she didn't seem to have that issue. She was out for blood, and Jesus, she was a killer. Had no problem going after Tabatha.

Tabatha was smaller, quicker, and obviously, more trained, but her trainee was giving her a run for her money. Which was good, since all the men were distracted by her. We were going to have to check our misogyny if we wanted to pass this bullshit. If I wanted to go home, I was going to have to get it together.

Saint clapped me on the back. "Let's go get some food."

I didn't know what possessed me, but as I walked by her, I could feel Saffron stiffen, and I couldn't help but ask, "Any other pointers for me?"

"Work harder," she said.

"Okay, maybe something more specific? What do you say maybe we grab a bite to eat, and you give me some pointers? Or are you a robot and don't eat?"

Her smile was beatific. "I know you don't like being beaten by a girl, but you'll have to get over it. I'm just better than you are."

I blinked rapidly. "That's not what this is. I was just inviting feedback. You're meant to be training me."

"You *think* you're just making an invitation. I get it. But you don't listen, so why waste my time? You can't ruffle me, King."

"I do like how you say King."

"The only capacity you will ever hear me say King in is as your trainer while I'm kicking your arse and trying to make you into anything other than a billionaire baby with a bad attitude."

I stiffened at that. "Well, tell me how you really feel."

She sighed. "Look, it's not personal."

"It *feels* personal. Go ahead and tell me. Why do you hate me so much?"

"Mr. King, your mistake is in assuming that I think about you at all. I don't."

I could hear the words she was saying, but the way her gaze flickered to my lips said otherwise. And it made the blood in my veins run hot and liquid. I leaned in, not too close, but just enough so only she could hear me. "You like me. You just don't *want* to like me. That sounds like a *you* problem."

"My only problem is overgrown children who think they matter to me at all."

I grinned. "I'm wearing you down. Might as well give in, because everyone likes me."

"Aw, then you should prepare for disappointment. Your first rejection. I am so happy to be able to pop that cherry."

I blinked as she sauntered out of the room, and Saint and Rookie ran over and jabbed me in the ribs. Rookie was cackling.

"Oh God, the two of you. Why do you keep trying to rile her? She's stone cold."

"It's fun."

Saint just chuckled. "Maybe your ego can take that beating, but mine could not. You should give up, because even if she gave you the time of day, Gabe would kill you."

I nodded. "I'm not touching her. But mark my words, before this is all said and done, she *will* like me."

Saint shook his head. "If you insist."

I did. Everyone liked me. What would I be willing to do to make *her* like me?

5

LACHLAN

I watched Saff intently. My new trainer who refused to train me.

She and Tabatha were sitting in front of our current training class, which included myself, Saint, Robert, Maxim, and Rookie.

And now it looked like we were all about to get the training of a lifetime.

Tabatha stepped forward. "We are going to test your tracking ability, your ability not to lose a target and to stay on point. We will be trying this on the Rogues campus first and then in the real world. In the real world, there will be a lot more obstacles. But that does not mean that you can believe everything you see on campus. Saff here will be your rabbit. Your job is to find her before your fellow competitors. While you are allowed to engage in hand-to-hand, you will not be getting live weapons. No real knives or guns, but you will have tranq darts and"—she held up one of the plastic knives that we often used —"these. You'll each return and then your markings will be tracked with this." She held up what looked like a light scanner, which she turned on, and we could see that she was completely marked up with pop song lyrics. She had one across her back that read *Give me more*. Next to her, Saff snickered but mostly kept her composure.

Tabatha continued. "There's no pretending you weren't hit or marked. You just better hope it wasn't fatal, because you will be docked points. The goal is to catch the rabbit, bring it back safe and sound, alive and unharmed. Saff's directive is to make sure you don't catch her, but if you do, to take herself out. So you will need to sneak up on her and restrain her."

Why did my blood hum at that?

Rookie asked, "And what if we're captured by her?"

Tabatha grinned at him. "I like how you think. She is very, very good. If you are captured by her, that's an automatic dock. If she comes back with you in restraints, it's an automatic extra month of training."

We all groaned at that. There was no fucking way she was bringing me back. Saff's gaze flickered to mine. Was that a smirk?

Jesus Christ, she thought she was capturing me? The hell she was. I just had to be smarter than yesterday. She'd caught me by surprise. Fool me once, shame on you. Fool me twice, never going to happen.

Tabatha was still talking. "Saff will get a head start of ten minutes. Remember, Saff is one of the most well-trained Rogue agents. If she doesn't want you to see her, you won't. So beware of the path that looks too easy. I'll say it again... *Beware of the path that looks too easy.* She is very, very good."

Saff grinned. She packed on her gear and turned. "Don't worry gentlemen, I'll take it easy on you."

Maxim and Robert were laughing. Maxim said, "You're going to beg me to take it easy on you."

The urge to throw my fist through his face was overwhelming. Tabatha turned around to sneer at them. "I hope she hands you your balls."

I couldn't help the chuckle that escaped, and her gaze snapped to me. And then her eyes went wide and she had the same confused look that Saff had gotten the other day when she first saw me. But unlike Saff, she didn't say anything. She just gave me a sharp nod and handed us all our weapons.

I generally had no problem with Maxim and Robert. They were lad's lads. Generally good blokes, but I didn't like how they talked about Saff, so I was going to have to watch out for them.

Stop watching out for her and watch out for yourself.

We were all watching the timer. Saff had headed east on the property toward the tree line, and Jesus, she was fast.

Tabs stood back with a smile. "Did I mention she holds Britain's under-seventeen record for the half mile? I should probably have warned you. She's going to be long gone by the time you lot get after her."

Next to me, Saint rocked on the balls of his feet as he watched the clock. Two minutes. I double-checked my pack and then grabbed an extra bottle of water because she might need one when I found her.

Isn't that sweet?

I didn't fucking know. I packed it anyway.

Saint smirked at me. "You think you'll be out of breath, do you?"

"This is a test. I don't know how long it lasts, but it's probably always a good idea to have an extra water. I'm sure there's water to be found in there, but I don't know if it's drinkable or not, so I'm planning ahead."

Saint watched me with renewed interest then. As if it had just suddenly occurred to him that I might be good at this. "You said you didn't have any training, right?"

I shook my head. "No, it just seems to make sense. Besides, everything I've learned so far while being here has taught me that it never hurts to be overprepared."

The clock buzzed, and we all went running. None of us stupid enough to go really fast except Rookie. He ran straight ahead of us. Sprinting really. Which concerned me. Did he know something we didn't?

I didn't have to be the first in, but I did have to be first to her. Which I planned to be. I just needed these other jokers to stay the fuck out of my way.

Saint matched my pace and tempo, so we reached the woods together. He searched the ground and frowned when he found footprints.

"Did you think it would be that easy?"

He shook his head. "No, but I'd hoped. And if she's as good as Tabatha said, she's probably also a climber."

My gaze automatically flickered to the trees, but I moved further into the forest, avoiding Maxim and Robert. Rookie was already way ahead somewhere, rushing about. Saint put out his fist, and I bumped it with mine. "See you on the other side."

"To the victor go the spoils."

Which made me think of Maxim and Robert. I did not want to think about them having *spoils* with Saff. I tried to keep my brain focused. The further I stepped into the woods, the more hyperaware I was that I might be underprepared for this. I stopped and finally opened up my pack. Inside, I found a compass, the water, and a knife. I put the knife in the sheath at my belt and held the compass. That way, at least, I wouldn't get turned around.

Somewhere to my left, I heard someone scream. And then they went silent. Oh fuck. I didn't know what games these were, but it would serve me well to be on red alert.

I'd been walking through the patch of forest for twenty

minutes when a scent on the air caught my attention. Roses. I checked the wind and headed north where the scent had come from.

Wasn't she aware her perfume was giving her away? Or was that on purpose?

I was moving quickly when my foot hit something, and then someone groaned. I kneeled down and found Rookie. He'd been tressed up like an offering and covered in mud. I kneeled down to remove the tape from his mouth, and he shook his head. "Ugh, I couldn't fucking help it."

"Was this her or the others?"

"Her, fucking her. I thought I'd run in here and track her electronic signature. I was so stupid. She walked right up behind me and zapped me with the tranq. I woke up like this."

"Sorry."

"Another fucking month. What does it matter? I just got here."

"Sorry."

I heard footsteps to my left and turned to find Robert, who asked, "Mate, is she here?"

"No, she's been here though."

He glanced down at Rookie and winced. "Some of us just aren't cut out for this."

I expected him to move on, but he lingered. Which had me on alert. "Where are you headed next? Back west?" he asked.

"I want to keep going north."

He nodded slowly and pushed past me. "It did occur to me that if you're not actually looking for her I had a better chance."

I laughed. "Aw, mate you don't really think that's going to work out, do you?"

He launched at me, but I'd already pulled my knife from the sheath at the back of my cargo pants. He kicked out a foot for me, and I caught it. Just like with Saff the other night, and I dropped him, using the knife to ink a nice arc on his chest.

"Ah, fuck you," he moaned.

"I didn't start this."

He tried to roll back up.

I laughed. "You are already marked. Stay down."

"I might be marked, but I'm happy to mark you back."

"That's not realistic, because you wouldn't be getting up from that wound."

"Yeah, I would."

And I realized he had no intention of playing by the rules. I was aware there were probably cameras in here, so I was following the goddamn rules. I didn't want to, but I was. He tried to lunge and kick me off my feet, like a full tackle. He got me, but I didn't go down alone.

He rolled on top of me, and I delivered an elbow to his face, which snapped his head back. "You think you're so fucking good, King? The rabbit is mine."

"You wish."

"Have you tussled with her already? Is that why you're so eager? You want another taste? Maxim and I had a bet going to see if you actually just shagged her. If she shagged you, she'll shag the rest of us. None of us are as ugly as you are."

"You're not going to fucking touch her."

"Sure, I am."

He held an arm to my neck, but I lifted my hips and rolled him off and delivered a blow to his temple. He groaned then. I pulled the zip ties I had stored in my front cargo pocket and trussed him up.

On the ground, Rookie wheezed. "Jesus fucking Christ, exactly what is this place?"

"You don't want to know, Rookie. I was very soft when I first got here."

On the ground, Robert was groaning. "Ugh, fuck you, King."

"No, fuck you. Next time, if you're going to aim for the King, don't miss."

It was something I used to hear Charlie say when I was a kid. It was cheesy, but that made me think of him. I left Robert trussed on the ground next to Rookie. I didn't bother covering him with mud. Let one of the others find him.

As I headed further north, her scent became even more prominent. It was like I was surrounded by it. Where the hell was—

I didn't even hear anything from the fucking trees until she landed with a soft thud next to me. "Looking for me?"

I whirled around, ready with my knife. But she was already there, delivering a nasty kick to my chest, and then she took off running.

I had to respect her hustle because the girl was quick. More than quick. She was resourceful. Hard to catch. Throwing things in my path. But a misstep took her down, and she gave a small yelp as she rolled to her side. She quickly rolled to her back and had her tranq gun at the ready. She fired off a shot that missed me by a mere inch.

I scowled at her. "We don't have to do this. It seems tiresome. How about you come peacefully, and then you and I can grab a pint and you can tell me just why you think I should remember you."

She growled at me and kicked out her leg. It almost caught me. I jumped back, but then I lost my footing and almost fell over. She used that brief moment when I lost my focus and went full rabbit, scrambling away. But I was hard on her tail.

When I reached her again and grabbed her around the waist, she screeched and kicked. "Easy love, I'm not going to hurt you. I'm just going to put on the zip ties and walk us out of here. Do you understand?"

"Over my dead body."

"Sweetheart, this isn't life and death. No one has to die tonight."

"It's always life and death."

I frowned down at her. She bucked and rolled. It was hard to hold onto her.

I finally had to flip her over and put the full force of my weight on her. "Christ, Saffron, hold fucking still."

"Never."

I growled down at her, finally grabbing her arms and pinning them above her head. "I said hold fucking still." I secured the zip ties and then began patting her down.

Her eyes went wide. "If you try anything like Robert did, I swear to God..."

I froze. "Robert? He tried something?"

Her voice went raspy. "Why the fuck do you think he was looking for me so intently? I took his friend Maxim down. He thought it'd be great to see if groping me was an option. It's not."

"That's not what I'm doing, Saff." But the more she wiggled beneath me, the harder it was to make that seem like the truth. What the fuck was going on? "Saff, I'm not going to hurt you."

"Sure, you're not."

"I'm fucking not. I'm just going to walk us out of here."

"Good luck. Maxim is down, but you still have Saint to contend with."

"Well, Saint won't be the winner."

"If you say so."

I frowned down at her. "Let's get out of here."

She bucked her hips then, bringing them straight into my crotch. And my brain, fucked up domain that it was, offered up a very detailed picture of Saff naked beneath me. Same position, writing, calling my name, her hands in my hair, fisting them as she begged me, *Yes, God, please. More.*

I shook the imagery and lifted her to her feet. "You're not going to bind my feet?"

I shook my head. "That's not necessary. It makes it hard to carry you through the forest."

I started to frog march her out of there. We'd only just reached the edge of the clearing where I'd left Robert when I heard, "You have to tell me how you found her so quick."

I found Saint leaning against one of the trees. "I figured, when I found Maxim and he was down that someone was taking this shit for brains down too. I wasn't sure if it was you or her. From the looks of it, maybe it was you. But then, maybe it was her."

"Are you going to fight me for her?"

He shrugged. "Nah. To the victor go the spoils. You won her fair and square."

Saff frowned. "This is such bullshit." She started to cough. "Can I have some water please?"

I nodded. "Yeah, are you okay?"

"Don't do that. I'm not your friend. I'm your prisoner."

Saint laughed. "I see the honeymooners are still in love."

I reached for a water bottle, and Saff leaned against the tree, eyeing Saint warily.

He held up his hands. "He caught you fair and square, so he gets the kill. But I do wonder, how did you know where to find her?"

I chuckled to myself. "Her scent. She wears this distinctive perfume. I don't even think she's aware of it. You know, if this was a real situation, she shouldn't wear stuff like that."

She stared at me. "My perfume? That's how you found me?"

"Yeah, it's unique. No one has ever told you that before? Someone probably should so you don't die out in the field, since that's what everyone keeps trying to beat into us. How much we're going to die in the field and shit."

She shook her head. "That's seriously how you found me?"

"Yeah. How else do you think?"

She shook her head. I lifted the water bottle to her mouth, and she took a few sips, nodding appreciatively. "Thanks."

I met her gaze again. Those sharp depths were searching mine for something. I couldn't identify what it was, but I knew I could feel her searching. "What is it?"

"I'm almost sorry."

"For what?"

She sighed and then brought her head hard against mine. I stumbled back. She brought her arms up with a quick jerk then down over the edge of her hip, and then she was free. She lunged at me and grabbed my tranq. Before I could roll her over, she fired two shots, hitting Saint center mass. He cursed as he went down. And then she pointed the tranq at my chest. "I'm sorry. You weren't a dick, and I appreciate that." And then she shot me point blank with the tranq.

Lachlan

I TOSSED IN BED AGAIN. My brain going to the one place I did not want to go.

Saffron Abott.

Why her? No matter what I did, I couldn't help but think about her. The more I thought about her, apparently, the less she thought about me. Which was just bullshit. She always had an encouraging word for one of the lads. At target practice yesterday, she'd offered Saint a full smile, and it felt like I'd been hit right in the center of my chest. That utterly gorgeous smile had never once been trained on me. It was more than irritating; it was debilitating because I couldn't do anything about it. The more I thought about her, the less she looked at me. Not that I needed it. Fucking hell, I did not fucking need it.

With her being assigned as my trainer, a part of me had thought that would mean more personal one-on-one time. But with me, she was hesitant. She didn't talk much. More a string of instructions than anything else.

The question was, why?

You want to know something? Ask.

And that was what I wanted to do. But asking with Gabe Webb looming over us all the time was going to be a problem.

My brain kept trying to conjure up as many ways as possible to ask a simple question. What's your problem? Why do you hate me? Christ, I needed to get those feelings under control. The buzz, the hum every time she was near me had to stop.

Easier said than done.

No, I could control this. She and I were just going to have a conversation. It would be easy. Why the fuck do you hate me? What have I done to you? Did I shag one of your mates?

I groaned at the thought of that because that could have been anyone. I knew for sure I hadn't shagged her. I would never have forgotten that face.

What the hell? There had to be a reason. I just needed to know what it was. I could apologize for it and move on. Because if I wanted to get out of here, I was going to need her to do it. And it wasn't going to help if she wouldn't talk to me or train me, or worse, just blatantly ignore me. It had been two days of no words from her. If we kept up like that, I was never leaving.

What the hell are you going to do about our little problem?

I glanced down at my rock-hard dick. Fuck. That complication wasn't going away. Every time I thought about her, and oh

God, that perfume she wore... I should have complained. She shouldn't be allowed to wear it.

Except she's a trainer who has your life in her hands. She can do whatever she wants. Including annihilate you.

I growled down at my currently unwanted companion.

Get your shit together. We can't have her. So what we're going to do is pretend we don't want her.

Sure, that should be completely easy to pull off.

6

SAFFRON

No, I wasn't gloating about the last trainee test. Okay, I was gloating a little. I'd given Gabe my reports. Maxim had been dropped. That was one thing I could say about my brother. He wasted no time on bullshit misogynists, especially not one who touched his sister. I wasn't aware whether or not most trainees knew that Gabe was my brother, but the whole point was, it didn't matter. I could have been anyone. That could have been Tabs. Granted, I had left Maxim intact. I wasn't so sure Tabs would have.

If I was being honest though, I had been surprised by Lock. I hadn't expected him to find me so quickly. I'd dropped Rookie easily enough, but Lock shouldn't have been able to locate me, which meant I was slipping. Jesus.

The look on his face had been worth it though. Today's training mission was different. We would eventually have to work as a team, but first he had to find me. And I meant to make it difficult. So I'd chosen one of my favorite disguises, although it was difficult to hide the hair. My braids were long and thick, but with enough bulky clothing and a hat, I would be hard to distinguish.

As we lined up in the training room, the trainees looked ready to go, dressed in black, tight-fitted shirts. It was bad that I quickly noticed how Lock's shirt fit differently over his shoulders. When he'd had me down yesterday, I couldn't help noticing how well his cargoes fit as they hung low on his hips. I'd known if I lifted his shirt, I'd have found the V leading down to a very promising heaven.

Thinking about him is not going to get the mission accomplished.

Gabe pointed to me. "Saff, why don't you remind the trainees of how the mission is going to go?"

I gave him a brief nod and stepped forward. "This mission will test out your ability to locate your target and then work with an asset. We'll know we've been located when you use the code word, and then we have to make it to our target location. There will be agents in the field. Some that you don't know and won't recognize, whose main job will be to make sure that we don't get to the goal. But we have to exhibit teamwork. Your trainers don't know the final target. So when you retain your clue, you'll have to do the majority of the legwork in figuring out where you're meant to be, communicating the information to us, and then working with us to get where you're supposed to be. You are not expected to complete the mission. I will repeat that just so it sinks in. *You are not expected to complete the mission.* But the trainees who can get the farthest will be the ones that we take note of."

Robert glanced around. "Where's Maxim?"

I slid a gaze to Gabe. My brother wasted no time. "Maxim isn't fit for the program anymore."

Robert frowned. "He was great yesterday. I was told he was taken in for medical and then wasn't told anything else."

"Sorry, that's how it happens sometimes."

Robert glowered at me. "What did you do to him?"

"Nothing."

He looked like he wanted to ask more questions, but Gabe stepped forward. That was one thing I had to say about my brother; he brooked no argument. You had to listen to him.

With our assignments complete, Lock strode over. "Do you feel like giving me a clue?"

I shook my head. "No. We're working together today, but it is my job to assess that you are fit and that you won't leave your team in a lurch. So I need you to not leave me in a lurch today."

"It would help if I knew what the disguise was though. I guess, I'll just have to figure it out. You're not going to tranq me today, are you?"

"That depends. Do you deserve it?"

He scowled at me. "It was a lucky shot."

"If you say so. So far, I've had a lot of luck with you, haven't I?"

Tabs came strolling over with an extra wiggle of her hips, and I could confirm that Gabe was, in fact, watching. "Ready to go?"

"Yup."

"Are you going with acting playful?"

I grinned at her. "Yeah, it works every time."

"You would think along the way, somebody somewhere would notify the team that you were the best at hiding, but maybe not. Maybe everyone's pride gets in the way."

I laughed as we headed out to the changing rooms.

As we both changed into our disguises, I wondered if Lock would have a tip to find me. He'd be given my coordinates, a list of potential favorite haunts, and then set out in the wild.

For this session, we'd all be doing separate missions. The trainees would be dropped together and have to find their locations and work on their own. Once Tabs and I were dressed, we marched up to the vans and were safely sequestered away before the trainees were brought out and led to their own vans.

It took us about twenty minutes to get into the city. Once we did, the van stopped to let me out. Tabs grinned. "Good luck."

"You too. You have Rookie, right?"

"Yeah. He seems smart. One hell of a hacker from what I hear. Hopefully he won't disappoint."

I was led into the Bubble Bar and Cafe. During the day, it was primarily a cafe. You could get a glass of wine after lunch time. It was an upscale place that working creative professionals liked to frequent. A Rogues member owned it, so whenever we needed it, one of us could fill in for a shift while undercover. My role, as I liked to play it, was called Ron.

Ron was short. Squat. Bit of a gut. Liked to believe he was a lady's man, but Ron wasn't particularly tall. And while I was five-eight and that worked for me, Ron at five-eight would have a bit of a Napoleon complex to him. And that's what we were going with.

Once I was situated behind the bar, all I had to do was wait. I knew that Lock would be given my coordinates, and it was his job to find me in the bar. The real question was, would he watch for me to come in or be looking for somone who was already there? Thus far, I had done maybe three or four of these training missions. Only one recruit actually found me, but sadly, he didn't make it to the end. Lock was made of sterner stuff.

For the next hour, I served drinks, kept to myself, and followed protocol. The chime of the door dinged, and the hairs at the back of my neck stood at attention. Lock was here. I couldn't explain it. Hell, I wasn't even sure I wanted to examine it, but I was well aware that he was in the room. His gaze scanned the bar, and I could tell he'd easily dismissed me. He was looking for a woman. A woman with long braids.

Thanks to the costuming, my braids were pulled back. I had on a fedora, because the way I figured it, Ron would love playing a character, and I'd concealed my braids behind my back. I'd had to put on more layers and a flesh suit to bulk up my figure, and the braids had helped achieve that. I just hoped the silicone of the mask would hold at my neck.

Lock sat at the bar and called over one of the bartenders, asking if anyone had seen me. He flashed a picture, and the waitress gave him a warm smile, shaking her head. I also saw the way she eyed him up and down.

Oh, fabulous. She was hitting on him. Awesome. The low simmering rage hit me tight in the gut, and I wasn't even sure what to do with that emotion.

Focus, Saff. He's not yours. He doesn't remember you. And this is a fucking mission.

The ever so helpful Katy, the waitress, called me over. "Ron, do you have any idea where this woman is? Have you seen her?"

I glanced at the photo and then deliberately lifted my gaze to meet Lock's. "Nah, mate, sorry." I was using a voice modulator, giving me a nice deep baritone.

Lock frowned at me. "Are you sure? She's supposed to be here."

I almost smirked to myself. He was going to lose. It's not that I wanted him to lose exactly. Hell, I hadn't had any time to even do any real training with him. I just liked the idea that he couldn't find me. That was the game. At the same time, I needed him to find me, to be as good as Gabe thought he was.

When Katy left and I was making another patron's drink, Lock seemed to kick back and take a sip of his. Then he called me over. "You ever have a woman you couldn't figure out, Ron? But she was like well fit, you know? And you would swear that there was something between you, but just when you thought the two of you were going to hit it off, she ghosted you."

I coughed. "It happens to the best of us."

"Yeah, but this woman... I don't even know her, you know what I mean? But every time I'm near her and get a whiff of her scent, I can feel it. It's amazing. It sets her apart from everyone. It's a distraction, because sometimes I just need to fucking focus on something else, and there she is with her fucking scent, you know?"

I nodded absently, meanwhile taking a step back. Fuck. That was how he'd found me in the woods.

It was at that moment that Lock smiled at me. "I give it ten-to-one odds Tottenham beats the Man U."

I scowled at the code phrase. How the hell had he known? "Meet me out back."

Lock grinned at me and winked. Then I turned to Katy. "I'm taking a break."

She sighed because she knew break meant I wasn't coming back.

I went around the back, and sure enough, when I shoved open the door, Lock was standing there. "That was a damn good disguise, but I can tell you your first mistake if you're open to the critique."

I lifted my brows. "Oh, you think I'm looking for a critique here?"

"Well, I figure we're all looking to get better at what we do, right? It's your eyes. They're distinctive. Oh, and that perfume of yours. I'd know it anywhere."

I frowned at that. "Anything else?"

He shook his head. "Otherwise, it's a damn good disguise."

I turned the voice modulator off.

"Right. You are good," he said. "I can tell you're used to being the best."

"We don't have to talk about this right now. We just need to get moving."

He chuckled as he walked. "I have the coordinates map. This is where we're going."

I knew what was meant to happen. He did not. But I could tell on the route he picked to his final goal that he might actually have found a way to avoid the counteragents. I frowned at that.

"What's the problem?"

"Nothing. It's a good plan."

"We're open in these places. I need you to ditch your costume. It's been tagged, right?"

I frowned. "No, they wouldn't tag it."

"You'll forgive me if I don't believe that."

I laughed. "I see you already understand Gabe."

He nodded. "Yeah, so we can't go anywhere until you've ditched that outfit."

I rolled my eyes. "You just tell me where I'm supposed to be going. I'll trust your directions and we'll go that way. In the meantime, you let me worry about the clothes."

As we moved swiftly among the pedestrians, I lost my neck prosthetics in the garbage. Walter from disguises was going to have a shit fit. And then as we went, I continued to drop layers.

He watched me in awe. "Jesus."

When he took me down an alley, I halted and discarded the rest of my uniform. I couldn't help but laugh as his eyes went wide. "Jesus fucking Christ, you look like a different fucking person."

I pulled out the dentures, and the nose prosthetic, and when I was finally myself again, he whistled low. "Do we get lessons on that eventually?"

I grinned. "Yes, eventually."

We finally ditched the alley and started making moves

toward Mulberry Street. Suddenly, he halted me, frowning as he glanced up at something.

"What's the problem?" I asked.

"I don't know. Just hang tight."

"Hang tight?"

"Yes. Something's not right."

I frowned. Having this level of awareness was unusual for a new operative. He paused, studied the surroundings again, and then backtracked me. "Nope, we're not going that way."

"What?"

"We're not going that way."

I wasn't supposed to help with this part. I just couldn't believe that he was sensing the danger. He backed me out the way we'd come through the alley and then paused and studied his map again. "We're going this way. There's a building there."

"Yes, I know."

"We're going through it."

I laughed for a moment, certain that he was joking. Then he gave me a look that said he wasn't.

"You're kidding, right?"

He shook his head. "Wasn't Gabe going on and on about thinking outside the box? I'm trying to Keanu it."

"Keanu Reeves?"

He nodded. "There is no box."

"Oh, a *Matrix* reference. Careful King, your nerd is showing."

"That's hardly nerd. That's part of the lexicon."

I had to laugh at that. He pulled down one of the fire escapes and adjusted it for me to climb up first.

"I have to tell you, I've never seen a trainee do this."

"Which makes me feel like maybe it just might work."

"I'm not allowed to tell you what will work and what won't. You just operate within the directive."

He nodded and then gestured for me to climb up. I did, and he followed behind, telling me where to pause and what apartment to climb into.

He couldn't know that we owned the building. But still, he was moving with the confidence of someone who did not care and had a mission to complete.

We paused outside a window, and he said, "I was watching the front of this building for the last hour. It's weird. Not a single person went in or out of this place, which makes me feel like it's not real."

I lifted a brow. "Oh, does it?"

"Yeah. And if it's not real, that means Rogues Division owns the building."

"Okay, is that what you're going with?"

"Yes. So when I break this, no alarm is going to go off, and the police aren't coming."

"That's a lot to stake your mission on, but you're free to try."

He laughed. "Yes, it is." And then he broke the window.

The next fifteen minutes were a mad dash. He led me quickly through the apartment, just in case he was wrong. And then we ran through the flat, out the front door, and all the way downstairs. But instead of going out the front of the building, we went through the courtyard to the next building over. With my hand tucked in his, he led the way.

His decision-making was fast. He'd studied the specs of the surrounding buildings and apparently knew this building was the real deal. It had real people. He still didn't choose to go out the front door, but instead led me around past the laundry room to a side exit.

He kept checking his watch. Just as we reached the fire door, he paused, holding me still. All I could do was wait for him to make a decision.

He took a deep breath then shoved it open. Right outside

were a line of taxis, and across the way, there was a theater. We hopped in a taxi before some of the waiting theater goers.

I lifted a brow. "Well then."

"Don't be impressed yet. Something tells me Gabriel Webb is not going to let me make it to the top."

He was right. But I was curious as hell to see how he was going to work this one. Lachlan King had deftly avoided capture twice. When he'd double-backed, sensing the charged air, I knew for a fact one of the agents was waiting to nab us if we came out that alley. When we'd gone inside the flat instead of going through the front door, we'd gone off the side, and across the courtyard. That was wise because there was someone waiting at the front door to grab us.

What was truly astonishing was his timing. He'd been given specs for the mission. He'd studied the area around it and used it to his own advantage.

I hated to admit it, but Gabe was right. He was good. The real question was, exactly who was Lachlan King? And how was it that the one man I'd let come near me in two years was also a skilled agent? I didn't want to give any credence to what Tabs said, that he was a plant by my brother, because there was no way my brother was going to plant somebody and let him touch me. So I was going to need to find out everything I could about Lachlan King.

When we made it to the target location, Lock leaned forward and told the driver to keep driving one more block. I pointed back at the building. "What are you doing? That's the way in."

He rolled his eyes. "You think I haven't learned by now that the direct way isn't the best way to go?"

I laughed. "You are a quick study."

"Come on, out you get." I followed him around the back of

the building where cargo were loading. "We're taking the freight elevator."

I chuckled softly.

"What's so funny?"

"I can see why Gabe likes you so much."

He shrugged. "You know, I'm getting the distinct impression, Gabe *doesn't* like me. Why do I think it has something to do with you?"

"I don't know. He likes you because you're smart. You think like he would."

"Is that a compliment?"

I shrugged. "It could be."

"Since we're locked in here together for another minute, you want to tell me why you hate me?"

I frowned at him. "What do you mean?"

"I get the impression you don't like me."

"You worry too much about what people think of you."

"I usually don't, actually. But I get the impression I've pissed you off. What did you mean when you said, 'You don't remember me?'"

What the hell was I supposed to say to that? "I don't know what you mean."

"Oh yes, you do. When we first met, I was unprepared for you. You kicked my arse and then acted like you knew me. Explain."

"You looked familiar. I thought you'd remember me from somewhere, but you don't."

"Are you sure I haven't shagged you?"

The way he asked that and the confusion on his face forced me to plant a look of derision on my own face. "I promise you, if you'd shagged me, you *would* remember."

"Something tells me I would absolutely never forget."

I rolled my eyes. "Let's just focus on the mission."

"No, tell me. What did I ever do to you? We just met. Or am I in the midst of some meddlesome weird game you and Webb are playing?"

"No. Gabe isn't playing a game with you. He's teaching you to survive."

"Are you sure? Because it sure as hell feels like a game with him."

"What are you going to do about it?" I asked.

"What? Are you one of those women willing to align themselves with the most powerful men around?"

"You don't know me."

"Sure enough, but I've seen women like you my whole life. You think he loves you or something?"

Of course Gabe loved me, but I held my breath because I realized he didn't know Gabe was my brother. Oh, this could get interesting. "Do you know what? You're better off when you keep your mouth shut."

"Hit a nerve today, princess? You know I'm still smarting from that tranq gun."

"Not my problem."

"If you say so."

"Don't be a sore loser. I beat you fair and square."

"You tranquilized me, and you didn't have to."

"How else I was going to get you across the clearing?"

"You could have walked me out like I was going to do to you."

"Sure, except putting you down was so much more satisfying."

"See? That's what I mean. You fight me like you hate me. Why?"

My mouth went dry. He hadn't moved. Hadn't gotten any closer. But somehow it still felt like he'd sucked all the air out of the room, and I couldn't quite breathe.

"Don't worry about it, King. You're about to do something no trainee has done in years."

"What's that?"

"Beat Gabriel Webb at his own game."

The elevator doors opened, and he took my hand. "Am I going to piss him off by holding your hand?"

"Nope. Because Gabe will know I'm trying to make an escape."

He frowned. "So you're really not going to tell me what it is with you two?"

"Other than none of your business, no."

"Fair enough, princess. I'll find out on my own."

"Yeah, you do that."

I couldn't help but be impressed. I didn't see eye to eye with Gabe on most things. My brother was a pain in the arse. Over-protective, overbearing. All of the things. But he wasn't was wrong about Lachlan King. He was good. Too good.

And just like that, he marched me up to the finish line.

Gabe looked up from the desk he'd put up in the corner, wide-eyed and confused. "You weren't supposed to help him."

"I didn't tell him anything. It was all him." I turned to Lachlan. "It wasn't badly done either."

Gabe stared up at Lock. "She didn't help you?"

Lock shook his head. "No, as a matter of fact, I'm pretty sure she tried to get me caught several times."

Gabe frowned at me. "He saw through your disguise?"

"Yeah. It only took him twenty minutes."

Lock just grinned at me then. "I think that's why she's really mad at me."

"Get over yourself."

Gabe stared at us during our interaction. "Well then, Lachlan King, it seems that I have underestimated you. Or maybe you have undersold yourself. Maybe soon you'll actually see your goddamn potential. No one's seen through her disguise in two years." He glanced at me. "Looks like you're going to have to change it now."

I scowled over at Lock. "Yeah, thanks for that."

Lock just smirked. "How no one has been able to see through her, I have no idea. Her eyes gave it away."

Gabe frowned at me. "Contacts next time."

"Whatever."

The two of them getting along was the last thing I needed. Lock seemed to be getting whatever he wanted out of this whole Rogues experience. I needed to know. Was he a plant by my brother? If so, why?

7

SAFFRON

I WAS JUST RETURNING everything to the disguises and weapons department when Tabs came out of the opposite corridor and snatched my arm tightly.

"Ow. What are you doing?"

"Come with me." She tucked me into one of the empty med bay rooms and glanced around the corner as if waiting for somebody to interrupt us. "We have to talk."

"What is happening?"

"We have to talk. You need to hear this right now."

"But I'm starving. Wouldn't you know, of course, Lachlan completed the mission. *No one* completes, but he did. So Lock is gloating, and then Gabe wouldn't even let me eat afterward. I'm hungry. Can we go get something to eat?"

She shook her head, practically bouncing from foot to foot, her ponytail swishing over the back of her neck and shoulders.

"What? Spill it."

She was vibrating so hard she might explode. "It's not his fault he doesn't remember you."

I frowned. "What?"

"Lachlan King. He doesn't remember you for a reason."

"Because, he's a dick? Or he was drunk? I don't know."

"No. That's not it." She reached into her back pocket and pulled out a photocopied sheet of paper.

"Is that part of a medical report? Please tell me that's not part of a medical report."

"I'm not saying where I got it or who I coerced it from. I'm just saying that I happen to have his."

"I don't want to see that."

"Yes, you do."

"No, I don't." I was worried about what I was going to find.

"Fine, I'll read it to you. *Subject displays symptoms consistent with an overdose of GHB.*"

I frowned at her. "Wait, like we roofied him?"

"Well, we gave him symptoms. We didn't really use GHB, but apparently the chemical compound that they used when they tranqed him and black-bagged his arse to bring him here mimics the effects. It's meant to be less stressful. Anyway, he didn't go down easy. He fought them, so they dosed him again."

"How many times?"

She screwed up her face with an odd grimace. "Twice."

I blinked rapidly. "What?"

"Yes, I know, that's a lot."

"But that's unnecessary. I've tranqed him since he's been here. He went down like a sack."

"Maybe because he wasn't fighting for his life or he trusted you. I don't know. But it says so right here."

I snatched the sheet from her hands. "What on earth?" I stared at the line from the doctor after they examined him. *Symptoms may include memory loss, fogginess, and missing patches of time from that period. Flashbacks may occur later.*

"Oh, fuck me."

"That's right. He doesn't *know* he fucked you."

"Oh my God."

"My thoughts exactly. So we can't hate him anymore."

"Oh, I can still hate him. He's *still* arrogant and annoying. And a prick."

"Well, maybe he's arrogant and annoying, but you liked him enough to sleep with him."

"That's not the point."

"I think that *is* kind of the point."

"Fuck, so he's not being a dick. He just doesn't actually remember."

Tabs nodded. "I figured you deserved to know."

I ran my hands through the braid over my shoulder, worrying one of the ends like I always did when I was nervous. "Fuck, he really doesn't remember me."

I didn't know why that knowledge hit so deep, leaving something hollow and empty in its place. Somehow him not remembering me now felt like I'd lost something. Like that part of Lachlan King who had seen me at that club, but seen more than just a girl out to celebrate her birthday, the part of him that talked to me about his brother and my parents, he was gone. What we'd shared was gone.

The irritation and pride I had felt for him not ten minutes ago evaporated, and all I felt was weighted down, rooted to the spot, unsure of what to do with myself.

"There's nothing I can do about it, right? Can't get his memories back. But I mean we should do something, shouldn't we? Are we going to tell him, not tell him, what's the plan?"

Tabs raised a brow. "Would telling him resolve it?"

"Well, it could trigger flashbacks." I coughed a laugh. "I was probably forgettable to begin with, and now we've just made it worse."

"Please, I wish you would stop doing that," Tabs said. "You are amazing."

"Sure, I'm amazing, funny, smart. But not exactly a sex bomb."

"That's because you don't let yourself be a sex bomb. And I'm pretty sure the way he looks at you indicates *he* thinks you're a sex bomb."

I frowned at that. "Do I smell weird?"

Her brows lifted. "What do you mean by weird?"

"My scent, is there something off about it?"

She leaned in and inhaled. "Roses. Vanilla. Something else. Lilies? I don't know, I can't tell notes of a perfume. I know you smell great. Why?"

"He was talking about it in the woods on that training day. He said he found me because of my scent."

She lifted a brow. "Really?"

"Right? And then today, he recognized me in my disguise within twenty minutes."

Her jaw hung open. "No one has recognized you in two years."

"I know. I'm annoyed. But he said it was my eyes and my scent that tipped him off, so I need to know if I smell weird."

She leaned back and folded her arms. "Oh, this is interesting."

"Why?"

Tabatha sighed. "Babes, you think I don't know you. You think you did something wrong and he forgot you, but obviously his subconscious hasn't. It's just a really shitty set of circumstances, and sometimes I think that you don't see yourself clearly."

"I see myself fine."

"Yes, love." She stepped forward, taking my hands. "You see yourself as smart and capable, which obviously you are. You're a badass. You are a Rogues agent."

"Not a full-fledged one."

She pressed her lips together firmly. "You don't need anyone to tell you that you're great."

"Like you said, I'm smart and capable."

"Yes, but you're also *beautiful*. And deserving of love. And more than just one thing. You're sexy and stupidly stunning without even trying. The fact that you don't even wear makeup is just like shocking to me."

"I'm not the sexy one. That's a fact."

"No, you feel that way because you've been dealing with men who aren't worthy and cannot see the inherent sexiness in you being you. Like it or not, Lachlan King saw it, and it hurts now that he's forgotten that night. And it's okay for it to hurt. That just sucks. But again, you didn't do anything wrong."

Hearing her saying that to me, I knew she was right. "It sucks."

"I'm sorry love. He's not just pretending not to remember. Those memories of you are actually gone."

My idiotic heart squeezed. He wasn't going to suddenly remember. That memory was gone and forgotten, and it would be better if I forgot it too.

Besides, he was a trainee. And Rogues agents weren't allowed to fraternize. So whatever the hell feelings I was having on the topic, they were a moot point. Nothing could happen either way.

Lachlan king wasn't for me.

———

Saffron

THE FOLLOWING MORNING, I was still reeling from what Tabatha had told me. It should have been easy to let it go and move on.

But here I was still thinking about it. About him. Obsessing over every whispered caress.

I'd been hands-off with him because I was hurt. I'd thought he was an average fuckboi who shagged so much he didn't remember me. Then I'd thought he was lying. Then possibly a plant by Gabe. When in truth, we had done this to him. Wiped me clean from his memory.

I'd been treating him like shit. In my defense though, he'd been flirtatious and I'd thought he was fucking with me.

I was so busy trying to put Lachlan King out of my head that I wasn't paying attention as I walked down the training hallway, and a hand clamped around my upper arm as another hand slammed over my mouth, and I was dragged into a medical supply cupboard.

"If you scream, we're both dead."

I glared up mutinously at the very same idiot I had on the brain. Lachlan.

"Do not scream," he repeated.

I narrowed my eyes, but I nodded. Slowly, he released my mouth. The moment he did, I spat out, "What the fuck do you think you're doing?"

"I could ask the same of you, sweetheart." He didn't put the requisite amount of space between us. I could feel every single one of his tensed muscles thrust up against me, and fuck me, my nipples were hard.

I swallowed hard as I glowered up at him. "You're in *my* house, arsehole."

"Might I add that's not entirely of my own free will. I heard what you said the other day about refusing to train me. My understanding is it's your job. And you just need to train me, or I'm going to die in the field."

"You seem to be doing just fine without me. You did so well

at your last training module that we don't actually have any need to train together."

The thing was, I had already decided to train him properly. Because he was right. If he didn't get refined one-on-one training, something bad was going to happen in the field. The fact that he made it this far was a testament to his natural ability.

" You really want me to go to Gabe with this?"

"Going to run off and tell, are you?" What the hell was wrong with me? Feeling him this close to me, his sandalwood musk wrapping around me, the way I could feel his warm breath against my cheek... How dare he stand in front of me looking so good while trying to force me into training him? Yes, I'd already been assigned, but I had planned on taking my own sweet time about it.

You've already taken your sweet time. And you are a Rogue. This is your job. Do it.

"Just tell me why you won't. What the fuck have I ever done to you?"

I had no answer for him. "How dare you question me?"

He chuckled then, the laughter triggering the motion of his muscles, causing them to rub against me even more. "I've tried speaking to you. I've tried being polite. You think I want to fucking walk into Webb's office and tell on you? I have no idea what the punishment would be for not following a direct order. I'm not a grass, but you need to let go of whatever is pissing you off. Did I shag a mate of yours or something and not call her back?"

I inhaled sharply. Well if that didn't just top it all off. "I really don't care who you shag."

His gaze narrowed on mine. He lifted a brow and smirked. "Oh, this is interesting."

"What the hell is interesting?"

"You're not as immune to me as you like to think."

A hot flush of embarrassment snaked up my neck, but I tried to cover. "Poor little rich boy. So used to the world doing exactly as he says. I don't work for you. I'm not your family. But I am the woman standing between you and your ultimate freedom from here. So maybe you'll think twice before you threaten me again."

He very deliberately shoved away from me. "I'm not threatening you. I'm just making it very fucking clear that whatever your problem is with me, we need to address it before it becomes a matter of my life or death."

"Tell me, King, what did you think you were going to get out of today? All you've managed to do is piss me off."

"Well, that makes two of us now. Start training me. I don't intend to die because you've got a stick shoved up your arse. The sooner you train me, the sooner I can get back to my life."

I went stock-still, remembering a conversation with Lock about sex. What we tried and hadn't tried. What we wanted to try. Not necessarily in that moment, but the kind of talk you have with someone you're interested in fucking again.

Lock had a habit of whispering dirty things he wanted to do to you as he was fucking you. One of those things was sticking that very large cock of his in my arse. The thought of it had excited me. But then, obviously, I hadn't intended on staying. And we had never gotten that far.

But now that he was goading me by saying there was something stuck up my arse, all I could think about was his hoarse, guttural voice asking me if I was a dirty girl who liked a cock up her arse or not.

I shook my head. "That family you're so desperate to get back to are the ones keeping you here against your will."

He flinched, and I knew I'd landed a solid blow. He'd told me his biggest fear was being utterly useless, and I'd used it against him. The shame seeped into my blood vessels, becoming part of me, and I knew I would not be able to take it back no matter what I said, so I clamped my mouth shut.

"You stay out of my way, and I'll stay out of yours. Nine months, and I'm out of here."

"Okay, deal. But you will have to pass on your own merit. I know that you're not used to that, but we don't play games around here."

He pushed himself away from me even further. "Do your job and I'll do mine." Then he opened the door and stomped out, leaving me alone in the dark.

———

SAFFRON

Just who the fuck did he think he was? That stunt in the cupboard... Just thinking about it had my core melting. Fucking hell.

I'd tried to interact with him as little as possible, only to have him full-on approach me and bitch that I wasn't teaching him. What the fuck did he know?

You're not teaching him.

Okay, fair assessment, but still, goddamn him.

"What's up, love?"

Tabatha's cheery voice dragged me from my reverie in the locker room as I sat with my face in my hands trying to scrub the memory of Lachlan King's hands on me out of my head.

"Nothing."

Tabs laughed. "Sweetheart, that is your frustrated look. You look like you want to hit something. What's wrong?"

"Nothing. I'm fine."

She laughed. "I know that face. That's the *I'm fine, but Gabe has ruined my life* face. What's he done now? Shall we kill him?"

"I do love a ride-or-die bestie. Honestly, I do. And thank you for offering to murder my brother for me."

"Anytime."

"But this time Gabe is not the problem; Lachlan King is."

She sucked in her bottom lip then and nodded while she was making big eyes at me.

"What's with the eyes?"

"Are you going to break down and shag him?" she asked excitedly.

I blurted, "What? Never."

"Oh, come on. You clearly want to. You wouldn't be so hard on him during trials if you didn't."

"I'm not being hard on him; I'm making sure he's a good agent."

"Then why are you mad?"

"Other than the fact that he appears to have completely forgotten that we hooked up, I'm not mad at all."

Tab winced. "Okay, it sucks, but at least you know now why that happened. He is a half-decent agent, and no one said you have to like him. Just that you have to train him. The sooner you train him, the sooner you get rid of him."

"He dragged me into a cupboard."

Tabs raised a brow. "What do you mean, he dragged you?"

"Dragged me, like hand over my mouth, the whole thing, demanding to know why I bloody hate him. Can you imagine?"

Her mouth hung open. "Are you going to report him?"

I frowned at that. "No. I'm not doing that. He wants to learn. And he's right; I've not been training him."

Tabs nodded, studying me some more. "Okay, so why aren't you training him? Isn't that the job? It's the punishment, right?"

"Yes. I just— I wish—" I sighed in frustration. "He looks at me like he remembers, but then I talk to him and it's like he *doesn't* remember."

Tabs frowned. "Do you know when he was brought in?"

I shook my head. "No, but I'm sure we can look that up in his file and figure it out."

"I have a theory."

"Okay, let's hear it."

She shook her head. "No, I'm not going to burden you with this theory until I have further proof. See if you can figure out exactly when he was brought in. Obviously, it was after your birthday at some point."

"Yeah, what are you trying to say?"

"Just see if you can figure it out. I'll do the rest."

"Tabs, you know I hate guessing games."

"I know, I know. I have a theory. In the meantime, he has a point. Your job is to train him. You're currently not doing that job."

I winced at that. "I'm damn good at my job, Tabs."

"Then show him. Because the job is to make sure that fine specimen of an arse and those gorgeous baby blues survive out in the real world, and currently, you're not doing that. You're focusing on Saint and Rookie, and Robert. You're not training him."

The sting of shame was almost worse than feeling Lock's warm breath on my face, knowing he didn't remember me.

"Okay, I hear you."

"Look, I'm not trying to make you do something. That's your brother's gig. But remember the job. We train them so that they all come back, right? So, whether you like him or not, you have to teach him how to survive."

I sighed. "Yeah, I know."

"Good. Now, hands off Saint. He's mine."

"I thought you wanted Gabe?" I asked.

"Oh, I do. Saint is just nice to look at. Now figure out what you're going to do with your recruit, and I'm going to do a little digging."

"Why does that scare me, Tabs?"

"What is scarier is how I plan on doing my digging."

I eyed her warily. "Oh God, please, please don't. I have this feeling it's going to have something to do with Gabe, and I'm not sure if I should be terrified for you or excited."

"Oh, relax. Take a chill. I'm not going to do anything illegal or anything that will get me kicked out of Rogues. I like this job."

"Fair enough. Won't you give me a hint?"

She shook her head. "Nope. No hints for you."

I rolled my shoulders and stood up. "Fine. Looks like I need to go find my trainee."

She grinned at me. "Maybe just plant one on him and see what he does. I guarantee you, he'll remember you after that."

"You're insane. I am going to train him though, because that's the gig. And despite hating my brother today, and all week really, I know how to do my job."

8

LACHLAN

I was just leaving the dining hall when the scent of roses brought me up short. I stopped in the path and immediately whirled around. From the shadows, Saff stepped out and studied me softly. "Have you eaten?"

"Yes. Is this where you tell me you're going to run me until I vomit?"

Her brow furrowed, and she shook her head. "No, although I wouldn't put it past Gabe to come up with training like that. So keep that in mind."

I groaned. "Okay, if you're not going to run me till I puke, why do I get the feeling this isn't a coincidence?"

"Because it's not."

I squared my shoulders, ready to hear that she'd reported me. That I would be going the same way as Maxim.

"You were right."

I frowned in confusion. "What?"

"You were right. I *haven't* been training you."

I breathed a sigh of relief. "Why would you admit that?"

"I admit my mistakes."

"Okay, let me ask... Why aren't you training me?"

"Because you are my punishment handed out from Gabe himself. So I've been resistant. But that's not fair because you need the training."

"Is there a reason you haven't been training me besides Gabe? Because I get the impression there is."

Her tongue peeked out to lick her bottom lip and desire went straight to my dick. Thankfully, it was dark out and she couldn't see it, because something told me she would have read me my last rights.

"No. Look, I've seen agents like you. Cocky. Think they know everything. Don't listen great. But my job is to keep you alive in the field, so I'm going to do my job. I can't let you walk out unprepared."

"Why help me all of a sudden?"

"It doesn't matter. I'm not going to let you die in the field."

"Well, I'm grateful for that, but I want to know the reason. You are very resistant to me, and I know it's more than the fact Gabe assigned me to you, so what is it?"

She looked like I'd put her on the spot, but she said, "It's like you guessed. You shagged one of my mates and then ghosted her."

"That doesn't even sound like me. I'm an asshole some-times, but it's usually because I'm blunt and direct. I never did like ghosting as a means to get rid of someone. It always feels like unfinished work, you know?"

"Yeah, anyway, you're at Rogues now. I shouldn't let that interfere."

"Would it help if I apologize to your mate?"

Her eyes went wide, and I could see the panic in them. "Um, no. I just plan on training you properly."

"Okay, but I'm more than willing to do it. Who knows, maybe it'll change your opinion of me?"

She lifted a brow. "Unlikely. But I don't want you to die on my watch, so don't suck."

I laughed at that. "Careful now, you're American side is coming through."

She laughed. "I spent half my life in the States. Mum was Ghanaian and Jamaican-American. Dad was obviously British."

"I can brush up on my American slang."

She nodded and turned to leave. "Oh, and King?"

The terse way she said my name had my dick swelling. "Yeah?"

"You ever pull some shit like you did in the cupboard again, and I will end you. I won't wait for Gabe to do it. I'll put you down again, permanently. Do you understand?"

I smirked at her. "Just one question." I knew I was playing with fire.

"What?"

"I know how good you are. You could have put me on my arse anytime while we were in the cupboard. Why didn't you?"

She pressed her full lips together and turned. "Meet me at the gun range in ten minutes."

"Now? It's dark."

"You afraid of the dark, King?"

And there it was again, the pull on my dick. "No, ma'am."

"Suit up then. I'll see you there in ten."

Well, it seemed that Saffron Abott was going to train me after all. The question was, why had she really changed her mind?

———

Saffron

"I HAVE TO SAY, I'm surprised by you. You normally wouldn't let a trainee get the best of you."

I frowned at Gabe across the dinner table. "What do you mean 'let him'?"

"Oh, come on, you really want me to believe that he navigated that last training exercise all on his own?"

"As a matter of fact, he did. I had nothing to do with it."

"He found you rather easily. Are you losing your touch?"

I knew what he was doing. This was his favorite game... to try and see if he could needle me, but I wasn't going to take the bait.

"You would think at some point you would get tired of this game."

"Tired? Of what game? Trying to see if I can get a rise out of you? Never."

I rolled my eyes. "He's very good." And that was all I could say about that. "You should be very happy. One of your recruits actually surpassed his master for once."

His brow dropped into a deep furrow. "I know it's weird for you, having me practically running things. But I'll have you know that most of my recruits perform well. I don't pick wrong often."

"Oh yes, it all comes down to your choice, not the training. If you say so."

Gabe put down his fork. "Is something wrong? You seem off. A little spicier than usual."

I shrugged. "Nothing's wrong."

"What is it? How did I irritate you today?"

"Did I say you irritated me?"

"It's usually the reason behind everything. I do something wrong, you don't tell me about it, and you expect me to read your damn mind."

"I don't expect you to read my mind, Gabe. I expect you to think. Have a little emotional intelligence, you know?"

He sat back from his plate of pork chops and wiped his mouth. "Saff, I don't want to fight with you. We get one dinner, once a fucking month that you'll allow me, and this is what we're doing?"

"You started this. I didn't start the fight, Gabe."

"Oh sure. Your maturity is astounding."

"You know what, Gabe?" I slapped my napkin down. I really didn't want to have this fight today. Or any day for that matter. But I did need to know why Lachlan King was so good. Too good. How much did Gabe know? Was Lock a plant? That would mean that whole night I hadn't been able to get out of my head for three months wasn't real. And I just needed to know. I deserved to know that much. "Where did you get Lachlan from? Where did you recruit him from, anyway?"

He frowned then. "Why do you care?"

"Jesus Christ, Gabe, can we just have one conversation where we don't fight?"

He sighed. "I'm not trying to fight with you." He watched me warily. "Fine, he's a classic recruit from a Rogues family. His brother, Charleston, was a Rogue. And their grandfather was a Rogue as well. But Charleston died when he was twenty."

"So you replaced one brother with another?" The night we were together, Lock told me all about his brother, how much he loved him, how much he'd idolized him, how much he longed to be like him.

"Not exactly. The old man has connections in Oversight. He wants one of his grandsons as a Rogue. I agreed to train him. That's it."

"And what, you discovered him just like that?"

"No. Not that it matters, but we've had our eye on him for a while. Recently, he got in a spot of trouble. He and his father disagreed about a business partnership. Lachlan refused to do business with someone, a good friend of his father's. He broke the deal. To add insult to injury, he took the man's daughter naked kite surfing."

My lips twitched.

"You seem to like this one. Like you want him to stay. Like you're willing him to be good."

"I'm not willing anything. He is good."

Excitedly, my brother leaned forward with his elbows on the table. "You've been training since you were a kid. He's good in hand-to-hand, you have to admit it. He almost got you in the woods."

"He did. I'm not saying he didn't."

"And he saw through your disguise in the last exercise. He has a sixth sense."

"You and I both know that's not how it works."

"Right. Well, I'm just saying he's a natural. He's only been training three months, and he's already that good."

My stomach turned because I could hear Gabe's glee at another billionaire Rogue. "Let me guess, he's been cut off and given a certain amount of time to get his act together, right? And what makes you think he's going to want to stay a Rogue?"

"I can see it in him. His focus."

"Did you lead his acquisition team?"

He shook his head. "No. The old man had a crew from Oversight do it. He wanted to make sure his grandson was unharmed, of course. Not that he doesn't trust us, but you know... He doesn't trust us."

I coughed. If Oversight's team had gotten him, it wasn't me they were watching. Fucking hell. So that meant Gabe didn't know. Which meant I should not be the one to tell him. "Well, he's not bad."

"Not bad? He's almost as good as you are. Which is high praise, right, sis?"

"If you say so."

"I say so. Why don't you like him?"

"It's not that I don't like him. It's just the way he does things, I guess."

"Oh, come on, I can tell you don't like him. You're tense and you're stiff. This isn't you."

"I'm being me." I lied.

"I'm not saying you're not being you. I'm just saying something's off. What's wrong? Are you still mad because I tied you to him? Look, I know you want to be in the field, but I just don't think you're ready."

I choked out a laugh. "According to you, I will never be ready. Which is neither here nor there. In some of these cases, I understand you keep me out of the field because I still have those nightmares. Other times, I'm just fed up, Gabe."

He pressed his lips firmly together. "Look, we just need to start small, okay? It's only been two years. I can't lose you too."

His voice was so soft I'd almost not heard him.

"What?"

"You heard me. I couldn't take it if I lost you, okay?"

"Gabe, don't give me that."

"You're my kid sister. I love you, and I just want to keep you safe for a little bit longer. And maybe I am holding on too tight. I could loosen the reins a little. If you want, maybe you can live off site. I just— I like seeing you every day."

"Give me something meaningful to do, Gabe. I graduated from uni a year early. I didn't come back just to sit here."

He nodded. "I hear you. And I think—" His phone buzzed on the table. I frowned at it because we had a rule of no phones during family dinner. But since Gabe was division lead at

Rogues, the phone couldn't completely be off. "I'm sorry, let me get this." He answered, "Webb."

Everything about him changed then. From the way he stiffened to the cold tone of his voice. "When? Where? I'll get the team." And then he hung up.

"What's wrong?"

He shook his head. "We've got a sighting on Massimo Igno. He and his girlfriend are going on a little vacation. Oversight wants them watched."

I sat up straighter. "That's good news, right?"

Massimo, as far as we could tell, was not involved with his father's business, but he was also hard to get a bead on. He kept a low profile. Rich lifestyle, but not too flashy. But now, he was dating a Spanish actress, Graciella Natanya, which meant more opportunities to get close to him.

Gabe pinched the bridge of his nose. "I have to go."

"You can't just go."

"It's important."

"If it's about Igno, I should be there too."

His gaze to me was direct. "No. You're staying out of this."

"I can help, Gabe."

"Forget it."

And then I watched my brother stride out of the room. Once again, I was left alone. Just like always. One of these days, Gabe was going to have to realize that I didn't need his protection. And every time he walked away from me and kept me out, he made me feel just as alone as I had in the days after my parents died.

9

SAFFRON

WHAT THE HELL was I doing?

You know what you're doing. He asked for a beer for a job well done. And now you're taking him a beer.

This was a stupid idea. We were *not* friends. I was his training officer, and this was dangerous.

Or, you're living a little. Trying to make a friend other than Tabs.

Speaking of Tabs, I hadn't filled her in on this little excursion because I'd known what she would say. She would've said, 'oh boy.' And then she would've made kissing faces, knowing full well I couldn't kiss him.

The problem was, now that I knew he didn't remember, it was harder to keep him at a distance because I *did* remember that I liked him.

He was still the same person. Brash but witty. He was also curious and eager to learn. He wanted to do things with integrity, but his impulsive nature got in his way. He was also a fast learner and didn't make the same mistake twice. He was shrewd and made good ops decisions. It was hard not to respect that.

I knew after today's mission, he was likely to go grab food and head back for his bungalow.

Tell the truth.

Fine, maybe I had watched for him. Which was ridiculous. Because I didn't care.

Sure you don't.

Liking him wouldn't get me far.

But, I knocked on his door, nonetheless. When he dragged it open with a rush, his eyes widened in surprise. "Fuck. Did I forget something?"

I shrugged sheepishly. "No. I, uh, brought these." I held up the beers and he grinned at me.

"Well, well. I knew I was wearing you down. I knew you would like me eventually."

"Let's not get carried away, okay?" It was impossible to suppress my smile.

He chuckled. "Oh, come on. You know you like me."

"You know what? I'm taking my beers and going," I said, turning back.

He stopped me with a hand on my shoulder. "Oh, come on, join me in the garden. You came all this way."

He walked me through the cottage, and I took note that the furnishings had been updated and refurbished. They looked modern and fresh to match the interior of the manor house. We reached the garden, and my breath caught. "Wow. I didn't realize the gardens were so well tended." There was honey-suckle and morning glories. Some roses too.

"Uh, that's not me. Surprisingly, that's Saint."

I wrinkled my nose. "What?"

"He's a regular green thumb."

"Well, will wonders never cease."

"I know, right? Sometimes I catch him out here talking to them. It's bizarre."

I chuckled at that. He motioned me to take a seat on one of the two loungers, so I did and handed him his beer.

"So, what made you decide to come have a beer with me?"

"Well, I realized it took me a moment to start training you, but you've progressed well regardless of that. And you did a good job today."

"Even though I missed the bombing target?"

I opted to let him in on the secret. "No one gets the bombing target. You're not supposed to. It's meant to be a lesson in keeping your guard up, I guess."

"You'd probably pass with flying colors."

"I don't count. I've essentially been training for this since I could walk."

His brow furrowed. "Explain that to me. You've just lived here your whole life?"

I rolled my shoulders back, thinking about how much to tell him. "Yeah. My great-grandfather helped found the Rogues. He had a whole thing about legacy I guess. He made the Abott manor our headquarters. He didn't have any siblings, and then he got married and had my grandfather who didn't have any siblings either. Grandpa had dad. You get the idea. And I was an only child until my parents adopted Gabe."

He frowned. "Gabe? He's your brother?"

I nodded. I had wondered if he would figure it out on his own or not. "Yes, he's my brother. Did no one tell you?"

His jaw went slack as he shook his head. "This whole time he's been your brother."

I laughed. "Yes, hence the overprotectiveness, the butting into my life, trying to control me, that whole thing."

"Fucking hell."

I leaned forward and took a sip of my beer. I didn't particularly enjoy beer, but it was something to do socially. "Why? What did you think?"

"Honestly? I thought you two were shagging."

I choked on the beer, sputtering and wheezing.

Lock leaned over and patted me on the back gently. "Let it out. Try and pull air through your nose. It will help."

I shook my head. "No. Too fizzy."

I coughed some more before the pain eased, and he didn't move from right next to me. "You thought I was shagging Gabe? Gross."

"What the fuck was I supposed to think? He essentially warned me off you. And he's very intense about you specifically. Doesn't want you hurt."

"Yes. Because he's my *brother*."

"Fucking hell. Why didn't anyone tell me?"

"It's not a secret."

"Wait. You're telling me Saint knew?"

I laughed. "Yeah, probably."

"I'm going to fucking kill him."

"Why were you and Saint discussing whether or not Gabe was my brother?"

His gaze met mine and then dipped to my lips. "No reason."

My whole body flushed under the close contact. His eyes stayed trained on me. This was the danger zone.

You can't have him. And he doesn't remember you, so watch yourself.

Right. I purposefully squared my shoulders and created a little bit more space between us as I inched backward.

"Your fucking brother?"

"Yep. My fucking brother."

"Goddamn it. How did I not see that?"

"I mean, he's white and I'm beautifully melanated, so I can see how our closeness was misinterpreted. Why would you assume I was shagging him though?"

"Do you have any idea that your brother is very intense about you and your safety?"

I shrugged. "Yeah. It's annoying."

"Why is that?"

"After our mum and dad died, he took it on to be my protector. He's essentially all I have left. And he takes it very seriously. *Too* seriously. I know he's looking out for me, but sometimes it feels like he's smothering me."

His voice went quiet. "How did your parents die?"

As usual, the pain wrapped around my heart and squeezed. But maybe, just maybe this time it didn't squeeze so hard that I couldn't even breathe. "Bomb."

"What?" His brows furrowed as if there was no way he'd heard correctly.

"They were killed by a bomb."

"I was expecting you to say something like an accident, or one from cancer and the other one from something else. Bomb was the last thing I expected you to say."

"Yeah. It's shocking for sure."

"What happened?"

I'd already told him this whole story. I'd already shared all of these details with him the night we met. And maybe that's what made it easier to talk about the second time around. Knowing that he'd already heard it. He just didn't know he'd heard it.

"They were visiting me at school. I had wanted one normal experience at uni, the whole bit. My parents at graduation." I shook my head. "If I hadn't insisted that they come, they wouldn't have exposed themselves."

"I know I wasn't there, but I really doubt that it was your fault."

"I know. You sound like all the shrinks that Gabe hired. Hell, you sound like Gabe. But I can't help but think if I hadn't insisted, would they still be here?"

"Speaking as someone who does this shit to themselves all the time, I'm going to tell you what everyone tells me. Well everyone but my parents. This isn't your fault. Things happen, but no one deserves bad things happening to them."

And I knew he would say that. It's what he'd said the last time.

"Yeah, I know. It's hard to shake though."

He ran his hands through his hair. "Up until two weeks ago, I thought I was responsible for my brother's death."

I furrowed my brow. "What?" That was one of the things we bonded over, both feeling responsible for the deaths of people we loved. "What happened two weeks ago?"

"Your brother dropped a bomb on me the day after you and I met."

"He did?"

"Yeah. He told me that Charlie had been a Rogues agent."

"Jesus."

"Yeah. And the night he died in a car crash wasn't an accident. It was deliberate."

My heart sank. My stomach cramped. "Oh, for fuck's sake. Lock, I'm so sorry."

All he did was nod and keep his eyes on his beer bottle as he shredded the paper label. "I guess I was meant to be collateral damage, but I survived with barely a scar."

I knew exactly where those tiny scars were. Along his back and his shoulders. I knew he'd covered them up with tattoos. But I couldn't tell him that I knew that.

Because this Lachlan King hadn't been naked with me.

I felt like a voyeur. I felt like I was lying.

I hated the feeling.

He continued. "The thing is you believe this one thing your whole life. And there's always a part of you that wants it to not be true. But still you believe that it is. Then you get information that it's in fact *not* true, and it spins your whole goddamn world. Because what does that mean for who I am? What does that mean for what I'm about? For the last five years, I've thought I was to blame. That I was the reason Charlie was gone. Now to find out that's not true, that part of my identity doesn't exist anymore."

"I'm so sorry."

He shrugged. "It's not like you did it."

"No, but that's a horrible thing to find out."

"It should be a relief, right? But somehow it's not."

"Even if you thought you were responsible I just want to remind you of what you just said to me... You weren't. Sometimes bad things just happen."

He gave me a nod and a wobbly smile. "Yeah. Sometimes bad things happen." He sipped his beer. "I'm not sure why it's so easy to talk to you."

"It might have to do with the fact that I decided to stop hating you."

"Told you I'd wear you down," he said with a laugh.

"You are persistent. I will say that."

"I should probably apologize to you."

I frowned. "For what?"

He gave me a sheepish look. "The pulling you in the cupboard thing. Maybe that wasn't my best look."

"Oh, you're fine. You were right. I wasn't training you. And not training you could get you killed out in the field. That's not what I want."

"So you *do* like me."

I shook my head. "Only a little. I guess you're not *always* annoying. You aren't always arrogant."

He laughed. "Well, there's that. So look at us, being friends."

"Not quite friends," I laughed.

"So if we're not friends, what are we?" he asked.

Why did it feel like he was closer now? Leaning in, so close I could almost touch him.

"I don't know. I guess I'm your trainer."

The crease in his brow deepened. "And why are you a trainer? You're really good. You should be in the field."

I winced. "It's a sore spot."

"Let me guess, hurricane Gabe?"

"On the first try. Well done," I muttered.

"That's bullshit."

"I don't want to talk about my brother."

"Brilliant. I don't want to talk about him either."

I nodded, and he nudged my leg with his. "Thanks for the beer. Being here can be isolating."

"Trust me, I know."

He turned to face me, and his gaze locked on mine again. He licked his bottom lip, and my insides melted and coiled all at once. God, that look could melt knickers from yards away.

"I feel like I know you."

"You do know me. I've been training you for two weeks now."

He shook his head. "You know what I mean. I feel like I know you from before I came here. This is easy. It feels good to talk to you. You're the first person I can talk to since Charlie died, and that's saying something."

I swallowed hard and shook my head. "Look, it's just transference. You have to trust me to train you, so it just feels that way."

He nodded slowly but didn't take his eyes off me. "Can I ask you something? How much of that is what you believe, and how much of that is the fact that you train me and are just following the rules?"

I swallowed. And then my gaze made a mistake of dipping to his lips and staying there. My brain gave all kinds of commands.

Lift your fucking gaze. Look up at him. Eyes on him. Not his lips.

But I couldn't. Because I did remember. Even if he didn't, I remembered.

He groaned low. "You look at me sometimes like you want what I want, Saff."

I cleared my throat. I tried closing my eyes and shaking it off. But still, that feeling had set low in my belly and was trying to claw its way out. Trying to seep its way into my bones. I could feel the desperation and need building. "I should go."

I pushed to my feet, but he took my hand and stood up himself. "Don't go."

"Whatever you're thinking might be a good idea isn't, Lachlan."

"I like how you say my name."

I swallowed again. "I should go. I'm going."

"You said that already," he whispered.

And while technically he was in my path. I could have easily sidestepped him. And we both knew I could put him down if I needed to, but I didn't. I stood in front of him, his hand holding mine, his thumb grazing over my knuckle.

"I'm not the only one who feels it, am I?" he asked.

I knew what would happen if I acknowledged it, but I couldn't stop myself from saying the truth. "It's not allowed."

"So I'm told. I just want to know I'm not alone. Because I have been obsessively thinking about you since we met. I can't get you out of my head, and I just want to know that I'm not crazy and alone here. Because the more time I spend with you, the more I feel like I know you."

"I'm—"

"You're my trainer. I get it. And you can't say anything. I just wanted you to know that I feel it."

I nodded slowly, not sure what to say. Knowing what I should do, but knowing that my body and my mind and my heart and my soul wanted to stay right there rooted to that spot with him holding my hand and my mouth begging him to kiss me. My core tightened around nothingness, desperate to feel the bite of having him inside me.

I squeezed my eyes shut. "We can't. *I* can't."

"I know." His voice was a low groaned whisper. But still he leaned forward. And I leaned up, tilting my face up toward his. His gaze was searching as he inched closer and closer and closer, the tension and the heat spiraling around us, sparking, threatening to set off an inferno.

An inferno that should not be. An inferno that was going to be a problem. An inferno that was going to get us in trouble.

"I know I shouldn't."

"You shouldn't." I tried to swallow around the sawdust drying out my mouth.

"But I can't help it." And as he leaned closer, only a whisper of a breath standing between us, I moaned.

"Fuck, I'm going to enjoy this."

The pull of the forbidden was so strong, I leaned into it. Then...

"Lock, where are you?"

We sprung apart, *caught.* I stumbled over the recliner and had to scramble to keep my balance.

Lock reached out and caught me with an arm around my

waist that brought me flush up against him. Reflexively, I shoved him hard.

The motion only toppled us both onto the lounger with him on top of me. In a panic, I rolled us to the ground with me on top of him, my hips astride his. He was gazing up at me, his eyes wide with surprise. "Fuck."

I tried to get up. But as I rocked backward, I felt the very hard, very thick length of his erection right against my core. And I closed my eyes and moaned, "Oh Jesus."

There was no choice. I had to work my hips up to get up. And when I did, he hissed and gripped them. Fucking hell.

I bit back a moan. "This isn't happening. I'm sorry. I have to go." I clambered off him and he sprang up with an intense look toward me like he was going to prowl toward me and consume me.

That sounds promising.

I shook my head. "I'm just going to—" I hooked my thumb toward the door.

"There you are," came a booming voice from the door of the cottage.

I looked around Lock to find Saint in the doorway. "Saint, hi."

He grinned at me. "Hey, Saff, did he fuck up today? Please tell me everything."

I gave him a tremulous smile. "Actually he did great."

Saint scowled. "Did he beat me?"

"I will leave the two of you to talk about it," I said, knowing better than to get between two competing males.

Saint laughed. "Don't let me run you off. I see you brought beer."

"That was his reward. It was what he asked for. But we're done anyway. You guys have a good night." I forced myself to turn to him with a smile on my face. "Good job today. I'll see you for training tomorrow."

He said nothing, his gaze intent on mine. And everything about his expression told me I should run and hide somewhere very far away, because when he caught me, we were going to break a whole lot of rules.

10

LACHLAN

I COULDN'T KEEP my bloody eyes off her. I wished I had a viable reason for why I couldn't, but every time I was near her, my mind took a mental vacation. I knew that I should be focusing. I had targets to hit. A course to run. Not to mention Saff was counting on me. If I'd been complaining that she should have been training me over the last two weeks, she made up for it in spades.

She woke me up at five a.m. sometimes to give me a surprise training exercise. Now that she was on board, she was taking no goddamn prisoners, and it would serve me well to understand that.

When she strolled out next to me, she raised a brow. "You ready?"

She stood just a hair too close and kept her voice low so I would lean into her. Jesus, fuck. That scent, the rose and vanilla, and... God, what was that other thing? I couldn't fucking breathe in all honesty. I'd learned to start holding my breath around her if I wanted to actually do any thinking, but she caught me by surprise with her closeness.

"Yeah," I cleared my throat. "A hundred percent ready."

She eyed me dubiously. "You've done the work, just stay focused."

"Right. Focused." Up ahead, I watched as Saint ran through the course.

Rookie was up next, then it was me. Two of the other trainees had already gone before us.

Essentially, we had to run a course at targets, shooting only viable targets, no civilians, all under duress with ample distraction. The distraction was tailored to us. So for Rookie, someone played the sound of his sister screaming for him. That had fucked him right up. He'd visibly struggled on the last three targets, but only missed one of them, which was still good enough for a pass.

Saint was having a harder time. He had to get a civilian out before he could annihilate the target. And the problem was, he had to make choices.

I didn't exactly know his story, because he kept his past pretty close to the vest. From the looks of it, he was struggling. There was plenty of time, but he was having a problem, and I could see him trying to make a decision about who to save first. The panic in his eyes was evident.

All we'd been told was that our training officer would be part of the course, but we didn't know how. Tabs had been there to distract him. He'd been able to counteract a sexual distraction easily. She'd wrapped her arms around him at one point during a bar scene. He'd hit that target dead in the eye and then quickly turned a charming smile on her. He looked like he might lean in and kiss her, but when she raised an eyebrow, he chuckled and released her. But what had tripped him up was the choice on who to save, his training officer or a child.

The child, as it turned out, was one of the daughters of someone on Oversight, and she was a volunteer. There were some pyrotechnics in there, and all she had to do was call out for help. I watched Saint as he went for the child and then went for Tabs at the same time. He was big. Not quite as big as I was, but broader. He'd thought he could save them both.

He whisked his arms around Tabatha's waist, and she fought him. Clawed at him. He was going to have to put her down and save the kid, but would he have time to come back?

And then he did the one thing I never expected him to do. He put the kid down for a second and restrained Tabatha. He winced as he hit her at a pressure point on the back of the neck, and next to me, Saff hissed.

Tabs went down easily, folding. And then he lifted her over his shoulder and bent down to lift the kid. He held them both, carrying them as easily as if they were nothing. Out the door, fire threatening to burn him. But he was nothing but grit and determination as he walked them out of the course.

He put the kid down first, and she grinned up at him and gave him a high five. Saint leaned over Tabs, wiping the hair away from her face and checking her vitals. All I heard was Gabe's whistle. "You make it a point to assault women, Saint?"

I watched Saint's jaw tick from where I was standing and he mumbled something in response. Something that made Gabe back off, which I had never seen before. Webb had a very clear fuck-around-and-find-out vibe, but Saint wasn't afraid of him.

A couple of minutes later, Tabs was sitting up, blinking and clearly annoyed. But then she grinned up at Saint and gave him a high five. When he helped her to her feet, she gave him a tight hug.

My gaze flickered over to Webb, whose jaw tightened. And I frowned at that. Wait a minute, now was he into Tabs? That was worth noting. Next to me, Saff's tension eased. "Oh, she's fine."

"You didn't think he'd actually hurt her, did you?"

She shrugged. "You never know about these trainees. But he did the right thing. Sometimes you have to neutralize an asset to keep them safe."

"That's good to know. Are you going to knock me out if I need it? Then carry me out somewhere?"

She shifted on her feet, just an inch closer to me, and her scent wrapped around me. It was like choking me from the inside out, and all I could smell was her. This was not what I fucking needed right now. Not at all what I needed. But this is where we were. "Of course, I'll carry you out. And I'm happy to shoot you with a tranq gun again."

I had to laugh at that. "You know, I feel like I owe you for that."

"Yeah, you can absolutely shoot me with a tranq gun, but you'll have to catch me first."

She sauntered away then, and I knew she was heading into my course. I also knew watching her arse as she walked away was a bad move. My gaze flickered over her once, and I made sure I took that photograph and stamped it in my head and kept my gaze resolutely forward. I had no idea what I was about to face, but I certainly didn't need Webb catching me watching Saff walk away. He would make it a point to murder me for sure.

Saint came jogging over, and I gave him a lifted chin in greeting. "Well done."

"Yeah, it got hairy there, but I didn't really have a choice. She's a hell of a fighter. Tiny, but... Wow."

"You look worried about her."

His lips pressed together. "I don't like putting my hands on women."

"Who the fuck does?"

His gaze met mine directly. "Too many."

Something about the way he said it made my jaw tighten. "You beat Rookie. I think Robert, too."

He nodded. "You're still up. I could put a wager on this."

I shrugged. "Sure. The problem is, I don't know what I'm facing, so it's a guess."

He laughed. "You scared?"

"Knowing that Saff is in there and she clearly has it out for me, yeah, I think I should be scared. Wouldn't you be?" Especially after we'd almost kissed. She'd been riding me... and not in a fun way.

"I don't know. She doesn't seem to hate you nearly as much as she did a couple of weeks ago."

She didn't. I wondered if she lay awake at night thinking about me like I thought about her.

"She's agreed to train me, that's it."

"Uh-huh." He eyed me then. "You two seem close now."

I shook my head. "I like my balls exactly where they are. Besides, no fraternization, remember? Or do you just not care about that rule or Webb severing your balls from you? I saw the way you were looking at Tabs."

"Nah, she's a mate."

"Oh, right. A mate. That looks like that."

He shrugged. "I like her. Besides, she's smart, funny, and she knows this agency like the back of her hand. It wouldn't hurt you to make a mate or two."

"I've been making mates."

"Yeah, sure."

"Well, if I were you, and Smith is just a mate, I'd watch yourself around Webb. He thinks of her as his."

Saint glanced back over at Webb as he was talking to her. Tabatha had her head upturned to Gabe's and was scowling at him and gesticulating wildly while Gabe frowned down at her.

"There's something there."

Saint narrowed his eyes. "Well, there can't be according to the rules. But if he can break a rule, so can I."

I chuckled at that. "Okay. If he tries to kill you, I want your album collection."

He laughed. "It's all yours. But who said I will be the one who dies?"

I glanced at Gabe and then back at Saint. "Please, you're my mate, but there's something about him that just says cold and deadly. The kind of bloke that will kill you in your sleep, you know?"

Saint shrugged. "I thought you were convinced he was shagging Saff."

"As it turns out, he's her brother. But you know that already."

He laughed. "Damn, who told you?"

"Saff."

He nodded at that. "Figures. You ready?"

"Is this the part where I say, I was born ready?"

He rolled his eyes. "You're such a twat."

I headed toward my course and tried to pull myself mentally back into the game. Saff had trained me for this. I just had to figure out what the hell my distraction was going to be and ignore it.

Ten minutes later I walked into my training course, and the sense of dread fell over me like a black sackcloth.

A little too much like a black sackcloth. Matter of fact, exactly like the one that had been shoved over me in my flat.

They'd recreated my goddamn flat.

Jesus fucking Christ.

I looked around and saw the markers leading to my starting point. My bedroom. Fucking hell. They'd left no detail untouched right down to the Xander Chase on my goddamn wall and the Z Con that was hanging next to the cupboard. Upon closer inspection, I saw they were prints and not originals, so they hadn't taken them from my flat. But Christ, if I hadn't been looking closely I would have mistaken them. It wasn't until I sat down on my bed that I realized what they'd done.

They'd sprayed perfume on the bed, and for some reason it smelled wrong. But something about it triggered a memory. Me waking up alone in bed. But the more I tried to tug on that thread, the more I rebelled and couldn't quite piece it together. I knew what was expected. So I laid down, trying to clear my head and wondering what the point was in replicating my loft. But I then shoved it out of my head. I didn't need to know the whys; I just needed to follow through, hit the targets, and make it out in the right amount of time. Easy, right? I cleared my mind and waited for the buzzer.

I heard the sound of gunfire. I could almost sense the person behind the door, so I rolled out of bed easily, palmed my gun that I'd placed right under my pillow, and fired. I didn't even wait to see the hint of green on the target's vest as I hit my mark. That person proceeded to lay on the floor in the doorway and I stepped over them easily.

I approached the stairs into my fake living area slowly. There was more of that sweet scent sprayed everywhere. What was that? It was wrong. All wrong.

From behind, someone jumped out. I blocked the hit, turned around to cast an elbow behind me, dropped my hips, and shoved them back. Pulling the person overhead and down, I aimed the gun and fired at his chest. Again, green light.

Before the other person from the doorway leading to the second bedroom could even step out, I hit that target.

It was like I knew where they were going to be. As if some part of my mind could sense it. I quickly whipped around, pointed at my loft, three, two, one, target hit.

What the hell? Why did I know where these targets were?

Saff had run me through all possible scenarios, but we'd

never done a version of this. Hell, how would she even know about my flat? So what was this? Why did I know where they were going to be?

I'd taken down four targets. I had to find my asset. I cleared each room, which finally left the cupboard, and it was the scent in the cupboard that stopped me.

Oh, fuck. Saff. I searched over my shoulder and saw no more targets were coming for me. When I pulled the door open, there was Saff in her bra and panties. Oh, Christ. I swallowed hard, trying to keep my gaze off her tits, but it wasn't even her state of undress, it was her scent that got to me. I liked how she smelled over the too sweet smell they'd sprayed over my loft. And Saff looked like she had blood on her side. I knew it wasn't real. I understood that. But something deep inside me broke just seeing her like that, lifeless. And the markings on her face... She looked like she'd been cut or something.

Rage simmered in my blood. I couldn't account for the anger. And maybe it took me a moment too long, but what appeared to be the front door of my flat opened. I aimed. And in that brief second, I knew it wasn't a target. And then I saw the baton and colorings of police issued jacket. The police. Fuck. "You'd better not be actually hurt," I said.

I picked her up easily. She was tall but easy to lift. I carried her in my arms and then shifted her in a fireman's hold so that I could still wield my gun. Two police officers walked in and headed for the upstairs loft. And as they were going, one of them turned around and aimed at me, but I fired first.

Green marker.

Oh fuck. Over my shoulder, Saff moaned.

"Are you fucking hurt?"

"Lock? What the hell?" She sounded disoriented. "What's happening? Is this your flat?"

I hesitated then. How the fuck did she know about my flat?

Another target came round the corner of the hallway, just in the doorframe. I hit them and got a green target on the shoulder, but they pointed their gun.

I cursed under my breath and turned to tuck Saff behind the door.

But she got hit. I heard the buzzer. I checked the target sensors on her body and saw they'd shot her in the leg. *Fuck.* I was going to lose points for that, but I needed to get out to wherever the fuck the exit was. The target was coming forward, sending an array of bullets toward us with not much more than the countertop as cover.

She was too disoriented to help. "Lock, why are we in your flat?"

"Why do you know what my flat looks like?"

"You don't remember." She muttered something under her breath, and I could tell they'd drugged her or something. "Saff, sweetheart, I need you to pay attention to me. Why do you know about my flat?"

"It's so pretty. So much light."

Except, my flat was dark, and God, they'd really given her something. I didn't know what it was, but I needed her to shake it off. "I'll be right back, okay? Stay covered. You're hit, I don't know how many points."

She smiled up at me, the way she'd never smiled at me before. "I'm sorry I left," she whispered.

I frowned. "Left where?"

"I really had fun."

I couldn't understand what the hell she was talking about or what she was saying. Before I could ask, she passed out again.

Fuuuck.

Suddenly, the target at the door was more than one target. I peeked out from around the cupboard, fired off two shots, and got one target down, but the other one nicked me. I cursed and saw that I'd taken a shoulder hit, which meant I had to shift my gun to my other hand. Fucking hell. Left-handed shooting. No wonder Saff had insisted I practice it at the range. Two more targets, then I could pick her up and carry her the fuck out of there.

I rolled out, trying to catch the target that was headed toward the loft. Probably to get higher ground so they could shoot down on me. I hit him, but again, only a hip shot. He fired at me again. I ducked and rolled behind the couch, and then I was up popping off two squeezes.

Green light.

Finally, the other target in the doorway was the only one left. I spun on my knee and got him.

I did a quick sweep, only popping my head barely up out of position to make sure I had all targets down. The hall had a lot of green lights. Excellent. And then I ran back to Saff and scooped her up. "You're okay. I've got you."

Her scent continued to wrap around me and then pulled at another memory. A fantasy that had been playing in my mind for weeks now. Saff over me, riding me, her perfect tits bouncing with each movement. Me sitting up to shove one of her pebbled nipples in my mouth, and the way she arched her back, smooth and lithe, giving me access. Fuck. Why that fucking fantasy? Why now?

You don't have time for this. Get out.

I didn't know how long we'd been in here, but I hoped to Christ I'd beat Saint. At the very least, Rookie.

As I carried her out toward the exit, I wished I could explain it, but there was that sense of unease that prickled. I put her down and placed her against the door, covered her body with mine, and fired at the target that had apparently been hiding in my cupboard.

Green light.

Behind me, gun still raised, I reached for the exit door, shoved it open, scooped her up, and walked through.

And all I heard after was the buzzer.

Saffron

I BLINKED SLOWLY awake and I winced at the brightness of the room. What the fuck? Why was I in med bay?

"Good, you're awake."

Startled, I snapped my head to the left and found Lock sitting by my beside.

"What are you—why am I in med bay?"

"I think they overdosed you for my trial."

His trial? Oh God. "Shit, are you okay? How did you do?"

That slow smirk I'd come to know and need appeared as he watched me.

"I passed, of course."

"So cocky."

"How about we say I had a good teacher."

I smiled at that. "Did you beat Saint?"

He grinned. "By two minutes."

"Now you'll be impossible to live with."

"I'm starting to think you don't believe that."

"If I were you, I wouldn't think that. No need for you to get cocky now."

"I have a question though."

I nodded. "What's up?"

"How do you know what my flat looks like?" His gaze didn't waver. His voice was soft but direct.

I didn't want to lie. But telling him now was too much. I couldn't have him anyway. "What are you talking about?"

"My trial was in a mockup of my flat."

"I don't know your flat, Lock." The lie persisted, but it had to be done.

"Do you remember anything about my trial?"

I could feel my brow furrow as I thought it through. I didn't remember anything about his trial. I remember going into his trial space, but before I could open the interior door, Gabe was there and— Blank. Seeing as I was in med bay now, obviously, they'd drugged me. Why had they drugged me? What had they done?

"I don't remember anything. The last thing I remember is talking to Gabe."

Lock nodded and swallowed. "Right. You were saying some stuff that didn't make sense, I guess, and you also mentioned stuff about my flat and... I don't know. It doesn't make any sense."

I searched his gaze. I could tell him. I could just blurt it out, like 'Hey, we shagged three months ago.' But what good would that do? That would only confuse him, and our entire working relationship would be destroyed. Besides, it was humiliating for me, so it was better to just keep that to myself.

"I don't know why they had you in your flat. But I don't remember anything about what I might have said in there."

He nodded. "You're okay, right?" He was watching me warily.

"I think so." I could wiggle my toes and feel the coolness of the sheet on me, but when I tried too hard to remember the trial, my head started to throb. "Yeah, if I try to think too hard about what happened, I get a headache. But other than that, I think I'm fine."

"You were shot."

I frowned hard at that. "What do you mean, I got shot?"

He winced. "Well, let's just say I was more concerned about getting you out and didn't anticipate they'd give me an extra target. Actually, a few extra targets."

"How many targets did you have?"

"Eight. You know what's weird? As I was going through my flat, it's like I knew exactly where they were going to be. At least the first set. I can't explain it, but it's like I had a cheat code. You haven't been giving me the instructions, have you?"

I lifted a brow and winced when my head throbbed. "As if I would."

He shook his head. "No, I didn't think so. Are you okay?"

I nodded. "But no, I haven't been subliminally sending you signals, sorry. You felt strong enough?"

He nodded. "I felt surprisingly good. All that good training."

"Don't be a smart arse."

He leaned back on his seat, watching me. "Why do you think they picked you as my asset to get out?"

"Well, because that's the deal. You have to be able to see your trainer down without reacting emotionally, I suppose."

"You know what's funny? They sprayed perfume all over my flat."

I swallowed hard at that. "What?"

"Perfume. They sprayed it all over my flat. It was too... I don't know, flowery, I guess. They like sprayed it on my bed, downstairs, the couch. The couch really smelled like it."

What was I supposed to say? 'Hey, we shagged that one time, but you don't remember, so I'm trying not to trigger anything. Please, dear God, remember me.' But I didn't say that. "Well, that's weird. Maybe it was supposed to remind you of a long-term girlfriend or something."

He shook his head. "I've never had anyone to my flat. I have another place for that. It was one of Charlie's rules. Never bring a girl back to the flat, because then you can't make them leave."

"Oh, charming."

"Well, there was an incident once when I was at uni. This girl, she kept showing up. That's when Charlie told me about his *no girls at the flat* rule. It seemed like a good idea at the time."

"I'm sure it did."

"Well, anyway, I just came to see how you're doing."

"Aw, don't tell me you care."

He rolled his eyes. "Easy does it. You're going to ruin my rep like that. Who said I care?"

"I see you, King. You're starting to like me."

He chuckled then. "Are you sure you're all right?"

"Yeah. You didn't react when you saw me, did you?"

His gaze was mysterious then. "No, of course not. I locked down all the emotions and did what a good agent would do."

"Glad to hear it."

When he pushed to leave, I called him back. "Oh, hey, King?"

"You know, I'm starting to like you calling me King."

"Ugh, please, get over yourself. But anyway, before you so rudely interrupted me, I was about to say good job today."

"Thanks. Start feeling better soon. I need my trainer, don't I?"

A smile tugged at my lips and my heart fluttered.

You cannot have him. He's forbidden.

It's best you remember that.

11

LACHLAN

I HADN'T EXPECTED to get called back into Gabe's office so soon. I spent the last day training with Saff, unable to shake the idea that I knew her. I couldn't shake that pull. Every time I was near the woman, I had a really unhealthy desire to drink her deep.

That would get my arse kicked by Gabriel.

Ever since we'd almost kissed, I'd been unable to think about anything else. When I was led to Gabriel's office, he was standing and pacing by the window. I didn't bother to sit. Instead, I inspected the books on his bookshelves until he turned around. "Those were my father's. He read a lot."

"These are all first edition classics."

"You know your bindings," he mused.

"You could say that. Mother founded a whole library somewhere."

"Yes, I feel like I knew that about you."

"Which one was his favorite?"

His voice coming soft, Gabe whispered, *"The Count of Monte Cristo."*

There was a thread in my memory. Something familiar. Like

that was someone else's favorite book, but I couldn't quite put my finger on it. And honestly, I was too tired. "Did I fail the mission in some way?"

He shook his head. "On the contrary. You were the only recruit to even come close. Saint came in second, but he got an extra set of bonus points because he got both assets out. Tough nut to crack, that one."

I smiled. "He's a good bloke."

Gabe nodded. "You know Massimo Igno, is that correct?"

It wasn't a name I'd heard in years. "Why?"

"He went to Eton with you?"

I nodded. "Oh, yeah. That's why the name is familiar. He was a couple of years ahead of me. Friends with my brother. What's the problem?"

"What were your interactions with him while at Eton?"

I shrugged. "Minimal. I was on the rugby pitch most of the time. I didn't pay a lot of attention to the upperclassmen. There were some legendary rumors about him and women, but I knew nothing else. Why?"

He walked over to his desk and clicked something, and when the screen popped up, Massimo was on the screen an older version of Massimo who I could only assume was his father. "This is the Igno family."

"All right. What is this?"

"This," Gabe muttered, "Is the mission."

My blood rushed at the word *mission*. "Are you shitting me? The Ignos?"

He shook his head. "No, I'm not. If you can pull off this mission, it will be something Oversight won't forget."

"What is the mission?"

"Massimo here has a new girlfriend. Usually, the Ignos stay off our radar. The old man has managed to amass a fortune in the criminal underworld. He's well connected and untouchable."

The way he said it, I could tell there was bad blood with the old man. I frowned. "What do you need?"

"Intel. The whole Igno family is private. Notoriously so. But recently, Massimo proposed to the Spanish actress and model, Graciella Natanya, so he's been more visible. We haven't been able to get close to him for any reason. But we have word that he is taking Graciella to the Winston Isles for a two-week holiday."

"Okay."

"I'm sending you in for surveillance."

I frowned at that. "Me? Don't you want somebody who has more field experience?"

He shook his head. "Not necessarily. It's strictly a surveillance mission. All you have to do is plant a few bugs, and then you're gone. We just want to be able to listen in on who he's talking to."

I hesitated. It felt like I wasn't being told something. I studied him. "What's the catch?"

"No catch. You do this mission, bring us actionable intel, and knock your sessions off to six months."

Holy shit. "You're fucking serious?"

"Yes, that's how important this is."

"And all I have to do is listen?"

"Yes. It shouldn't be too difficult. One small thing. You won't be doing it alone." Gabe frowned when he muttered this. "We don't want to rouse suspicion, so we are sending you in as yourself, but you will be going in with your wife."

"What? Who?"

"Since you two have been working so well together, you'll be going with Saff."

The other shoe had dropped. It was one thing to obsess

about her, have her walk around in my dreams. But it was a whole other kind of temptation to be stuck on a mission with her.

———

Saffron

"Do you want to tell me what your problem with King is?"

Gabe had waylaid me in the hallway on my way to training and pulled me into his office.

"I don't have a problem with King," I lied smoothly.

He lifted his brow and crossed his arms after tossing his tablet on his desk. "You forget, I grew up with you. I know when you're lying. Is he a problem?"

"What?" I shook my head. "No. He's fine."

"All right, then what's going on?"

"Nothing."

He frowned. "Look, Saff, you and him obviously have a thing, and I need to know if it's going to be a problem."

I sighed. "No, it's not. He's not bad. He's a little cocky. Hand-to-hand is pretty good, actually. He has never been put in a position where he has had to fight for his life, but I think that he will rise to the occasion. He got a little distracted today, but also, I wasn't actually trying to kill him. I think he'll be fine. We've got months left before his final evals."

Final evals were essentially hell week, where we took the recruits out in the middle of nowhere. They had to survive, and we could jump out at any point. Attack, attempt to kill them.

We did that in a closed environment because the last time we tried to do it in a real-world scenario, we almost lost an agent. That had been mum and dad's era.

"I need your honest opinion because I'm about to put him on a mission."

My brows lifted. "What? You're putting someone untrained in the field?"

"I thought you just said he was pretty good."

"That was before I knew you were putting him in the bloody field. Are you kidding me? I've been out begging for field duty for over a year. You won't put me in the field, but you'll put him there?"

Gabe held his hands up. "Settle down."

"No, I will not settle down. What's the billionaire got that I don't have? Because I have the chaps, I have the heart, and I've been pissing my life away."

"Saff, I know. I know it's all you've ever wanted, but I've been trying to keep you safe."

"Bullshit, Gabriel. I've done everything that's been asked of me. Everything. I watch these trainees come in and out of here. I turn them into great fighters. Good strategists. And when I ask for a shot and you sideline me, I know it can't be because I'm a woman because we've turned out female agents who could kill you in their sleep. So what is it?"

My brother scrubbed his hands over his face. "Look, when I came to live with your mum and dad, it felt like Christmas. Like an actual honest-to-God miracle. And I swore that I would do anything to stay. It didn't matter what. When dad pulled me aside, I thought he was going to tell me I had to go because my grades hadn't really been enough, but he told me we were going to work on it. The only thing that he asked from me was that I look out for you always. And I have done my best to do that. I am supposed to look out for you."

"You know what's funny? You keep trying to tell me how irresponsible I am, how not ready I am, always making emotional decisions, but this is *my* legacy. I was born to do this,

Gabe. And you seem to not see it. That and the fact that you're keeping me from it."

He frowned then. "I'm not keeping you from your legacy, damn it."

"You want to put the billionaire in the field. A guy who's done nothing more than slum his way through half of Europe on his daddy's money."

"Your daddy had money."

I cringed at that. "Yes, I had the privileges afforded to me, but I'm no billionaire's kid. And I would trade all the money in the world to have my fucking parents back."

"There are extenuating circumstances, Saff."

"What do I not understand? Don't you think I want to serve and protect people like my parents did?"

"Of course, Saff, of course. I just— I'm trying to keep you safe."

"Maybe you should trust me, trust my training."

"Fucking hell, Saffron, are you in a hurry to get yourself killed?"

I folded my arms. "It's not about that, Gabe. You know it. I deserve the right to prove myself."

He glowered at me, his piercing green eyes so familiar to me after all these years, that firm set of his mouth. I could see why Tabatha was so enamored with him. He was good looking. He was also stubborn. Mule-headed. Obstinate.

The point was, he was a pain in my arse. Had been since the moment he showed up on my doorstep.

He was never going to see me as an equal.

He sighed and pinched the bridge of his nose. "You know, Saff, if you would let me get a word in, you would see—"

"I would see what? I'm sorry, Gabe. I can't just sit back and do nothing. For years, I watched everyone go out, waiting for my turn, and now you're putting the billionaire bad boy into play? How can I sit back and not say anything?"

"You're looking at it the wrong way."

"I am embarrassed, Gabe."

"Enough. Tell me about your King hesitation."

"I'm hard on him because he's cavalier and brash. He's good, and with more training and toning down his assholery, he could be *really* good. But he's not ready, and you're putting him in the field. That reflects poorly on all of us. Me especially, because I'm his training officer."

"It can't be helped. This is from Oversight. It pertains to the sighting of Massimo Igno."

My eyes went wide then, and I scooted to the edge of my seat. "Massimo? Are you kidding me? He's a ghost."

"Yes, but he is getting married to Gabriella Natanya. She was saying to her sisters that he's taking her on a pre-wedding vacation to the Winston Isles. I need eyes and ears on him."

Massimo Igno was number five on so many international wanted lists. Weapons, especially technical ones, were his specialty. And he'd proven slippery. Hard to catch. We thought we had him in Spain once, years ago. Dad had been leading the team then, but he'd slipped the snare. I had to ask the question. "Will his father be there?"

Gabe met my gaze with a grave one of his own. "No. As far as we can tell, Antonio Igno won't be in attendance."

Drake Webster, Igno's right hand was the man who killed my parents. And I had vowed when they died that I would be the one to bring them down. "Massimo's our intel. It's just him and Graciella."

"You're going to put King in that den of beasts and terrorists? He's not ready for that. You need someone with experience. What are you doing, Gabe?"

"Well, I'm doing my job. Oversight wants it to be him."

"He's only been training for a little more than three months."

"I know. It's a surveillance op. All he has to do is watch, and he'll be going in undercover with his wife."

My stomach sank. I knew what that meant. "You're sending Tabs in with him? Oh."

The flash of white-hot jealousy sliced through me. Tabs *was* a field agent. And she was damn good. And she was unbelievably sexy. She was good bait. Perfect, actually. Except, I wanted to be the one in the field. I wanted the opportunity. But I knew that wasn't going to happen.

My brother crossed his arms and his head hung. "No, not Tabs. You. That's what I've been trying to tell you, if you would give me a chance to talk. You'll be going undercover as his wife."

I stared at him, trying to understand the words that were coming out of his mouth, letting them soak in. I got about as far as, 'you'll be going undercover' and my heart stuttered to a stop. And then I heard the rest of it. *'You'll be going undercover as his wife.'*

12

SAFFRON

INSOMNIA WAS A BITCH. I'd been steering clear of Lock all day as much as I could. And trying not to see Gabe. But when I'd tried to sleep, the turmoil in my brain and heart had kept me up.

Tabs found me on the first floor kitchen. How did people even have relationships with this life?

Are you asking for a friend?

No.

Tabatha hopped up on the counter and swung her feet. "So, you want to talk about it?"

I grabbed the ingredients for cookies. Flour. Sugar. Vanilla. Eggs. Chocolate chips. "No, I don't want to talk about it."

"Okay, who said we're going to make chocolate chip cookies? Honestly, are you going to eat all of these?"

"I don't know. Baking helps me relax."

I started cracking the eggs and she studied me. "Trouble in paradise? I've been thinking, since it's clearly eating at you, would it be the end of the world if he knew about the night you guys spent together?"

I slid her a sidelong glance. "Yes, it would."

I didn't know how else to explain it to her. There was a sense of security in him not knowing. That tension that crackled between us was just curiosity as far as he was aware. He wouldn't attribute it to any feelings I had buried. But if he knew, God... That would just be worse. And I would be humiliated.

"So what are you not telling me? I mean, how good can a dick really be anyway?"

I slid her a glance. "Tabs."

"What? So you shagged once, and then he promptly forgot about it. But we know it wasn't his fault."

"The worst thing is that I can tell he doesn't want me to do this with him. I think he wants me to say no. I can see him *waiting* for me to say no. And I don't want to. I just wanted Gabe to put someone else in. Put in Saint. Saint is good. Or Rookie. He looks like I could crack him in two, but I like him. He's earnest."

"You know what we can do to earnest."

"Tabs."

"What? He's cute."

"He is very cute. But so young. I think he's, what, nineteen?"

"And what? At the ripe old age of twenty-two, you are far wiser than him?"

"Okay, fine. Hardy-har. I've just been doing this my whole life, that's all."

Tabs rolled her eyes. "Honey, I know. Look, you have a chance here to prove yourself. This is your chance to shine. Are you really going to give it up because you shagged a bad boy and he didn't call after?"

"It was I who didn't call him."

"Even better."

"Except, he doesn't know I'm better."

"Honey, we take our wins where we can get them. He knows you're a killer agent. Are you really going to give him the satisfaction of making you run from the things that you're going to be great at?"

I licked my lips. "Ugh, he's just so annoying."

"Who knows? On missions, people sometimes get close."

I glowered at her. "It's the last thing I want."

"If you say so. I'm just pointing out that it could be fun."

I shook my head. "You are deliberately trying to make me crazy."

"Maybe a little. But come on, are you going to run? He doesn't remember. So what? It's fine. You're Saff Abbot and you don't need him, but you *can* work with him. For whatever reason, you unsettle him. And that's good." She winked. "Bring out your inner sex goddess."

I laughed. "If she still exists.."

"Oh she's in there. Now pay attention to your damn cookies because I want to do a taste test. Also, hand me the rest of the cookie dough."

I shook my head. "Ugh, raw eggs."

"Live a little, Saff. Remember, *when* you're on this mission, I know the version of you that you want to be. Outgoing and bubbly and fun, and all those things I know you can be. You just get caught up in the rules a little."

"The rules are there to protect us."

"Yeah. But you will be *undercover*, so you get to be whoever you want. And you get to show Lachlan King what he is missing. If he doesn't remember, that's on him."

Lachlan

Her scent wrapped around me like a vine intent on seeing my demise. Roses, vanilla, and God, what was that secret ingredient?

And at night, the dreams... Jesus fucking Christ, the dreams. My hands on her tits, her lips on my chest, kissing down my abs. Her mouth... that full pouty mouth. Jesus. My hands on her braids, fisting in them, tugging on them slightly as I angle her face just the way I like so I can kiss her. I could almost taste her.

Fuck. I'd wanted a woman before, but this was some other level bullshit. When I went to sleep, I dreamed of her. When I was awake, it was maddening to try and get on some kind of even ground with her. I didn't think I'd ever had a thing this bad for someone before, including my horny teenage years.

I watched her across our planning table as she leaned over. There was nothing overtly sexual in her V-neck fitted tee, except it hugged her breasts in a kind of way that gave way to my imagination. And she had joggers on, same as the rest of us. But hers molded to her arse. Fucking hell. This had to stop. I had to find a way for it to stop or I was going to go mad. Because every night, I could almost smell her on my sheets.

Next to me, Tabatha snapped a hand in front of my eyes. "King, are you paying attention?"

I realized then that Gabe had asked me something and I'd missed it. "Yeah, I'm with you."

Gabe raised a brow but continued, nonetheless. It turns out it hadn't been Gabe's question. It had been Saffron's. "What's our position here?"

Gabe pointed at the map. "Here's the palace, here is Massimo's villa, and you'll be located right next door. Our people are already there moving things around. The bedroom where we positioned you is right next to where Massimo's is, so you'll be able to have full access. You'll leave in three days, and we'll have some help from the Winston Isles royal security team. They're called the Royal Elite."

I nodded at that. "Word is their weapons laws don't meet our requirements."

"Just like the UK. No concealed carry unless you are armed police or have special dispensation. Luckily, you *will* have special dispensation. I don't want you going anywhere without being armed."

Gabe turned his gaze to Saffron. "That is an order, even though this is a surveillance op. Your job is to go in, get close, listen, and that's it." He turned his attention to me. "That means no cowboy shit."

I lifted a brow. "Why are you looking at me when you say that?"

Gabe narrowed his gaze. "King, it's no secret you want to fly this coop. You will do this mission and you will stay on the book. If anything happens to her, I come back to you for blood."

Saffron tilted her chin up. "First of all, this is my team, yes?"

Gabe lifted a brow.

"Yes or no?"

He looked like he'd swallowed a lizard. "Yes, Saffron is team lead."

"In that case, I'll be making the proclamations. We are a team. Everyone comes home, everyone does their job, and everyone keeps their mouth shut."

Gabe glowered at her but muttered, "You'll have some support staff outside of the Royal Elite. So you get to pick who comes with."

"All right, Tabs, obviously."

Gabe shook his head. "Nope, Tabs is needed here for another mission."

Saff bit her bottom lip. "All right, I'll take Saint then."

Gabe's eyes went wide. "Are you sure?"

"With Massimo's expertise in technology, I'd like to have someone who knows what they're doing on that front."

"Fair enough. We'll get him ready and introduced to the Royal Elite as well. Send him the day after you, maybe."

She nodded. "Um, how much backup will we have from the Royal Elite?"

"They will be your support, your egress, your safe house, all of it. You will also have help from the royal family, but obviously, they cannot provide you overt support. Understand?"

Her brow furrowed. "The queen is a Royal Guard, right?"

He laughed. "Of course, that would be what you remember about the Winston Isles."

"Hey, I remember when they got married. It was the hottest news."

Gabe dismissed the rest of the team and spoke to Saffron and I alone. "The two of you need to learn and work together. I want you to memorize these dossiers backward and forward. You need to be good enough to convince me, do you understand?"

Saffron gave him a brisk nod and he gave me a narrow-eyed glare. And then we were alone.

"Do you want to explain to me why your brother keeps looking at me like he wants to put a hole in my face?"

"That's just his face."

"Right. I feel like he didn't hate me as much a week ago."

"Do you think everything is about you?"

I shrugged. "Well, most things are."

She scowled at me. "Do you have your dossier with our undercover story? Have you even looked at it?"

"Yes, I've already studied it."

"Where did we meet?"

I grinned down at her. "It was actually a fix up. Your sister thought we'd be a good match, so she set us up on a blind date. And wonder of wonders, you actually tried to run away from me. I chased you down and talked you into going out with me for real."

She lifted a brow. "Yes, but can you say it with more passion, so someone would believe it?"

"You really want me to show you passion?"

She was so fucking hard to read. Yes, I was pushing her. Honestly. "Just tell me, why do you hate me again?"

"I don't hate you. I just don't think of you."

"Now that's not true. I've seen you watching me, Saff."

"That's Agent Abott to you."

I glanced down at the dossier. "Actually, no. It's Angel. It says right there that I'm supposed to call you Angel because you are the angel of my life. And I'm supposed to say it lovingly too, I assume."

She just narrowed her gaze at me. "We have a job to do, King."

"For fuck's sake, call me Lachlan."

"Are we on a first name basis?"

"Considering we have to pretend to be married, yes, we need to be on a first name basis. I'm trusting you with my life and hoping that whatever chip is on your shoulder isn't going to give away the job."

She squared her shoulders. "It won't."

Her gaze was slightly guarded. She never looked at me directly with those eyes, and it irritated me. Scooting around the desk, I marched toward her. And when she realized what I was doing, she backed up a step. "What are you doing, King?"

"As much as I love hearing you call me King, we're going to have this out. What the fuck is wrong with you?"

"Me?" She still didn't meet my gaze.

"You won't look me in the eyes. You won't address me

unless you have to. I know you're hard as hell on my assessments."

"Ever stopped to think I'm just trying to make you a better agent?"

"You and I both know I'm not going to be an agent. I'm not cut out for it. For me, this is the worst detox of my life. And I got the message. I need to clean my shit up. Fine. So we'll go to the Winston Isles, we'll sniff out a bunch of people, we'll come back, and I'll leave. But this is about something else for you, and I don't believe for a minute it's because I shagged a friend of yours. So what is it? Just tell me. The way you're acting it's like we fucked or something. And I know we didn't because I would remember that mouth. You see, I keep having dreams about your mouth and what it's capable of. So since I know that's not it, why don't you tell me what the fuck it is so I can, you know, get to the business of making you feel better about it and we can move on."

She looked like she'd seen a ghost. She hadn't paled exactly, but she looked stricken. She shook her head, this time lifting her gaze to meet mine levelly. Fucking hell. Those whiskey brown eyes could strip you clean to the soul. And I was the fool who'd insisted she look me dead in the eyes. Bloody fabulous.

"You're right. This mission will get you wherever the hell you want to go. And it'll give me what I want. So let's figure out a way we can work together."

I studied her warily. "So you're going to stop fighting me?"

She glanced at the dossiers. "You understand we're going to be in stupid-close proximity for the next several days. Like there will be no privacy between us. But while I might not be your biggest fan, I'm willing to put that aside for us to do this job. Because it is about to get vulnerable and intimate in a way I'm not sure either one of us really wants, but it can't be helped. The question is, can *you* handle it?"

13

LACHLAN

SHE'D ASKED me if I could handle this. And the truth was, I didn't know. The atmosphere on the plane was tense. I could feel her practically vibrating as the flight circled over the Winston Isles. I glanced out of the window, marveling at the striking azure blue water. Sure, I'd been to the Caribbean before. I had been on a million private jets all over the world. But there was still a part of me that was like a kid. I used to love traveling private with mum and dad. We would swear we could see specific people on the land below. It was hard not to continue the game in my head even as I looked down now, determined to try and see the king and queen on their balcony of the palace in the distance. I knew, of course, it wasn't real. But still, I looked. The pain of missing my brother was extra tight today. Would he be proud? Would he have so many questions about what I was doing and where I was going and how I had ended up like this? Probably. Would he have thought I was fucking cool that I got to be James Bond even for a few days? Hell, yes.

Saffron looked less than thrilled. Her face had been buried in our dossier from the moment we took off from London.

Hours and hours of pouring over our backstory, hours and hours of studying. Oh, I had studied too because I knew this mission stood between me and going home, going back to my life. Sure, I learned some cool things. And my grandfather was right; I had been lacking purpose. I thought sending me to the Rogues was bullshit, of course, but still, I could see why he'd done it. I felt more settled, but I was no spy.

So, I just had to do this mission well, and I could go home. It was easy surveillance. We'd get in, watch the couple, and report back.

I glanced at Saffron. "You know that dossier inside and out by now."

Her shoulders stiffened, and I knew I should have just left her to it. Maybe this was how she calmed herself on a flight. I didn't know.

"Do you know who Massimo Igno is? Do you have any idea how many people he's killed?"

"It's in the dossier. I read it. I studied it. I reviewed it. I know it."

"Do you know what he will do if he so much as suspects who we are?"

I swallowed. "I know. This is serious. I get it. But isn't there such a thing as being overprepared?"

She clenched her jaws together. I could see the delicate muscles ticking back and forth. She shouldn't do that. She would likely give herself a headache from all the teeth grinding.

"From the moment we get off this plane, we have to *be* who we say we are."

I nodded. "Yeah, right. Hold hands, smile, watch them. Do you have a problem with that?"

She sighed and leaned forward, placing her forearms on her knees as she did so. She'd worn a cream-colored India Rolan suit. It was exquisite on her dark skin. She'd changed her hair too. Her braids were different. One side had more of a wave or curl to them. I knew better than to touch her hair without her permission, so all I could do was stare at it, trying to identify how she'd done it.

Maybe she'd had someone do it for her. Hell, what did I know?

"From the moment we arrive at that villa, we will be watched. And you better get ready soon, or at some point he is going to get fiber optics in that house and spy right back on us. I know that you think you know how to do this, and you think you're going to just wrap your arm around my waist and call me sweetheart or love from time to time, but you shouldn't forget; we are faking this until we make it. There is no reprieve unless we are somewhere like the palace or the Royal Elite offices. Everywhere else we have to assume, as public space, we can be viewed without our permission. You can't ever call me Saff. I can't ever call you Lock. From the moment this door opens, we are on. And when I tell you it's tiring, I mean it."

"Won't we be safe in the villa?"

"I don't know for how long. We're better off having any conversations we need to have privately in the shower."

I swallowed convulsively. "I hear you. I hadn't realized we would be *that* together."

"I know you think it's a game, but this is life and death. Massimo Igno could be our ticket to Drake Webster. If we can get to Webster, that's a jackpot."

I frowned then, watching her closely. I could see it in her eyes. This Webster guy was the one she wanted. "Is he part of this? Drake Webster?"

She shook her head. "He is Antonio Igno's right-hand man and the person responsible for the death of my parents."

I winced. "Shit. I'm sorry. I didn't know."

She shook her head. "You weren't here then. It's not your fault."

"Are we going to have any moments of privacy?"

She shook her head. "Not safely. Like I said, Royal Elite offices but nowhere else. This needs to be the best acting job of your life. No mistakes."

"I hear you. We are a team, right?"

Her gaze lifted to mine. "Yes, we're a team."

"So you trust me?"

"In terms of this mission? Yes. You want something out of it, and so do I. Because of that, I think we make a great team."

She wasn't saying the one thing I was curious about. "We're meant to be a married couple, Saff."

She nodded absently.

I continued. "The thing about married couples is they have to, um... You know, touch at some point. Is that going to be okay with you?"

She nodded curtly. "Get ready. We're landing soon. Welcome to the Winston Isles."

Saffron

I WAS STRESSED and it showed.

Yes, I knew what I was getting into when I agreed to this. I just had to get used to being locked in a house with Mr. Sex on a Stick. Ever since the incident in his cottage, I'd been careful with him. Distant. At least as best I could. It wasn't like he made it easy.

I hadn't even told Tabatha what had happened at the cottage. Because Lord only knew that she was inclined to forget about the rules and insist that I needed to have some sort of torrid affair. Sometimes Tabatha could be so by the book. And other times, when it came to me, she thought the rules didn't apply. Or that they shouldn't for some reason. That never made any sense.

Maybe because you need to live a little.

Lock drove us through the winding streets of the main island's old town, and it was beautiful. The sunlight on the azure blue waters was mesmerizing, and on the streets there was such a mix of new and old culture. There were traders along the road, selling everything you could possibly want from batteries to coconuts to sunscreen to fish. I loved it for its eclectic nature.

It reminded me of times when I'd traveled to Jamaica with my mum. The street hawkers were such a juxtaposition to the skyscrapers of steel and glass. All I could do was take it all in.

I'd have to come back to the Winston Isles for a vacation when I had more time.

Lock seemed to manage driving on the wrong side of the road fairly well. "You're actually half decent at this."

He lifted a brow. "I am surprisingly stressed out."

"Sorry," I winced.

"You're driving next time."

"Must I?" I whined.

He nodded. "Yup. You're the training officer."

"Oh, *now* you acknowledge that I'm your training officer?"

He gave me a tight smile at that one. "I acknowledge it. It's just hard for me to take orders."

"Let me guess, every one of your school reports said, *Lachlan has a problem with authority figures?*"

He grinned then. A real grin. One I hadn't seen in a week. "Exactly. How did you know?"

"Because it's something I wrote in my report to Gabe on you."

He made a mock shocked face and clutched a hand to his heart. "Wow. And here I thought we were friends."

"Is that what we are?" I asked softly.

His gaze looked into mine for a brief moment, and I shifted uncomfortably in my seat. We hadn't talked anymore about what had almost happened. We hadn't acknowledged it. And honestly, I'd pulled back from him. Way back. I dragged my gaze away. If I had to, even for a moment, relive the feeling of his hard erection between my legs, I was going to lose it.

One more round with my battery operated boyfriend probably would have really helped me out. But mostly it just intensified the need, so I was going cold turkey.

Oh yeah, that sounds like a fantastic idea when you're locked in a house with him.

I had to do something. Lock on the brain was a problem. And I was finally getting what I wanted. A field assignment. Maybe it was just observation, but there was still a dangerous element to it, so it was something I could cut my teeth on. To show Gabe that his trust in me wasn't misplaced. Focus on the mission and not on my partner. Easy.

When we pulled up to Royal Elite, Gabe's shoulders finally relaxed as he parked in front of the flat-roofed contemporary building. The white columns gleamed and the glass walls glittered. It looked modern. Just as I pushed open the door to get out of the car, an enormous man stepped out of the front door. At Rogues, we had all kinds of agents. Some of them former military and enormous. Many of them played bodyguard roles. We had spies who were meant to blend into the background. But this guy was stupid good looking. Massive. He was bigger than Lock. Had more muscle on him too. His light brown hair, blue eyes, and clean-shaven jaw screamed *I could have been a pouty Abercrombie model in my youth.*

And then he unleashed his smile. *Dear Lord.* "Let me guess, you're Saffron Abott?" he asked in a low timbre.

I nodded, barely able to croak out a hello. "Yes. That's me. This is my partner, Lachlan King."

He gave Lock a nod and shook my hand, completely encompassing it in his. "I'm Jax Reynolds. I'll be bringing you up to speed. Ariel Winston's on her way."

"Right."

The whole recent history of the Winston Isles fascinated me. Ariel Winston had been a Royal Guard in the palace. And then somehow she'd left her employment there to start her own security agency. But her security agency still worked closely with the palace. It was fascinating. And she'd married a prince. An actual prince.

Not that I paid a lot of attention to the gossip rags.

Who are you kidding? You live for that.

It was my one guilty pleasure, really. I loved anything about royals and celebrities. They led a life completely different than my own. Yes, the Abott name afforded me money and access, but I lived a life with no lights and parties and dancing until the wee hours of the morning. I didn't get to experience that aspect, so I didn't know those people. Hearing about their lives was endlessly fascinating.

Ariel was also best friends with Queen Penny, who had also been a Royal Guard. Eventually, she'd married the king. She stayed on as a guard too, which I found so modern. She was my hero. Able to have both. And I couldn't quite squelch that inner teenage hope that I might actually meet the queen.

"Thank you so much for taking the time to set things up for this."

"It's not a problem. Gabe and I go way back."

"Oh, I wasn't aware you knew my brother."

He nodded. "I was sorry to hear about your parents."

I swallowed hard and forced a thankful smile on my face because that was what people expected. "Thanks, I appreciate it."

"Should we go in?" Lock asked.

Jax nodded and led the way.

As we followed him, I noticed Lock was glaring at him. "What's wrong with you?"

"I don't like the way he was looking at you."

I choked out a laugh. "Are you serious right now?"

He shrugged. "Yup."

"Then maybe you didn't notice the ring on his finger?"

Lock frowned. "That doesn't mean anything.

"Wow," I said, laughing.

"It doesn't."

Almost as if on cue when Jax opened the door, a squealing toddler ran out. "Daddy, daddy, daddy, daddy, daddy."

With a laugh he stooped down and picked her up. She had a head full of curls and was mostly cheeks and dimples. "Mayzie, I told you not to run. You can slip and fall, especially in this office."

"Yes, but I wanted to say hi, Daddy."

"Okay, Mayzie, why don't you say hi to some new friends of daddy's. This is Mr. King and Miss Abott."

The little girl blew Lachlan a kiss, and he grinned back at her, a full smile showcasing dimples of his own.

My stomach squeezed. It was adorable. So was I really jealous of a toddler?

She eyed me. "You're pretty."

Way to melt my heart. "Well, thank you, but I'm not as pretty as you are."

She giggled and tucked her face into her father's neck. "No. I'm not as pretty as my mommy."

"I'm sure your mommy is beautiful." I gave her a soft smile.

A harried woman came running around the corner. "Oh Jesus Christ, there you are, Mayzie."

Mayzie clapped. "Mommy, you found me. You seeked me good."

The woman took her from Jax and admonished her. "Mayzie, I told you if you wanted to play we had to stay in the back of the house, remember?"

Mayzie frowned. "I sorry. I forgot." She pointed at Lock. "Isn't he cute, Mommy?"

Her mother laughed. "Oh my God. This child. She's boy crazy already and she's only a toddler."

Jax frowned down at his daughter, who looked nothing like either of the two of them. Mayzie's mother looked maybe like she was Indo-African? Her skin color was deep brown, though not as deep as mine. But her hair was a silkier texture with a slight curl to it. "Hi, I'm Neela. This one's mum. His wife."

I gave her a grin and shook her hand. "Hi, I'm Saffron."

Jax scowled at Lock as Lock turned his charming grin on her. "Lachlan King. It's nice to meet you. Your daughter's adorable."

Neela rolled her eyes. "Don't buy it. She's a ridiculous flirt and will use her dimples to get whatever she wants."

"I can see why."

With a laugh, I added, "Lachlan sees no problems with that strategy. That's how he gets through life."

Jax laughed at that. And then Neela excused herself and leaned in to give her husband a kiss. Jax lingered just a second too long, and Mayzie pushed at her father. "Ew, daddy, stop slipping your tongue in mommy's mouth. Gross."

All of us laughed. And as the two of them were leaving, Jax's gaze stayed on his wife's arse. Oh boy, that was a man in lust with his wife, which was amazing. How did these kinds of things happen where people were so besotted with their significant other that they just couldn't keep their hands off each other? Trying to think back, I thought my parents were maybe past that point in their life. Well maybe not. I did see them sneaking kisses every now and again. But they weren't nearly as demonstrative as these two.

When Jax led the way back toward what seemed like offices, I raised an eyebrow at Lachlan, and he shrugged. "Okay, fine. He's married."

He said it with such a snotty countenance I had to giggle. To cover, I asked Jax, "Is this a work-life situation?"

He nodded. "Yeah, it is sometimes. We have a couple of agents who stay on-site. When Tristan travels, Ariel will stay here. As she says, it's better for her health to not have to go blind up in the palace with Penny and Sebastian."

I frowned at that. "Go blind?"

His ears turned bright red as he lifted a brow.

I snorted a laugh. "Ah, got it."

"When Tristan's there, I think they're more discreet because Sebastian is very protective of Penny. But when his cousin is gone, they're more liberal. There isn't a member of staff who hasn't walked in on them at least once."

I hid a laugh. "Oh my God."

"Yes, yes, it is in fact an oh-my-God situation."

Lachlan was loving every bit of this. "Oh man, Saint's going to be pissed he's missed this briefing."

Jax led us into the conference room, and we took seats next to each other with Jax at the head of the table. "Your other agents are coming in tonight, correct?"

I took out my tablet. "They made a stop in New York for some extra equipment."

"Ah yes, Blake Security's Matthias."

"Yes, actually. You know Matthias?"

"Yes. He got us a new set of bulletproof vests last time they came through. He's the best in the business when it comes to tech and gear."

I nodded. "Yes, he is. So they'll arrive tonight, but we wanted to get situated."

"Excellent. My team's already set you up with equipment in the villa. Anything else you need, just let me know."

"Thank you."

The conference room door opened, and in walked a stunning brunette. She looked an awful lot like a Bratz doll. Barely over five feet tall, full lips, big dark eyes, and inky black hair that cascaded around her shoulders and down her back. And then she grinned at me and Lock. "Oh, you guys are here already. Nice to meet you. I'm Zia Barnes."

Then the rest of the members of the team rolled in. Once we had a full house, Jax started the meeting, but then a redhead rushed in. "Sorry I'm late. Sorry, sorry, sorry."

Jax threw up his hands. "My God, woman, can you let a man finish? Are you running the meeting, or am I?"

"You're running it. I'm just observing." The redhead flashed me a grin. "Saff Abott, right?"

I nodded. "Yes. I stood to shake her hand, and she swatted my hand away and gave me a tight hug. "I met Tabatha last time I was in London. She couldn't stop talking about you, so I feel like I know you." She cocked her head and glanced at Lock. "Oh well, Tabatha did not tell me you looked like that."

Lock gave her a bemused smile. "Lachlan King. Nice to meet you."

"I'm Ariel, obviously."

She indicated the red hair and rolled her eyes.

I laughed. "That's perfect."

"My mother was obsessed with the movie. This is the result." She plopped into her seat. "Okay, Jax, carry on."

Jax walked us through protocols that we'd have to follow to

keep the Royal Council happy. And while the palace couldn't *officially* assist us, they were absolutely assisting us. "This is perfect. Thank you so much."

He gave a nod. "And as additional backup, if you have an event to go to, we will try and get at least two of our men in there."

"Do you think that's necessary?" Lock asked.

"Just for added security. We know the Ignos' reputation, so we want to make sure that you're covered."

"This is amazing," I said. "We couldn't have expected more."

"Our pleasure," Ariel said with a smile.

"You know how you're going to make your approach?" Jax asked.

Lachlan looked at me. " I will be using my official ID. She will be Saffron King, my wife, and we're here on our honeymoon. Having the extra identification helps a lot."

Jax nodded. "Excellent. I've got her ID here. If you need anything else let us know."

Ariel interceded. "So Lachlan, do you know Massimo Igno?"

"Only from school. We weren't friends, and he was a couple of years ahead of me. Maybe he won't even recognize me, but we'll need to be a little hands-off if that's the case."

"Okay. I'll have my people stay back just in case."

"That's helpful, thank you."

Ariel grinned at me, and I couldn't help feeling like her smile was a warm hug. I said, "Tabs told you, huh?"

"Your first field mission, yes. She's very excited."

I groaned.

"Don't worry about it. We're all here to support you. And this is your show. You just tell us what you need. Welcome to the Winston Isles. Try and have some fun."

Lock deliberately bumped my leg. "Oh yeah, fun is Saff's middle name."

I scowled at him, and Ariel laughed. "Oh, pretend married couple. You guys are going to be great."

Jax rolled his eyes. "If you need a deeper cover, let me know. Zia came up with those. She's a great hacker."

Ariel cleared her throat. "I came up with those, thank you very much."

I lifted my brows. "You're a hacker?"

"It's one of my skillsets."

Jax rolled his eyes. "You'll have to forgive my boss. Sometimes she likes to gloat."

I chuckled, loving that we had this team as our backup crew. With them, I felt infinitely more secure. We had this in the bag.

Famous last words.

14

SAFFRON

LACHLAN WAS RIGHT. Driving on the wrong side of the road was nerve racking to say the least. By the time I reached the villa, I was exhausted.

We'd both agreed to head off to freshen up, get some rest, unpack, and spend a little more time with our new IDs. Lachlan got to be himself. Which was hardly fair. But he had to remember things like calling me Saffron and not Saff. And remember things that Saffron loved. And while he was fine, a little practice never hurt anyone. Besides, I needed a moment to myself. Watching all the loved-up couples today hadn't necessarily been a revelation, but it had made me hyper-aware of just how alone I was.

For the most part, I didn't feel my loneliness. But watching everybody else together, hearing Jax and Neela's daughter, Mayzie, laughing, I realized I wanted that too. The life that I'd started to craft for myself, or the one I was thrust into if I was being honest, I didn't want that. I wanted *real* friends. As much as I loved Tabs, I wanted more friends than just her. I wanted a family.

I had to figure out how the hell I was going to get that. Or if that was even possible for someone like me. My whole life, the Rogues had been everything. But maybe there was more to life than that. It hardly seemed fair that I couldn't have both. That I couldn't *be* both.

I should have the opportunity to be more than one thing, shouldn't I? Wasn't that a possibility, a thing that people wanted? Those were the kind of things I wished my mum was around to talk about.

But she's not, is she?

And Gabe didn't let anyone in. Not even me. The only other person on earth who knew what he could be going through, and he didn't even let me *see* him. My brother angered me, suffocated me, and sometimes pushed me to the point that I honestly considered shooting him. Not a fatal shot, but like a shoulder or a kneecap. But even worse, he pushed me away, refusing to accept even the slightest bit of love. Or giving it to me. And I needed it.

I dragged myself out of the melancholy and started to unpack. I knew the guys were bringing in our bulletproof vests and additional specialized items. I had a couple ball gowns coming that had cameras built into the fabric. We were also getting more audio equipment. But for now, I could unpack the rest of my things. Tabs had helped me put together the things that I would need for the mission.

Because, hell, I didn't know what I needed. But she had been on dozens of missions.

When I opened my suitcase, I immediately started to hang up the usual things. Dark jeans, sundresses. But when I got to the toiletries, what I found made me frown.

Yes, she had put knickers in. It's not like she'd left them out. But it was the *kind* of knickers she'd slipped in.

I picked up my phone, quickly dialed the routing number for the secure line. And waited.

When it chimed, I gave them my code. "Alpha-Tango-Whiskey-Sierra-five-seven."

That was a code line for Tabatha.

It rang once and she answered. "Oh my God, you're there. How is paradise?"

"Are you fucking kidding me right now?"

"You sound unhappy. Is Lock irritating you already? Or is it just the foreplay?"

"Can you explain to me why you packed me sheer knickers and thongs? So many thongs."

"Oh, yes. That's to help, you know, get in the *vibe* of your character."

"You're joking."

"Why would I kid about something like your character? You are Mrs. Saffron King. Your undergarments should reflect that."

"You do know we're not *actually* married, right?"

"But you're playing a married couple. You have to believe it. As a newlywed, you would have very sexy things. What if this Massimo character breaks into the villa and snoops around? He's going to wonder why you have granny panties. Also, why the fuck do you have granny panties? You're young and hot."

"I do *not* have granny panties. I have seamless panties. They're perfectly respectable. They're even low-rise." I sniffed indignantly.

"Yes, they're serviceable, and they don't leave panty lines. But you need thongs and lace. Lace is *sexy*."

"I cannot believe you switched out my underwear," I grumbled. "Where did these even come from?"

"La Perla."

I dropped the offending pairs in a drawer. "Are these yours?"

"No. I ordered them as soon as I knew you were going on a mission. What's the problem?"

"I'm going to kill you." I shuffled through the bra and panty sets. "There isn't a decent regular set in here except what I have on."

"Thank God. You need to see yourself as a sexual being. Someone who gets shagged."

"Oh my God. I hate you."

"You're welcome." She hung up the phone.

She was making me insane.

But she also had a point. Our characters needed to be foolproof.

I just had to hope that Lock didn't notice. Because he was not seeing my panties. Ever.

———

Saffron

This was it. We were doing this.

I was fine. Not nervous at all. Not terrified.

Okay fine, a little terrified.

I was Saffron King, Lachlan King's wife. My husband was part of the famous King Media empire. And I loved him.

As we started the stroll from the car park, Lock threw his arm over my shoulder, and I purposely reached up and intertwined my fingers with his.

He pulled me in and gave me a brushed kiss on my forehead. "You ready?"

"Look alive, King."

"You know I will always love hearing you say that."

I lifted a brow and just shook my head.

I could feel his chuckle vibrating through his body. And of

course, it vibrated through me, making me warm and squishy and desperate to be even closer to him. *Like a fool.*

We hadn't talked about anything. And I was not about to start now. Nope no talking necessary. We were going to do this mission. We were going to pull this off and it was going to be fine. I was going to be fine.

"Relax, Saffron. You're holding on real tight."

I realized my arm around his waist was bunched in the fabric. I unclenched my hand and smoothed the fabric, not sure what else to do with my hands.

"Go on, you know you want to. Put your hand on my arse."

I burst out laughing. And then he very deliberately pulled me in. He leaned down, and I stiffened.

Oh fuck.

He would know. The moment he kissed me he would know.

I knew that was irrational. I completely understood that I was not being a rational person here. He wouldn't know. Those memories of me were gone.

And while I was trying to come to terms with that, indulging in this feeling was a bad idea. I knew it. I needed to stay focused. Eyes on the prize. We had a mission to complete. And I could do it. It was just Lachlan.

He was good. If he was himself, we could do this. We just had to be in the right place at the right time.

Lachlan's voice was soft. "Would you relax? You can do this."

I nodded and relaxed into him. "Okay, sorry."

He leaned over and kissed me properly. It was brief. Soft. Honestly no more than a peck. But it was just the peck I needed. It wasn't demanding. It wasn't sexual. It was more like reassurance. Like we were a team. And then I relaxed into him.

He pulled back, his gaze lingering on my lips for a moment. Then he nodded, and we resumed our walk.

We very deliberately paused in boutiques, and I tried on hats and scarves while he nodded and smiled approvingly. Snapping pictures. It was almost easy to pretend.

We'd already gotten word from Zia that Massimo Igno was on the island. He was with his fiancée, and we'd seen them leave their villa. Their driver was a Royal Elite informant, and he had notified Zia, so we had their exact location. It was only a matter of time. And well, being seen, being out, being a loving married couple.

We stopped for Lock to grab me a gelato. And as I took a lick, Lock leaned over and whispered to me, "Showtime."

I nodded. Lock turned with a wide smile. "Oh my God. Igno. Is that you?"

He kept a broad smile on his face as he pulled me close and kissed me on the forehead. "You okay?" he whispered.

I nodded at him, and he dragged me over to his "friend."

The woman next to him, Graciella Natanya, looked confused.

The two men embraced and clapped hands on each other's backs. I was always fascinated with how men could do that. Pick up and resume friendship right where it left off as if no time had passed.

Massimo said, "Mate, I can't get over how much you look like your brother."

Lock shrugged. "Yeah well, the King genes are strong. How are you? I haven't seen you since Eton. I expected you at Cambridge, but you never appeared."

Igno shook his head. "My father had other ideas. Wharton, Harvard, you know the deal. I'm not really a Harvard man though, am I?"

Lock laughed. "To be honest, I wouldn't know. You ran more with Charlie when it came to that."

"I miss him. I can't even imagine what it's like for you."

"Yeah. I appreciate it, mate. It's been rough. I miss him every day."

Graciella cleared her throat. "Sweetheart, who's your friend?"

He sighed. "Sorry, love. This is an old mate, Lachlan King. This is my fiancée, Graciella Natanya."

Lock turned on the charm. "Ah, lovely to meet you. This is my wife, Saffron King."

Massimo guffawed. "You got married? You?"

Lock shrugged. "What can I say, when you know, you know. And one look at Saffron and I knew I wasn't giving her up."

"Wow." Igno stepped forward and wrapped his beefy arms around me, inhaled deep, and squeezed.

I expected Graciella to narrow her gaze at me, but she just looked at me curiously as if completely unaffected by her boyfriend's overly long hug.

"Hello."

"Sorry, you have to allow us an indulgence. We haven't seen each other in a very long time. Since school. This is my fiancée, Graciella. I'm sure the two of you will get along great."

But Graciella just gave me an exasperated laugh. "Men. They don't know anything, do they?"

I chuckled. "It's nice to meet you."

"This is such a lovely coincidence. How long are you staying on island?" she asked.

We made small talk before Lock found his way back to me and pulled me to him, kissing my temple. "There you are. Don't run far."

Graciella had me walking a little bit, looking in the shop windows, but Lock was wise not to let me get too far.

This only worked well if it was the two of us together. A team. The idea was no separation unless it was absolutely necessary.

It was easier to sell the couple, sell the connection. And it was just safer.

I had to keep reminding myself this was a sneak and peek mission only. We were only there to observe.

As the four of us walked through the old town, Graciella occasionally wandered into a boutique and pulled me along. She was beautiful. Lovely.

When she looked at me and asked me what I did, I told her I was still in graduate school. Art history.

She laughed as if that was the most delightful thing she'd ever heard.

Whatever. I just needed her and Igno to buy the act.

And they did. Lock and Igno laughed once or twice about an old mate of theirs. To wrap up the "accidental" meeting, I strategically yawned.

Lock groaned. "Ah, my darling wife, you're exhausted already?"

"You were the one who wanted to go cliff diving this morning at the crack of dawn. And then you wanted to go see the king's museum. And then on a photo tour. I am beat, Lachlan."

"Well okay, let's get you back to the villa."

He turned to Igno then. "It was good to see you, mate. But she will murder me if I don't get her back for some rest. Where are you guys staying? We're at the palace villas at the edge of the old town. We should catch up more, drinks tomorrow or something."

Igno's eyes went wide. "No way. That's where we are too."

I laughed. "Oh my God! Fantastic then, the two of you can catch up tomorrow and leave me to rest. I'm so sorry. I don't want to be horribly rude, but I am knackered."

Igno laughed and started to wrap his arms around me again. But this time Lachlan stayed locked tightly to my hips.

"One hug, Igno."

Igno laughed. "Ah, I'm Italian. I love beautiful women. See, Graciella doesn't mind, do you?"

She only rolled her eyes. "You'll have to ignore him. I do."

I assumed they were joking, but I made a mental note to double-check how their relationship was going just in case there were problems we needed to know about.

When we separated, Lock picked me up around the waist and tossed me over his shoulder. "Now, woman. Come with me. I plan to ravish you before you sleep."

I giggled and mock slapped his back. And all I could do was lift my head slightly and shake my head at him. Just enough so that Massimo and Graciella would see it.

At the car, he eased me down, every inch of my body sliding against his, and I could have sworn to God that underneath his clothes he was rock hard.

He watched me smoothly and bit his lip. "They watching?"

My gaze flickered over his shoulder.

Massimo and Graciella had wandered over to the other side of the boutiques, and she had a clear line of sight to us. "Yes."

"Relax... or try to. I'm kissing you now, okay?"

I couldn't help it. I went stiff again. He leaned in, dropping his lips low and sliding his hands into my braids, pulling gently and angling my head, turning our bodies so that Graciella and Massimo would absolutely see us kissing.

He pulled back slightly, and against my lips he whispered, "Try and swoon a little, okay?"

He kissed me again, and when he released me, I didn't have to pretend. I *did* swoon just a little, my body unsure of exactly what had happened. The kiss had been just as hot as I remembered, and I was left dazed and confused.

Damn it, he knew what he was doing to me, and he relished it. It was hardly fair.

"All right let's get in the car."

When he opened the passenger side door for me, I eased in. He gave a nod. "Looks like that went well."

All I could do was nod because I still couldn't quite stop the buzzing and humming in my head.

How the hell was I going to survive any more kisses from Lachlan king?

15

SAFFRON

OF COURSE I TOLD TABATHA. I kept telling myself I was calling her for advice because she had experience as a field agent. But really, obviously, I had just kissed the man I fancied, and I needed someone to dish about it with.

After the rigamarole of entering all the clearance codes, Tabatha answered on the second ring.

"Hey, how's it going?"

"Good as can be expected. I will say Massimo is very creepy. He looks at me like I'm a gelato on a hot summer day."

Tabatha, best friend that she was, made gagging noises. "I've seen photos of Massimo. He's not necessarily bad looking, but there's something very sweaty looking about him. Is that wrong?"

"No, that's exactly it. Look, he's Italian, tan skin, dark hair, deep-set eyes. But it's like it's all paired together wrong. You can see in a photo how some women would find him handsome, but in person there's this slick quality to him. I can't explain it, but I do not want to be left alone with him."

"And how is it going with your delectable husband? They

say the first year of living with someone can be the true test of a relationship."

"Oh, very funny. He's fine. Except yesterday..." I let my voice trail off.

Tabatha took off running with that kernel of gossip. "Oh my God, we wasted time on all the niceties for the last whole minute. Tell me everything. Did you two shag?"

"What? No. But we did kiss."

On the other end of the line, Tabatha whooped. "I knew it. I knew being in paradise would ignite the passion. And does he remember?"

"You said yourself, the effects of the drug we gave him are like GHB. He won't remember. And I very much think the kiss was for the mission, not because he wanted to."

"Bullshit. Was there tongue?"

I thought back to the way his tongue slid over mine. The way his hand fisted in my hair, tugging just a little to give enough bite to excite me but not so much as to hurt. I thought of the way he groaned low in his throat. And I thought of the way the thick pulsing length of his erection had nestled up against my core, practically begging for entrance. But I didn't tell Tabatha any of this. Instead, I just said, "Yes, there was tongue."

There was more whooping on the other end of the line. "Honey, he's so into you. Even if he doesn't remember. This is some love shit."

There was no way I was entertaining this line of conversation. "No, this is some chemistry shit. We find each other attractive. How do you do it? You've been on missions where you have to pretend to be the girlfriend of someone. How do you pretend and not get a little affected?"

Tabatha sighed. "Honey, that's very different. Sure, maybe I find my fake person attractive. But I look at it like an acting job.

You and Lachlan actually have a thing, so it's going to be harder for you to separate fact from fiction."

"That was the last thing on earth I wanted to hear from you."

She laughed softly. "I'm sorry. I wish I could give you, if not good news, easy news. But there is no easy news. You two will just need to figure out your feelings."

"That's just it. I'm trying to ignore my feelings, thank you very much. There was nothing wrong with Elsa and her conceal-don't-feel methodology."

"Yes, but we all know how that ended up. Stuffing your feelings is never good. You have to look at them and deal with them properly. And in your case dealing with it might involve just shagging him and getting him out of your system."

I laughed. "You're no help."

"I'm sorry. I shouldn't tease you. But I do think you should shag him. Because orgasms are good for everybody. And it will be like a reset. Maybe that can be your starting point."

I groaned and rolled around in the bed, pulling the pillow over my face. "This was not helpful."

"On the contrary, I find this very helpful. Now I have the play-by-play. So how are you going to play it when you see him this morning? Cool, casual, completely unbothered? Or are you going to really lean in, give him another smack on the lips and see what happens?"

"You would really like that wouldn't you?"

"I would actually."

I rolled my eyes. "No, I am going to play it cool. This is a mission. And I need to remember that. This isn't real, and I can't have Lachlan."

"Well, if you insist on being boring, fine. You wanted my advice, and I gave it. Enjoy this time. Really lean in. Get him out of your system, get some orgasms in, then go back to your normally scheduled programming."

"Ugh. That doesn't help Tabs."

She laughed. "Look, I'm mostly teasing. But enjoy it. Experience what it's like to actually be in a relationship. Think of it like a test run, minus all the ghosting and mediocre boys."

I hung up with her on a laugh and forced myself to climb out of bed. I couldn't hide in there all day. I was going to have to face him. And it would probably be best if I acted like I wasn't one giant walking hormone when it came to him.

———

Saffron

"ARE YOU OKAY?"

Something was off with Lock. When I'd come down for breakfast, he'd been uncharacteristically quiet.

Lock watched me carefully. "Yeah."

"Are you sure? You seem off." He looked fine, but he was quieter than usual.

"I'm good. You good?"

Last night had been intense. I wasn't ashamed to say I'd had two cold showers since he'd kissed me. Today, he was acting off. I needed to figure out what the hell it was, because tonight was a party that Massimo and Graciella had invited us to. I needed him on his game. But first, I needed to get my brother up to speed. "Totally good."

There was something like resigned reproach in his eyes when he said, "Good. Let's go."

An hour later, we were meeting in the Royal Elite conference room. Jax started the meeting a little late with an apology.

"Sorry we're late, everyone. Ariel had a last-minute thing up at the castle."

Zia nodded and quickly dialed London. Gabe answered with his typical, "Webb."

I almost had to laugh at my brother. He was so predictable. "Gabe, it's us."

There was a part of me that thought there was some warmth in his voice, but I could never tell. "Saff, you all right?"

"Yeah, we're fine. We're just calling in for a status check."

"Tonight's the party, right?" he asked.

"Yes, the plan is we'll go to the party, find a reason to get into the bedroom, and plant a bug in the cupboard. Lock will take care of the balconies, providing we have access. Back up will also be Jax and Zia. Saint will be our waiter. He'll give us our kill code if we have to abort. The ultimate goal is to get into the library."

Gabe listened to me silently. "Don't take any unnecessary risks. This is just surveillance."

I clenched my jaw, trying to dissipate the annoyance at his admonishment. "I understand the assignment, Gabe."

"Good. Anything we get, make sure we've got photos on everyone."

"We're on it. We'll have additional help tonight too. Queen Penny and Ariel will be in attendance."

"Make sure the whole team knows the abort code."

"I will make that determination in the field," I said through clenched teeth.

Jesus, even from thousands of miles away, he was still trying to control exactly how I managed everything.

"How is Lock managing?"

I tried not to grumble. And despite his surly demeanor today, he was helpful by jumping in.

"Lock is fine. Listening to Saff. Staying the hell out of trouble. Mostly lending my name and trying to be a billionaire dick so I can play the part."

"Massimo's believing it? You two are old chums?"

"Yeah. Although, I will say, I don't love his fixation on Saff."

I scowled at him then. What the fuck was he doing?

Gabe's reply was tense. "What fixation?"

I stared at Lock. "Our new recruit thinks Massimo is fixated on me. That isn't accurate. We will proceed with the mission as outlined."

My brother's voice was hard. "Do we need to pull you?"

"No. And remember, I'm the lead agent in the field."

I could almost see his jaw tensing from here. "Saff, we're not taking risks with your safety."

"No, but I'm the agent in the field, so I'll make the determination."

Lachlan scowled at me. What the hell was his problem? Everything had been fine yesterday. I'd have to ask him about it later because I did not have time for his attitude right now.

"Have we heard any chatter on our actual targets?"

Lock sighed. "No, but we've got a keen ear. All the intel so far has to do with his businesses. As far as we can tell, legitimate ones. He's doing some entertainment management thing. Presumably for Graciella, but I know the Ignos, and there's no way that's on the up and up."

"Fine," Gabe said. "Keep doing what you're doing. We'll find a way. We know wherever Massimo is, Drake isn't far behind."

I shivered just thinking about him. But I squared my shoulders and resolved to get my job done. My team was counting on me.

When we finished with my brother, Jax nodded at me. "Would you like more men tonight?"

"No. I know you guys have to assess security for the queen. I don't see any problems. It's a party. But obviously, have as many men there as you think you need to have."

"I'm not worried about the queen. Penny can handle herself. We're only there to make Sebastian happy. Ariel and Penny make a hell of a team on their own, so you won't have to look out for them. She may look like a fairy princess, but she's not bad at hand-to-hand combat, and she will be armed."

I blinked slowly. "I knew, she was a Royal Guard, but I guess I assumed she wasn't combat trained."

Jax and Zia chuckled. Zia's smile was broad. "Oh, you don't know Queen Penny."

As we left Royal Elite, I couldn't shake the feeling something was wrong with Lock. Every time I snuck a glance at him, his jaw was tight, a frown marring his forehead. I headed to the driver's side, but he shook his head and scowled. "I'm driving."

I tried again. "Is there something wrong?"

"Nope. Nothing."

"You've been weird since last night."

"I'm not weird." His response was terse.

"Are you sure?"

He turned to me then. "Question, how did you get assigned to me?"

I frowned. "Gabe. He assigned me to you after our initial debacle outside of the bungalow."

"So before then, you didn't know me?"

I frowned. "What's going on?"

"I just assumed you'd seen my file or something."

I shook my head. "I had no idea you even existed at Rogues until you tried to put me on my arse."

"Almost managed it too."

"You wish," I said, rolling my eyes.

For a moment, the teasing was back, the effortlessness. But when we climbed back in the car, he was all tense again.

"Do you feel uneasy? Did you see something? You have to talk to me."

"I'm just trying to figure out why this is your first mission."

I frowned. "We're doing this now?"

He nodded. "Yeah, we're doing this now."

"Well, do you want to start driving so I can fill you in with all the boring details while we're on the road?"

He frowned at that and started the engine.

"When my parents died, I wasn't twenty-one yet. I couldn't fully step into the legacy, and honestly, I don't like to admit it, but Gabe's right. I don't think I am ready. I want to be ready, and God, being a field agent has been all I have dreamed about my entire life, but I was too young. And now it's like I can't get any experience because Gabe never lets me out of his sight. But suddenly, you turn up, and you get this fun mission."

"Well, it's not exactly a walk in the park. I think I was chosen for it because of my school connection with Massimo."

He started to ease out onto the king's road and hit the brakes. "But Antonio, he's the big bad. Papa evil. And then his second in command, Drake Webster."

I shuddered. "He killed my parents. Antonio ordered it, but Drake carried it out. Massimo is below Drake in the pecking order. He doesn't know anything. And for the most part, he's been kept out of the family business. Drake isn't blood, but he's the adopted heir to the arms dealer throne."

Lock cursed under his breath. "And that's why everyone's tense when we talk about the Ignos. I didn't fucking know."

I turned to face him then. "I get the impression you're trying to ask me something? Like you're uneasy with this."

He shook his head. "No. Not with the mission. It's *you*. You, make me uneasy. *We're* the problem."

16

SAFFRON

OKAY, I was nervous as shit.

Especially given what he'd said. *We're the problem.*

God, how were we going to get around this tension? We needed to figure out a way around it or we wouldn't make it.

As we stepped into Massimo Igno's party, I was hyper-aware of every move, every angle, what the job was. My comms had been hidden in my lipstick and when I'd gone to the loo, I'd slid it into my bra, pulling my braids forward to cover just in case. When I stepped out of the loo, Graciella was waiting for me. "Oh, there you are."

"Ha, sorry, I was just in the loo."

"Wow, you look gorgeous." She looped her arm through mine. "You must tell me what your hair stuff is. It smells divine."

"Um, it's pretty ordinary. It's shea moisturizing conditioner."

"Maybe it's not your hair stuff but your perfume. What do you wear?"

"Oh, it's this perfume my mother used to wear. She had it custom made."

"Of course, it's custom made. God, that's not even fair. Do you remember the perfumery? I have been trying to hunt that scent down since we met the other day."

"Trust me, I've tried. I just know she always wore it."

"Ugh, is it one of those things you can call her and ask?"

I cleared my throat. "No, unfortunately, my mother died a couple years ago."

Her face fell. "Oh gosh, I'm so sorry. Listen to me going on and on about perfume. I'm sorry, that was insensitive."

"It's okay, you couldn't know."

Except, it wasn't okay.

Why was she obsessed with my scent anyway?

Lock's obsessed with it too.

Yeah, but his obsession didn't annoy me at all. Hers, did.

"Why don't you come out to the balcony. This is quite a crush of people. You know Massimo... He loves to be social."

"Okay."

She led me to the side balcony, and I knew that if he'd been able to put his coms in by now, that Lock had me. I wasn't getting lost. Still, I couldn't help but feel uneasy. It was hotter out in the balcony that she led me to.

"So, why don't you tell me about your relationship with Lock? You two seem so in step. It must be that flush of honeymoon, right? He's hardly left your side since he walked in."

"Yeah, I mean, we do like each other a lot."

"And you met at a party, right?"

I was very careful to recite the exact story. I added a few slight embellishments as a normal person telling the story would, but I was careful. She was prodding, and I wanted to know why.

"I mean, he must have been one hell of a playboy before you caught him, right?"

"That's... You know, that's what I hear. But with me, he's so different."

"Yeah, that's what I say about Massimo. I changed him."

I blinked slowly, fighting against the urge to say you can't change a person, because that's what *Saff* would say. But here, I wasn't Saff. I was Saffron. "I mean, that's what love can do for you, right?"

"You guys are such a sexy couple. It's just so delicious watching you together."

I frowned at that, unsure of where she was going, but I let it go. In my com, I could hear Lock's choked laughter and then he muttered, "I told you I was sexy."

I resisted, just barely, the urge to roll my eyes.

"I mean, you two are young. I feel like getting married young means that you're a little wilder and a little more open to everything, you know?"

I had no idea where this was going. Graciella still had her arm wrapped around my waist. What was she doing?

Her hand stroked my hip, and I frowned at the contact because I wasn't usually comfortable being touched by someone. "Um, yeah, you know, Lock always does push me to think outside my comfort zone."

"I love to hear that because Massimo has me doing the same."

"Oh, really? Like what?"

I kept the conversation going the best I could, because at the end of the day, she was giving me yet another place I could bug. We reached the edge of the balcony and I gently slipped my finger into my clutch, palming the little keys that held the listening devices. "I mean, you're young too. And God, you're a movie star."

"Only in Spain. I haven't really broken into the international market yet, but I'm working on it."

"That's honestly impressive. I'm still trying to figure it out. I work at King Media for Lachlan's family."

"Right, King Media. Let me guess, you're in marketing or something where the cute girls hang out?"

I ground my teeth together. "You guessed it."

"Ah yes, young and impressionable. I could see the appeal."

"I don't understand."

"You know, powerful men do love a young and impressionable woman around."

"I suppose so." Where the hell was this going?

Lock's voice was in my com. "Incoming."

"There you are, Graciella. And our guest of honor. I was just talking to your husband, reminiscing about our days at Eton and some of what we used to get up to."

"Oh, you know, he doesn't really talk about his school days much."

"I wouldn't imagine he would. You know, he was a bad boy then."

I shuddered at the way he said it. "I'm sure he was."

"Graciella, why don't you be a dear? I left my drink."

I knew I didn't want to be left alone with him. "Oh, I'll get it. I want to check on Lock anyway."

Massimo wrapped his arm around my waist where Graciella's had been. "No, you stay. I want to get to know you better."

I swallowed hard. This was not good.

When Graciella was gone, he turned his attention to me. "She's beautiful, yes?"

"Graciella? Yes, but of course she is."

"You know, before she was an actress, she was a model. And she was a muse at Valentino."

"I didn't know that. She's stunning, of course."

He frowned at the door she'd just slipped through. "Yes, of course she's stunning. You know, sometimes I wonder, how people get married."

I shifted in his hold.

"Um, I suppose they just do? You find someone you love and off you get."

"Yes, but how do you *know*? I always feel like you have to sample all the goods."

I tried not to purse my lips at his use of the word *goods*. "Well, when you find the right person, maybe you feel like you need to stop sampling."

"I hate to think people get married and lose themselves entirely. You can't even recognize them for who they once were," he said.

"I'm sure that happens more often than not." Once again, I tried to escape his hold. The way he was holding me was too close. Too familiar.

"Don't you worry that Lock will be unfaithful?"

I swallowed hard. "That's not even a question." I had a strong conviction when I said it. I just knew him. When Lock was in, he was in. He'd made that clear the night we spent together, and that was it.

"Ah, Graciella always worries that I'll be unfaithful, so she's even agreed that we're open, did you know that?"

My brows lifted slightly. "Well, for some people that works."

"Would it work for you?"

I blinked slowly. "No. I'm far too jealous. And Lock is quite demanding. He almost extinguishes all the oxygen in the room. He's all I can see."

He leaned in close to me. "He's a lucky man."

I swallowed hard. "I'm lucky too. After all, he chose me, didn't he?"

"What that means is that he's smart."

"I suppose that's true."

"Do you think being open is a mistake?"

"I think whatever works for the parties involved is what's important. And good communication." This conversation was making me more and more uncomfortable.

"Do you think you would ever consider being open?"

The moment he asked that question, Lock's growl was audible through the balcony door. "No, she wouldn't. If you don't mind, Massimo, I'd like your hands off my fucking wife." His voice was all gravel, and there was a hint of ice in it that sent a shiver down my spine.

I purposefully turned with a smile. "Oh, sweetheart, there you are. Massimo was just asking me questions about—"

"I know what he's fucking asking about. I can hear. He was putting moves on my wife."

I gave him a tremulous smile. "It's not like that. Tell him, Massimo."

Massimo gave me a sheepish smile. "He wouldn't be entirely incorrect. Graciella and I, we're looking for a third."

I swallowed hard. I knew what he was doing, but I deliberately shifted my stance and stepped out of his hold.

Lock took my hand and tucked me into his side harshly. His hand wrapped around my waist and hip, his fingers imprinting on my flesh. "Mine."

Massimo's brows lifted. "Oh, I didn't know it was like that. Possessive. If you hold on too tight to your toys, sometimes you break them."

"Let me be clear. I will break anyone who touches what's mine." He glowered down at me. "Looks like you need to be reminded who you belong with."

Massimo gave him an angled nod. "If you two will excuse

me, I need to get back to my guests. Enjoy the view. Join us when you're able."

Lock snatched my hand in his and pulled me toward the stairs that led down to the beach. "We're taking a walk."

He looked angry. Genuinely ticked off. But we'd been following the script.

"Lock? What's wrong?"

"You mean besides Massimo's hands all over my *wife*?"

I frowned at his tone. Something was going on. "There's no reason to be jealous. You're the only one. Only you can make me feel the way you do."

When we were down the stairs, we paused and he led me toward the gazebo. He pulled me in close, his lips hovering close to my ear. "I don't know how much of this place is bugged, but I just heard from Saint. Massimo's men are in our villa now. They're bugging it."

My breath whooshed out, and for a second I forgot to breathe. The burn in my lungs forced me to inhale sharply. *Fuck.*

"He clearly wants you."

"That's not on the menu."

He snorted. "Yeah, well, I think I made it perfectly clear you're not down for that."

"Shit. Did Saint say why they think he's bugging us?"

He shook his head. "He slipped me a note that we should go to Royal Elite."

"Why?"

"I'm not sure. The queen's here with Ariel. Maybe it's to get us out?"

"Okay, I suppose we'll go with them."

"I think that's the plan. Are you okay? He had his hands all over you."

I nodded. "I'm fine."

He pulled back and his gaze searched mine. "Graciella left you with him?"

"Yes. She found me after I'd bugged the library and bedroom."

"Do you think she knows what he's up to?"

"I have no idea," I muttered. "But remember, we know very little about Massimo. He's a blank slate. The real question is if we can get any decent intel on his family. So don't worry about Massimo. We can handle him. You and I, we're a team, right?"

His gaze fell to my lips and he nodded. "Yeah. We'd better get back before I do something reckless."

<h1 style="text-align:center">17</h1>

LACHLAN

I HAD no idea how in the world we were going to leave with the queen. But it seemed she and Ariel had a plan of their own.

Over the course of the last hour, the queen had been getting steadily and steadily louder. And finally, at one point, she and Ariel stumbled into each other. Then the queen murmured to Ariel that she'd had too much to drink. Ariel countered with she was the one who'd had too much to drink. Then they started to squabble.

If we weren't in real danger, I would have found this hilarious.

The queen looked regal and normal all at the same time with her dark skin, updo and mermaid style dress.

Since Massimo hadn't allowed any cameras in the party, there was no danger that there would be some tabloid report about the queen's behavior. I recognized that they were playing their roles well. Ariel turned and leaned on Saff then. "Can you take me home? Some best friend she is."

My eyes went wide, because just as she leaned into Saff, Penny shoved her. Ariel turned as if to shove the queen, and then a hulking brood of a man came out of nowhere. "Princess Ariel, it's time to go."

She shook her head. "I'm not going."

Penny just laughed. "You're being escorted out."

Ariel shrieked. "You're the one who's being escorted out."

And suddenly, another hulking man came forward. "Ladies, time to go. The king calls."

Ariel shook her head. "I'm not going anywhere without my new best friend."

Saff's eyes went wide when Ariel's arm wrapped around her waist and dug in. "Oh, um..."

Massimo looked irritated. Graciella's face, while attempting to remain neutral, held sort of a secret smile as if this was something she wanted. Massimo tried to call one of his men forward. "They'll escort you, make sure that you get back safely, Your Highness."

Penny shook her head. "I have my own men. I'm also making sure she gets home safely."

Ariel snorted. "I'm not going. Not without my new bestie."

The more Massimo's men tried to advance, the louder Ariel got. And finally, Penny just shoved her, making Ariel stumble two feet, almost taking Saff with her. Saff saved them both. "Okay, we'll make this easy. I'll come and make sure you both get home safe and sound."

Ariel grinned at her. "See? I knew we were going to be besties."

"I'm already your bestie," muttered Penny.

They were doing their *drunken best friends out on the town* act so well. I would have almost believed that they were two girls in their twenties who'd had way too much to drink at a party.

When we were outside, Graciella stopped me just outside the door. "We'd love to take you to lunch since you won't be able to stay for the rest of the party."

"Yeah, I think you have Saff's number. Just give her a call and we'll arrange it."

She nodded. "And please, tell her I'm sorry if Massimo made her uncomfortable on the balcony. Sometimes he gets ideas in his head, and she didn't do anything wrong."

"Give her a call. Arrange that lunch." And then I followed my wife and her new best friend to the waiting car.

Once we were in the limo with the privacy partition up, Ariel and Penny high-fived. "Oh God, it's been a minute since we've done the drunken-girl-fight thing," Ariel said, laughing.

Penny giggled. "In case you haven't noticed, we've done this before."

Saff just laughed. "For a moment there, I almost believed you two were having a legitimate squabble."

Ariel snorted. "She's so bossy, right? I should get a new best friend."

Penny just laughed. "Good luck. You're stuck with me. Besides, we're also sort of family now, so you know how that goes."

Ariel rolled her eyes. "Can't get rid of family, can you?"

Penny shook her head. "Nope. Might as well get used to me."

When` we arrived at Royal Elite, we all jumped out of the car and followed Ariel into her office, the heels of the women making soft clicking noises on the marble as we walked.

"So what are we going to do about our villa?" I asked.

Ariel was already calling Gabe when we all filed in. Gabe's terse one-word answer let us know he was on the phone. "Webb."

"Gabe, it's Ariel Winston. I've got the queen with me and your agents. We notified you earlier that the villa has been compromised. How do you want your agents to proceed?"

Gabe's voice was tense. "Is my sister there?"

Saff answered, "Yeah, I'm fine. Massimo tried to recruit Lock and I into some kind of poly situation, but Lock shut him down pretty hard."

I could almost hear Gabe choking on the phone. "King, I owe you."

"Trust me, it wasn't hard to decline."

"You're being watched now, so you'll have to be extra careful inside the house. We can't dismantle the bugs they planted without alerting them, so you'll have to follow strict protocol."

"Yup, we're on it."

"Your devices should still be safe, but let's save any phone calls back to base unless absolutely urgent."

Penny added, "I'm going to make a big deal about an apology to Graciella and Massimo too. Maybe invite Graciella to lunch as well."

Gabe's voice was terse. "Your assistance is greatly appreciated, Your Majesty."

"Please, it feels good being back in the field." She did look like she was happy, despite being in the presence of a man with potential ties to weapons manufacturing.

"Gabe, can Lock and I speak to you privately for a second?" Saff asked.

Ariel and Penny excused themselves. Saint tried to stick around, but Ariel tugged him along. "Something tells me, she doesn't want you there."

Saint frowned but complied the moment Saff gave him a sheepish smile. When it was just the two of us and Webb, she muttered, "What do you want me to do? They bugged us, so that means that they're going to expect something."

"Yeah, about that. You're not a honey agent, I know."

I frowned. "What's a honey agent?"

She flicked me a glance. "Uh, a honey agent is, you know, a honey trap. Agents trained to use *every* tool in their arsenal?"

I frowned at that. "You would let your sister be a honey agent?"

Gabe cursed low. "Of course not. And trust me, having this conversation is uncomfortable enough, King. But you two are going to have to put on a convincing enough show."

"Show?" Saff's voice squeaked out. "What do you mean by show?"

"Massimo is listening in, and he just attempted to proposition you. I have confirmation that the bugs are audio *and* visual, so you will need to play the part. Obviously, King, keep your fucking hands off my sister, but make it look real, yeah? Unless it's a fucking problem."

My gaze locked on Saff's. Her eyes were wide and unblinking. "I'm going to defer to my partner and team lead in this situation, sir."

There was a long pause, and then Gabe exhaled slowly. "Good answer."

Saff cleared her throat. "Right. Um, I guess we'll figure something out."

Gabe's voice was low. "Saff, you don't have to do this."

"What else are we going to do, Gabe? Massimo was never supposed to bug us. If he's in our villa, it means he doesn't believe us. Which means we have a problem. How are we supposed to surveil him and get the intel we need if he suspects us?"

Something occurred to me. "What if it's not about suspicion? Maybe he's trying to get in Saff's knickers and this is more about his obsession than our cover being blown."

Gabe was silent for a moment and then said, "That's a good point. This could have nothing to do with your agent status at all. It could have to do with you, Saff."

"I spent my whole life with men ignoring me, and suddenly a potential arms dealer wants to stalk me? That's a lot."

When Gabe hung up and I was left alone with Saff, I swallowed hard. My fingers were already tingling with the anticipation of touching her. "We don't have to do this. We can fake it."

She folded her arms. "How are we going to fake it? We don't know where the cameras are."

"Look, it just has to look real enough in some random cameras right? It's highly unlikely he's got night vision in there. I get you upstairs and we put on a good show, no big deal. Get you on the bed, and we just—" What the fuck was I saying? I cleared my throat. "Fake it. We don't have to actually, um, have sex."

Her eyes went wide. "Jesus fucking Christ, things were not supposed to go like this." She started pacing back and forth.

"It's fine, Saff." I strolled to her and put my hands on her shoulders. "You trust me, right? You wouldn't have agreed to come on this mission if you didn't trust me in the field."

Her gaze lifted and met mine directly. "Yes, I trust you. You're my partner. But Lock, from the moment we step back in that villa, it has to look real. If that matters to you too, are you going to be okay to pull this off?"

She had no idea I'd been fantasizing about what she would feel like for weeks. And now I had to go and live out my fantasies. But only to a point, and fake it. Yeah, easy. "You're my partner and I want you to trust me."

She nodded, her gaze never straining from mine. "I do trust you. We're in this together, and we can do this. I also think you're right. I don't think this is about us as agents. The stuff he was saying out in the balcony makes me think it's more about wanting me to be some kind of third in a poly situation than anything else."

"I think so too. Also, I think Graciella was hinting that she was going to call you and apologize. I think she knows something is not right."

She shook her head. "We're just going to go in and play the part. I'm sure you've hooked up in a million bars and clubs and with all kinds of women, right? We can do this."

"This is different. We're a team, and this is awkward."

She gave me her determined smile. I'd seen it before when she was about to do something she didn't want to do. "We can do this. We're adults."

"It's just for show. If you don't want to do this, we won't. You're my partner. I only care about your safety."

She put her hand over my heart, and I knew she could feel it trying to jump out of my chest.

With her eyes locked on mine, I watched hungrily as she licked her bottom lip. "I want to."

Her voice was a low whisper that went straight to my cock, "Fuck." My brain offered up all the ways I could consume her. My throat constricted as I asked, "Anything off limits? Something you don't like?" We wouldn't be able to ask real questions once we were inside the villa.

Her eyes went wide. "No. I guess I'm pretty vanilla."

"Nothing about you is vanilla. Just touching you is hot to me."

She swallowed. "This is only the one time."

I knew what she meant. Didn't mean I had to like it. "Guess I better make it count then."

18

LACHLAN

I WANTED HER.

From the moment I'd seen her outside the cottage in the dark, I'd wanted her. From every moment we fought, to hearing her laugh, or seeing her smile when I actually got something right in training, I'd wanted her. Everything about her determination and grit, and God, that fucking smile. The way she just turned it on me and something deep inside would ache, as if I knew that smile. As if it called to me. I wanted her. But could we do this?

If you're smart, you'll take her any way you can get her.

When we were back in the real world, there would be rules that said I couldn't touch her. I was only getting one shot at this. One chance to make her mine, even if it was only for the moment.

We approached the door, and I lay my hand on her lower back. She turned to me with derision. "I don't know what your problem is, Lock, I didn't agree to anything."

Confused I searched her gaze. She lifted a brow as if trying to get me to catch on. Oh, we were starting.

"I saw how you were looking at him."

"I wasn't looking at him in any way. He was looking at *me*. Jesus Christ, I was minding my business. It's not my fault that he made an indecent proposal. How are you blaming that on me?"

"You are my wife. *Mine*." I ground out. "My pussy." I palmed her arse and pulled her to me. "My arse."

Her laugh was melodic and quick. God, I love that laugh. "You are out of your mind if you think that I'm going to let that fly. Let's be really clear; I need someone who's confident. You know how I feel about you. I fucking want *you*."

To hear her utter those words was like a shot to the solar plexus. I knew it wasn't real, but God, to hear her say them. "If you love me, what the fuck were you doing with him on the balcony?"

She stepped past me and used our key to open the door.

Now it was real. There was no backing out of this.

"Graciella brought me there. I'd gone to the loo, and when I found her in the hallway, we got to talking, then she invited me out on the balcony. I didn't have anything to do with it. I didn't know he was going to be there."

"Don't you lie to me." I forced my voice to an even lower register.

Right in the doorway, she turned in my arms and planted a hand on my chest. "I only want you."

"Someone needs a reminder of who they belong to."

"Oh, yeah? Are you going to remind me?"

She tried to shove away from me, and I grabbed her wrist and pulled her back. "Are you sure about that? Maybe it's him you want."

"You wanker." She shoved at my chest hard. She didn't budge me, because she wasn't using force as much as she would have if she was actually pissed, but if she had, I would have moved a step or two. "This has nothing to do with me. They have some weird kink going on, and it's none of my business. Good for them though, because I have the man I want."

"Do you?"

"Maybe if you would spend more time fucking me instead of worrying about who else wants to fuck me, I wouldn't be entertaining other offers."

I grabbed her then. My hands twitched as she trailed a hand on my chest. "You are playing with fire."

She shrugged. "Am I? I'm dying to see that fire in you."

Her brows lifted ever so slightly, and she was telling me she'd ratchet it up. Fucking hell. With a strong grip on her upper arms, I pushed her ever so slightly into the villa and I used my foot the kick the door shut. "You're spoiling for a fight."

"If you say so."

With a firm grip on her arms, I backed her up against the wall in the foyer. "You are mine. Say it."

Her eyes flared, and in the moonlight, I could see her pupils dilate.

Oh, shit. That tiny reaction sent blood rushing to my cock, and that fucker strained against my trousers. "Say the words, Saffron."

I almost made a mistake and said Saff, but I'd corrected it.

"Why don't you prove that I'm yours?" She said it with a little laugh in her voice, and I nearly choked on desire. She tried to shove at me again. "I want a man who wants me. Who can stake his claim. Is that you? Because I feel like Massimo is trying to stake a claim."

She was pushing my control. Everything I'd learned from her about being an asset and being in the field, and I finally surrendered.

"Did you want him?"

"I don't know. He was offering me pleasure."

I turned her around, my hands firm on her hips, gripping tight. Her dress was short, flirty, hugging her hips in a body-con style. With a firm grip on the hem, I pulled up the fabric, and she breathed harshly. "What are you doing?"

"I'm taking what's mine."

"Are you punishing me?"

Fucking hell, Saff Abott was fire, and she knew it. Her skin flushed, and I glowered down at the flesh exposed to me now. Smooth, supple, brown skin that ached for my hand, completely untouched. I wondered if all that pretty brown skin would flush with a spanking. I leaned in tight. "You're playing with fire, sweetheart." I spanked her bare flesh. "You're a naughty thing. Tell me no."

Her breathing was deep, and then she moaned out a single word. "Yes."

With a grunt, I reached up under the tight fabric and hooked my fingers into her knickers. "Am I going to find you wet?"

Her breathing was deep now, heavy, labored. "Lachlan."

My fingers brushed against the soft flush between her thighs and she hissed. "Oh God."

Fuuuck. I couldn't think. The blood was humming in my veins. She was in front of me. Her dress up and her pussy feeling like sweet silk. "Tell me you don't want me. Tell me you prefer him."

All she did was moan my name. With rough tugs at the buckle of my belt, I wondered just how far we were going to take this. This was a show. This wasn't fucking real.

But we had to sell it because Massimo Igno was watching.

Fuck him. This is ours.

"You are in so much trouble."

"Lock, hurry."

I moaned into her hair. "Tell me to stop." I realized it was a plea. My voice was harsh as the words tore from me. "Tell me no."

But she didn't. She just swiveled her hips, tempting me.

Once my cock was freed, the steel length of it brushed against her ass and she draped her forehead against the wall and groaned. "Lock, hurry."

I bit down on her shoulder, and she pushed her ass back. With my hand around the base of my cock, I bent my knees so the tip of my cock brushed the space between her thighs. With a grunt, I kicked her feet apart. "Saff." I froze when I realized I'd used her nickname.

She just whispered my name, and I kissed the nape of her neck. "Saff," I whispered.

"It's just us, Lock. It's just us."

I could feel the heat of her pussy, and I swallowed hard. "No condoms," I whispered.

When her answer was a murmured, "I'm clean," a spike of electricity shot up my spine.

My whisper was in her hair. I knew Igno couldn't hear us, but something told me that this wasn't about him. It really was more about us.

Her hand gripped my thigh and I paused, the head of my cock against her slickness. "Lock, please..."

In her hair, I whispered. "Tell me no, Saff. Fucking tell me no."

In the tense silence of our foyer, instead of the two letter word I expected her to whisper, the short word she whispered was, "Yes."

She tilted her hips backward, and the tip of my dick slid right into her wetness. I froze, gritting my teeth, gnashing my jaws, fighting for control.

Saff whispered, "Oh my God. More."

And I knew I was in trouble. Because when I slid a hand into her hair, angling her head so I could lean in and kiss her properly, the tip of my dick slid right in, and she clenched around it as if trying to suck me deeper into the abyss of a torment I knew I would never escape from. "Saff..."

Her gaze lifted and she met mine directly. Her pupils were completely dilated now and her eyes were heavy lidded.

I searched her gaze as she squeezed around me, and with a groan, I slid all the way home.

She was hot. So fucking hot and tight. Flashes of the fantasy that I'd been having all week bombarded me like rain as I held on to her tight. One hand on her hair, the hand I had on her hip sliding up over her breast and squeezing. "Fuck, you are so goddamn hot."

My brain kept offering all kinds of images. Saff on top of me, her breasts in my face, the inescapable urge to suck on them. Another of Saff bent over my bed, her ass in the air, and me devouring her pussy and arse.

The hint of her taste was on my tongue, and it was like I knew how good she would be.

She pushed back against me as I fucked her. The tingle started down my spine, and all I could do was grind my teeth and stop moving. No, I was not going to come like this. Not without her.

Frustrated, she ground her ass against me. "What the fuck are you doing?"

I leaned in and whispered against her ear. "We're going upstairs."

"What, we're stopping right now?"

She squeezed around me like a tight fist, and I cursed into the softness of her hair. Coconut and hibiscus mixed with her own scent, intoxicating me, and I almost fucking came. The electric buzz threatened at the base of my spine, and I forced a deep breath. "Fucking stop. I— We're going upstairs."

She whimpered and rolled her head back and forth on the wall. "Um, okay."

I turned her around and tipped her chin up so she would meet my gaze. When she did, her gaze was unfocused, aroused. Her lips were swollen from our kisses, and my dick screamed to be let back in where I'd been.

"Fuck, Saff."

I bent and picked her up and wrapped her legs around me. Without any preamble, I slammed home again.

She was easy to hold, her hair cascading down her back as I braced her against the wall.

"Oh, fuck. I meant to get you upstairs."

Fuck. Fuck. Fuck.

I eased her away from the wall, because if I kept fucking her like this, I was going to come before she did, and mission or not, that was not the way I rolled.

I held her easily, my hands on her ass as I started toward the stairs. Saff wrapped her arms around my neck and held on. Her gaze searched right into mine, and it almost felt like she was looking for something. Expecting me to say something. I couldn't imagine what it was, but every step, I had to fight hard not to drop her down on the floor and just fuck her senseless.

I made it to the stairs and realized there was no way I'd make it all the way up, and fucking her on the stairs would be uncomfortable for her. So instead, I turned around and headed the opposite way into the living room. Her eyes went wide. "The stairs are that way."

"I know. I'm not going to make it," I growled.

In the living room, I skirted around the corner tables and then eased her down onto the couch. When I pulled out again, she gave me a frustrated wail. "Fucking hell, Lock."

"Easy does it. I'm hungry."

With her splayed open on the couch, it was easy to kneel before her. She started to close her legs, and I braced my arms on her inner thighs, my thumb stroking her clit. "Oh no, you don't. I'm going to eat and make you come. After I'm done with that, I'm going to fuck you and make you mine again."

Her dress was a problem, so I pulled her forward and attacked the zipper with relish. When I finally managed to get her arms out and lift the dress up over her head, I didn't bother with the strapless bra. I just plucked the cups down and leaned forward for my reward.

Blindly, I found a nipple and started to suck with enthusiasm. She tasted even better than she smelled. Sweet with a hint of spice. "Jesus, you are so soft," I murmured against her skin, losing myself. I knew this wasn't real. I understood that. But that didn't stop me from relishing the opportunity, even if it was just for now.

Every cell in my body fought against that idea. Soul deep, I knew she was *mine*. I ran my nose along her sternum to the flat taut planes of her belly, inhaling deeply. "This scent has been driving me insane for weeks. Why do you smell so good?"

Her fingers slid into my hair, and my name fell off her tongue. "Lock, oh my God, Lock."

I kissed down her belly, marveling at the softness. Damn, my hands were shaking as I splayed her legs wide. Fuck me. A neat strip of hair pointed to the promised land, but other than that she was bare. With the moonlight peeking through the living room, I could see her arousal on her lips. I knew I was supposed to be playing a part, but to me this was real. And I dropped the act for just one moment. "Do you know how long I've been dreaming about being here?" My question was soft and hopefully wouldn't be picked up on the mikes. It was a risk but I had to say it. She needed to know.

"Before I get started, I'm going to need you to tell me who's pussy this is." I blew gently on her clit while I waited for her answer.

At first I thought she would be stubborn. But when the answer came, it was a whispered, "Yours, King."

I smirked at her use of my last name. Suddenly, we weren't playing a game. We weren't acting for the cameras. This was real. In this moment, it was just me and Saff and the rest of the world didn't matter.

My hunger overtaking me, I dove into her pussy, wrapping my lips against her clit and sucking hard. She immediately dug her hands into my hair, holding me in position she screamed out my name.

I licked from the bottom of her slit to the top using the flat of my tongue, letting her flavor soak into me. She melted over me, tasting so damn sweet, and fuck it was all I ever wanted.

She started to rock her hips into me, and I dipped my tongue inside, fucking her with my tongue, going as deep as I could. When she tugged on my hair and dragged my face into her cunt, I growled.

Fuck yes. I licked and sucked and fucked her with my tongue and my fingers. She was open and willing and everything I could ever ask for.

I scooped my hands under her arse, holding her cheeks firm, unrelenting. When I spread them with my fingers, she froze. "Lock? What are you doing?"

"Did you really think there would be any part of you that I wouldn't touch? That I wouldn't like? That I wouldn't finger? That I wouldn't fuck?"

"Oh my God." Her eyes widened, and she flicked her tongue over her bottom lip. I groaned watching her.

"Or do you not want me to? Don't you want me to make every part of you mine?"

She hesitated for only a second before she nodded vehemently. "Yes, oh God, yes."

"That's a good girl."

When my tongue flicked over her pucker, Saff let out a low, guttural moan that I could feel all the way to the tip of my cock. That was the only encouragement I needed. I went to town, licking and rimming, using my fingers over her clit in a tight circular pattern.

When her legs started to shake and she tried to clamp them over my ears, I knew what was happening. With my fingers on her clit, I slid my thumb into her pussy and rotated my wrist to find just the right angle. When I stroked her pussy and her G-spot at the same time, with my tongue rimming her asshole, she screamed my name loud enough for the neighbors to hear even without their sneaky listening devices.

With her legs still shaking, I finally came up for air, and I couldn't help the cocky smile as she lay open to me. But I wasn't done with her yet. I could lick her all day. But the way she was shaking in my arms made the blood rush to my cock, and I knew I wasn't going to last very long.

I grabbed her ass, pulling her just off the edge of the seat, and then I knelt in front of her, positioned my cock, and slid home.

Her eyes rolled in the back of her head. "Oh Lock... Lock."

It was easy to find the rhythm this way. I knew her body like it had been imprinted in my mind. It didn't matter if this was our first time together. I knew her. Every little shift, every little moan, I knew what it meant. I knew when to pick up the pace, when to slow it down. I knew that sliding my thumb over her clit just so was going to make her shake her head and say, "Oh no, no, no, no," as she tried to beg off another orgasm.

But then I would slow the motion down ever so slightly, just soft little strokes. Then as I picked up my pace, she arched her back, head thrashing. "Oh, shit, Lock. Oh my God..."

She broke apart under me, and I forced my eyes open so that I could watch her lips part and her eyes glaze, watch her body go taught and bow for me as the earthquakes overtook her.

I shifted positions by bringing her to the edge of the coffee table. And then gently I scooted her and rotated her over until her arse was bared to me.

I leaned my body over hers, my dick sliding against her pussy, eager for re-entry. With my hands wrapped in her hair, I bit her shoulder. "Now be a good girl and tell me who's pussy this is."

When she hesitated, I bit her a little harder, scraping my teeth over her skin, waiting for the shudder. Waiting for her to relent. "I said, whose pussy is this?"

I gave her a sharp tap on the ass as I drove all the way home, and she screamed out my name. "Lock. Oh my God. Yours. Only yours."

I reached around her to find her clit. Her juices flowed over my fingers, making both of us slick and wet and hot. As I gripped her ass with my other hand, I drove home again and again. Leaning over her, I whispered all the filthy things I'd been dreaming of doing to her against the shell of her ear.

When I could feel her pussy start to quiver around my cock again, I straightened and found her asshole with my thumb. As I drove home, over and over again, my balls slapping against her flesh, my thumb inside her arse, Saff came all around me.

I picked up my pace. Faster and faster, knowing I could only capture this moment in time. This moment when we were Lachlan and Saffron and nothing else mattered. And she really was mine. The trick would be holding on to her.

I was assailed by fragments of images of all of the ways I

could fuck her, make her mine, claim her, and make her come, and come, and come.

The lightning was barreling down my spine in that moment, and I clamped a hand on her shoulder to hold her in place as my pace tipped into fever pitch.

I slammed into her again and again, her hips meeting me thrust for thrust. And in that moment, I knew she was mine. And as I exploded hot jets of my release into her with my brain struggling to hang on to reality...

I knew I had fucked her before.

19

SAFFRON

Once we finally made it to the bedroom, he'd stayed.

And stayed. And stayed.

Next to me, he stirred. When I tried to shift out of his hold, he dragged me closer. "Where do you think you're going?"

His voice was full of deep, gravelly cement, and a deep ache started at my pussy again. *Fucking hell.*

You cannot have him. Okay fine, you can have him now, but you cannot keep him.

Better not to have him again.

"Lock, remember we're supposed to meet Graciella this morning?"

Behind me his cock instantly nudged my arse. "Saff?"

"Yup, that's me. Sorry if you were expecting someone else."

I kept my voice just at a whisper because I knew prying ears were listening. I dragged the duvet over my head and encouraged him to do the same.

Once both of us were under the duvet, his gaze searched mine and he mouthed. "Are you okay?"

I nodded. "Yeah, I'm fine."

His gaze dipped to my lips, and I couldn't help it... My pussy clenched because I knew exactly what that look meant now. Oh, he'd given it to me before, not just the first night we met, but several times in training. The other day when we'd been practicing touching one another like a couple, I was quite convinced that was the *I need to eat your pussy now* look. "Lock."

"There are still cameras everywhere." His voice was a low whisper.

"I know."

He smoothed his hand down over my hip and then shifted to move between my thighs.

"Oh fuck me, Lock..."

"Is this still the mission?" He dipped his finger deep and I moaned. "I like it better like this, when you're just for me." Another finger probed the entrance of my arse gently.

My gaze flickered to his face and I blinked rapidly. "I—"

"I know. This is the mission, right?"

The way he said it was as if he knew exactly how I tried to play this all, that this was just a mission, that what we were doing wasn't real.

"Lock, we can't—"

"We can. Remember, the cameras are still on."

I groaned as he finger fucked me.

"Do you know how you taste? Like spun sugar and vanilla. And how am I supposed to look at you like I don't know that now?"

"You know the rules."

"Fuck the rules," he muttered as he rotated his hips into mine.

"You can say that. I cannot. This is all I've ever wanted."

His thumb smoothed over my clit, and he smiled at me. "So you're telling me you don't want this?"

"That's not fair," I whimpered.

"Sure, it is."

"Lock—"

"Oh come on, just one teeny-tiny orgasm? Just let me give it to you."

Was I weak? A hundred percent. Should I have left myself open and vulnerable? No, absolutely not. But we were still on a mission, and we were playing husband and wife. Newlyweds at that. And we did have a madman who was apparently filming our interactions. Which was creepy. But I knew that required us to play the part. So I wasn't being selfish. I was doing my job.

When Lock leaned in, he kissed along my jawline. His whispers of, "Yeah, that's it. I love the way you're cunt is squeezing my fingers. I like it better when you're squeezing my dick."

I gasped when he pressed harder on my clit, and I knew this was possibly the worst idea I'd ever had, but still, I couldn't quite make myself stop.

And when the orgasm rolled through me, when my back started to bow and I started to chase his fingers as he retreated and slid in, I knew that this had absolutely nothing to do with the mission.

Was it selfish? A hundred percent. Was I going to enjoy it? A hundred percent. When I called out his name, loudly, he grinned at me. "I do like how you say my name."

"Lock—" I broke off not sure what to say.

He leaned in and kissed me softly. "I know. I love fucking you too."

"You can't say that to me."

With a smirk, he said, "I really want to fuck you everywhere. I want your mouth .I want to watch your arse take my cock. I want to hear you whimper as I slide in and out. I want to come in your arse, come down your throat. Come on your tits. I want to watch cum ooze out of you then push it back in with my fingers, tongue, and dick."

I shivered at his words. "Lock, we..."

"I know. I know. This is just for the mission, but we are far from done. We will do this again." And then he lined up his dick to my pussy and fucked me until there was no question.

I could not give him up.

————

Lachlan

TWO THINGS TO NOTE. One, I had definitely shagged Saff Abott before. And part of me was sure it was during my missing forty eight hours. The second thing I knew was that I had every intention of doing it again. But first I had to figure out what the fuck was going on and why I didn't remember ever sleeping with her.

Shouldn't I know her?

That instant connection to her had to come from somewhere. It did. I had always felt connected to her, and maybe that was why. I knew her. Which meant I had to figure out *how* the fuck I knew her. I couldn't count on her for the truth, obviously.

Yes, we were on a mission, but there was no fucking way I was going to just pretend I hadn't tasted her. I wasn't going to pretend that I didn't have that desperate clawing need to be with her again.

The more I thought about it, the more I knew there was no way on earth I'd just forgotten her. This wasn't some drunken night. This wasn't some sloppy shag in the loo of a pub. For the last several weeks, I'd kept having flashes, fantasies of her in my flat, in my bed, on the couch, and I knew she'd never been there before. And then I remembered our trainee simulation. She'd said, "We're in your flat." *My flat.*

She knew my flat. She hadn't just seen a photo of it. She'd been in it before.

When I tried to think of the scenarios, none of them made sense.

Except you have two missing days in the timeline of your life. Maybe she's hiding in there.

When I arrived at Rogues, my grandfather had been waiting to give me the ultimatum. One year at Rogues, one year to clean up my life. It had been hard to accept that my family had been responsible for putting me there. But the question was, how?

Sure, I'd woken up with a black bag around my head. But how had it happened? Where had I been? Who had I been talking to? Was Felix involved? Hell, was he worried about me now? Felix was used to me going off grid on occasion when I just needed to fucking be alone. He was an easy friend. But hopefully he would ask some questions about where the hell I was.

I didn't have any of the things from my past life. No phone. No nothing. But I was going to make a phone call. One that couldn't be traced. I had to know about Saff. And if I could piece together what had happened to me in the forty eight hours before I was forcefully constricted into Rogues, then I would finally have some answers. Because there is no way on earth that Saff Abott wasn't mine. I could feel it. I knew exactly how she liked to be touched, exactly how she tasted. I knew it all.

That morning, there was something in her eyes when I said I'd been dreaming of her taste for months. Something told me she understood what I meant. She knew that I meant it when I said I trusted her. And I wanted her to trust me, but she was hiding something from me. So the question was, what was it?

The only way I was going to find that out was by going off the reservation and making a fucking phone call.

It wasn't going to be easy. I was due at Royal Elite at noon. It was supposed to be an easy day. She and Graciella were having breakfast in the morning. She was recording that conversation, and while she was recording that, we had eyes on Massimo at the house. We'd managed to get a bug into his car, so we'd have a record of those conversations too.

I checked the clock, took a quick shower, and grabbed some coffee before asking Saff, "Are you going to be okay?" I ran the faucet to make it difficult to hear.

She frowned up at me. "Yeah, it should be easy. I've got Zia for backup. And if anything goes wrong, I know how to handle it. I'm good."

"All right. I'm going to work out before the meeting with Jax."

"Okay, be careful." Her smile was easy. As if we hadn't just spent all night with me inside her.

I stepped to her, wrapped my arms around her, and whispered "You, too." And then I leaned in and gave her a quick peck.

Her quick inhalation of breath made me smile. And like a fucking masochist, I leaned in for more, sipping at her lips, sliding my tongue inside, waiting until I heard her moan before drawing back. "Have a good brunch."

She slowly blinked at me. "We're in trouble."

"I know." Boy, did I ever.

When I left her, I took the same path I'd taken the other day toward the king's beach. But this time, instead of heading down the promenade along the water, I headed up the steep stairs toward the old town.

At the old town, I went to the heart of the massive market and found the first vendor that could sell me a sim chip. I quickly paid the man and then found a café to sit down in and make my call.

Felix answered right away. "This is Felix."

"Mate, it's Lock."

Felix cursed under his breath. "What the fuck? Mate, where the fuck have you been?"

"That's a long story. And sorry I haven't called until now."

"Did you know I've been fucking worried? All your plants are dead. I assumed you were too."

"Let me guess, you checked with my parents and they told you I was just fine?"

"Your mother implied that you were drying out somewhere. Which I knew wasn't you. You party, but you don't need to dry out. Where the fuck are you?"

"Let's just say it's something like that. I have a question for you, mate."

"Yeah, shoot. Are you okay, though?"

"Yeah, mate I'm good. Probably better than I have been in a bit. Listen, this is going to sound weird, just answer it best as you can."

"Okay. Is this about a woman? Are you shacked up with some bird?"

It was surprising how accurate that was, but I couldn't tell him that.

"No, it's not like that."

"What's up?"

"About four months ago, right after I sold off Charlie's subsidiary company, did anything happen? Anything weird?"

"Your old man was pissed. He insisted that your grandfather had to do something. Why don't you know this?"

"It doesn't matter. Keep going."

"Your grandfather said you needed to lay low."

"Yeah, that much I remember. I don't know. You dragged me out maybe a couple of nights after that."

"I remember. We went to the bar near your place."

I frowned at that. "That I don't remember. What exactly happened?"

"Mate, are you losing it? Tell me, have you been kidnapped to a desert island, or is some woman using you as a sex slave?"

That was eerily accurate. Very specific, but okay.

I tried to get him back on track. "No, not at all. But I have questions."

"What? You have to remember this. You were dancing with that girl. Very fit. Black woman. She looked like fucking Naomi Campbell with braids. She was hot. And then I left with Angel."

My stomach sank. "What?"

"Yeah, I ditched with Angel. I sent you a text, but I never heard back. I figured you and the bird hooked up. Didn't really think about it until I couldn't reach you for the next several days. Then I went to see your folks, and they said you were out of town, drying out."

"Oh, Jesus." My skin grew cold and clammy. Saff. He'd just described Saff. She had been part of this. That hole in my memory, this was her doing. Fucking hell.

My stomach rolled as I thought of it. Every touch, every kiss, and the way she'd avoided me during my training until Gabe had forced her hand. Fucking hell, that whole time, she'd known. She'd fucking known. I wanted to kill her. I was going to fucking put my hands around her neck and squeeze.

Oi, mate. Not before you shag her again though, right? One for the road?

My dick couldn't be helped. Even the thought of strangling her, just being anywhere in her vicinity had him ready to go. Fuck. I wanted some goddamn answers.

This whole time, she'd been lying to me. How the fuck could

she? After all the bonding? Granted, that was her job, wasn't it? Making me believe I could trust her. I was the asset. Me. She was working me. Had been ever since. She was the one responsible for my missing time.

"Mate, thanks. It's been really helpful."

"Are you sure you're okay? When are you coming back?"

"Hopefully soon. If you can do me a favor, get the housekeeper to come through my place. Put some more plants in it."

"Yeah mate, of course. Are you sure you're okay?"

"Sure," I lied. Then I hung up with him and dropped my face into my hands.

Saff lied to me. And I was going to make her pay.

20

SAFFRON

Something was wrong with Lock.

He was off. I couldn't figure out what it was, but I didn't have time to worry about it at the moment.

When I approached the restaurant, Graciella was there at a massive table by the one of the windows.

She stood and smiled as I approached. "There you are."

"You weren't waiting too long, we're you?"

"No, not too long. You look fantastic."

I'd worn my set of pedal pushers and a cropped lightweight blouse and paired the outfit with flats, topping my vacation-chic vibe with my enormous shoulder bag.

The buckle on my shoulder bag had a mic in it and was already recording, which was handy.

Graciella said, "Thank you for joining me for breakfast this morning."

"Of course. How are you feeling?"

Graciella covered her face with her hands. "I'm really embarrassed about yesterday."

"Whatever you have going on, it's not really my business. As long as you're okay."

She sighed. "I'm fine. Sometimes we disagree."

"Well, that's normal. You guys will figure it out."

She nodded and pushed up her glasses. I could tell she was trying to hide her emotional tears and couldn't quite manage it. "It's just— It's so embarrassing. We were having such a lovely party, and he had to go and be Massimo. I hope he didn't make you too uncomfortable."

"Again, you don't have to explain yourself to me. But he did make me very uncomfortable and really made Lachlan angry. I'm glad we have met, and I want to be your friend. If you need anything, just tell me."

"You're so sweet. This is why I feel even worse about what he made me do."

"What do you mean?"

She sighed. "Cornering you on the balcony, that wasn't okay. I'm so sorry. God, I don't even know why I stay. At first, it felt like I was being seen, you know? And it felt amazing. It was romantic at the beginning, and then it turns out he's actually very controlling and not very nice, and all that other bullshit."

"That's terrible. I'm sorry."

"It's all right. I made my bed. Now, I have to lie in it. And then there's his family."

I leaned forward, trying to appear casual. "Not nice?"

"They're perfectly *nice* on the surface, but they're not *kind*. There's something off. Every time I turn around I feel like I'm being judged."

"I'm sure you have family, right? Someone you can talk to?"

"I came into this relationship with family and friends, and now it feels like I have no one. I'm the odd one out. I'm the one without anyone to love them and look after them. And it feels deliberate." She leaned close. "Once, I met his father, Antonio, and he sent such a chill down my spine. He wasn't cruel, or mean, or anything like that. It's just that look, completely vacant. Like he could easily have me killed or something."

"That sounds very discomforting. Did you tell Massimo about it?"

"Yeah, of course, I did. And of course, he brushed me off, saying I was being paranoid. I know it's my fault."

"Nothing is your fault. There's nothing to be ashamed of here."

"I don't know. I feel like there is. Like I've spent my whole life making poor decisions."

"I hardly believe that. You're beautiful, which, yes I know, wasn't exactly your choice, but you are a successful actress. And you know, maybe trust yourself more because it sounds like you know what you want and what you don't."

"I don't even know how to extricate myself out of this situation."

And there was my opening. My opportunity to take advantage of this situation. I should have had some sense of remorse, and I did, because for the most part, Graciella seemed like a nice woman. She didn't deserve to get taken advantage of. But at the end of the day, this was my job. This was an opportunity to prove myself. So I was going to.

"Listen, I get it. Sometimes you're in a situation that is not exactly of your making and we don't know how to find a way out. But if you need a friend, I'm here. I'm happy to help you find a way out. Do you need somewhere to stay or something?"

She shook her head. "You're so kind." She glanced around then leaned forward conspiratorially. "Also, I've met someone."

My eyes went wide. "Oh, Lord have mercy."

She waved of my warning. "It's dangerous, and I know Massimo is going to go crazy."

"Maybe now isn't the right time for something new."

"I know but I can't help it, and we're in love. In fact, you can help me with him now."

"What do you mean?"

"I need a way out. Just for thirty minutes. He's here in the islands, and he wants to see me."

"What?" The fuckery with this couple knew no bounds.

"I know. But I didn't have a way out of the house on my own."

My stomach churned. With a new player we didn't account for, this was dangerous. "Look Graciella, maybe just tell me what's going on, and I'll see if I can help you. We don't want to make entanglements all the more difficult."

"It won't be more difficult. I know I made a mistake with Massimo. And my new man, he's amazing and great. He really looks after me and cares for me."

"And I love that journey for you. But listen, we don't want to jump out of one fire into another."

"I'm not. Honestly. And I appreciate you just looking out for me. It's really kind."

"Sure. I like you. And if you think you're in danger, then I want to help you in a more tangible way. Maybe get you somewhere safe. It seemed like you were friendly with the queen, and I'm sure she can get you help. We can get you away from him."

"They mean well, but Massimo and his father are too powerful."

"Do you think his father will hurt you?" We had no protocol for her extraction.

"I think he could. But I'm in love, and I want to be in love, and I think it's okay."

She was delusional. "You know, if you love this new person, that's great. And hopefully they can help, but we could think of real opportunities, real chances to get you away from this situation."

She nodded. "I know. And I will. I just... I need to see him."

"So he's here on the island?"

I didn't like the idea of working with a new player, but we needed Graciella as an asset, and I was unwilling to lose her.

"He's going to meet me, and I need you to tell Massimo that you're with me. I know it's not fair, but I need your help."

I stared at her. "This is not a good idea." Oh God, that sounded terrible. Not at all helpful.

"I know. But please, help me, okay?"

It felt like I was being worked. "Look, I need to meet him and make sure that he's not a bad guy, okay? And then we'll go from there. How's that?"

"Good, okay. Here he is."

I turned my head to the left and saw several men, all good looking, heading up toward the beach. Two came from the side stairs up toward the restaurant, presumably from the board-walk. They had that look to them. Polished. Sophisticated. And they were led in by an enormous man in a light-colored suit. I tensed. His walk was familiar. Was that one of Massimo's men?

"Graciella, why don't we head to the ladies' room? We can freshen up, and then we can go meet your guy, okay?"

She shook her head. "No, he's here."

I glanced around again, trying to look for which man she meant. My stomach sank as the man in the light suit pushed closer. My skin went clammy, and my heart started to beat fast. Too fast.

"I'm actually excited for you to meet him. I've told him a lot about you."

"What did you tell him?"

"That I've made a new friend and her husband. And I wanted a love like that."

"Oh, that's sweet."

The man approached, and I knew instinctively that I'd seen him before. I couldn't breathe, and alarm bells were ringing in my head.

As he approached the table, I frantically reached for my purse to pull my gun. I knew I couldn't have a shootout right there. I knew that was against protocol. Fuck, I didn't want to sound alarms, but I had to. I grabbed my phone quickly and then said to Graciella, "Hey, let's take a selfie before he gets here."

She groaned. "Oh my God, my face."

"Hey, you're the one who declined to freshen up."

I leaned over quickly and angled the phone as if I was shooting us and grabbed several photos of the man approaching us. I quickly tucked away my phone and then searched for my exit, but the men that had come up from the boardwalk were blocking them all.

My only shot was going to be to the fucking front door, and if he was smart, he would have that exit blocked too.

It was either the beach, which offered no security, or the front door. I scooted to the edge of my seat, ready. Waiting as Graciella smiled up at the man as he approached.

"Darling." His voice was velvet.

I knew that voice. My stomach pitched, and I fought to keep down the bits of egg and toast I'd just eaten. She stood and wound her arms around the neck of the devil. I wanted to tell her run. I wanted to tell her he was not her friend. He was the enemy. But Graciella, poor, sweet Graciella, was winding her arms around the man who killed my parents. Drake Webster. The right-hand man of Antonio Igno.

Fucking hell.

I tried to duck my head. "I'll just leave you two lovebirds alone."

But that voice, smooth as silk and cold as ice, said, "Oh, don't run off. I didn't mean to interrupt your breakfast. Why don't you introduce me to your friend, Graciella?"

Her laugh was high pitched and bubbly. "This is my friend I was telling you about, Saffron King. She's here with her husband."

I still had my sunglasses on, and I prayed that they gave me some coverage, but I knew they didn't give me enough. I was the spitting image of my mother. He would know. One look at me, and our whole mission was over. All this time we'd been working Graciella, Drake Webster had been working us.

He took his aviators off, his bright blue eyes shiny as always. And then he stuck his hand out. "Any friend of Graciella's is a friend of mine. I'm Drake."

For a long sickening moment, all I could do was stare at his hand, willing the bile to stay down, willing myself to have the courage and strength to stare him in the eye and spit. To hurl myself at him and call him a murderer in front of all these people. But I couldn't do any of that. All I could do was stare.

Graciella bumped my shoulder. "Saffron, this is Drake. Say hi," she laughed nervously.

I swallowed hard and stood, sticking my hand in his. "It's a pleasure to meet you."

The moment I spoke, his brows furrowed. "Have we met?"

I shook my head. "I don't think so. Actually, you know what, Graciella? I'm just going to head to the ladies. I'll be right back."

"All right. Hurry back. Drake and I want some time alone, and that doesn't work if you're not here."

Right, she wanted to use me. "Maybe you should come with me."

She stood abruptly, bumping the edge of the table, which bumped me slightly. It unsettled me, and my sunglasses fell off my face. I scrambled to pick them up. I slipped them back on, but not before Drake met my gaze and his eyes went wide. His nostrils flared. His lips parted, and I didn't wait for him to say anything.

I ran.

I bolted for the front door, but I knew he had men out there. And of course, I could see them as well as Massimo's men. So all I could do was pray for a back entrance. But he was too smart. There would be men back there too.

The loo? A higher floor? How was I going to get out of here?

I booked it into the ladies' room. I reached for my purse and pulled out a hundred pounds, handing the money to the startled attendant. "I'll give you a hundred pounds to keep that door closed."

She just nodded and then shifted her chair and adjusted it under the knob. "Okay."

I ran to the windows. "Will these open?"

"Yeah, the lock is tricky though. Are you trying to run away?"

"Bad date."

"Surely you can go out the front door."

I shook my head. "I can't."

Her brow furrowed. "Is someone hurting you? I can call security."

I shook my head. "No. I just need to get out. Please help me."

She nodded and stood on the counter, fiddling with the window lock. When it finally gave way, I shoved the window open. "Do you mind giving me a boost?"

I was tall, but I still needed several inches before I could get my fingers to find purchase enough to pull me up and over. It was then that I heard the banging on the door. It sounded like Graciella. "Saffron? Are you in there? The door is locked. Are you okay?"

Drake hadn't just seen me. His men were looking for me too. Fuck.

The attendant shrugged at me. "I won't let her in. But if she's determined enough, she could probably just have security shove the door open."

"It's okay. Just hoist me up."

She did so inelegantly, but I wrapped my purse over my shoulder and climbed. When I cleared the window in the soft grass outside, I breathed a sigh of relief and then did the only thing that I could do. I sent a distress call. I didn't do it lightly because it would mean every single one of us would have to leave quickly. Get to the safe house and then make it off the islands. We couldn't risk going to the palace and tying Sebastian and Penny to a covert op. We weren't supposed to be here, and that was the joy of the Rogues Division. We were invisible. The royals would help us get off the island, but we couldn't be found in the palace.

I sent a text to the encrypted number. Three words, *the heir's ruby*, and then I ran like the devil himself was chasing me.

———

Lachlan

RAGE WAS AN INTERESTING EMOTION. It could flash hot and burn brightly, or it could simmer. But more than the rage I felt was a sense of sadness that I hadn't expected.

I had to find out what the fuck was going on. I liked her. Trusted her. She was more than just my training officer. I cared about that woman. And to realize that she'd done this to me, brought me here and then looked me in the face every single day and said nothing. She made me her partner. Made me care about her.

Fucking hell.

My phone chimed, and I forced my brain into compliance. We had a mission to complete. I sure as shit I wouldn't be touching her again. It was like my dick was mocking me though.

Oh yeah, sure you won't.

I scowled. "We won't."

Uh-huh, whatever you say.

It was like my dick full-on understood the theory of hate fucking. It was her fault I was here.

My brain kept trying to offer other potential and valid reasons for Felix to know her, but there weren't any. I had been her mark. There was no other explanation.

But why would your grandfather bother?

Maybe they needed me in a softened, weakened state. I would have fought back, wouldn't I?

I was just on the edge of the old town, my trainers slapping on the cobblestones, when the alert came in. I frowned at it, not sure if I was seeing it right. It was the emergency code.

Red. Red. Red. Saff had called in The Heir's Ruby.

I saw Saff's message, and my heart sank. Adrenaline flowed in my veins. Fuck. Fuck. Fuck. She was in trouble. My rational brain had a lot to say about that.

I thought we hated her.

Fucking hell. I knew what the protocol meant. Find an exit route immediately. It didn't matter though, because I was still calling her.

I knew she wouldn't answer. *Think fucker, think, think, think.* Where was she? She'd gone to breakfast with Graciella, right?

From there, what would be the egress route she'd take? I had a whole map of the big island. Memorized it backward and forward. She was in trouble. Where would she go? If she was seeing red, that meant she'd had made a hasty exit out of somewhere. She needed help. I ran quickly, nearly taking out pedestrians. I had to get through.

My skin was too cold and flushed hot at the same time. At one point I slid and stumbled over someone's fallen gelato. I managed to stay upright then kept going. Fuck, I had to get to her. I *had* to fucking get to her.

Fucking Saff. I was furious. More furious than I'd ever been in my entire life. She had betrayed me. But still, I couldn't leave her to die. Protocol said I was fucking supposed to get to the pier. Anyone who didn't make it on time would be left behind.

But I couldn't leave her. My phone buzzed. It was Saint.

"Saint," I answered, huffing. "The fuck are you doing? You're breaking protocol."

"You answered. So are you."

"I'm trying to get Saff so we can get out of here."

"That's against the rules."

"I know."

"Where are you?"

I told him my location.

"If we do this, we're all likely going to miss the fucking boat," Saint groaned.

"I'm not asking you to do this. I just— I can't leave her."

"Yeah, keep going, I'll meet you on Winston Walk."

I quickly did a mental assessment of where Winston Walk was. "We'll be there."

"You better be there, because I'm going to borrow some wheels."

I laughed. "Aren't you a demolitions expert? How are you going to borrow these wheels?"

"Don't ask questions."

And I didn't. I just hung up and ran for my life, because I knew that if she had called red, she was in trouble. And I had to get to her. It didn't matter what she'd done, or how, or what that meant. When we got back to London, then I'd talk to her. But for now, the only way I wanted out of this was for *all* of us to be safe and sound. But her most of all. And I was willing to risk everything to make sure of that.

There were throngs of people on the streets. It was a bank holiday, so everyone was on bloody holiday time. Fuck. The streets were teeming, and I knew I was not going to make it.

I made an ill-advised left, and it took me straight into the path of an impromptu parade with buskers up ahead. I cursed. The crowd was so thick I knew I wasn't getting through. And then I saw a retaining wall, so I hopped up and worked my way up and up. A couple of people were in their yards and shouted a warning, but of course I didn't listen. I couldn't hear them for the fear and the worry that had pierced my gut and gripped it, refusing to let go, the claws of it digging in tight.

Her first mission. Her first fucking mission. She could not die.

Fuck. Fuck. Fuck.

I made a right on Penelope's Place and waited for her. This was the path she'd come down. If I could grab her, we could rendezvous with Saint. We'd be out of here in no time.

I just prayed to God I wasn't too late, that she was okay and safe.

For someone who's angry, you sure are concerned about her safety.

I needed Saff to myself to discuss our issues extensively. I was going to tan her hide first though.

Her arse is plenty tan enough.

Fucking hell. The last thing I needed was to think about her arse and how it felt to touch her, her body pressed up against mine, riding me, taking everything I had to give her. Fuck.

I wasn't much for God or religion, but now was the time to pray. I hoped to God I knew her well enough to assume that she

would come this way. Of all the things she'd taught me in
strategy and ops, she would have insisted I follow the path of
least resistance straight to the pier.

So in the shadows, I waited for her. At the small of my back,
I palmed my gun and waited, hoping to God that Saff followed
her own advice.

21

SAFFRON

I RAN like the devil himself was chasing me. I had no choice.

Drake fucking Webster?

What was he doing here? Our intel hadn't told us he was here. There was no calming my heart. I couldn't process it because there was still a part of me that wanted to run back and make him pay for what he'd done to me, done to my family. Because of him, I never felt safe in my own skin. Because of him, my parents were gone. He took everything from me, and I wanted to kill him. But I was also terrified and didn't know what to do, so I just kept running. Despite the panic though, my footing was sure.

I reached inside my purse and grabbed an elastic, and as I headed toward the shopping district, I made a sharp left, dropped twenty pounds in a shopkeeper's hand, and grabbed a scarf. As I exited hastily, she called after me. I saw the label that said the price was only five pounds and called back, "Keep the change," as I kept moving, pulling my hair into a pony tail and quickly wrapping the scarf around it.

I moved as quickly as I could, trying not to draw attention

to myself in the packed streets. I didn't dare look behind to see if someone was following me. As I turned on one of the streets in the shopping district, I heard a commotion behind me.

When I hit the corner, a mirror posted in one of the shop windows showed cars approaching and two men in heavy jackets running in my direction. Fuck. Drake's men.

I had to move. I sprinted through the crowd, frantic now as I glanced at my watch again. There was no way I was going to fucking make it on foot. I needed to steal a vehicle. But that could mean more trouble because getting caught in a stolen vehicle meant police. Police meant I'd be a sitting duck and Drake and his men could find me. It also meant that I'd likely already missed the rendezvous with my team and I would have to get myself out.

Penny and Ariel would try to help, but the whole point was that we weren't supposed to be there. The Royal Elite team would try to help, but any association with me would mean trouble for them.

Think, Saff, think.

A motorbike would probably be the fastest. A car would have to stay on the roads, but for motorbikes, alleyways were an option. I had a whole map of the main island imprinted in my brain. Because if there was one thing that I did, at the very least, it was mentally prepare.

I saw a big group of people and inserted myself in the middle of them. Just in time, because one of the men in a heavy jacket ran past the group, scanning over the top of it. He headed to the right, searching in the boutiques along the way. The crowd I was in began to move up ahead. They were probably headed to one of the first churches built on the island. It looked like a tour group.

I made a sharp left into an alley that I knew was full of

motorbike parking. When I did, a hand clamped over my mouth and dragged me into the shadows. "There you fucking are."

I shrieked internally, though I made zero sound. I quickly turned my head sharply to the right, putting my face in the crook of his arm so I couldn't be choked out. I shifted my hips in the same direction, bringing my palm down, but a hand caught mine. "Ah, you fooled me once."

The voice was familiar, and it wasn't Drake. I forced my brain to calm the panic, to take a deep breath, and to ignore the adrenaline. It was Lock.

His hand clamped around my arm and softly traced over the skin of my inner wrist. "I'm going to let go. Are you okay?"

I nodded and he released me. I turned in his arms and he put his finger to his mouth. "Shh."

Relieved, I wrapped my arms around him. "You're not supposed to be here."

"I know. But did you really think I would leave you?"

"This isn't protocol."

"Fuck protocol. We need to wait here for another thirty seconds. They're doing a sweep of those stores over there. Which bike do you want?"

I peeked out around his shoulder. "The black one. There are two helmets on it."

"Okay, are you good?"

"Yeah."

"When we stop, you're going to tell me what the fuck is going on."

"Yeah, but we have to get to the pier without being seen on the bike."

"Don't worry. We'll ditch it about four blocks from here. Saint is waiting."

My brows lifted. "Saint ignored protocols too?"

"Are you insane? You're our fearless leader. We weren't going to leave you in the field."

My brow furrowed and I shook my head. "Lock, you're supposed to—"

He didn't let me finish. Instead, he grabbed my hand and took off running toward the black bike.

There was no time to waste. I climbed on the bike on the driver's seat. Lock shook his head, scooted me back, and climbed on.

The ignition was digital. He laughed as he pulled out his phone with a decryption device that we'd been given for the mission just in case. It took several precious seconds, but the bike revved and I could feel rather than hear Lock chuckle. I just prayed to God, he knew how to ride the thing.

Oh, holy shit. He *did* know how to ride this thing. As the bike roared, he charged forward, careening down the alley without a care. Not even pausing as we hit the end of the street and made a sharp right turn directly into traffic.

Somewhere behind us a car honked and there was yelling, but we were already on the road, weaving in and out of traffic. He made another sharp left, and I held on tight. My hands flattened against his taught abs and all I could do was suck in a sharp breath. Fuck. Fuck. Fuck. My brain kept going over and over where we'd gone wrong. Where the intel was wrong. Drake Webster was not supposed to be here.

We took another sharp right, and I heard a ping and saw the cement wall next to us chip as we charged into an alley. I cursed low and shouted, "Bullets." I didn't know if he heard me, but Lock drove like the devil himself was behind him.

He made another sharp left and looped back around until he made a full circle and we were behind the man chasing us. I knew what he wanted me to do then. I grabbed the gun out of his holster. I really did hate to shoot up the Winston Isles, but for fuck's sake. Lock increased our speed until we were within a hundred meters.

I was a hell of a marksman, but on a motorcycle? Lock, for his part, did his best to keep the bike straight. Using his arm to brace, I palmed the gun using both hands, one hand for support, one on the trigger. As we got closer and closer, I aimed for the tire. Fired.

There was a massive pop that sounded like an explosion, and as our bike popped in the air for a moment, the back end of the car in front of us seemed to lift several feet off the ground before spinning and careening out into a barricade.

I brought the gun back, put the safety back on, and kept it tucked in front of me, with one arm holding tightly to Lock.

Lock made a sharp right, and then another left before driving us into an alley. "Come on," he said as he swung off the bike. He took the gun from me and shoved it back into the waistband under his shirt. He held my hand easily as he tugged me along. At the entrance of the alley, he tried to walk forward, but a shiver stole up my neck and I held him back.

He frowned at me, and I shook my head. "Wait."

Suddenly, one of the hulking men drove past us in another car. Lock cursed as we stayed in the shadows. "Jesus, fuck."

Across the street, we saw Saint idling in a car.

Lock glanced around the street, saw nothing else suspicious, and tugged me forward. As we booked it through traffic, weaving in and out of the oncoming cars, several people honked at us. But once we reached the car, the door swung open and Saint grinned back at us. "Can't take you two lovebirds anywhere. Always causing trouble."

I rolled my eyes. "Just drive."

He gave me a wink and a nod before muttering, "Yes, Ms. Daisy," as he sped off.

I slumped down in the back seat with Lock as he used his whole body to practically shield and guard me.

In the safety of his arms, with my heart hammering against my ribs, my brain started to finally make sense of what had happened. Drake Webster was here. The man who had killed my parents. I'd had him within my sights. And instead of staying and fighting and killing him where he stood, I'd run. What the fuck did that say about me?

It says you know how to survive.

Lock's hands rubbed my arms. "You okay?"

"Yeah." I sighed. "But we got bad intel. We need to find out why."

22

SAFFRON

"WHAT THE FUCK HAPPENED?" Gabe's voice boomed.

Twenty faces turned to stare at me. I knew what debriefs were like. They were immediate and stressful, and I was the agent who had fucked up in the field.

Gabe scowled at me. "Are you sure it was him?"

"Yes. I took photos so we would have proof of a sighting. I didn't just abort a mission for nothing. We made eye contact. He recognized me."

"Are you sure he recognized you?"

I glanced around the room. Everyone in there was a senior agent. My team was there. Saint and King, both looking at me with a grim determination to the set of their lips. They were going to back my play, whatever I said. But I didn't want them going down with me if this went sideways. Why didn't Gabe believe me?

"All I can tell you is what happened. I was working Graciella, and she told me she was having an affair. I gave her the standard *we'll take care of you, and if you need a friend, I'm here for you* speech. She was asking me to cover for her while she spent time with her new boyfriend, who was on the island."

Gabe frowned. "We had no intel that Webster was on the island."

"I don't know what to tell you. Maybe he came in on a boat. Maybe he's got someone on the docks who brought him in quietly. I have no idea. On the way back, we spoke to Ariel on the sat phone. There was no record of him coming or going."

"He's a ghost. We know that much." Gabe ran his hands through his hair. "What the fuck, Saff?"

I lifted my chin. "Don't you mean Agent Abott?"

A hush fell over the room. I shouldn't have said that, but if he was going to ride me like I was just another one of his agents, he couldn't pretend I was his sister today.

Tabs spoke up. "If Agent Abott says that it was Drake Webster, I trust her instincts. She's one of the few people who has managed to get a recorded sighting of him. Everything else we have is blurry at best. And if she says he recognized her, he did. Which means she's in danger."

I shook my head imperceptibly at her. I didn't want Gabe punishing her for defending me. "If we can get to Graciella, we can get to him."

Gabe laughed. "You are not going back in the field."

"We have an asset who trusts me. It's ridiculous to pull me now." I wasn't being petulant; I was making a good argument. At the end of the day, everybody wanted Drake Webster. All of us. My parents were legends, and I was the heir. Webster had taken them from me, which meant I owed him a debt. Whether Gabe liked it or not, he could shuffle this all the way up to Oversight, but they would agree.

That's if they believe you.

Lock came to my rescue, which I didn't need. "I broke protocol. I knew the route agent Abott would take, so I waited along that route to provide back up."

Gabe lifted his brow as Lock spoke, but he said nothing. Because, of course, Lock was new. And a man. Although, half of the best agents in this place were women and could run circles around my brother.

Lock continued, undeterred. "We were definitely shot at."

Gabe crossed his arms and eyed Lock up and down. "Did you ever stop to think that maybe it's because of how Agent Abott responded?" he asked derisively.

I squared my shoulders, ready for this fight. "For starters, I followed protocol. You can track the routes I took. I made an escape out the window. According to Ariel, someone broke down the door of that loo coming for me, and then broke the window. I didn't break it on my way out. I was chased through the Winston Isles. Last we spoke to Ariel, she was pulling video footage. I'm sure you will find Webster's men looking for me. And finally, we were shot at. I know what I saw, and Graciella is the way to get to him."

"We'll send Agent Smith then."

Tabs looked up, frowning. "What the fu— No. I can't identify him. She's the one who knows who he is. And as good as I am in the field with assets, Saff—Agent Abott," she corrected with an apologetic smile, "is the one who has established a relationship. It doesn't make sense to send me."

Gabe's jaw ticked. He wasn't used to anyone talking back to him. The other agents in the room said not a word, not even a murmur. But they were all leaning forward, watching the show.

"Agent Abott has a point. We can send her back with more support," Tabatha concluded. "I'm happy to support her, but she should be the lead agent on this. I'm sure it's Oversight's call, but this is the closest we've been to Webster in two years."

Two years exactly. I would never forget those bright blue

eyes as he leaned across the picnic table while I was saying goodbye to friends on the main quad a couple of days after graduation. I'd just lost my parents. He had come to campus where my friends were trying to console me, and he'd told me, plain as day, 'Get the hell out of dodge or you will die too.' I saw it as a threat, but it felt like a warning. Why not just kill me then?

He'd stalked me for months. How he even knew I was there was beyond me. But he'd stalked me and used me to kill my parents. It was my fault. If I hadn't insisted they needed to see me graduate, they would still be alive, and I lived with that every day.

I inhaled deeply and lifted my gaze to my brother's. "I know the players. Webster recognized me. I'm the only one who knows what he looks like. You can tell from that video that he is perpetually in a blind spot. He's that good. So I'm your best bet at getting him in the field."

"Let's see what Oversight says." Gabe was not used to me fighting back... ever. Let alone publicly.

Saint tried to be helpful. "For what it's worth, I got the distinct impression that they were trying to capture, not kill."

Gabe lifted a brow. "How can you even discern that?"

"From the video footage we've watched, it appears they were trying to corral her, using a grid pattern to hem her in. They wanted to capture her, which is... concerning."

He gave me a shrug, and I lifted a brow. Saint hadn't told me that. Why had he not told me that?

Gabe nodded. "I'll speak to Oversight and see how they want us to go forward. Dismissed."

When we stood, I tried to approach Lock, but all he did was give me a grim nod as he went out the opposite exit.

What the fuck was that? We didn't have much opportunity to speak alone on the way back and frankly, we were exhausted.

Completely shredded from the adrenaline of the day. But I expected him to say something to me. Anything about what had happened with us.

Fuck.

Saint approached me. "Sorry."

"No, it's fine. You spoke the truth. Next time though, tell me first?"

"Yeah. Got that. I should have, and that's on me. It won't happen again." He gave me a nod and then stepped away.

It was Tabs who found me after everyone was gone. "Jesus, come on. You look like you're ready for war."

"I just need to get some rest and get back out there. But you know, Gabe."

"I think Gabe is worried, love. Something could have happened to you, and I was terrified myself."

"That's the whole point. I'm an agent. And he doesn't respect that."

"Well, he might have to because what I said was true. You're the only one who has seen him. And Graciella knows you. She won't trust me or anyone else who comes to her, especially after the madness of everything that happened. Looks like you'll finally be getting your wish and becoming a full-fledged field agent. And honey, we all want him, but we have to follow strict protocol. We'll get him."

"Not we, *I*. I will get him. I owe him."

"And you have back up. Hang tight on Gabe. He'll come around."

"Well, for once big brother is not going to have a choice."

As we walked out and headed for the elevator to take me upstairs to my quarters, she frowned and inclined her head toward the rear entrance of the debrief room. "First, are we going to talk about what the hell happened on the island with you and Mr. Sex on a Stick?"

Despite feeling completely wrung out, I had to laugh. "I don't know. He performed well on the mission."

Tabs smirked. "I'll bet he did. So was the first time a fluke?"

Heat rose up my neck and splashed into my face. "No, Tabs, but that's none of your business."

"If that means no, it was not a fluke, are you going to talk to him about it?"

"Well, it doesn't look like he wants to talk to me. And I am wrecked and tired. So I am going to rest. If I'm going to war with Gabe over this, I need to be fully armed."

"Okay. I'm on rotation tonight until six, and you can come home with me if you want."

"I might do that. I need to get the hell out of here."

"All right, I'll text you."

She left me and headed down toward the training tunnels. When I turned left toward the elevator to the main house, I found Lock suiting up for what looked like target practice outside the weapons department. "You're going to do more target work?"

"Yup."

"You don't want to come down after the mission debrief? That was stressful on all of us."

"Nope." It seemed one-word answers were all I was getting out of him.

I frowned at him. "Is something wrong?"

"No, nothing is fucking wrong."

I squared my shoulders. "Lock, maybe we should—"

"Let me stop you right there. You're going to say something about 'Hey, we should talk.' There's nothing to talk about. We did what we had to do for the mission. That's done now. We're safe."

I jerked as if slapped. There were many other agents milling about, so I lowered my voice and deliberately kept my distance.

"Do you want to actually have a conversation about this, or are you going to go off and sulk?"

He smirked. "I think I'm going to opt for sulking. Except in my case, it won't be sulking." He leaned forward then. "I'll be too busy pondering why the woman I haven't been able to get out of my head for fucking weeks is the entire reason I'm here. You and I have fucked before." A cold wash of tension and anxiety slipped over my body, like a suit coating me in electrified jelly. I gasped and his silvery gaze searched mine. "Deny it. Go ahead."

When I couldn't, he smirked and nodded. "Yeah, so instead of shooting you, I'm going to go shoot a target, and we'll pretend it never happened."

All I could do was stand there. The shock of it hitting me, word for word. *You and I have fucked before.* He knew.

And like my worst nightmare, he assumed I'd done it on purpose.

———

Lachlan

Two hours later and I still hadn't calmed down. I lined up my targets and fired, trying to put all my focus and my anger to directing exactly where that bullet was going to go.

I couldn't talk to her. Not yet.

The things I had to say, I couldn't take back.

Or maybe you'll beg her to take you back.

Nope. For weeks now, she'd lied to me. We had definitely shagged. She was lying. Pretending she didn't know me, pretending I didn't know exactly how her pussy tasted.

So there was nothing to say. Nothing to do except to stay the fuck away from her. No matter what I did, I was still going to be haunted by the dream of her. Because life wasn't fair. I finally gave a shit about someone else since Charlie died, and it turned out she was a liar.

But at least I could have some semblance of sanity. Fucking hell. What had I done to deserve this? For weeks, we'd been training together. We'd been getting close.

Or maybe only you thought you were getting close.

Maybe she wasn't getting close at all. Maybe she was doing her damn job.

All the scenarios ran through my head, every single one, as I tried to force an outcome. But every time I closed my eyes, all I could see was Saff laughing, smiling at me, rolling her eyes, doing that pursed-lip thing that she did when she was trying really hard not to laugh at me.

The more I focused on her, the more I could see snippets of me and her in my flat. I'd danced with her. I had fed her cake? Frustrated, I blasted my last bullet into the target and then dragged my headphones off as I called it forward. Waiting for the sheet, already knowing that half of my bullets had gone wide.

I needed to get a handle on this. If I couldn't get a handle on my emotions, I was screwed.

"You are certainly in a mood, aren't you?"

I frowned at the sound of a familiar voice. "Agent Smith."

"Oh, shut up. Call me Tabatha."

"Tabatha, anything I can do for you?"

"You just came back from a mission. Standard protocol is down time, forty-eight hours, whether you like it or not."

"I don't need it."

She laughed. "Oh, so you're special. You are a very special agent that somehow has managed to counteract the effects of adrenaline and stress. I didn't know you had a medical back-ground. I knew you were pretty, and you know, had all the makings of a bad boy with a decent brain. But I did not know you were also a medical doctor. I will make it a point to remember that in the future."

I frowned. "Okay, I hear you. I just... I needed to blow off some steam."

"We will get Webster. That's what we do. Gabe is not going to let anyone rest until we get him. He lost his parents too."

"Yeah, sure, whatever."

She frowned at me, and I reloaded the clip. But before I could put my headphones back on, she put a hand on my arm. "Listen, whatever your problem is, I saw that little interaction with Saff. What's your deal with her?"

"No deal."

"Oh, bullshit."

"No deal. She's my supervising officer, right?"

"God, so pretty but so dumb. Your memory starting to come back yet?"

I furrowed my brow at that. "I don't know what you're talking about."

"Yes, you do. You know exactly what I'm talking about. I read the brief. And I talked to Ariel. I know that you guys had to pretend for safety."

I clenched my jaw tight. "The full details were in the report to Gabe?"

She shook her head. "No, he just has ops details. So the fact that the place was bugged, yes. What happened after it was bugged, no. That's all I'm going to say."

"Oh, this just gets better and better."

"It's confidential. Even Oversight doesn't see it, so you're fine. Gabe won't know that you deflowered his sister."

"Jesus fucking Christ." Had she been a virgin the first time we'd been together? And I didn't fucking remember? If that didn't take the cake, I didn't know what did.

"Is that or is that not what happened?" Tabatha demanded.

I cleared my throat. "That is not any of your business."

"All right. If you say so. But why are you in here with her face on your targets?"

"You don't know who I'm shooting at."

"Oh, after a mission like that, either you are real pissed off at Drake Webster because he ruined your mission, or you're mad at someone else. I'd bet cash money that someone who you're mad at goes by the name of Saffron Abott."

"I'm not doing this with you."

"Okay, but you should talk to someone because sometimes what happens in the field can get dicey. And it's hard to separate."

"I'm fine. Everything is *fine*."

She laughed. "When did you start to remember?"

I blinked rapidly. "Remember what?"

"Let's not do this, okay? Let's not do the thing where you and I pretend that nothing major is going on. That you aren't stupid in love with my best friend. Let's have an honest conversation. So, when did you start to remember?"

I stared at her and crossed my arms. "I feel like that also falls in the category of none of your business."

"Okay, none of my business then. But I can tell you're in here shooting because you think she played you. But obviously, you don't know anything about Saff. It's not her style. It's not what you think it is. Maybe you should talk to her before you make judgments."

"So what you're telling me is, before I judge her, I should go ask her to give me details of what the fuck happened?"

"Yeah."

"And completely forget the fact that she's been lying to me all this time?"

"Has she, though? Or was it that she came to work one day

and the guy she hooked up with walked into her place of employment and did not seem to remember her at all."

I scowled at her, but it didn't seem to have any effect.

"But hey, by all means, you feel free to punish her for something she has no control over. You didn't remember. So if you were her, what would you have done?"

I frowned. "I know you want me to believe you, but I really don't."

"That's on you. You can believe what you like. But I'm telling you that's not how Saff operates. She would have told you, but there was no point. You didn't remember, and there was also the whole no-fraternization thing. So welcome to hell. Now imagine you're Saff and she's been assigned to train you."

I swallowed hard at that.

"Ask Gabe if you want. See what he says."

"Look, I know she's your mate and you want to cover for her—"

"Don't be a twat! Listen to your instincts. She was horrified to see you here. However you got here, she had nothing to do with it. So if you want to make someone's life hell, make Gabe's life hell. Or your grandfather's. Or whoever it was that didn't love you enough. Don't take that out on her. In a perfect world, she would have told you. But the world isn't perfect, so what was she supposed to do?"

"Are you going to let me go back to shooting things now?"

"The real question is whether you think you still need to shoot things or if maybe you just use your words."

"It's been a long couple of days, Tabatha."

"I heard. Imagine what it's been like for Saff. I know you don't remember, but I told you in that club that if you hurt her I would sever your balls from your person."

I lifted my brows. "I don't doubt that you're capable."

"Good. You shouldn't. And honestly, I could eunuch you any

time. It could happen in training. It could happen as an accident. But she likes you, so I'm giving you an option to fix it.
Whatever you have going on with your family, however you
ended up here or if you even want to be here, *don't* take it out on
her." She turned and stalked toward the door. "Oh, and P.S.,
Gabe's looking for you. You fucked up."

23

LACHLAN

IT TURNED out I wasn't the only one getting a private ass chewing from Gabe since Saint was waiting on me in his office.

"Have you two lost your fucking minds? We have protocols for a goddamn reason."

Saint was relaxed, as if he'd anticipated this ass chewing and was taking it on the chin with his characteristic seemingly good nature. He nodded. "Yes, sir. We know, but it was necessary." He was clearly unbothered that Gabe was well ticked off.

"And you, King, you *knew* better. You had one task. Stay on target. It's not your fault the devil incarnate turned up, but you broke protocol. Went out on your own."

I met his gaze coolly. "Would you rather I'd left your sister to die?"

He sat on his desk and leaned forward, glowering at me with a raised brow. "You see, that's the thing. Saff, in case you haven't realized, is the fucking heir. She knows how to survive. She's been training for this since she was in diapers. She doesn't need saving. Not by you."

That one line pierced my soul, because it had been instinct

to help her, despite how angry I was. Yes, of course, she was my teammate, but still, she was Saff.

"I know. But we were assigned to be a team. And we don't leave each other behind." Maybe he would buy that I had full-on committed to a team.

Instead, he growled at me. "A *team* operates when we follow bloody protocol. What if you'd saved her only to be captured?"

Saint held up his hands. "I'm too pretty for jail." He was such a twat. But still, I wanted to chuckle. He *was* too pretty for jail. He would be very popular wherever he went.

Gabe looked like he wanted to throw something. He didn't look at Saint when he spoke. "Saint, get out."

Saint was up and out of his seat in less than a nanosecond. Gabe didn't have to tell him twice. As he strolled by me, he muttered. "Wanker." He grinned at me good-naturedly. "See you back at the flat, mate."

When he was gone, Gabe ran his hands through his hair. "Speaking as Saff's brother and not your superior, thank you. I owe you a debt."

I frowned. "Weren't you just chewing me out because Saff knows how to survive on her own?"

"She does. She probably would have made it off the island before you did. It doesn't change the fact that I'm happy some-one's looking out for her. I'm also thrilled you seem to under-stand teamwork."

"You know, she's really good. I made a dozen mistakes on our little jaunt. Without her, I might not have survived."

"I know."

It wasn't my place, but I had to ask. "Then why the fuck isn't she in the field? Is there something wrong with her?" Maybe I didn't have the right to this line of questioning, but I needed to know. Because Saff had been responsible for my current residence here, and I wanted to know everything.

Gabe crossed his arms and sat back. "She's not ready."

"Bullshit. You wouldn't have sent her on the mission if she wasn't ready."

"You don't understand. Drake Webster... She handled that better than I would have."

I cursed under my breath. "He's the one who killed her parents?"

He nodded. "Yeah. Saff sees herself as responsible. Webster approached her when she was at uni. Classic asset recruitment. Except he pretended to be interested in dating her. While Saff was cagey, she couldn't find anything on him. He looked legit. While he never progressed their relationship beyond friendship and mild interest, he kept a close eye on her, watched her for months. Stalked her and pretended to be interested."

Hearing that he groomed her, that she'd been that close to danger made a pit form in my gut.

"Our parents weren't going to let her graduation day go by without being there for her. All Webster had to do was sit on Saff and wait until they turned up. Our folks were careful. They flew private on a small commuter plane in and out of a private airstrip. At least he let Saff have her graduation first, but when they were leaving, he bombed their plane. Saff saw the whole thing. She's never really recovered."

I winced.

"He found her afterward. Said that if she identified him, what happened to our parents would happen to her."

"Fucking hell, I'm going to kill him."

Gabe nodded. "Get in line. Of course, Saff knows protocol. When we lose someone in the field, everyone comes home to their respective base. *Everyone.* We take all precautions, new passports, wash everything, close down that base, and return to central command. We scrubbed IDs and sent everyone back out to new posts."

"Jesus fucking Christ. And Saff? What about her?"

Gabe exhaled. "Because she wasn't an active agent yet, she couldn't just come home. She buried her parents and then had to find her own way to safely return using her actual name and ID. She backpacked across northeastern America, made her way into Canada where she made it to a safe house, grabbed new IDs, and came home. It took her a month."

"Fucking hell."

"Yeah, she was paranoid. She didn't want to lead anyone back to home base."

"For fuck's sake. How did they even know who she was in order to target her?"

"I don't know. We were hoping our new mission with Massimo would give us some more of the inner workings of the Igno empire. At the very least, we'd be able to listen in."

"What about the bugs we have planted?"

"The moment we got the red notice, we sent a cleaning crew. While you lot were vanishing into thin air, we scrubbed the listening devices. At most, Igno might wonder where you went. We very publicly cleaned out your villa and had new agents move in just to make it seem as if the honeymoon was over. We've also planted some tabloid rumors, with your grandfather's permission of course, about how you were seen with a secret lady love in the Caribbean and then in Ibiza."

"Wow. Well, at least that tracks with the whole playboy image Massimo had of me."

"Thanks for laying the ground work on that."

"Is Saff okay?"

He shrugged. "I might not have been helpful on that front, but my sister knows she needs to play it close for a bit."

I lifted a brow. "Jesus, mate."

Gabe's brow furrowed. "She's your teammate and your training officer, but I'm in command, do you understand?

You can either speak to me as her brother or as commander. You can't do both." He sighed. "As your commander, you broke protocol. You have to stay on and finish the mission."

"What is the mission now?"

"We have to regroup. Figure out where we are. I have to talk to Oversight."

"And my status?"

"For the meantime, you're still a Rogue."

Two weeks ago, before I left for the islands, all I wanted was out. But now, I owed Drake Webster a bullet to the skull.

And here I thought we were done with Saff.

Done or not, that twat deserves to die.

"As Saff's brother again, thank you for watching her six. You're dismissed."

"Is Saff grounded?"

"No. She's finally getting her wish, actually. To become a field agent."

I nodded. "Well, at least there's that."

I pushed to my feet and made to leave when he called out, "And King, whatever happened between you two in the Winston Isles, I don't want to know about it. But you understand the rules at Rogues Division, yes?"

I knew what he was asking. I turned slowly. "I know the rules. They won't be a problem. But I do have a question for you."

He shrugged. "What is it?"

"The forty-eight hours before I turned up here..."

"Yes?

"Was Saff responsible?"

His brow furrowed. "Why would you ask that?"

I scanned the way his eyes widened at my question. "I don't know. She said something in training that made it seem like she'd been in my flat before. And she was a little too familiar with my file."

"We don't disclose those details for a reason."

The only way you're going to find out is to ask her directly.

Too bad I was just as likely to throttle her as I was to kiss her. And either option could get me killed.

24

SAFFRON

THIRTY MINUTES after arriving at Tabatha's house, she texted me that she'd been called in on another brief and was going to stay on-site.

Jesus Christ, that sucked. I could almost see Gabe doing it on purpose to make sure I was alone. He had texted and called once, but I wasn't inclined to answer. I made my check-in calls as required, but I couldn't speak to him right now. Not after he'd essentially questioned my sanity and my leadership in the debrief.

The only thing worse than being stuck on campus was being stuck alone. As much as I wanted to eat junk food and watch movies and relax and pour a glass of wine, none of that seemed the same without Tabs here.

You should be sleeping.

I should. But I was too keyed up, too wired. I just wanted to get back out in the field. Normally, I had a routine, but this was my first time coming back from an actual mission. Sure, I had been coms lead before, supporting other missions, but I'd never been in the field. It was completely different.

Maybe Gabe was right and I didn't belong in the field. Because fucking hell, this feeling, the unease, the restlessness was driving me crazy.

The doorbell rang, and I frowned. Tabs wasn't here and this was her safe space. She had an address that she would take men to, but this was her *private* place. No one came here except for me. So who the fuck was at the door?

I palmed the gun under her coffee table and pushed myself up from the couch.

I stayed out of range of the windows and watched the door, sticking to the side in case someone attempted to shoot through it, though I knew for a fact her door was steel. And there was a panic room.

But still, I quickly checked the security monitor, and my stomach fell when I saw who was on the other side.

I pressed the speaker and forced a deep, long breath. "What do you want, Lock?"

"Can we talk?"

"No. I need to get some rest. We'll talk when I'm back on campus."

"Do you understand what I had to do to get off campus? Tabatha had to write me a special note and everything."

"I don't care. I'm not opening the door."

"Are you going to make me test out my lockpicking skills? You know I struggled with that in training."

"That's not my problem."

He held something up to the camera. "See? Here's the note."

I squinted to read it better, and there was Tabatha's perfect handwriting in bold script. "Let him in. Talk."

Damn it. Sometimes having a best friend was a pain in the ass. "Lock, if you are here for retribution or you're angry, I understand, but I cannot talk to you about this right now."

"That's fine. I will sit out here and talk through the door and make sure the neighbors know all of our business. I'm perfectly okay with that if you are."

I dropped my forehead against the door and then used my thumb to disengage the lock, and then the deadbolt, and then the chain. When I swung the door open, I scowled at him sitting on the floor.

"There you are. That was going to get embarrassing. Thank you for saving me from that."

"I don't have anything to say to you."

"Don't you think the two of us probably should start saying a lot more?"

I ran my hands through my hair, half expecting to find the pile of braids there. I was getting it braided again tomorrow, so I wouldn't have to feel as if I was partially naked. "Lock, let's not—"

He barged past me, leaving me no option but to close the door and lock up behind him. I turned to him, angry now. "I tried to talk to you earlier. Didn't you already say what you have to say?"

"Why didn't you tell me?" His question was an anguished snarl.

"What was I going to say? How was I supposed to explain that to you exactly?"

"You didn't try."

"When I say Rogues don't date, it's not some little thing. Relationships of any kind are frowned upon. You are forbidden from divulging anything about Rogues. And it is expressly forbidden for agents to bang, even if it's just to let off some steam, get the lead out, work out some kinks. Strictly verboten. So what did you think I was going to say to you? 'Hey, that gap in your memory... Funny thing is it happens that I'm in that gap.'"

I could see his jaw working. "How am I supposed to feel?

I've learned to trust you. You've become my anchor point since I've been here. And you've been lying to me the whole time. How that's supposed to make me feel?"

"I don't know what to tell you. You weren't supposed to ever show up."

He gaped at me in disbelief. "You really didn't know that I was going to be picked up?"

I whirled on him. "No. I had no idea."

"If you had known, would you have told me?"

I stared at him, my heart sinking because he'd truly believed me capable of harming him. "If I had known you were going to be black-bagged, I wouldn't have slept with you."

His gaze was fiery and intense on me. So hot, I could feel the heated tracks his eyes took as they flitted all over my body, leaving little volcanoes of awareness and need in their wake.

"Do you know that since that night we first fought, I've been having flashbacks?"

I hadn't known that. "I'm sorry. I didn't know. At first I thought you were pretending that you didn't remember me. Then I thought maybe you were a plant, that you were someone Gabe was using against me. I thought you'd shagged me as a mission and he was going to use you to keep me from the field."

Lock frowned. "He wouldn't do that."

"You've met my brother, right?"

His brow furrowed. "Okay, yeah, fair enough."

"So what was I supposed to do? That's why I pretended. And I am good at pretending. I acted like everything was fine, even if it wasn't. I didn't know what else to do. And then of course, as punishment, Gabe assigned me to be your training officer. My brother, ever diabolical."

"Why would he assign you to me?"

"Because I've been wanting to be a field agent. Because I

was sneaking off campus. If I'd just told him, he would have sent me with six armed guards."

"Fuck, your relationship is so screwed up."

"You're telling me. I just didn't know what to say when I realized that you didn't actually remember me, and I wasn't sure what to make of it. I had Tabs looking into it, and she said it was because we changed up the drug protocol because psych ops said it was less traumatic for those that needed black bagging."

"Oh, newsflash, it's still traumatizing."

"Do you remember the team picking you up?"

He shook his head. "All I remember is you. Do you know what it is though? It's your scent. It's like I'm attuned to it."

A soft smile tugged at my lips. "You asked about it that night, about my perfume."

"Even then I knew. Can you tell me more details about that night? I don't like having these holes in my mind. My brain is not to be trusted, like I can't rely on what I know to be true."

"I'm not sure it'll be helpful, but what do you want to know?"

He took a step, closing the distance between us. "It's helpful to me. Do you know what it feels like not to be able to trust yourself? To keep running over every thought you have, every desire you have, thinking you're going fucking crazy?"

"I do, actually. After what Webster did, I kept seeing shadows everywhere, even when there weren't any. I couldn't trust anyone. I kept going over and over all the seventy-five ways I could have saved my parents."

He sighed and then hung his head. "Shit, Saff, that's not what I meant."

"No, I know what you meant. And believe me when I say I understand that not being able to trust your instincts or your brain are equally as important. I get it." I wrapped my arms around myself, praying that I could piece myself together. "I'm sorry, Lock. I am. I was between a rock and a hard place. If I had told you, I risked you not believing me. I risked you asking a lot of questions. And that would have put both of our paths at Rogues Division in peril. You didn't remember, so there was no point in bringing it up again."

"There was no point?" his voice was strained, a note of anguish in his eyes. "I have been tortured for weeks with images of you in my bed, calling my name. I haven't been able to get you out of my head. I was going fucking insane wondering why I felt so connected to you, so attached. And you think that I wouldn't have believed you?"

"Are you hearing yourself? Would you have believed me, if I was like, 'Hey, I know you don't remember me, but you know, before you came here, we shagged our brains out one night.'"

He opened his mouth to speak, and I could see it, the determination on his face that he would have believed me. But then his shoulders sagged. "No, I probably wouldn't have. I would have made a lewd joke about you giving me a refresher."

"Exactly. And then you probably would have said something to Gabe or someone else. And then instead of getting your time served at Rogues Division, your family would have found another creative way to keep you in line."

He frowned at that. "Fuck."

"Yes, exactly. Fuck."

He ran his hands through his hair. "Fuck, I can't—" He started to pace. "Walk me through it. What happened?"

I sighed and returned to the couch and my wine, not bothering to look at him. "It was my birthday. Tabs dragged me out, despite the fact that I didn't want to go. I thought we'd come here and watch movies, have a low key night in. In case you haven't figured it out, I'm not really the club and party type."

"Yeah, I guess not. I've seen you in action."

"I'm just socially awkward. Part of me thought that being a field agent would make me somehow cooler. As if I could put on a suit of armor, I guess. My own Sasha Fierce suit."

He cocked his head. "Sasha Fierce?"

I gawked and blinked at him. "Beyoncé?"

He shrugged. "I mean, I like her songs, but who the fuck is Sasha Fierce?"

I rolled my eyes. "Never mind. It would take far too long to explain it to you. Anyway, we went out, and there was this bloke. We were dancing. He was getting handsy, so I sent him packing. Then I noticed you watching me."

"Yeah, that sounds like me. You're stunning, but then you know that."

He set an arm on the couch and watched me intently as I talked. "You came over and we danced."

His brow furrowed. "The touching in the kitchen, it was familiar."

"That's how I touched you on the dance floor."

He let out a long breath. "I have to tell you, I'm relieved to know I'm not fucking losing my mind."

"I'm sorry you thought that."

"Go on."

"I had to do a check-in call with Gabe, and while I was out there, the bloke from earlier turned up in the alley, thinking I owed him something because I'd been rude to him on the dance floor."

Lock cursed under his breath. "What the fuck?"

"It's fine. I handled him easily, but he did pull a knife." I lifted my chin and showed him the fading scar on my neck. "Anyway, you came out to find me fighting him, and when I put him down, I had to stop you from killing him."

He shook his head. "I remember none of this. I hate that I remember nothing."

"You're not supposed to remember. Then, you picked me up and tossed me over your shoulder and took me home. We were maybe a few blocks from your place."

"Yeah, my place is not far from there."

"I know."

His teeth worked over his bottom lip then. "At the training simulation, you said, 'This is your flat,' and I wondered how you could possibly know."

"Yeah. I was disoriented. I don't know why they chose that, but I think I do now. Very likely, they simulated your bag and tag."

"Fucking hell. I remember feeling like I knew exactly where they were going to be."

I shrugged. "I wasn't there, so I don't know. But I think it makes sense."

"Did they grab me then?"

"No. You insisted on celebrating my birthday. You ordered me cake. And then you made me dance to Stevie Wonder."

His gaze went soft. "I love that album. It was Charlie's. All of the albums were his. Since he died, I play them a lot when I'm missing him."

"Yeah, you told me that." I gave him a soft smile and continued. "And I don't know... One thing led to another. And then... We shagged."

"You say that so easily as if it wasn't a big deal."

"Oh boy," I muttered. "Is this the part where you want me to rave about your very big dick and that you kept me busy for hours and then I could barely walk after?"

"It depends. Is any of that true?"

A hot flush crept up my neck. "Yes, actually."

He perked up then. "I must have really liked you. I don't take women to that flat."

"You said that, too."

"You know, maybe we should have all the conversations that we had then. Just so I can catch up."

"Sorry. This is probably so disorienting."

"Sounds like we had one of those kismet nights."

I frowned. "What's a kismet night?"

"Oh, I didn't tell you about this?"

I shook my head.

"Charlie used to think of all those perfect nights in the movies as kismet nights. Whenever he thought he'd met the girl of his dreams, he always described it as a kismet night. Though it didn't work out until he met his fiancée. She was who he would have married, I think."

"That's sad."

"Yeah, she's married now with a kid. I'm glad she was able to find love again. Most people don't get that chance. She was a good friend. Anyway, he called those kismet nights."

"You know, I like it. And it did feel like that, but..."

His gaze sharpened on me. "What do you mean, *but*? You're not like pregnant or something, right?"

I blinked at him, and then a laugh sputtered out. "Oh my God, no. Can you imagine the disaster?"

His brow furrowed. "It wouldn't be that bad, would it?"

"Coming back pregnant? There is no way Gabe would have let that fly, ever. He would have hunted you down."

"You know what, I believe it."

I shrugged. "Anyway, I... left."

He lifted a brow. "What do you mean?"

"I'd been there, till... I don't know. It was four in the morning maybe. And I had to go before you woke up."

His brow furrowed. "You just left? No goodbye or anything?"

"Yes, I left. I had to. I couldn't stay."

"Wow." He looked dumbfounded as he stared at me.

"What? No one's ever left you before?"

He opened his mouth and then shut it abruptly. "That's not the point."

"I think it *is* the point. You were used to being a playboy."

"Fine, I was. But you left me?"

"I couldn't stay. It would have gotten very complicated trying to explain why armed men were at your door threatening to break it down because I'd missed reporting back to campus on time."

"All right, fair enough."

"So I came back to Rogues and didn't think I'd ever see you again. Fast forward three months, and there you were. I had a bit of panic. I hadn't even thought to guard what I said. Then I realized you didn't remember me. So that was ... easier. I didn't have to explain anything to anyone."

"You could have said something."

"I could have, but we already covered that, Lock."

"Shit. You've got to give me a minute, because this is hard."

"I recognize that. But you asked. You told me to tell you. So I'm telling you."

"I just don't know what I'm supposed to do with this information."

"Well then, don't ask for it. That was what happened. It wasn't some nefarious thing. I wasn't hiding from you. I didn't deliberately not tell you just to fuck with you. I just *couldn't* tell you, so I didn't. But in the Winston Isles, you started to remember after we kissed, didn't you?"

He lifted his gaze to mine and nodded. "Yeah."

"I thought so."

His eyes narrowed, and his voice pitched low. "I remembered how you tasted. And that sound you make in the back of your throat when you're having fun."

My belly flipped and my brain was quick to hop on that.

Nope, we are not doing this. You cannot.

"I had an inkling. I thought maybe we just hooked up at a party or something. But that night after Igno's party, that's when I knew."

I licked my lips nervously. "It had been months and you hadn't figured it out, so I thought maybe those memories were gone forever."

His voice went gravelly and seductive. "Maybe I just needed a stronger memory to pull it out."

"I'm sorry, Lock. Sorry it hurt. Sorry you thought that I was capable of lying to you. If I had been part of your bag and tag, I never would have slept with you."

For a long moment we sat and stared at each other, and everything that happened between us hung in the air. Lock reached out and touched my hand. "Now that I know, I'm sorry that's how it went down."

"What do you mean?"

"The islands, I wish that's not how I remembered. I've had a million memories of you for weeks. Little things that cemented to my soul."

"We were between a rock and a hard place."

His lips quirked, and I could see the smile he was trying to hold in.

"Oh, come on, really?"

He shrugged and gave me a teasing smirk. "I mean, it's hilarious."

I laughed. "You are incorrigible."

"Yes. So I've heard."

"Are we good?"

He blinked at me. "You're asking me if we're good? If I'm okay with the fact that I can't have the woman I have feelings for?"

My heart cracked in two as he spoke. "What are you saying?"

"Jesus Christ, how can you be so bloody brilliant and not know? There's a reason I remembered."

I could see it in his eyes. The determination. He wasn't walking away. He wasn't giving up. "Lock, we can't. There are strict rules about this for a reason."

"After all the shit we survived in the Winston Isles? I know it's against the rules, and I'm pretty sure Tabs knows it's against the rules. But she sent me here hoping that this was what would happen, so I'm going to take your hand, and I'm going to lead you into the bedroom. Please tell me it's not *her* bedroom because that would be awkward. And then I'm going to hold you, okay? Can we make that work?"

I swallowed hard and looked down at his hand. So many times I'd wanted to do the thing that I *wanted*, not the thing that I *should*. But I almost always picked the thing that I should. And for once, I couldn't. I couldn't say no to him. Because I was wound tight, and I was scared, and I trusted him. So I took his hand and let him lead me down the hall into the guestroom.

If I was going to have to give him up, we should do it with a bang.

25

LACHLAN

I KNEW WHAT THIS WAS.

As far as Saff was concerned this was a goodbye.

But that was bullshit.

For months, I'd had the feeling that I was missing something. That there was some kind of glitch in the matrix. It felt like a part of me was missing. Something important. A part of my life I couldn't access.

And now I knew what it was. All along, it was her. Now that I knew, I couldn't give it up.

So while for her this might be one last chance, little did she know I was playing for keeps. She wasn't getting rid of me. Tonight was just the beginning.

Saff led the way into the bedroom, giving me full view of everything I couldn't wait to get my hands on. Her leggings encased her arse, and I watched her gentle sashay. Fucking hell, she was stunning.

Once in the bedroom, she turned in my arms, looping hers around my neck. "I've missed you."

I slid my hands into her braids, fisting gently, angling her head. I knew they were fresh. I didn't want to hurt her. But I did want to leave a mark.

I leveled my gaze on her. "This isn't goodbye for me, Saff. I plan on keeping you. Our situation is just a little bit more challenging than most. But so we're clear, this isn't some goodbye fuck you're going to walk away from." A hint of anger seeped into my voice. She'd walked away from me once before. And even though I'd forgotten, knowing now that she'd walked away burned. I had every intention of making sure that this time she couldn't walk away. Not without great difficulty anyway. "You are mine. Do you understand that?"

"I've always been yours. It's always been you." Her gaze met mine and lingered as if looking for something. Maybe she was looking for an assurance that I meant it.

But all I could do was show her, so I did.

When I pressed my lips to hers, I wasn't gentle. I tugged her body into mine, holding her in place and savaging her mouth, taking everything I wanted from her. I didn't ask; I demanded. Kiss by kiss, stroke by stroke, I tried to mend the broken fissures in our hearts.

It was raw, and visceral, and I couldn't stop. Since the islands I had thought she'd been playing me, but really, I was playing myself. I was a fool thinking that I wouldn't give everything I had to be with her.

In the end, even if she had been the reason I had ended up at Rogues, I still would have wanted her. And eventually I would have cracked. And once I tasted her again, the outcome would be the same. The desperate, cloying need would take over, and I would refuse to let her go. Because she had been made for me.

I backed her up step by step until the back of her knees hit the bed.

I wasn't gentle when I shoved her back. She fell with a little bounce and a giggle. But I was already bending down, my fingers hooked in her leggings, tugging them down over her long expanse of legs.

I wished I could pretend like I was going to take my time, that I was going to savor every morsel of her. And maybe eventually I would. Maybe eventually I would have a session where I went slow and coaxed every orgasm out of her. But no. We were going to be rough and fast, and only after I had taken this edge off, would I be gentle and take my time.

I tried taking her leggings down while I kissed her, which was just a tangle of tongue and teeth, but eventually I had to break our kiss to get the job done. Pulling the tight fabric over her ass, I stopped when her leggings and panties were midthigh and shoved her back, pushing her legs all the way up and exposing that gorgeous ass and pussy to my view.

Saff gasped, and I gave her no time to even realize what was happening before I planted my face directly in her pussy. I didn't even give myself a chance to inhale. I just planted my mouth over her clit and sucked.

Her gasping moan sent an earthquake straight to my cock. Yes, that was the sound she should be making always. Surprised, on the edge, and fucking horny.

I dove into her pussy like a man starved, licking and stroking and fucking her with my tongue. I brought my fingers into play so I could focus my mouth on her clit. I just wanted one quick and dirty orgasm from her, unexpected and explosive, as a reward for being mine.

As my fingers hooked inside her pussy, pressing up and curling ever so slightly, I sucked hard on her clit and then pulled back, scraping the bundle of nerves gently with my teeth.

She screamed, her hips bucking off the bed and her hands attempting to drag me off her pussy. But I wasn't going. Not now, and not for a very long time. I had plans for her.

"Lachlan. Oh my God. Lachlan. I can't—"

But she could and she would. I did it again. This time using the flat of my tongue to keep stroking over her clit, hard and fast just like she liked. Short strokes. And I dragged a second orgasm from her.

The scream she let out had me grunting against her clit, satisfaction coursing through my veins. I continued licking her, burying my face completely between her thighs, lost to the pleasure of hearing her beg.

When I replaced my fingers with my tongue, her whimpering moans turned to something deeper, more primal and guttural. And then suddenly she wasn't trying to pull me away but holding me steady, lifting her hips to meet me stroke for stroke.

I slid my hands under her ass so I could bring her more fully to my face and control every angle. When I dipped down to tongue her arse, she let loose a string of inventive curses that made me grin. My girl was a dirty girl.

"You like that don't you, Saff?"

She didn't answer me right away. All I got was a muffled moan. I lifted my head to meet her gaze and chuckled low when I realized she'd pulled a pillow over her face in an effort to be quiet.

I waited for her patiently until she started to writhe in my arms, and finally she pulled the pillow away and scowled at me, her little pout so unbelievably sexy.

"Why did you stop?"

I flashed her a grin. "I'm waiting for a response."

She groaned low. "Did you ask me a question? I was a little busy."

"Well, allow me to reiterate." I bent down and gave her a long lick from her dewy center to her clit. "I was just asking if you liked it when I licked your arse."

Her eyes went wide. Her skin was too dark for me to tell if she was blushing or not, but the way her lips parted and her gaze darted away, I could tell. "Lachlan, I—"

I licked her again, and her breath caught. "All you have to do is say one little word. One little word and I'll do it again."

She dragged the pillow back over her face, and my name was a breathless whisper on her tongue.

I couldn't let her get away with hiding. I wanted to hear her words. I needed to hear them. I focused my attention on her clit again sucking deep. "I said, do you like it when I lick your arse?"

In my hands, she trembled, and I could feel the impending earthquake. "Yes. Yes, Lachlan, I like it when you lick my arse."

"Well then, I aim to please."

I lifted her easily, ducking my head, leaving no part of her unloved, no part of her pussy or ass untouched, unlicked, or unfucked by my tongue and my fingers. When Saff started to shake all over, I slowly drew back and glanced up her torso to find her hair a wild cascade somewhere over the center of the bed and her T-shirt partially pushed up, exposing her taught, flat belly.

Her chest was rising and falling rapidly. Her tongue peeking out to moisten her lips as she struggled for breath.

This was how she should always look.

With a smirk and a quick tap on her arse with my palm, I rocked back on the balls of my feet then stood and proceeded with the removal of her leggings and knickers again.

Saff's eyes were glazed over as she tried to focus on me. "Jesus, Lachlan, what the hell have you done to me?"

I could have said something snarky along the lines of, 'Oh we're just getting started sweetheart.' But the truth of it was, I couldn't find words. There was a feral monster inside me, and he needed to fuck her right the fuck now.

When her gaze met mine, her brows lifted and her lips parted in surprise at the expression on my face.

I dragged my shirt up over my head by reaching behind my back and tugging. Three swift movements and it was gone. The button of my jeans went next. Saff's eyes were glued to my fingers as they worked. When she licked her bottom lip and followed the tiny pink muscle with the scrape of her teeth I growled. "You keep doing that, and I'm going to fill that pretty mouth of yours."

She did it again. As a taunt? As a promise? Jesus Christ, I wanted her mouth. But I needed to fuck her first. She could suck me off later.

What I should have done was remove my jeans. Hell, I still had my shoes on. The problem was that feral monster. The one who knew exactly how she would feel squeezing around my cock. The one who knew the sound she would make as she was coming. The one who knew exactly how hot, tight, and wet she was, and he wanted out. He'd been denied for too long, and he wasn't playing. Taking time to remove my jeans and boxers was going to be too much. So letting him free was going to have to be enough... for now.

Saff's eyes went wide as they roamed down my body and settled on my cock. He, gentleman that he was, twitched at her as if in greeting. Because the fucker was cheeky like that. I kneeled at the edge of the bed again and spread her thighs wide with my hands, forcing her to make room for me. And I kissed her pussy again.

I made sure she was wet, ready. But the joke was on me. Because as I licked her juices, all it did was make me burn even hotter.

"Fuck," I muttered under my breath. I was supposed to be driving her mad. But she was owning me. Sending me careening in the wide abyss of desire.

I pushed to my feet, scooping my hands under her arse, squeezing and lifting her. Moving her back until she was farther up the bed, making room for me. When she was far enough up that my feet could find purchase, I notched the broad head of my cock against her slick wetness, and her eyes went wide.

My name was both a curse and exultation on her tongue as I rocked my hips ever so slightly, teasing her entrance. Teasing that bite of pain and pleasure.

I knew she knew what was coming. We'd done this before. I was giving her body time to adjust. Time to remember. I was big, but she would fit around me like a glove.

For this part, I would be patient. I could wait. I knew she would be the one begging me. And sure enough, she whimpered and lifted her hips.

"Hush. You know we need to go slow."

"And if I don't want to?"

Jesus fucking Christ. With those words alone, I notched further inside of her, my tip sliding past her entrance. I hissed and dropped my forehead to her chest. Why the fuck was she still wearing a T-shirt? Why couldn't I take her fucking nipples into my mouth right now? I glanced longingly at the pert tip poking through the lace of her bra and her T-shirt, trying to get access to my mouth.

I know exactly how you feel my friend.

With a frustrated growl, I leaned over and sucked her through the cotton and lace and pulled deep just as I swiveled my hips and sank the full length of my cock into her.

She was all heat, soft glide, slick wetness, and bliss.

Her hands sank into my hair again, tugging sharply, and I lifted my gaze to watch her. Fucking hell, was I hurting her?

Her eyes were wide, but not with pain. With pleasure and desire and something else I couldn't quite name. With her gaze focused on me, her lips tipped into a soft smile. And I rewarded her with a slight retreat and a sharp hitch forward. Her lips formed that *O* expression again.

"You like that?"

I slid my lips over hers before pulling back and doing away with both her T-shirt and bra. With her tits exposed to me, I was going to play.

I palmed her breasts, teasing a nipple with my thumb, fully intending to bend down and suck the other peak into my mouth, when she started to squeeze me. I could feel her little Kegel movements. A long pull followed by short, pulsing ones.

And fuck me, a bolt of electricity started to sneak up my spine. I tried like hell to ward off the impending orgasm. I tried to think of cricket stats. What could be more boring than cricket? Except that wasn't working because I could feel the orgasm barreling toward me.

I was caught between tucking my face into her neck and fucking her for all I was worth and slowing down, taking my time, making this last.

But I was too far gone. I wasn't going to make it. She knew it. I knew it. When I lifted my gaze to meet hers, she had that exultant smile on her face again. The one that said she was going to get what she wanted. And who was I to deny her? I leaned down and licked her nipple, which made her gasp.

"I know what you're doing, and I'll give you what you want. You want it hard and fast. I'm so far gone it's all I *can* give you. But we're not done. We are *far* from done, princess."

"Are you going to come inside me, Lachlan?"

I blinked at her words filtered through the two brain cells I had left. *Come inside her. Come inside—* Fucking hell, I wasn't wearing a condom. We both knew it. That should have doused me with a cold splash of water. But it didn't.

"Would you like that? Would it be a disaster if you were

pregnant? Or would you like it?" I punctuated my question with a sharp rock of my hips.

Saff gasped. "N-no. Not a disaster."

Her eyes were clear and bored straight into my soul. *Not a disaster*. And suddenly it was all I wanted. I could see her round with my child. After all, hadn't I gone down this path without the condom in the first place?

"You're such a dirty girl. You want me to fuck a baby into you because I want to come inside you so bad."

And then Saff did something I didn't expect. She dropped her legs around my waist and locked them. Giving me no room to escape. She wanted this. She wanted us.

"Yes, Lachlan, yes. I want you to come inside me. Please, I'm begging you."

With my hand palming her breast, I pinched a nipple slightly, tugging playfully. I reached my other hand between us, my thumb finding her clit and bringing her to the edge. Her fingers were clamped on my back, sliding into my hair, tugging, pulling, and her lips were against my skin, begging.

I could feel the telltale pulsing around my cock. She was coming. Oh Jesus, she was coming and it felt divine.

This time when the electricity started clawing its way up my spine, threatening to blow me apart, I went with the feeling. I didn't fight it. I just wrapped my arms around her softness and dug my face into her neck. And as I made love to her, I let the ecstasy take me until there was nothing left but bliss.

———

Lachlan

I woke up to Saff's scent enveloping me and her heat wrapped around me. "Good morning," I murmured.

She was snoring inelegantly, and I had to smile. Her hair was fanned up on the satin pillowcase. Sometime after our third round, she'd grabbed a satin scrunchie and piled her curls on top of her head. When I'd asked her about the pillowcase, she said her hair needed a lot more moisture than mine did.

As I played with the strands of her hair, rubbing the soft tresses through my fingers, I wondered if she was going to get braids again. Or maybe she would wear it curly. Either way, I wanted my hands on it. As long as she was okay with that. Which last night she hadn't seemed to mind.

It's funny that you think this has a happy ending.

I was not going to listen to my brain, because what Saff had said was right. This was not going to be easy. It wasn't going to work out exactly how I thought it was going to.

No. Gabe would have a lot to say.

Oversight would have a lot to say. Last night was an anomaly. We weren't going to be able to keep this up. Sure, Tabs could help, but we could only do this for so long before someone became suspicious.

Saff finally stirred in my arms and blinked awake. I smiled down at her. "Hi."

"Were you staring at me?"

"Staring is such a strong word. More like a little light watching while you slept."

"God, that is so creepy."

I leaned forward and kissed her nose. "Maybe a little. Did you sleep okay?"

She stretched with a wide smile like the cat who caught the canary. The sheets shifted down under her breasts, exposing a nipple to my view. My gaze immediately homed in on it, and I leaned forward, pressing a kiss to the soft dark tip.

She automatically arched her back, moaning into the caress.

But suddenly, her hands slipped into my hair and she pulled me off. "Lock, food. I need food."

"If I feed you, will you feed me?"

She giggled, and I moved to shove the duvet off to head into the kitchen to see what we could scramble up. If I couldn't find anything, I'd just have to order in.

"What do you feel like eating?"

"Tabs has some eggs. I think waffles too. We made some the other day. And she likes to make them fresh."

"Tabs can cook?"

"Oh, yeah. Tabs can one hundred percent cook."

"You know, she never struck me as the cooking type, but I kind of love that."

"She does it when she's stressed. Which meant she was worried about us, or me anyway."

I leaned over and kissed her lips. "She's a good friend. She really loves you."

"Yeah, everyone's in love with Tabs."

I was in the kitchen about twenty minutes as I found the waffles, heated them up, and then brought her breakfast in bed. "I feel like we're back in the Winston Isles now. I wish we'd been able to stay longer."

Her eyes went stormy. "Yes, but duty calls."

I whispered, "Hey, don't think about it. We've got a couple more hours, okay?"

She nodded. "You're right. We shouldn't think about it. We already had more time than I ever thought we would."

"Don't say that either. Because I didn't even know having time with you was an option. Now that I've had a taste, well, letting go will be a problem."

"Lock..."

I kissed her lips. "Nope, sit up and eat. I don't want to hear anything negative right now. When I crawl back into bed with you, I'll force you to share your waffles with me. And then I'm going to lick syrup off your body. And after that, I'm going to have *my* breakfast. And then maybe after that I'll give you a moment to rest."

She giggled. "You're so generous."

"I am."

She ducked her head, and I could tell she was embarrassed. "Hey, you're beautiful."

She smiled at me. "Thank you."

"You're welcome. Now eat. You have to keep your strength up. I calculated, we have four hours before I have to report back, and I want to use that wisely. We have a lot to talk about."

She shoved a piece of waffle into her mouth and mumbled, "Like what?"

"Well, for starters, that perfume. What is it? I need to spray it all over my sheets or something, because it's like the only way I can sleep now."

She shook her head then, her eyes going sad when she spoke. "I can't find it."

"What do you mean? Has it been discontinued?"

"No, Mum used to have it made. On her first trip to Paris, she went to a perfumery and they crafted it just for her, based on her body chemistry. I've got a few drops left, but that's basically it."

No fucking way. "Are you kidding me?"

"No, I wish I was." She touched the chain at the base of her throat. "I used an atomizer to get some of it in here, and it's basically all that's left. I've got maybe three sprays left in the big bottle, and that's it. I used to have this diary of hers too, and I thought maybe I'd look in there for a clue as to where it was made, but I think that diary got sold along with a whole bunch of other used books after she died. So this is all I have left."

"Shit, I'm sorry, Saff."

She nodded her thanks. "Me too. I've gone and tried perfumeries, but none of them can quite get it right. They've tried to make me replicas, but it never works."

"There has to be a way."

"Trust me. If there was a way, I would have found out by now."

"Of course, leave it to you to be extra. A very special perfume for a very special lady."

She grinned. "She would have liked you. My father would have hated you."

I laughed. "Let me guess, Gabe takes after him."

"Oh yes, a hundred percent overprotective."

"I keep trying to remind myself that he loves you."

"Yeah well, he has a very specific way of doing things."

"Was he closer to your dad?" I asked.

"Yeah. He wanted to be just like him. You should have seen Gabe following after him with a clipboard, taking notes on how to be the perfect agent. I just liked the combat training. I loved hand-to-hand. I think I'm like my mum. She was known for being somewhat impulsive, but she was great in the field."

"That's a hell of a legacy, Saff."

"I know. And I just hope that I can make them proud."

"You already have," I assured her.

"You seem so sure of that."

"Well, I've been in the field with you. I know how good you are. Sooner or later, Gabe is going to have to realize it too."

"I hope so, because I'm exhausted trying to pretend like it doesn't hurt every time I submit for field op and get declined."

"Are you going to be mad at me if I say I understand where he's coming from?"

She scowled at me. "What?"

"I'm sorry. I do. You're his family. He wants you safe."

"Says the man whose ass I can kick."

I threw my head back and laughed. "Touché." When she was done and we'd cleaned up and showered, I carried her back to bed. "I was dead serious. You're not leaving this bed for another three hours and thirty five minutes."

She laughed. "You can't keep me prisoner in bed."

"That's exactly what I intend to do."

"But the real world beckons."

I dived under the covers and pulled her to me. "But what if it didn't? What if we just don't tell anyone?"

Her eyes went wide. "Lock, we can't."

"Look, I'm hearing a lot of reasons why we can't. But this, you and me, I had full-blown amnesia, but I *still* remembered you. If that doesn't mean something, I don't know what does."

"I know what you're doing, Lock, but it's a fantasy. There will be consequences if we get caught. You want out of Rogues, and Gabe will find a way to make that difficult. I want to be a field agent, and he'll make it next to impossible."

"We can try."

She ran her hands through her hair. "Lock, I want it too. I feel like you *see* me, but this is all I've ever wanted. And now you expect me to just give it up?"

He shook his head. "No, of course not. I just... Fuck, I don't want to let you go."

"I'm not sure I want to be let go. But what are we supposed to do?"

"We'll figure it out, okay? We just have to try."

"Gabe will kill you, and he will lock me in a tower. Let's just enjoy the next three hours, okay?"

"Three and a half." I pulled her to me and tucked her into my arms. She might think it wasn't possible, but I was going to find a way. I wasn't giving up. I had to have her.

She was mine. And no one, not her brother, not Rogues Division, not Oversight itself was going to keep me from her.

26

SAFFRON

I COULD FEEL Lock's gaze on me. The hot lick of every caress of his eyes.

I tried to ignore it. After all, what choice did I have? I'd made it perfectly clear that what we had done was a one-time thing. It couldn't happen again.

You're kidding yourself.

I *was* kidding myself, because I was weak and any moment now, I was going to cave and give in and turn up at his cottage and just beg him to take me.

No. Stay strong. Stay strong.

I had to. What was I going to do? Lose it and start climbing him like a tree?

That's always an option, my libido offered.

Tabs nudged me. "Earth to Saff. Are you ready?"

I blinked at the question. "What?"

"R-e-a-d-y?" She pointed toward the group of trainees. "Training mission? Basic evasion? Remember, we're supposed to be tracking these people."

"Right. Ready, a hundred percent."

She stared at me. "You've been so out of it ever since you got back. Are you sure you're okay?"

"Uh-huh."

She eyed me warily. I knew she didn't believe me. And honestly, she shouldn't. I tried to keep my lies as close to the truth as I could, but Jesus, it was getting impossible. I could barely hold anything back from Tabs. But secrets couldn't be kept by more than one person, so I kept my mouth shut.

"Yup, let's do this."

"Okay," she said sarcastically. "Run me through the plan so I can make sure you remembered."

"Basic deal. Me in the woods. I run and they, uh, hunt me."

She grinned at that. "You know, there are women who are into that sort of thing. I'm not, but there is something about when they catch you," she said with a wink.

I rolled my eyes. "Tabs, I think you've been reading too many of my romance novels."

"Hey, a girl can dream. You ready?"

"Yeah."

I headed to my starting line, and she called me back. "Hey, you forgot your bag. You'll need supplies to bag and tag 'em, remember?"

"Yup. I remember."

She shook her head. "Maybe Gabe is right and you should sit out some of the training stuff."

"Have you heard anything from him?"

She shook her head. "No. He's with Oversight now. So he'll be in Berlin until tomorrow."

She knew what I knew, but because she was a field agent, she had more access to operations' movements. All Gabe would tell me was that he was going out of town, not exactly where he was going or when he was expected back.

"Oh the joy of having a brother who still treats me like a child."

"Yeah, that's all I've got," she said. "When I know more, I'll let you know."

"Thanks." I swung my bag over my back and slid both of my arms through.

Saint smirked at me. "You're not putting me down this time."

"Sure. Whatever you need to tell yourself to sleep at night," I teased.

Saint frowned. "You seem a little too excited about putting me down."

His smile was infectious. "Excited is the wrong word, Saint. I'm merely doing my job."

He shook his head. "God save me from a woman with an evil streak."

"Keep your head up and wits about you," I reminded him.

As I approached the line, I strolled past Lock and he grinned at me. His teeth grazed his bottom lip, and I felt like his mouth was on me. I swallowed hard and deliberately turned my back on him. I could have sworn I heard him chuckle. He was insane.

It had been a week since we'd been together. I had tried to go back to pretending that he wasn't on my mind every moment of every goddamn day. But I couldn't help it. With every look, near caress, smile, I felt like I was doing something illicit. The problem was that pretending he wasn't there, pretending I didn't see him looking at me, pretending I didn't ache every night wishing my fingers were his own, that all just made it worse. I was desperate now. And he must have known it because I looked a wreck. I was a wreck. I was so distracted.

Tabs squared me up on the line. "Are you *sure* you're okay?"

"Stop asking me that."

"Stop being a space cadet. Jesus Christ, you look like you

have someone on your mind."

She stopped talking and then turned toward Lock before turning back to me. "You look like you've been dickmatized."

"That's not a word."

"Yes, it is. It absolutely is, and this is a look of someone who's been dicked so good, she cannot think. Please, God, tell me that he has dicked you so good you can't think."

"Christ, Tabs, Winston Isles was over a week ago."

"You know that's not what I mean."

"I plead defeat," I sighed. "Now, can we get on with the show?"

"You are going to tell me everything, okay?"

"I'm telling you nothing because there's nothing to tell. Can I go now?"

She rolled her eyes as I took my position on the line. "Sure, run along. But I will corner you. I will get answers, and then I will want all the gory details. You've been holding out. And I will make you pay for that. Sorely."

I knew enough of Tabs to be scared. She would find a way to make me talk. But this was one of those secrets that had to be taken to the grave because there could be trouble.

I took my mark. I could still feel Lock's gaze on my ass. Very much like the hand print he left there a week ago. I could still remember the shock of it.

And then the shock of other things. The way both of his hands had smacked on to my flesh, squeezed, grabbed hold and pulled me backward right into his mouth. And then all the places he had put his tongue. I shivered and tried to focus. If I was slow, one of them was going to catch me. And I'd be goddamned if anyone other than Lock caught me.

If Lock catches us, please God, let it be dirty, my libido called out.

Nope. No dirty. Focus. Just focus.

My brain locked in on the tree line as my target. When the gun went off, I ran and I felt free. Like no one could catch me, almost as if I had a say about what happened in my life. I made it to the tree line easily, and I wasn't even breathing hard. But I could already hear the thunder of footsteps coming for me.

I grabbed the branch that had been conveniently placed at the entrance and proceeded to jog backward, covering my path with nettle leaves as I went. When I hit the boulders, I took my brush branch with me, scrambling up and over them. I headed west purposely to make footprints leading that way for about fifty meters before hopping the boulders and tracing my path backward. And then I headed east. Sprinting. Moving. Hearing the call of their voices just outside the tree line. I needed to hurry.

I had twelve trainees today, Lock and Saint being two of them. Sadly, Saint was going to have to go down first because he would be the most problematic next to Lock. Lock, I could fuck with. Saint though... If I wasn't careful, he would have me trussed up like a Christmas goose in no time. He was good.

When I finally hit the caves, I picked my high target and climbed. I had no trouble making it up. It was a warm day, but the falls hadn't yet started, so it was still dry enough to use my hands instead of having to use equipment to climb.

When I scrambled up on top of the tallest boulder, I climbed into the bolt hole I'd used for months and pulled out my gun and tranqs. I almost felt bad. I took out the slowest target first, right at the tree line with a simple *pop*. He went down quietly, so the others didn't hear him. They were busy thrashing through the forest.

From my vantage point, I could see most of them. This time, the competition was designed so that they had to take each other out. Most people tried to find me first and then take out the competition. But I saw Saint was not taking that tactic. He took out one target about fifty meters in. I accessed the mic in that region of the woods and heard her saying something about an alliance. Working together.

Saint's voice was light when he said, "That sounds like a great idea. Except those aren't the rules." And then he shot her with a tranq gun. I chuckled at that.

When she sagged, he caught her easily. And Saint being Saint, he lifted her and placed her against the tree with a yellow flag over head, marking that she'd already been taken and the others had to leave her alone.

Jesus, that was one and two, I had ten to go.

Rookie actually took out Robert, who was so busy thrashing around that he hadn't even seen Rookie hiding behind a tree. Rookie was coming along with his combat skills, and he just stepped around the tree, clotheslined him, then hit him with a tranq dart. I winced, almost feeling the pain for him. And wonder of wonders, Rookie didn't even flinch. He just planted his flag and kept moving.

Sadly, he was going to have to go. I took out him and two more targets by the lower falls, making sure to mark each of them by the tracker in their tranq dart. And on and on I went until only Saint and Lachlan were left. So much for my plan of taking Saint out first. I couldn't even see Lachlan. He had gotten better. Far better.

I still could see Saint in the bushes. He started to go west, following my tracks, and then something stopped him just at the boulders. He glanced at the ground again and then started to laugh, shaking his head as he turned east.

Which was going to be his downfall. I didn't have much time and space, but just as he headed down the tree-lined path, I aimed and fired.

But just before my dart went in, someone tackled him to the ground.

Son of a bitch. I hit the mic for the region he was in, and sure enough, it was Lock. "Sorry, mate. She's mine."

Saint laughed. "It should stand to argue that whoever catches her, she's *theirs*. And I intend to catch her."

"She's mine."

"I let you have her last time."

"I'm not letting you have her, mate. Sorry." Lock's voice, while light, was all menace.

Saint, just laughed. "I see you've got it bad."

Lock winced. "Nope. I just have every intention of being sent back in the field. And I've got to get good."

Saint laughed. "I do love how you say that. Got to get good. Meanwhile, I was born good."

Lock laughed as they danced around each other. "I see you're delusional. That's okay. I like you anyway."

And then Saint lunged at him, but Lock had gotten good. Very good. He was quick. Efficient. He anticipated movements. I knew even I might have a difficult time with him in hand-to-hand combat at that point. He'd taken all of the fight training and paired it with his finely honed instincts. He was going to be a problem.

It took him no time to deal with Saint, and then he put a tranq in his friend's neck.

Oooff, cold.

He was coming for me. And it was time I let myself get caught.

Anticipation hummed in my veins. Technically speaking, this wasn't part of the skill. But we had to talk, and this was the most privacy we were going to have for several days. Inside the cave, I paced. He had to have known I was coming here. It provided the best vantage point, and if he'd seen me shoot at Saint, he knew the trajectory of where the tranq dart had come from. It only took five minutes before I heard his footsteps outside. And even that was more of an instinct than anything. He was being very stealthy. If my brother knew what was good for him, he would make him a field agent.

"Sweetheart, I know you're in here," he said sweetly.

"You're not supposed to call me sweetheart."

I stepped out of the shadows, and he relaxed. "There you are. That was dirty with Saint. You tried to tranq him."

"Sorry, but isn't that the point? It's his job to avoid getting tagged."

"Yes, but I wanted the honor."

"Are we going to argue about who the right person is to tranq him? Your job is to tranq him before I do. You did your job. Well done."

He stalked toward me. "I know that look."

"No."

He frowned. "But I missed you."

"You have to stop looking at me the way that you look at me."

"Do you really want me to stop?"

I swallowed hard. "You *need* to stop. How's that?"

"Still not an answer."

"Lock, we can't."

"I know. I know we fucking can't. Except I can't go another day and not taste you. Sorry. You're going to have to stop me."

I pleaded with him. "Lock."

He stepped toward me. "You know how to stop me, just say the words. Tell me, 'Stop, Lock, I don't want you to touch me.'"

"That's hardly fair."

"Who said anything about fair?" he chuckled. "I crave you. Do you understand? I can't think. I can't breathe. I can't fucking sleep. God, do you know how many times I have jacked off to dreams of you?"

I swallowed hard then backed up, hitting a ridge with my

ass. "Lock, this makes it so much harder. I can feel you watching me all the time."

"I can feel *you* watching me."

"Oh right, so this is my fault?" I countered.

"Well, yes. I need you."

"Lock, we can't."

"Fuck the rules," he said as he closed the space between us. "Tell me to stop. Use your words, Saff. Tell me you don't want me."

I swallowed hard, backing up ever so slightly. "That's not fair."

"That's what I thought." His lips crashed down on mine, hard and unyielding. He backed me up against the wall, and I shivered with need.

Jesus fucking Christ. It felt good. So good. Always so fucking good.

He ran his nose along my neck. "Do you know how many times I have thought about this scent and what to do about it? I need more of it all over my fucking room. The moment I went home, I could smell you. It's almost as familiar to me as your cunt."

"Lock, you can't say that to me."

"Why not? I want you. And I know what the rules say. You don't have to tell me." His big body crowded me against the wall. And then his hands slid around my waist and scooped down to my ass, lifting me. And then, bracing me against the wall, he said, "Tell me no, Saff, and I'll walk away. Tell me you don't want me."

But he knew I couldn't say that, and all I could do was moan his name. *"Lock..."*

"Say no. It's just one little word."

Then his lips trailed where his nose had been, and the only word I was able to whisper was, *"Yes."*

Lachlan

WE DIDN'T HAVE TIME. Not the kind of time I needed with her. These stolen moments were barely keeping me going.

It's not like she didn't warn you.

She had warned me. But true to form, I'd thought the rules wouldn't apply to us. But they had. I knew what she stood to lose, but that didn't stop me from craving her, from needing her. Didn't stop that feral, burning lust under my skin.

As we kissed, her lips on mine felt like a soothing balm after being on fire for weeks. But then her tongue teased out, and all it did was stoke the flames again. It was her, always soft, always driving me mad. She would be my undoing. Hell, she already was.

I kissed her thoroughly, bending my knees ever so slightly to give us a better angle. As always a slow teasing start led to a frantic tangle of tongue and teeth and moans. My thumbs played across the exposed expanse of skin at her belly just above her cargos. My thumbs dipped down below the waistband, and her breath hitched.

In the background, I could hear the walkie talkies going. Other trainers speaking as they were dealing with the rest of the incapacitated trainees. It was my reminder that we had no time to waste.

I kissed her hungrily, licking into her mouth, trying to capture a part of her. Something to tide me over until I could taste her again. But the deeper I delved, the more I craved, and I knew was this was a hunger I could not satisfy.

Saff tugged at my T-shirt, sliding her hands underneath it. Her fingertips were cool, but the higher she slid the hotter her palms got. Teasing, she flicked her fingertips over my nipples and I hissed. My skin was on fire. Hypersensitive. Desperate for her to touch any piece of it.

I didn't care where she was touching me, I just wanted her to touch me. My cock fought against my zipper. He wanted out. He wanted in Saff.

Fucking hell. I was desperate to give him what he wanted.

With a frustrated groan, she angrily tugged at my T-shirt.

Chuckling, I helped her and pulled it all the way off. Then she went for my cargoes, and those slid down more easily.

Saff sank to her knees and said, "You're not the only one who's been craving something."

I froze with my hands braced against the sharp edges of the cave wall as I watched her in the darkness. "Saff—"

"Shhh. I'm busy."

She wrapped both hands around my cock and stroked down the length of me to the base of my shaft, one hand anchoring a firm grip, and already my eyes were ready to roll in the back of my head. With her perched on her knees in front of me, her breath on my tip, I was done for. I could even feel the bead of precum threatening to leak. Fucking hell, she was going to kill me. I had survived the other trainees only to have her kill me while she was the one on her knees.

With her thumb, she spread the bead of precum across the tip of my cock, making me strain even harder. My skin was stretched so tight that every stroke felt like blissful torture.

And then she leaned forward, and with the tip of her tongue she licked all around the head of my dick.

I grunted, dropping one arm to fist a hand in her hair, trying to drag her forward. "No teasing."

She peered up at me from her knees, her position one of submission, but she knew she was absolutely, completely in control of me. As always, Saff Abbott owned me. I knew it, and so did she.

Her dark eyes shone, and she tentatively licked again.

Fuck. My knees started to go right away.

I fought for control. Fought to keep myself standing. Fought not to embarrass myself by coming within five seconds of her putting her mouth on me. And it was a fight of a lifetime.

Leaning forward, she took me all the way to the back of her throat. When my cock met with resistance, she inhaled then slowly relaxed her throat, taking me even further down. All I could do was watch in mystified awe as her lips wrapped around my cock and she took me all the way down.

I moaned, "Fuck you're so sexy."

She pulled back slightly and took me down again, all the while, stroking with her hand in time with her mouth. It didn't take long. I was ready to come. Ready to blow and I hadn't even been inside her yet.

With a sharper grip than I meant to use, I tugged her braids, trying to force her to stop. Her eyes glittered mutinously, and then she took me once more down her throat and made the swallowing motion.

The zing of electricity up my spine was enough to make my knees shake. And I had to pull hard to tuck her off my cock. "You naughty thing. I'm not coming yet. Not until I'm inside you."

"Hurry up then. We are out of time."

"Sorry, sweetheart, this isn't something I plan on rushing.

I turned her to face the wall, planting her hands up above her head. And then I reached for her hips, pulling her ass out. I release the button of her cargoes, making sure they dropped to the ground. When I leaned down, placing a tender kiss on the cheek of her arse, I made sure to lick her pussy just like she liked. Just a few short strokes because she was right, we were running out of time. I also reached into the pocket of my cargoes and popped open the bottle of lube I'd brought, spreading it over my cock.

I bent my knees, sliding my dick between her open thighs, groaning at the sensation.

"Oh fuck, Lachlan, your so slick. Am I that wet?"

I smirked down at her and bit her shoulder. "Yes. And no. I brought a little help."

She was still then. "Lachlan, we don't have time."

"We'll make time," I ground out.

With her ass turned up toward me. I lined my dick up along her crease and moved my hips, sliding back and forth along the length of her. "Spread your cheeks for me. I want to see what I'm playing with."

With a quivering gasp, she nodded. "Oh God, yes. Yes, Lachlan."

She did as I told her, and I could see the tight pucker of her gorgeous ass. I certainly did not have time to go slow and fuck her ass right now, but playing was an option.

With my thumb, I slid over the tight pucker massaging the muscles and sliding a finger inside. When I did, she gasped, "Oh, fuck."

At that very moment, I bent my knees, lined my cock up to her slick center, and drove home. She released a cheek and braced a hand against the wall, muttering a soft curse. "Oh my God. Oh my God."

I whispered into her shoulder, "I know. I fucking know. I've missed you so much."

I slid my hand up her belly, over her ribs, and palmed her breast. I loved her fiercely and quickly, demanding she give me everything she had to give in a short amount of time. Biting her on the delicate skin where her neck met her shoulder, marking her as mine.

The only question was if I'd be able to hold onto her if someone tried to take her from me.

27

SAFFRON

I WAS TOAST.

For sure, Gabe was going to be able to tell that I was lying. I'd never been able to lie around him. Even when it would have served me best, I still couldn't lie to my brother. He had that way of staring at you, peering into your soul and plucking out the one thing you didn't want him to see.

Like your pussy still aches from Lachlan's dick.

Like that. My pussy, of course, was no help because she was too busy throbbing and insisting she wanted to see Lock again. Which, after Tabs point blank catching us eye fucking each other that afternoon, was probably the worst idea I'd ever had.

"What's wrong with you?"

Gabe's voice was tight as he stared at me from across the dinner table. In the main part of the house, we still kept things like mum and dad had by some unspoken pact.

There was a large living area, dining room, and a kitchen that was mostly used only by the staff unless I was baking. We'd left dad's office intact. But both of our bedrooms were upstairs along with three others. The middle of the house was divided by a massive courtyard, and on the other side it was all Rogues business. All the offices, conference rooms, briefing rooms, and accommodations for senior Rogue members. The trainees stayed in the cottages on the property. Those that had completed their Rogues training and passed all security clearances were allowed to move offsite if they wished. Underneath the manor house were the training facilities. Even before it was a thing to do in London homes, my grandfather had chosen to build underground. We had a gun range, sparring rooms, locker rooms, and classrooms. Outside on the property, there was a track, more sparring areas, and a long range gun course as well as some other outdoor courses. My father had added a basketball court too.

The estate was massive. I didn't venture to the other side of the house often unless it was to go to Gabe's office. I was mostly downstairs in the training facilities, the gym, the pool, or on the grounds. Literally, it was my house. I was the heir, after all, but there were whole spaces I never ventured into because I felt unwelcome.

I had security clearance, but since I wasn't ops lead, there would be people who would ask what the fuck I was doing there. They'd grumble and let me sit in, but I had no role, no purpose.

"What do you mean? Nothing's wrong with me."

"I mean, I'm looking at your face. Something's wrong. It's all pinched. I know you don't like asparagus, but just fucking eat it."

I glowered at him. "You realize I'm not ten anymore, right?"

He grinned. "Yeah, but when you were ten, I'd do you a favor and eat the asparagus off your plate. You're a grown up now, so eat the fucking asparagus. It's good for you."

I shoved aside the asparagus on my plate. "I'm not going to, because guess what— I'm an adult. I'll make a smoothie after dinner."

His fork clattered to the plate and he steepled his hands. "Must you always be like this? What the fuck is wrong now? How have I insulted you this time?"

I blinked at him. "What's wrong with you?"

"Me? I'm fine. But apparently, I can't make my sister happy for shit."

Were we going to bloody do this right now? "Well, for starters, you can stop fucking talking to me like that, Gabriel. I might technically work under you, but the only thing keeping me out of the field is you. You're holding me back. I'm not scared of you though. Remember, you're not actually in charge of me. Which is hilarious. Have you stopped to consider that I *let* you boss me around?"

His gaze narrowed. "I am your supervising officer."

"You are, but I'm the actual heir, remember?"

His lips pressed into a firm line. "Yes, I am your goddamn seat warmer. I know that."

Shit. That was not what I'd wanted to say. I sighed. "Gabe, can we just have a night where we don't fight? Please, I do not want to fight with you. I just want a truce, okay?"

He sat back. "Fine. Sorry."

My eyes went wide at the grumbled apology. Gabe didn't do apologies.

"I'm sorry too. And you're not a seat warmer, Gabe. You know that."

He nodded, but I could see that it still rankled. My grandfather, before Gabe had come along, had put in his will that someone with Abott blood would always own the estate and everything on it. And that his official seat in Oversight and the Rogues Division would always be in the hands of an Abott by birth. How was he supposed to know we were going to find Gabe and adopt him? He died before it happened. So I was technically in charge of this ridiculous inheritance, and my brother was working his ass off for nothing. I knew it sucked.

"Gabe, what do you say we maybe save the pork roast and the asparagus for tomorrow and order some pizza?"

He glanced down at his plate and something warmed in his face. It made him look young for a minute, like the kid he'd once been.

"Yeah, probably pizza is a better idea."

"And while we're at it, let's eat in the living room and watch TV or something."

He rapidly blinked at me as if he wasn't sure what to say, and I quickly retreated.

"No, it's fine. We don't have to do that. I'll let you know when the pizza is here and you can grab a slice and go to your office or something."

He shook his head. "No, we can watch TV."

When had we become like this? There had been a time when Gabe and I were thick as thieves. He was the one who'd convinced mum and dad to let me go to school in the States, instead of going to Oxford or Cambridge. He'd suggested that the freedom would be good for me, give me a chance to grow up outside of Rogues and provide me with opportunities that didn't involve training nonstop.

It wasn't that our mum and dad had been taskmasters; it was that I saw Rogues as my whole life. Everything I did, I looked at from the lens of the Rogues legacy. It was everything I wanted to be, everything I aspired to be, and Gabe had thought I needed perspective.

He was right. Going to school in the States at my mum's alma mater, having friends, that had felt like real life. Until it hadn't.

Gabe studied me long and hard. "Come on. Let's put this away."

We packed up the leftovers silently in the kitchen, and then he followed me to the living room after grabbing a beer for himself.

"Oh, look at you, living life on the edge."

He smiled at the Stella Artois. "I guess I should have asked if you want one."

I blinked at him. My brother had never in his lifetime offered me a beer. "Um, I actually can't stand the taste of beer. It tastes like piss. Whether it's warm or it's cold, it doesn't really matter."

Gabe's eyes went wide, and he choked a laugh. "You just haven't had the best beer. Because if you tried some of these lagers—"

With a laugh, I shook my head, heading for my favorite spot in the corner of the couch, which was also Gabe's favorite spot from when we were kids. We both took a look at it and immediately dashed for it.

He made it first. Damn him being bigger. He winked at me, and for a moment I just sat there on the opposite side of the couch, blinking at him. *This* was my brother. He was still in there. To his chagrin though, I held the remote.

"In your haste to take the seat, you forgot to grab the remote first. She who holds the remote controls the room. Rookie move."

His brows furrowed as he took a sip of his beer, shaking his head. "You always were smart."

"Yes, I sure am. And we are watching *Love is Blind*."

His brow furrowed. "What is that?"

I gawked at him. Full-on open mouth, eyes wide, the whole bit. "You don't know what this is? What are you, living under a rock?"

He chuckled. "I like it when you're laughing. It looks good on you."

I cocked my head. "I could say the same for you."

He shifted uncomfortably. "All right, tell me about *Love is Blind*."

"So there are these pods, right?"

And for the next twenty minutes while we waited for pizza, I regaled him of the stories of how the show worked.

His brow furrowed. "People actually use this as a method to date? Why don't they just go out and meet people?"

"The point is you're not supposed to see them. You're supposed to fall in love with their spirit."

"Yeah, but what if you don't want to fuck them?"

Again, Gabe had never really spoken that directly in front of me, and I snorted in surprise. "Ah, well, I suppose that happens."

"Fine, turn it on. I have got to see this ridiculousness for myself."

We ended up bingeing two episodes before the pizza turned up. And then my brother, my uptight, stick-in-the mud, pain-in-the-ass brother, was screaming at the screen about how one of the douche bro idiots was playing two girls. "Oi mate, that's out of order. He just told her that..." When he caught me looking at him, he shrugged. "What?"

"You're really into this."

"I don't exactly have a love life."

I laughed. "You could easily have one. You know that."

He shook his head. "Have you seen my schedule?"

"I have. But I know you. If you actually want to do something, you'll find a way of making it happen."

He shrugged. "I don't know. The last two years it's just been full push, you know? Settle everyone at Rogues, secure a legacy for you."

That made my heart squeeze. "I never asked you to do that."

He folded a large slice of pizza and shoved the end into his mouth, wiping the oil off his chin with a napkin. He chewed fully before saying, "I don't just do it because of you. It feels good to do it. Mum and Dad, they saved my life, you know? It's an honor to their legacy. No way could I have ditched this or let someone from Oversight run Rogues Division. So I do it until you're ready to. And then you can make your choices about what you want from there, and I'll know that I did right by them and by you."

I rapidly blinked the tears away. "I love you. You know that, right?"

He blinked at me rapidly, then with a gruff clearing of his throat, he turned his attention to the television. "Yeah, I know. And despite what you think, I love you too."

We ate in silence for a minute, watching the couples on TV. Then he broached a subject which made me go stock-still. "What about you? Do you date?"

I stared at him. "What?"

"Do you date? I don't know. Men? Women? Are you pan? I have no idea."

I stared at my brother, wondering how in the world he had missed so much of my life. "You realize that you don't let me out of this house very often, yeah?"

His brow furrowed. "You get out. You go out with Tabs all the time."

The way he said her name was through his teeth.

"Yeah, I do."

"And I know she has a place in London, so you stay there sometimes. I just... I guess I figured you were attempting to date."

"If I was attempting to date, wouldn't you have already run background checks on everyone?"

He chuckled. "Do you really think Tabatha wouldn't have beaten me to it?"

"That's a solid point. I'm surprised you haven't dug. It just seems like something you would do."

He pursed his lips. "You're not one of the regular agents. You can be afforded some privacy. I just need you to be safe."

"You recognize that your version of safe is not conducive to me dating, right?"

His brow furrowed. "So, you've never dated?"

How the hell did I answer that question? "Yeah, I dated in college. Far away from here. I haven't gone out with anyone in a couple of years."

That's a lie.

Not really a lie. We hadn't gone out; we had gone in.

He sat back. "Let me guess, you blame me for that too?"

I blinked in surprise at how quickly he'd reverted back to his usual form. "You know, contrary to popular belief, I don't factor you into everything that I do. I'm not blaming you, Gabe, though I know that you probably see it that way. I'm just saying, with this life, I can't date anyone."

"You know field agents don't really date. It's not encouraged."

"I know."

He muttered under his breath. "I don't want you to not date because of the Rogues. You're young, have fun, be out. Shag some bloke or some girl. Hell, shag two of them."

I made a gagging noise. "Can you please not talk about me shagging? That's just weird."

He sighed. "I just want you to have all the experiences you're supposed to have when you're young, because eventually, this is going to be it. This is all you will have, and it's lonely."

I watched my brother, my heart breaking for him just a

little. He'd taken on so much when our mum and dad died. I'd never asked him to, but he done it because he loved me. Because he loved them. And he respected their legacy and the life they'd given him.

"No one is asking you to be alone Gabe. You've given your whole life to this. To me, to protecting this legacy. No one asked you to do that. I don't want that for you. I miss my brother. The one who laughed on occasion. The one with the quick smile, the quicker comebacks. The one with warmth in his heart. I know he's in there somewhere."

Gabe swallowed hard. "I don't get to be that guy anymore, Saff. I have to make sure you don't have to deal with the things I've dealt with. When I know that's set, then maybe I can let that guy out again."

I expelled along breath. "Gabe, we've got to start doing something different.

Maybe ease up on me a little, because it's exhausting for the both of us. Ease up and give me a chance to be my own person. Give yourself a break for once."

He shook his head stubbornly. "I just have to watch out for you to make sure that you're making good decisions."

"You're not my parent."

"I'm the next best thing, aren't I?"

My frustration bubbled to the surface. "You're not listening. Why do you think you deserve to be alone? You don't have to get mad every time I try to remind you that you're my *brother* and not my father."

"Well, if he was here, he would—"

I pushed to my feet. "He would have what, Gabe? If he and Mum were still here, sure, he would try and lock me in a tower. I get it. It's weird. But Mum would talk sense into him. And she would have asked him if he wanted me to be alone, feeling unloved and unwanted everywhere I go."

His brow furrowed. "I'm sorry I make you feel unwanted."

I ran my hands through my fresh braids, almost ready to pull them out. "Fuck, why do we always do this?"

He shook his head. "You know what? Thanks for dinner and the show, but I need to get back to work."

"Gabe, you cannot run away when I want to talk to you about this. You're my brother. I miss my father, but I *need* my brother."

He pushed up, strolled over to me, and then pulled me close and planted a kiss on my forehead. "I'm sorry. Tonight was nice before we fought. I just have to make sure nothing happens to you. That's just what it is. If you want more freedom, you can stay with Tabs more often, I guess. I insist on you staying here, not just to keep an eye on you, but in hopes that someday you'll talk to me more."

"I wish I *could* talk to you more because I need you."

"I'm always right here."

I nodded my head, knowing that wasn't exactly true. But he needed to believe it was. And then I watched my brother stalk out, knowing full well that he would never understand what I was doing with Lachlan. Also, he was very likely to kill him, which meant I was going to have to keep it secret. The question was, how long could I keep up the lie?

———

Saffron

AFTER DROPPING off a report on one of the trainees we'd been having trouble with, I was heading back to the main office when I passed by the briefing room. To my surprise, Lock was in there. As were Saint, Tabatha, Gabe, three other agents, and a representative from Oversight named Madeline.

What the fuck was she doing here? All their heads were bent over briefing packets, and I scowled. My brother had kept me away from this? What the fuck was going on?

Gabe had sent me on an errand taking things to our secure post in the village down the lane, but one of the senior level agents had already been on his way down, and I'd handed it to him.

I pulled out my phone and checked my texts. There's no way my fucking brother had gotten me out of the building to have his meeting. Tabatha and Lock were seated next to each other, and both had been whispering. A text hit my phone.

Tabatha: *Where the fuck are you?*

Me: *Gabe sent me on an errand, but I'm walking in.*

Startled, her gaze lifted and met mine as I headed toward the door. She elbowed Lock, and his gaze skittered up as well.

When I opened the door, I smiled at my brother. "I'm sorry I'm late. That errand you had me run didn't take nearly as long as you probably thought it would."

Madeline lifted a brow in confusion. "Agent Abott, I didn't think you were available. Your brother said you were tied up."

"Oh, I'm available. I just need a briefing packet."

Madeline shifted one over as if it was nothing, as if she'd expected me to be in the room. The hurt piercing my heart was so sharp I couldn't meet Gabe's eyes as I said, "Thank you."

"You're welcome. And Agent Abott, I know I told Gabe to tell you already, but your work in the Winston Isles was well done. Quick thinking in the field. You have the instincts of your mother."

The bittersweet wash of the compliment hit me like a two ton force. She'd told Gabe to tell me how well I'd done? All he'd said was how I'd messed up. He'd never told me anyone at Oversight even cared or had anything to say about my mission.

I finally met his gaze, knowing the fury was clear in mine. His was more sheepish.

"That's very kind, Madeline. I was just doing my job, along with Agents King and Saint. They were great in the field."

"They said the same about you and your great leadership. You know, I'm surprised that you haven't wanted to take a more active role. You'd make a great field agent."

I blinked at her. "Well, you know, Gabe is a little overprotective."

She frowned. "Oh, I was under the impression it was you who didn't want to be in the field."

My mouth went drier than the Sahara.

He'd lied to me all this time. I had been begging him for something, and he'd told everyone that I didn't want it. I could ruin his career with one comment. If I let my rage out, it could cause him the same kind of pain he had caused me for two years. Instead, I gave my brother the trust he refused to give me. "I think after our parents' deaths, everything was a bit raw. But I'm more than ready now."

Her smile seemed genuine. "That's what we love to hear. Your training is exemplary. Make sure you stay and talk after the meeting."

"Yes, ma'am."

I took a seat across from Lock and kept my gaze resolutely planted forward. I wasn't supposed to be in this meeting. If Gabe had his way, he would have left me out of it, and then I wouldn't know he'd been deliberately benching me. For two goddamn years.

So much for our bonding the other night.

Madeline signaled for Gabe to resume the meeting, and he pressed on. "Team, as you can see in the briefing packet, this is everything we know on Massimo Igno, Drake Webster, and Antonio Igno. Thanks to the work our team on the ground in the Winston Isles did, we now have the opportunity to get close and move on Antonio through his son. But we're going to have to move in quickly because the Ignos have gone even more underground.

"If Webster is in fact courting Graciella Natanya , then we need to get to her before they see each other again. As outlined in your packets, Graciella will be attending an awards show in Los Angeles. That's our shot to approach. More than likely, Webster will also try and approach her. It's the perfect opportunity to get to her first."

Tabs raised a hand. "Is Saff making the approach?"

Gabe shook his head. "My thoughts are that you will."

Madeline frowned at that. "I think that's a mistake. It should be Agent Abott."

I watched the muscle in Gabe's jaw tick. "Saff will be occupied. She'll be on coms."

Madeline laughed. "Of course, you are ops lead, but we have an agent who not only knows the asset, she's also well acquainted with the target. It doesn't make any sense to not use her."

There went Gabe's jaw again. He had really thought to leave me out. But he was between a rock and a hard place. Madeline was here to observe. If he was making poor decisions, then they would remove him. Or worse.

I spoke up. "I'm happy to go in and make the approach. She does know me. Just a reminder though, my supposed husband and I left in rather a hurry, so our cover story would have to stick.

Gabe met my gaze, and his expression was unreadable. I couldn't tell what he was thinking. At the same time, I didn't really care. What was I supposed to say to him? You were supposed to have my back and you betrayed me? He clearly didn't give a shit about that.

Madeline said, "It's something to be discussed. For now, carry on."

The rest of the meeting went fine. Gabe ran us through the scenarios for approach. He went through tactical planning, personnel, not exactly who would go on the mission, but more along the lines of what tactical skills we would need.

When the meeting adjourned, Madeline stood. "Agent Abott, I'd like to speak to you. And Gabe too. I think we're missing an opportunity here. Let's discuss it."

He scowled at me. He thought I'd arranged this.

Yeah, well, when you lie, and get found out, what do you expect?

The rest of the team was dismissed, and Madeline frowned. "Gabe, obviously, we are using Agent Abott. I didn't want to undermine you in front of your team, but she's the best person for this op."

Gabe wasn't having it. "With all due respect, Madeline, this is my team. I run it how I see fit. And Saff isn't ready."

She laughed. "She followed protocol on her own and got herself out of a dangerous situation."

"Because her team hung back for her."

"She engenders trust and camaraderie. Let me just remind you that she didn't break protocol. They did."

"That's not the point."

"I think it is. And given the video footage we've seen at Oversight, she was right. It was Webster. So what is the problem with your sister going in the field?"

I hadn't dreamed that this would happen. That I would have an ally at Oversight. Someone else who saw the problem.

Gabe bristled. "If I may say plainly Madeline, she needs more seasoning. She's not ready."

Madeline laughed. "Neither were you. Hell, neither is anyone. Give her a good team." She turned to me. "Agent Abott, you're going in. You are going to make your parents proud. Keep up the good work."

When she stalked out, Gabe clenched and unclenched his jaw. I watched the muscles work. This time, I was not going to jump in and rescue him. I was not going to offer up a filler for the silence. He was going to have to sit in it. Drench in his own betrayal.

"Saff, I—"

"Go on, I'm waiting. Let's hear what excuse you have this time."

"Fuck, I'm trying to keep you safe."

"What you did today was undermine and embarrass me. You told Oversight that I had an errand to run, and you treated me like your assistant to keep me out of the way. Good thing Tatum was on his way out. He's level six and perfectly capable of carrying the package."

He sighed. "Fucking Tatum."

"Let's get back to the fact that you tried to lie and keep me out of something that was important."

"I didn't lie. I just said I needed you to do something. Which I did."

"You *lied*. A lie by manipulation is still the same."

He rolled his eyes. "Don't be so dramatic."

"Of course, you would call me dramatic after you screwed up and got caught."

"You're all I have left. What the fuck am I supposed to do if something happens to you?"

"Not my problem. Maybe act like my fucking commander instead of my brother next time."

"I am acting like your commander."

"No, you're not. My commander would never humiliate me and hurt me like that. I don't know who you are, but you're not him."

28

LACHLAN

THANKS TO TABATHA, I found Saff in the sparring room. She was going to town on one of the bags. "Do you want to use me and get some of that energy out?"

Her scowl landed on me, and I kept my expression neutral, knowing she had to be hurting. What Gabe did was out of order. The moment I saw we were having a briefing, I asked Tabs where the hell she was. We'd been so confused, especially since it was about a mission to go after the Ignos again. I understood Gabe's hesitation, but still, this was Saff. The Ignos owed her blood.

"Put on gloves or get out. I'm not in the mood."

I stepped toward her. "Look, I know you need to blow off some steam, and I'm happy to be your punching bag. There are other ways we could work out some of that energy, but I mostly want to give you a hug."

"There are cameras in here."

"Tabatha turned them off. But that's not the kind of hug I meant. I meant one that comforts because you look like you could use one."

She swiped her nose with the back of her glove. "I'm fine."

"Right. Of course. *Fine*, like always."

I walked around to the other side of the bag so I could watch her face. Tears were streaming down her cheeks, and she was gritting her teeth, clamping too hard on her mouth guard. "You're too tense. Just let it go."

"I will not let it go. Oversight said I was good. He purposely didn't tell me."

"I know, baby," I crooned.

"He didn't tell me, Lock. He *kept* it from me. He made me feel like I was useless. Like I wasn't ready. And when she said she was confused that I wasn't a field agent yet, I'd thought Oversight had said no. It turns out this whole time it was Gabe. He was keeping me from all of it."

I could kill him for hurting her, but I knew he was her brother. There was a line, and I had to tread lightly. "What he did is bullshit. I know that. You know that. He knows it. He still did it anyway. There's a part of him that is trying to protect you because he's your brother."

"I don't have a brother."

"Saff, you do have a brother, and he does love you. He just royally fucked up."

"This isn't fucking up, Lock. This is lying and manipulation. Which, you know, we're clandestine agents, so I guess it's par for the course. God. He humiliated me on purpose. In front of everyone."

"No one else knows what's going on."

"Oh, they know. They know."

I didn't want to defend him, but at some point in the future when she was ready to talk to him again, she would need help seeing things differently. "No, they don't. Gabe loves you. He doesn't want to embarrass you. You saw how Madeline looked confused as to why you weren't in the meeting. She has no idea what's going on. Which means no one else does either."

Her brow furrowed as she tried to work out that fact, and she nodded. "I can't do this right now, Lock. I just—"

"I know. I'm just here to help you hit stuff." She lifted her head, our gazes finally meeting. "I'm here for you. So, how about I give you a hug and then help you figure out all ways we can kick your brother's ass?"

"He's not my brother."

"Yes, he is. As mad as you are at him, as shitty as what he did was, he's still your brother. That doesn't change just because you have a fight."

Coaxing her into my arms didn't take much once I stepped around the punching bag. She came in easily, tucked her face against my chest, and sobbed.

She was always so independent and strong, always holding it together. But Gabe had broken her. He'd hurt her in a way that no one else could, and she deserved to cry. I wasn't sure how long we stood like that. Me holding her, rubbing her back, soothing her. When she finally pulled her head back, she gave me a nod, once again using the back of her gloves to wipe the tears away. Then she did the unexpected and swept my leg. When I was lying in a heap, staring at the ceiling, coughing, she shook her head. "Like I said, always keep your guard up."

I laughed. "I hear you, Saff."

She was in there somewhere. Pissed off, I could work with.

"Now let me get gloves on and actually give you a fair fight."

"You still can't take me."

I grinned as she helped me up. "I do relish the attempt to try."

———

Saffron

GABE and I hadn't spoken since the meeting with Madeline. He also hadn't said a word when I got a roller bag, tossed some things in it, and walked out of the residence. Of course he wouldn't say anything. Who was I kidding? My brother was not going to apologize. Not for anything. He still believed that he was doing the right thing. At least that's what he thought. Never apologize. Never say die.

Right. Whatever. Tabs was on tonight, so I was in her flat by myself. Which was fine by me, because I wasn't in the mood to talk to anyone.

Lock was off as well, and not twenty minutes after I walked in, he was knocking on my door. "Do you have room for one more in here?"

"Lock, I'm not in the mood."

"Is that your way of telling me that you don't want to shag me? Because honestly, I mean to cuddle."

I smirked at him. "You're incorrigible."

"Come on. Grab a change of clothes. We're going to my place."

I wrinkled my brows. "You are probably being surveilled. I can't go to your place."

"Sure, you can. What's Gabe going to do, fire you?"

I frowned at that. It had never really occurred to me what would happen if I broke one of Gabe's rules. I didn't ever flaunt that I was the heir, but honestly, I could probably get away with breaking some rules if I really chose to. "Lock, I really just want to crash."

"It's been a hard couple of days, so you really should. I just want to take care of you."

I smiled up at him. "What did I ever do to deserve you?"

"You were either very, very good, or very, very naughty. I'll choose naughty. It works with the dynamic I'm going for here."

"Oh, yeah? What naughty, nefarious thing did I do?"

"I'm not entirely sure, but it was really naughty and super nefarious. And honestly, I'm surprised I haven't punished you before now."

I laughed again. "I don't want to feel better. I want to wallow."

"Fine, then come wallow at my place. Either way, you're not staying here by yourself."

"Why are you forcing me to do this?"

"You've had a really rough couple of days. As someone who cares about you, I just want to see you feel better."

"Thank you."

He grinned. "So let's go. I have a surprise for you."

"How do you have a surprise set up? You didn't even know I was going to come."

He smirked. "With me, coming is a guarantee."

I smacked his arm, but I grabbed my weekend bag and put some clothes in it.

He took it from me and said, "Come on, we're going to have some fun."

Reluctantly, I followed him. "Fun, what's that?"

"Well, believe it or not, I know a thing or two about having a good time."

"You do? I'm shocked. I cannot believe it," I said, clutching a hand to my heart.

He rolled his eyes. "Hardy-har."

I snorted a laugh. He was being silly, playful, fun, and it was exactly what I needed. He led the way out of Tabatha's, and the evening lights of London showed off the night life that was about to kick into gear. Everywhere we looked, young professionals crowded bars and eateries, desperate to get the drinks flowing to forget their days. I sighed. "Sometimes I envy them lot."

"Who's 'them'?"

"Normal people. People who don't do what we do. People who can look at the world and just see the world. They don't have to see any of the ugliness."

"Nah, I'm pretty sure you always want to be you. Saff Abott. Protector of the free world."

I shook my head. "I don't necessarily want to be a protector all the time."

"You still make a great one. Because if it's not you, then who will it be?"

I smiled at that. "Why are you so good to me, Lock? You say the right things. You feed me the right things. It's like you were built for me."

"Yes, me and my big cock were built for you."

I coughed a laugh. "Lock!"

"What? I'm just saying. As a matter of fact, he rather insists on being near you twenty-four seven. Since we can't do that, I spend a lot of time in the shower calling your name."

"You fantasize about me?" My skin flushed thinking about him in the shower.

"I sure do. Your mouth, your body, the way you laugh when you say my name."

His voice was low and husky and turned my insides into liquefied mush. "This is dangerous. You can't say these things to me."

"Are you telling me to stop?"

The moment I did tell him to stop, he would. He would still think things, but he would never tell me. And I didn't really want him to stop. Far from it. I loved how he made me feel with his words alone. "No. I love hearing that you can't get me out of your head."

"I had a training op today with Robert. I swear, I caught a whiff of your perfume and got a boner. It was awkward."

A laugh tumbled out of my chest. "Oh my God, did he notice?"

"I think he thought it was for him. Whatever."

I rolled my eyes. "Oh my God, you're ridiculous."

"Yes, I am. But look, you're laughing."

"Thank you. I appreciate it."

Despite wanting to be alone, the walk to his flat was idyllic. Even though we weren't holding hands or anything, it felt like the kind of warmth that you would take from someone you cared about. It was easy and light. I realized how little time and opportunity I got to be light and easy.

When we reached his flat, I hesitated. "You're okay with me being here?"

He nodded. "Yeah. I know you weren't part of what happened that night."

"Is it awkward?"

"I've been back once or twice already. It still smells like you."

I inhaled, unable to pick up anything. "I don't know what you're talking about. I can't tell."

He rolled his eyes. "Of course not, but you've been torturing me with your scent for months."

"Sorry."

"No, it was the best torture."

He walked me into the flat, and I said, "Wow, they really did get all the details right."

"Yeah," he said absently. "Do you think they were watching us?"

I shook my head. "Gabe would have said something by now. Maybe they would have separated us."

He squeezed my hand then. "Well, I'm not going to let that happen."

I started to shake my head and say something, but the look in his eyes was a stormy gray, like he was ready for a fight if I even mentioned anything about it. I wanted to be here. I wanted to be in his arms. I wanted to be held by him. I wanted it all. I wasn't greedy. I knew I would have to give him up at some point, but I just wanted to prolong that for as long as possible.

"What's on the agenda, Lock?"

"I'm so glad you asked, because we are having a picnic."

"Are we now?"

"Yes. And then there will be card games."

"Card games? I'm not playing strip poker with you."

"Who said anything about strip poker? We're playing rummy five hundred."

I blinked at him slowly. And then despite myself, I laughed. I knew what he was doing, and the more outrageous he was, the lighter I felt. He was taking care of me. When he took my hand and led me upstairs, I blinked in surprise at the array of candles.

"What in the world?"

He licked his bottom lip. "I called a friend. You didn't meet him at the club that night, but my friend Felix set it up for me."

"Did you tell him you have some girl you were trying to impress?"

"He wouldn't have believed me if I had, but are you impressed?"

I laughed. "A little."

"Good. I'll take a little. I can work with that. I said I was going to take care of you and I meant it."

I stared at him for a long moment. "You're serious? You want to take care of me?"

"I've never met anyone who needed being taken care of more. And no one ever takes care of you. What Gabe did to you, that was shitty. I don't know what to do with it. I don't know how to fix it for you. But what I can do is draw you a bath, feed you, give you eye candy in the form of naked rummy five hundred, give you a massage, and put you into bed, you know, with a couple of orgasms."

I choked a laugh. "These wouldn't be solo orgasms, would they?"

"You want to watch me give myself one?"

"No, that's not what I meant."

"Tonight is about you. You've had enough bullshit to deal with."

"Why are you so good to me?"

"Haven't you figured that out yet? You matter to me. You are everything—." He cut himself off and dragged in a deep breath. "When I thought I might lose you in the Winston Isles, I was mad. Really fucking pissed off. The idea of losing you... I couldn't. I just... " His breath hitched again. "I couldn't."

"You didn't," I said, shaking my head

"So, what do you say?"

"You're on. And I'll warn you... I really do hate to lose at cards."

His chuckle was low as he left me in the bathroom. "Saffron Abott, you act like I've never met you before."

29

LACHLAN

THE BUZZING on the nightstand woke me out of a deep stupor. But this time, I didn't wake alone. I had Saff in my arms. The buzzing continued, and I couldn't make it stop. I frowned. When I checked the clock it was two o'clock in the morning. What the fuck?

Saff stirred. "What is it?"

"Someone's calling."

She was up immediately, throwing off the covers and reaching to grab her clothes. "Answer. You're being called in."

"What? I thought I was off."

"If you're being called in. We're in trouble." She grabbed her phone, but no one was calling her. "Okay, maybe it's just you."

"It's two in the fucking morning. They'll go away."

She grabbed my phone out of my hand and peered at it. "Yeah, Rogues Division. Answer it or they will send someone for you."

I growled when I thought of who they might send for me. "The result will not be the same as the last time."

"I promise you it will. You have to answer. Let's go."

I couldn't believe I wasn't even getting the whole night with her. "Fucking hell."

"If you're being called, it means something."

"But why aren't you being called then?"

"I don't know." But even as she spoke, her phone also buzzed, and she answered on speaker right away. "What is it Gabe?"

"You need to come in. When you get here, come to my office."

"Is that an order?"

He sighed. "Saff, my office. Thirty minutes."

She hung up with him. "We have to go."

I was slow to move, but she was already dressed and shoving my clothes at me. "You can shower on campus before you go out on mission."

"You think it's a mission?"

"Look at the protocol. One-five means mission. I didn't get a one-five. Gabe is calling me in personally, which means I'm likely on coms."

"This is bullshit. If I'm going, you should be going. You're my training officer."

"I don't have any control over that. Move."

Once I saw the urgency with which she was moving, my head started to clear. "I want more time with you."

"We'll get more time later. Time to go."

That was what I admired about her. Her single-minded focus. We were going in. That was that.

This is her whole world. Are you ready to compete with that?

I frowned at that thought. This wasn't Saff's whole world. She had lots of other things.

Are you sure about that?

I didn't want to think about it.

Thirty minutes later, we were hustling through Rogues

Division. I was called into the briefing room, but Saff headed for Gabe's office. "Are you okay?" I asked.

"I guess so. We'll find out what's going on."

I didn't want to let her go. "Be careful, okay?"

"Same goes for you."

As she walked away, my heart squeezed at the idea that I might not see her again.

———

Saffron

I PARTED ways with Lock and headed to my brother's office. He was pacing when I walked in. "What's wrong?" I asked.

"Thanks to your little stunt earlier we have a fucking problem."

"I swear to God, if you called me in here to give me bullshit, you can fuck right off. It's two in the morning, Gabe. Neither one of us has time for bullshit right now."

"When will you understand that Oversight doesn't give a fuck whether you die or not. They want you in the goddamned field. I got the chewing out of a lifetime because I was protecting you."

I was not here for the fuckery today. "No, Gabe, you were trying to look good. You don't care about me."

"Why do you think I've been doing this? I'm trying to keep you bloody alive, goddamn it. Just because you don't have the good sense to run away from this place."

"Gabe, has it ever occurred to you that you never once asked me what I wanted? You never asked me how I feel. You presumed to know. Even Mum and Dad weren't this bad. Yes, Rogues Division is my legacy, but you just assumed control of everything, and now it's blowing up in your face. What's the mission?"

His hands were shaking as he ran them through his hair. "We aren't waiting for the awards show in LA. You're going back in the field with Lachlan now. Graciella is in New York. Oversight wants you to make the approach there."

"Maybe next time deliver the message without any of the additional bullshit."

He sighed. "For the love of God, I was wrong, okay? You have to understand, you are my responsibility. And if I lose you, I'll have failed. And every time I turn around, there you are trying to do something to put yourself into more danger."

"It's not your call. You're my brother, and I love you, but it's *not your call.* Every time you make a decision for me, you're taking away my agency, and that sucks."

"Well, you got your wish. You are a full-fledged field agent, effective immediately."

My heart stopped and something clogged my throat, making breathing impossible. "What?"

"If I had my way, you would never see the field."

"You recognize that makes me leery, right? Because the only way to hold *your* job is to have field experience."

"You think I'm keeping you out of the field because of job security?"

"What am I supposed to think?"

He shook his head, his shoulders hunching as if he was tired. "If that's what you really think of me... Maybe I deserve that."

"Is my team briefing right now?"

"Yes." With a huff, he added, "You may hate me right now, you may be pissed the fuck off. I don't really care. But you fucking stay alive in the field, do you hear me? Because if you do not, I will revive you and kill you myself."

I could see pain in his face. He was trying to protect me. He'd just gone about it the entirely wrong way. I was finally getting my wish. I was going in the field. And I was getting this much closer to getting vengeance for my family.

I reached the door, and he stopped me. "Will you ever forgive me?"

30

SAFFRON

A DAY LATER, Gabe's last question still rattled in my mind. Could I forgive him? I didn't really know. And the not knowing was distracting me from the mission at hand. I dragged myself out of my reverie to focus.

"Are you sure this is the play you want to make?"

I frowned at Lock. "Yes, it makes sense because you have media interests in New York, and the Caldwell is the place to see and be seen if you're in the city. It's also private and discreet."

He nodded as he stared up at the meticulously maintained prewar exterior. "Okay. It's your call."

And it was my call, wasn't it? No matter what happened on the mission, it was all my responsibility. And I wasn't entirely sure how I felt about that.

The Caldwell was an upscale, boutique hotel on the Upper East Side. They were known for their exemplary bar and their discretion, which made it a haven for actors and musicians, and it had become Hollywood's quiet spot on the East Coast.

My mission brief had us going in as a couple yet again since there was always a chance Graciella might believe that we were running into each other given Lock's status and hers.

"Do we have eyes on her?" I asked into my comm unit. Instead of Saint this time, we had Rookie. Just as well. He was excellent with tech.

His voice was low but clear. "We have her on the terrace. Be aware of your exits. There are two on the way up there. We don't want her vanishing on us. You are clear to make your approach."

This should be simple. Easy. Deliberately walk in front of the bar. Act as in love as ever with my husband and make sure she saw us. Immediately, Lachlan wrapped his arm around my shoulder. Fingers getting dangerously close to my breast.

"Would you behave?"

"I'm just getting us in the right frame of mind. Playing the part."

Sure enough our bait worked. "Saffron? Lock? Is that you?"

We both slowed and glanced around, and sure enough, there was Graciella, looking beautiful, stunning, and completely unbothered. I forced my eyes wide. "Oh my God, Graciella, how are you?"

"Me? Sweetheart, where have you been?" She stood and sauntered over, arms outstretched. "I thought something had happened to you. What are you doing in New York?"

When she hugged me, I placed the tiny tracker on the back lip of her belt. She wouldn't notice it until she undressed. She seemed genuine, and I *was* fond of her. But she kept strange bedfellows, so it was better to keep an eye on her.

That was the thing about being a field agent; you learned to never trust anything at face value.

Lock said, "Gracie, it's good to see you. Apologies that we had to leave the Winston Isles in a bit of a hurry."

"What happened? I mean, I saw Saffron for lunch, then she went to the bathroom and just vanished."

Lock continued squeezing me tight into his side. "I am sorry for all the dramatics. I had a business thing come up unexpectedly. It couldn't really be helped, so we had to go in quite the hurry."

"You couldn't even say goodbye? I was concerned, and Massimo was quite cross. He thinks you two deliberately didn't say goodbye."

"Like I said, it couldn't be helped." Lock gave a shrug as an apology.

On the surface she seemed to buy it. "In that case, let me buy you a drink."

Very intentionally, Lock shook his head. "No, we're just trying to have a quiet night."

"Ah, you two lovebirds. Please, it will be an insult. Massimo will want to know what you two are doing in New York." When she said Massimo's name, she gave me a pointed look.

Lock said, "I've been working for two weeks solid. If I didn't take her out there would be hell to pay. After this, we'll continue our honeymoon."

Graciella made googly eyes at us. "I swear, you two are the cutest. You have to hurry and procreate. I love children."

I smiled and coughed. "I think we can wait on that."

"Oh, don't wait too long. You won't be able to chase them around."

She showed us to her table. There were several bottles of champagne and food laid out. "I've been here for a minute. I have some friends who are just in the washroom."

I stood straighter at that. Friends?

"I insist you join me."

"Then join you we shall," Lock said.

Once our glasses were poured and we were settled in, I felt

on edge, and Lock's hand pressed my lower back trying to rub soothing circles on my skin. I was waiting for Webster to show up. But he didn't come.

After about five minutes, Graciella's phone buzzed and she looked at it. She rolled her eyes dramatically and excused herself. "If you'll just pardon me for one moment. I'll be right back. You keep on enjoying your drinks."

Before she even stood, my instincts told me she was up to no good. I watched her closely as she headed toward the loo, and then Lock and I were on our feet. Him to the first exit, me to the other.

In our comm units, Saint was monitoring her movements. "It might be a false alarm. From the looks of it, she is actually going into the loo. But watch the exits anyway."

After five minutes with no sign of her from either of us, I headed into the loo just to be sure. And it was empty. *Fuck!*

I ran out pressing my comm unit. "She's gone. Where the hell did she go?"

Lock and I had a shorthand between us now I didn't even need to tell him to start a standard grid search. If she wasn't where she was supposed to be, chances were we'd been made before we even walked in there. The likelihood that Webster hadn't told her about me was slim, but it had been worth a shot. Unfortunately, our only lead had pulled a Houdini.

She'd played us. And now we had nowhere to go. We were dead in the water.

That inner voice started to pick at me.

Of course you failed. Did you really think you were going to be the one to pull this off? Gabe was right.

I shook it off. There was no time for that bullshit. I had an asset to find.

———

Saffron

I HAD MADE A MISTAKE. I should've listened when Gabe insisted we just snatch her up and secure her in a safe house until she agreed to cooperate. I thought working our angle would be better for us.

I was wrong.

I ran down the east corridor, making sure to double-check my map. There was no street exit there, so she would have had to backtrack. Saint was checking hotel security cameras. So where the hell had she gone?

"Saint, come in."

"I've got you loud and clear, Heir."

I startled. Being in the field meant people were going to use my call sign. I wasn't sure I'd thought about that, but it was a problem for another day. "Got anything on the cameras?"

"I've got nothing. There are a couple of blind spots. She could've gone down the service elevator, or hell, even into a guest room. I have no idea."

I ground my teeth. "King, what about you?"

"Nothing yet. Let's just run the pattern."

Yes, that was protocol, but something was eating at me. Something was not right. I double-checked my exit, heading down to her floor again. "I'm headed to her room. I'll just double-check that we didn't somehow miss it."

"Copy," was Lock's response.

"Rookie, can you get me into room 604?"

"Hold please."

Ten seconds later, the lock flashed green and I pushed the door open.

I saw nothing of importance. I didn't even know what I was looking for, just following protocol. I'd lost my asset, so I had to assess the environment, assess where I'd gone wrong, and make notes for next time.

Yes, but you are also sulking.

Okay, fine, I was sulking. I had messed up. Gabe had tried to give me advice, but I had been so convinced I knew what to do. Fuck.

Empty. Damn it. There was nothing in there. Nothing that said anything about her. I had trusted her, and instead of me building the asset, she was playing me.

And like a fool, I fell for it.

Asset development 101: Don't become *their* asset.

I was a fool.

You can focus on being a fool or focus on fixing it. Now, think.

If I were her and I was being watched, what would I do? What were the possible scenarios? Then it came to me. We hadn't tapped her phones, so she'd likely gotten a call out. A call could be traced.

I mentioned the idea to Rookie, but he was already checking, so what else? What had I missed? She'd made us think she was buying our act, which meant she was already wise to us.

But why even call out our names unless she knew *exactly* who I really was and had been watching us.

She'd known that we had eyes on her, which meant everything had to happen quickly and quietly without us noticing. God knew, she had some help, but she wasn't with anyone in New York as far as we knew.

Unless...

She *wasn't* alone. That meant either we'd had bad intel again or she was with someone who could vanish or who didn't exist. I quickly searched the room looking for signs that I was right.

We'd wanted her to lead us to Webster, thinking that he

wouldn't be with her, especially not after what happened in the Winston Isles. But what if he was?

Jesus.

Oh fuck, he'd been here with her all along. We'd been expecting her to lead us to him, and he had been here right under our noses.

I started dialing Lock, but before I could get a call through, a hand clamped over my mouth. "You always were too smart for your own good."

31

LACHLAN

SAFF SHOULD HAVE BEEN BACK ALREADY. Searching Gracie's room should've taken no time at all. It was clear she was in the wind. Except how the hell had she gotten past us with no help?

"Hey, Rookie, give me a location on Saff."

His voice was concerned when he said, "I keeping pinging her, but her comm unit isn't on."

Fucking hell. I ran toward room 604. When I shoved the door open, my heart stopped.

The room was in complete disarray, and there had clearly been a struggle. The desk lamp was knocked over, papers were strewn around the room, and there was a shoe print on the wall. Saff had fought someone, and now she was gone. Something had happened to her.

Fuck, she'd been taken.

I wasted no time. I quickly searched the room in case she was just down. And as I ran back to our working suite, I was already on the phone with Tabs.

"Why are you calling me, Lock?"

"We have a problem. Saff's gone. And I don't think she's gone by choice."

To her credit, Tabatha didn't ask a lot of questions. "Fuck. All right, we launch Babylon protocol."

"What? We're not fucking leaving her."

"You need to familiarize yourself with all the protocols. Babylon protocol is when your teammate is captured. Get to a safe house. If she's conscious, she'll activate her secondary tracker."

"That's bullshit. I can't leave her."

"Listen to me. She knows what happens, and she knows what to do."

"I shouldn't have left her. I fucking knew it."

"We will get her back. But if you're going to be in the field, you have to learn the way we do things. Don't forget, preserve the mission at all cost. If the mission cannot be preserved, we return, regroup, and analyze. Now focus, so you can go get Saff when we locate her."

This was my fault. I hadn't listened to my own instincts telling me something was off with Graciella. I ignored it all. And now Saff was gone and I had no one to blame for that but myself.

Fuck.

Saffron

When I woke, my hands were tied.

Of course, the motherfucker had tied them.

"Glad to see you're awake. Now maybe you and I can have a conversation." His voice was smooth and deep like I remembered. His cultured accent gave no definitive clue as to his upbringing. He could be British, Swedish, hell, even an American who had spent some time in boarding schools.

I struggled against my restraints.

Drake Webster leaned forward into my view, and his dark hair fell over his brow. "Easy does it. I don't want you to hurt yourself."

"Why? You want the pleasure of doing it yourself?"

He grinned. "I'm not so much into the physical pain thing."

"Hey, if that's your kink, have at it."

I struggled some more. All I had to do was activate my secondary tracker in my belt.

Webster leaned back and tsked, his dark hair flopping in his face, his blue eyes bored. Why was he bored? He had me in his grasp, so I expected more from him.

"What the fuck do you want?" I demanded.

"You, my dear, have caused me more than my fair share of trouble."

"Well, considering you murdered my parents, I figure your debt is eternal."

Emotion crossed over his expression. "Look, about that—"

"Nope. I have zero intention of hearing whatever you have to say about that. You lied. You gained my trust. You used me, and then you murdered them."

His brow furrowed. "I know what you think but—"

"No, fuck you. The moment I get free, I am killing you."

"I don't think you have it in you."

"You don't know me," I scoffed.

He chuckled then. "Ah, little one, you have grown into a feisty cat. I can see why he likes you."

He leaned down to brush some of my braids out of my face and I jerked back. "I swear to fucking God, if you touch me, I will kill you."

"You don't understand, do you? I'm not trying to hurt you."

My stomach rolled over as I considered. "If you don't want to hurt me, what do you want?"

"Can't you see I'm protecting you?"

"By murdering my parents?"

"Like I said, what happened to your parents was not the plan." He shook his head. "I never intended for them to be harmed."

"Bullshit. You put a bomb on their plane."

He swallowed, looking almost contrite. "I'm sorry for what happened."

"I swear to God, the moment I am free, I am going to murder you."

"You already said that. Now, love, I know you're mad. But we can't focus on our past right now. By the way, how's the new boyfriend? I like this one. I'm sure Gabe probably likes him too."

"What? You think you're my brother now?"

"Aren't we bathed in the same blood? That makes us a family of sorts."

"Fuck you."

"While you have grown into one hell of a feisty hellcat, which I do appreciate, you're not really my type."

"I swear to God, I'll kill you."

"You keep saying things like kill and maim, but you and I are going to become very, very special friends."

"When Gabe gets his hands on you, you're done."

"Are you sure about that? Look, as much as I would love to keep arguing with you, I need to go. And I made sure you're safe and secure while I'm gone."

"Fuck you."

"You know, I don't remember you being quite so sassy. I love the spunk, but wow, you probably drove your brother insane.

"Why did you take me?"

"My darling girl, stop asking why and start living up to the legacy. You are the goddamn heir. Act like it."

"You don't know anything about me."

"I know *everything* about you. I have been there from the beginning. I know who you are, and you have no idea what you're fucking with. So just stay put. Do not interfere, and no one will get hurt."

"Except I've already been hurt."

He frowned. "No one in your past has laid a hand on you. I know that."

My eyes went wide. "How do you know that?"

He lifted a brow and gave me a beaming smile. "Do you really think I haven't kept a close watch on you all this time?"

"Are you playing Graciella like you played me?"

"What's the matter love? Are you jealous?" He chuckled softly then added, "You, were a flirtation. We didn't shag, remember? I do have some integrity. You were so young."

"Thank God for small favors. I always thought you were kind of creepy. What was someone your age doing hanging around a college student? Do you really think Antonio is going to let you live when he finds out you're shagging Graciella? His own son's fiancée?"

He lifted a brow. "Do you really think I was shagging Graciella? If we're going to have this conversation, can we talk about your boyfriend? Does Gabe know? I can't imagine your big brother is going to be very pleased about you breaking all the rules against fraternization. Fucking another Rogues member, *tsk-tsk*. You know, I must say there's a part of me that's a little bit impressed with you. I don't have to say that, but I can't help it. Just look at you breaking the rules like that. You're a far cry from that little girl I once knew."

"God, I hate you."

"I know. You're supposed to hate me. I'm responsible for your parents' deaths. Hell, if I had a heart, I'd hate myself. But I did away with that bullshit years ago. Now, you're going to stay here. I need to go find Graciella."

"What the fuck do you mean, find her? She's with your men, right?"

He laughed then. "You still don't get it. You are a pawn in a game you do not understand. I can't wait until you figure it out. I would say I'm surprised that you haven't quite figured it out yet, but I'm going to give you the benefit of the doubt. You've been distracted by a lot of things that don't matter. And that's okay. We've all been there before. But you're smarter than this, Saffron. Pay attention to what you're being shown." He leaned in close then. "I need you to see the truth."

"Then will you let me go?"

"I would. I actually would, because I don't know how to deal with you. You're going to follow me, and that's not what I need from you right now. I have a few more things I need to lay the groundwork for to get ready for our last powerful dance. In the meantime, you just sit tight, okay? I won't hurt you. You have my word."

"Fuck you and your word. I remember once you pretended to be a friend. I won't make that same mistake again."

He sighed. "I'm sorry it's come to this."

I prayed to God my team was getting my tracker information. If I could just keep him here and talking, they would find us. They would be coming for me at any moment.

"You did grow into a beautiful young lady and one hell of a badass. I hope your brother can see that."

"What's your obsession with Gabe, anyway?"

"Ah, Gabe and I go way back. Tell him I said hi, will you?

Now, I'll leave you here, so you can't cause trouble, okay? Be happy that I didn't kill you."

"You're a sick freak."

"You know, that one I have heard before. You'd just better hope you don't have to find out how sick I really am."

I fought against my restraints, but they were too secure. I prayed to God Tabs was already on her way and not following protocol. I'd been a fool. I had walked right into the trap, and I just hoped my team was good enough to figure out what had happened and come for me.

Because right now, all I could do was scowl at the villain as he prepared to walk out the door.

———

Lachlan

TABS WAS RIGHT. Saff had activated her secondary tracker. And thanks to some New York contacts, I'd tracked her to a small house on the edge of the warehouse district.

I approached from the south where there were fewer houses.

This doesn't feel right.

Maybe I needed to stop relying on my feelings and instincts.

Except my feelings were driving me. The terror and fear and frantic worry. And the rage. I was going to tear this fucker limb from limb. He'd taken her from me, and I owed him pain.

Stay on mission. I had a job to do. I needed to make sure she was safe first, and then there would be blood. With a grim determination, I approached the south side of the house but could see no movement.

Using my infrared, I searched inside and identified one person in a chair in what looked like maybe a living room. That was probably her. I headed along the back side of the house, moving swiftly and noticing there weren't even any cameras back there. Fuck. Who had this level of confidence in their safe house that there was no security?

As I approached the side of the house, I quickly pulled out my lockpick kit, and just when I heard it click, I heard something else click too.

"Fucking hell. You're certainly better than I expected."

I put my hands up. "Webster?"

He chuckled. "Yes, boyfriend. See this is why you don't fuck your partner. Because you make mistakes."

"Fuck you, Webster."

"Well, come on then. Since you're breaking protocol and coming after her in the first place, let's get this over with."

I whirled around, knocking his wrist with mine, and his grip on the gun loosened. I rotated my wrist to grab his, bracing my other arm on his shoulder while delivering a knee. He grunted as I made a connection.

But then he whipped around with his other arm, delivering a back hammer fist that was just shy of my face. I was barely able to dodge it.

He laughed. "As much fun as this would be, we don't have time for this. Bad shit's going to happen if you don't let me go."

"Yeah, bad shit's going to happen to *you*," I muttered.

"I have fucking work to do, and you're standing in the way of it. But I do have to say I'm impressed. Honest to God, if anyone had told me that you would be a Rogues Division recruit, I would've laughed. Of all the legacies, you have been the most disappointing."

"What the fuck do you know about me?"

"Your grandfather, Isaac King, is connected to Oversight. You think nobody outside of Rogues knows anything about you? Yes, you're a secret government organization, but really, you should watch who you tell your secrets to."

He lunged for me, and I remembered the shift of the foot motion that Saff always did just as she angled out of position. I did the same and caught Webster in the temple. He grunted as it dislodged him from his path. I launched myself at him and delivered a couple of sharp punches. The first one made contact, but the second one he blocked.

He dragged me forward by the lapels, banging his head against mine. With my brain rocked, he jumped on top of me. "I don't have time for this, and you're in my way. Stay the fuck down. She will be cross if I maim you so, I'm inclined to keep you alive. But I will make it hurt."

"Who the fuck are you talking about?"

Webster laughed. "Saffron, of course. Who knew she was going to grow into such a beautiful woman?"

The growl bubbled up from somewhere deep in the center of my body, and I grappled with it. All the while he just laughed.

"Oh, mate. Does Gabe realize you're shagging his sister? When he does and realizes that you can't give her up, that is going to be a fight I wish I could watch, but that's for another day. While I admire what you're trying to do here, it's time for you to stop." He pointed the muzzle of his gun at my shoulder, but I struck out, dislodging it.

The gun went clattering, and Webster's eyes went wide for just a millisecond before he delivered another elbow that rocked me.

My world spun and I fell back, desperate to get back to my feet, but I couldn't. The oddest thing happened though. When Drake had his gun back in hand, he turned to me and shook his head. "You should have just listened and stayed fucking down. Now it's going to take you longer to get to her."

He raised his gun, and I knew I was done, and I'd never told her the truth. That I loved her. That this was real. She would never know.

But instead of shooting me as I expected, Webster shook his head, tucked his gun back in his holster, and ran.

All I could do as the gray closed in on the edges of my vision was watch as the woman I loved was consumed in a ball of fire.

32

LACHLAN

I woke up to ringing ears, a blasting headache, and one word on my tongue. "Saff." Saff had been blown up. The house... Barbed wire squeezed around my heart, but my brain refused to acknowledge what had just happened. "Saff?"

"Would you quit your bitching? I'm right here."

Her voice was clear, right bloody next to me. I frowned trying to blink as I came fully awake. Obviously, I was dreaming. "Saff?"

"That's my name. Don't wear it out."

I dared to turn my head, and there she was, sitting upright. Her face was smudged with dirt, and she had some cuts and bruises, but otherwise, she was fine. "B-b-but you... You were in the house."

She nodded. "Yeah, Webster set some charges. I was closer to the front of the house and the explosion took out the back. I was barely touched. There was some flying debris which accounts for my scrapes, but otherwise, I was not hurt. I'm really lucky. Are you okay?"

I winced as I sat up. "Yeah, but I'm not sure why. He could have killed me, Saff, but he didn't."

She nodded. "Same for me."

Rookie groaned from the corner. "Well, he actually shot me. So, fuck that guy."

When I glanced around, I realized we were in some kind of white medical looking room. Tabs nodded at me. "Surgeon's office. He's a friend."

I lifted my brows, but she didn't elaborate. "Did we get Webster?"

Tabs shook her head. "No, but Saff has an idea."

"Yeah, we didn't catch Webster, but we all kind of brushed with him and he didn't kill any of us. Sure, he shot Rookie, but it could have been worse. It was through and through and completely superficial. He didn't hit anything vital."

I frowned at that. "He hit nothing vital?"

Rookie shook his head. "It was like he just wanted to slow me down."

"This doesn't make any sense."

Saff nodded. "Exactly. But seeing that he didn't hurt any of us"—she held up a hand toward Rookie—"*seriously*, I don't think he wants to. Which means he also wants us to find him, or at least find what he's going after."

Tabs crossed her arms and leaned against the door. "And what do you think he's going after?"

"I think he's going after Graciella."

"But why does he want Graciella?" she asked.

Saff shrugged her shoulders. "I don't know. All I know is that I misread the situation. From some of what Webster said when he had me, I don't think she's dating him. I think she's seeing the old man. I also think she was really hoping Webster would eliminate us, which means she has something major to hide.

And while I want him in custody with the strength of a thousand suns, I still think we can get them both. He mentioned something about the Highland. We need to find out what that is."

Tabatha nodded. "I know some locals I can ask for help. I think it's a hotel, but you never know."

Saff agreed. "Perfect. I think we can get two heads for the price of one. If we can get local help, even better."

I frowned at Saff. She couldn't be serious. She'd nearly been blown up by a psychopath. That same psychopath who had shot Rookie. We needed to regroup, not jump in head first.

Are you thinking that because she's putting herself in more danger, or because you honestly think she's mishandling the mission?

It didn't fucking matter. She wasn't seeing this clearly. She was being driven by revenge and her emotions. I was afraid she was going to get herself killed, and just the idea of losing her had that barbed-wire feeling wrapping around my heart again. There was no way this was a good idea, and I knew I had to speak up.

"We've taken enough hits today, don't you think? You were just fucking kidnapped by that psychopath."

Saff pursed her lips. "That's just it. I think he only took me because he had to. I don't think he wanted to take me with him, but he couldn't risk leaving me where I was for some reason."

She was grasping at straws, and I pressed on. "Is this your gut talking? Because it's already been wrong today."

She frowned at me. "Our mission is all that matters. Yes, there's some risk, but I will call it in and get it cleared. Right now that's the job."

"Are you so desperate to prove Gabe wrong that you're willing to throw yourself headlong into danger?"

The moment the words were out of my mouth, I knew I'd made a huge mistake.

"This is the gig, Lock. We catch the bad guys. And we don't

give up. That's what you signed up for. It's what we *all* signed up for. Either you're with the team or you're not."

I ground my teeth together in frustration. "You keep saying these things to me about teamwork. But what happens when your team leader can't see the bloody forest for the trees? Your single-minded focus could get us all killed."

"It's a matter of trust. When we go into the field, there are orders for a reason. Now if you're too injured to go back out, fair enough. Get back to the safe house. The rest of us are going after Webster and Graciella."

Tabs glanced between us, and so did Saint as he popped up out of bed. "Well, I'm not that hurt, so Tabs, why don't you help me find something to eat. Then we'll figure out what this Highland business is."

When the two of them were gone, Saff turned to me. "Look, I know it's been a hell of a day. Nothing has gone right, but we are on a mission."

I shook my head stubbornly. "Do you have any idea what it's like to watch the woman you care about nearly get blown up? I can't watch that again, Saff."

"You have to trust that I'm actually good at my job."

The next words out of my mouth were born of fear and worry. "Maybe Gabe was right. You're not thinking clearly, and you're going to get yourself killed."

She jerked as if I'd slapped her. "I think one of us is experiencing an overwhelm of emotions right now. Newsflash, it's not me. Like I said, we're going after them. If you're not up to it, head back to the safe house. But this mission is still on."

I knew I was saying exactly the wrong things. I knew that I was fucking this up. But panic had me by the balls, and I couldn't let her walk into danger. I had to say something. I had to *do* something. "This is reckless, Saff. Maybe we should call this in and get our directive from Gabe."

She blinked at me slowly and said. "You don't believe in me."

My heart sank. "I'm not saying I don't believe in you. I'm saying maybe your judgment is compromised."

Way to keep digging yourself a hole there.

She crossed her arms. "We are field agents. We could die any day. I'm not going into this with zero intel. We are the team on the ground. And last I checked, I was mission lead."

I pursed my lips then. "Right. Back to that again. You're taking risks I am not comfortable with you taking."

"You sound just like Gabe."

"I never thought I'd say this, but maybe he's right."

She flinched. "Wow. Tell me how you really feel."

When she turned to leave, I grabbed her hand. "Don't do this, Saff. It feels like a trap."

"I have to follow my instincts on this one," she said and pulled her hands free.

At the end of the day, she was there to be a field agent, not the woman I loved. But all I wanted to do was hold her in my arms and keep her safe, whether she wanted it or not. And to prevent that from happening, I let her walk out the door.

33

SAFFRON

"Are you mad? Because you look mad."

"I'm not mad, Tabs."

"Do you want to talk about it?"

"No, I don't want to talk about it. I just want to finish this mission and get back."

"He doesn't understand how it works."

I shook my head. "It doesn't matter."

"I think it does. It feels like he doesn't believe in you."

"Tabatha..." I gave her a firm press of my lips and my serious eyes.

She strapped on her bulletproof vest. "Look, I know how this goes. I understand it. I've been in your shoes before. And let's face it, he's a man. He hasn't done enough of these missions to know that sometimes you have to go on your instincts. And I trust yours with my life."

I frowned at that as I checked my magazine. "I don't want your life to be in danger. I know that's part of this. I understand. It's a hazard of the job. I still don't like it."

"He'll come around," she said, trying to soothe me.

"I'm not sure I want him to come around. This is too hard, Tabs."

She finished strapping on her vest as she studied me. "You love him, don't you?"

"I don't love him. That's bullshit."

"Honey, I can see it. You're completely smitten. For weeks, you two have been running around here sneaking glances. You've gotten better at hiding it in the building, but you forget, I see you when you wake up. I see the smile on your face. I see how he makes you feel. You are giddy and excited. And that's fantastic."

I felt like a vice had wrapped around my heart. "I don't want this. I don't want these feelings. I have so much to do, so much to prove. If I make one wrong move, I could get everyone killed. I nearly got everyone killed yesterday."

"That was not on you. You were following protocol."

"Yeah, protocol. But I didn't clear the room. Rookie move. I made a mistake."

Tabs sighed and then strode over to me, planting her hands on my shoulders. "Do you remember Berlin?"

I frowned. She'd had several missions there. "Which mission?"

"You know, the one where the bomb was left behind. That was my fault. I got made. Simple as that. And as a result, the guy left his bomb behind instead of taking it to the actual intended target. Luckily, no one died, but several were injured. And that one haunts me. We all make mistakes."

"I know." And I did, or at least tried to. "But how am I supposed to trust my instincts, which I can feel in my bones are right, when the one person who's supposed to believe in me doesn't?"

Tabs whacked me on the arm. "The one person?"

I laughed. "I'm sorry. You're right, actually. You, I can count on."

"Always. Now, what do you say we go pick up that stropping cunt?"

I laughed. "Tell me how you really feel."

"How I really feel is that she lied to us. She played us, or played you, from the beginning, and no one does that to my best mate."

"Sometimes I feel like I'm going completely crazy."

"Maybe you are. Maybe we come up snake eyes on this. I don't know. But you have a hunch, and if you back it up with some intel, I'll follow you over a cliff. As long as you're Thelma and I'm Louise."

"Whoa. Why do I have to be Thelma?"

"I don't know. You just look like a Thelma."

She tried to hit me again, but this time I blocked her easily. "I'm Louise."

She winked. "If you say so."

I knew she was doing anything she could to make me smile, and I loved her for it. "You're right. Let's go get this stropping cow."

"Cunt. I said, cunt, okay?"

I laughed. "Yeah, stropping cunt, got it. I love you, Tabs."

"I know. I'm pretty awesome. And just so we're super clear, you love Lock too. And he loves you. Though how you two are going to make this work in Rogues, I have no idea."

"I really don't want to think about that. I'm not sure it can work. I don't know. I feel like I've been fooling myself this entire time. And it's too complicated now. I'm just worried about everything."

"Focus on things you can control and the rest will be okay."

"Are you sure about that?"

"I'm sure."

As she turned to leave with her bag of equipment, I called out to her, "Hey, Tabs."

"Yeah, babe?"

"Thank you."

"Anytime. Now finish getting suited up. We're going to show everyone how it's done."

Did I have any idea what I was doing?

34

SAFFRON

As it turned out, the Highland was a hotel featuring luxury bungalows. And when pressed, our contacts had in fact seen Graciella on the premises, and they even gave us her exact bungalow. It was quiet, closer to the water, out of the way. And hopefully no one would see us coming.

I was surprised to see Lachlan step out of the safe house fully geared up.

I frowned at him. "So, you're coming?"

He nodded. "This is the mission."

As if that answered every question. As if yesterday, he hadn't directly questioned my ability to run this team, to run this mission to success. All I could do was give him a brusque nod then load my team into the van.

From the safe house, the drive out to the Highland was only about twenty minutes away. The sun had just started to go down, so luckily, we would have some cover.

As we sat outside the property waiting for the security guards to make their shift change, my knee started to bounce up and down.

Tabatha and Rookie didn't see it, but Lock did. He placed a hand on my knee, gently squeezing it. All I could do was stare at him. We were not ok. How did he think we were at all ok?

I cleared my throat, checked my magazines again, and resolutely turned away from him. Despite what I had allowed myself to believe, he wasn't mine. And despite what he believed, he wasn't the one running the mission. I was. I didn't need his reassurance.

"Let's go."

I could hear his frustrated sigh behind me. "I was just trying to be supportive."

"Now is not the time for that, King. We have bad guys to catch."

Tabs gave me a fist bump as I clambered out with my two hulking agents next to me. The Winston Isles felt like a baby mission compared to this. It hadn't been classified as active and dangerous. But marching into the Highland to catch Graciella and Webster, the adrenaline that poured through me was off the charts. This was the kind of thing that I had dreamed of my whole life. Vengeance for my parents, but also putting a dangerous man away. One who had no qualms about killing people.

At the fence, Lock set a small explosive charge, and we backed up about twenty feet. When he hit the button on his detonator, it blew, breaking open a hole for us in the wrought iron.

We climbed through and headed around the east side of Graciella's bungalow.

I placed my tech wand on the base of the window. Rookie said that it would track any electronic activity inside the house like alarms, phones that sort of thing. And since it was on the same frequency as our equipment and our phones were already calibrated, it wouldn't pick ours up. But when I flipped the switch, it showed nothing, no electronics inside. That was bull-shit because we knew Graciella was here.

Unless your intel was bad again and you made another bad call.

I couldn't think like that. We need to clear the house, and if neither one of them were here, we'd regroup. But I wasn't letting Lachlan's doubts get to me. That could be death out in the field.

I signaled for us to move. I was heading for the main door, Rookie for the back, and Lock for a side door leading out to a large veranda. Saint was in the van on Coms and Tabatha trailed Rookie. The adrenaline barreled through my veins, making my heart pump excitedly and my breathing go shallow.

Easy does it. Breathe. Nice and steady. You have this.

At the front door, I used the key code given by our contact. The door eased open with the audible grind and click of the heavy duty lock. One by one we cleared the rooms downstairs. As we were coming back around toward the kitchen, I heard footsteps. Someone was moving fast. Someone big.

I signaled to them that I was going after him. Lachlan tried to reach for me, but I shook him off and ran up the stairs, my gun trained for anyone coming down. I heard him curse under his breath as he followed me. Despite his hesitance, he had my back.

We moved quickly from room to room clearing then. And then I heard a crash in the master bedroom. We both went running, with Lock watching my back and Rookie coming up the stairs. When I kicked open the door of the bedroom, there was Drake Webster throwing something out the window. I shouted, "Of course, it's you. Why is it always fucking you? Going somewhere Webster?"

He chuckled low. "Would you believe I think we've both been played?"

"Doesn't matter. You're the one who's going to be in cuffs."

He eyed me up and down then assessed Lachlan and Rookie. "Are you sure about that? Tell you what, how about we fight for the privilege of bringing me in? You win, I come willingly. I win, you let me go. Hell, I'll even throw in that I take care of your Graciella problem for you."

I stepped forward, and Lachlan cursed under his breath. "Fucking hell, Saffron."

He really thought I was going to take this monster at his word? That I would fall easily for the nonsense? Did he think I was that naive, that dumb?

Still, I stepped forward and removed my jacket.

Even Rookie seemed concerned "Boss?"

I paused in the room full of three of the biggest, baddest men I'd probably ever met in my life, and I knew I had the upper hand.

Webster smiled when he saw me taking off my jacket, and he tsked. "I can't say I'm disappointed, but at least you're predictable. Come on now, why don't you give me the beating you're so desperate to hand out so I can hurry up and get out of here. Because you can't win. You won't win."

I shrugged. "You're right. If I play the way you play, I can't win. But if I play my way, I always come out on top." Then I palmed the gun that I'd pulled up from the holster as I was removing my jacket, and I tranqued him in the dead center of his chest.

There was nothing more satisfying than watching a massive tree go down.

Saffron

I wish I could say I felt something, anything other than pure numbness.

But I didn't. Okay, fine, maybe exhaustion. On my first mission, I had nearly gotten my entire team taken out, been kidnapped, gotten blown up, fought with my boyfriend, then broken up with said boyfriend. Then as a final topper, I'd captured one of the most notorious criminals in the world, the same one who happened to have killed my parents.

I was long overdue for a nap.

Yes, we had captured Webster, but even that felt too easy and not quite right. It was almost like he wanted to be caught.

And I had no idea why.

In our pursuit of Drake Webster, Rookie had been shot, Lachlan had been injured trying to get to me, and Tabs... Well, Tabs was just pissed right the fuck off.

All because I made the wrong call about Graciella.

One bad call and we had lost Graciella, and I'd almost gotten everyone killed.

This was why they didn't let agents date. Too many distractions. There was a perfectly good reason for it, other than my brother being a dick.

But in this case he had good reason to be. And sure enough, even Lock questioned my judgment.

So yeah, everything was shit.

There was nothing worse than having the man you loved—okay, fine, I said loved—question your call in the field because you'd already made the wrong one.

There was nothing worse than having your own team doubt your competence because you'd already screwed up once.

Yeah, there was a reason they didn't let agents date.

I hadn't believed in it, hadn't wanted to adhere to that rule. I thought I was exempt and that the rules didn't apply to me. But even funnier was that they applied to me most of all.

The fucking heir. What load of bullshit was that?

I didn't have some great legacy to uphold. I was like every other rookie agent trying to survive. And I made a colossal mistake.

After the prisoner transport at the airport and during the long drive to Rogues Division, I was just relieved to be in one piece, prisoner intact, ready to go.

But I knew what was waiting. There would be no hot shower, no moment of respite. My brother would have a lot to say to *me*. And sure enough, he was waiting for me.

He glowered at me then at my whole team. "Mission debrief, now."

I could have argued. I could have pushed, but he had the right to be pissed the fuck off. Exhausted, I followed behind Gabe, and my team followed me. Because at the end of the day, we all screwed up together. In the debrief room we all took seats, and I glanced around at my team. They were all road weary. Tabs though, ever the faithful sidekick, was glowering at Gabe. Lock's expression was stoic.

My brother turned to me. "Explain yourself."

"Any mission protocols broken were mine. My team only followed my lead."

"That's what you have to say?"

I nodded. "Graciella Natanya evaded capture for now. But we brought in number two on Interpol's list. Drake Webster."

Gabe sat back and lifted a brow. "Right. How did you lose Graciella?"

I squared my shoulders, leveled my gaze on him, and told him the truth about how she'd disappeared pretty much right in front of us.

"Right. And then you got yourself nicked."

Yes, there was that. "Obviously, I didn't realize that was going to happen."

"You let an asset, one that you insisted you could cultivate, walk."

I swallowed hard. "Yes. I did."

Gabe just stared at me. "There could be consequences." Then he turned his attention to the rest of my team. "And you lot?"

But before he could start, I pushed to my feet. "I accept full responsibility for their actions. The breaking of protocol was a pattern I established early on to get the job done. They weren't wrong. Because they are responsible for capturing Webster, not me. I was merely the bait."

"Well, these sacks of shit have actually passed the team-work marker," Gabe said. "Congratulations. You are all grounded. No one leaves the campus."

When Gabe dismissed us, I turned to go with my team, but he held me back. "Oh no, not you, Agent Abott."

When they were gone, I turned to him. "Can't this one wait? The lecture, the grounding, stripping me of my Rogues agent status, whatever it is? I am knackered."

His voice was low and gruff. "Are you all right?"

I frowned at that. "What do you mean?"

"Are you harmed in any way?" He couldn't meet my gaze.

"I'm fine. Scrapes and bruises. Nothing permanent."

His shoulders sagged a little. "I died a thousand deaths when Webster took you. Do you understand that?"

"That wasn't my intention, Gabe."

"I know, it's just—"

"Yeah, I already know. I'm a shitty field agent. I understand."

He sighed. "That's not what I said. Look, off the record, every first mission goes shitty. That's why I wanted you to have more seasoning. They're all supposed to go shitty. Your first field agent op wasn't supposed to be something like this. Oversight interfered, and I have no idea why. They've been happy to let me run the show up until now. I don't know what possessed them."

"I'm fine, Gabe."

He cleared his throat and nodded. "Yeah." And then he dropped his head and rubbed at something on the end of his nose before inhaling deeply and blinking rapidly. I frowned. Was he crying? There was no way he was crying.

"You ever scare me like that again, I swear to God, I will kill you myself."

I shifted awkwardly from foot to foot. "I really am okay, Gabe."

He nodded. "Fine. Yeah." He cleared his throat. "Get the fuck out of here before I remember how mad I am."

I nodded and headed for the door. Pausing, I turned to him. "I really am okay, Gabe."

"Go. And don't let me see you for at least twenty-four hours." He paused then added, "Well done bringing Webster in. I've been trying for two years, but you actually managed it."

I'd never seen him like that. "I owed him."

"One more thing, agent."

I cursed under my breath as I turned to face him. "Yeah?"

"Did you really think I wouldn't notice?"

"Notice what?"

"You and King. I trust you know what to do about that?"

I sighed. Tears started to prick my lids, but I held them back. "No need for concern. It's over. Has been over." And then I stalked out to go and shatter my heart into a thousand pieces.

35

LACHLAN

I KNEW WHAT WAS COMING.

It didn't mean I could do anything about it. All I could do was wait, see her face, and take it.

She came straight to the cottage, and I was grateful that Saint wasn't there. He had taken one look at me when we came back and headed straight back out with his gym gear.

She was just as knackered as I was. We were all wrecked. I could tell by her beautiful face, her chin uplifted, her shoulders squared. "Can we talk?"

I sighed and stepped aside. "Look, I know that things got a little heated in the field. But that's no reason to walk away."

"It's all the reason, Lock. When it came down to it in the field, you didn't trust me. That's a hundred percent my fault, and I own that. I needed to be your supervising officer, not your girlfriend. And because I was your girlfriend, you couldn't follow an order I gave you in the field."

"That was my fault, not yours."

"That doesn't really matter, does it? At the end of the day you and I shouldn't have been together."

"Stop saying that. We'll just work it out so we're on different missions."

"It's not going to work, and we cannot do that. Gabe knows."

I frowned at that. "What the fuck do you mean he knows?"

"Gabe, my brother, our operations commander. He knows."

"You told him?"

She chuffed a laugh. "You think I had to tell him?"

The anxiety in the pit of my stomach twisted and gnarled, trying to claw its way out. "Saff, I fucked up. It was my fault."

"No, it was mine. I never should have let it get this far."

My gut twisted. "You don't understand. I'm... I'm..."

"Lock, I love you. And for the first time in my life, I felt seen in your arms. But I need to be with someone who trusts me. Who believes in me. Who will back my plays."

"Saff, don't."

A sob tore from her chest. "You broke my heart. And maybe you were right. But the moment you treated me like I couldn't trust myself, I knew I had to walk away."

"Fuck, I'm so sorry. I just panicked because I almost lost you. Before I met you, I thought I had to be on my own. I thought I didn't deserve anyone. And maybe I don't, because when you needed me, I couldn't get past the possibility of losing you. But I can work on that. I won't love it, but I can figure it out. Give me a chance."

"We have no chance. We were never supposed to be together. This—us—it's against the rules."

"I will break every rule for you." I tried to hold her again, and she stepped out of reach.

"You have a job to do, Lock. You've got six months. Fucking hell. Just do your job. Go back to your life. This *is* my life. Now I have to figure out how I can salvage it."

"You're giving up, Saff.

I leaned down, my forehead pressing into hers. Our lips were a whisper from each other, and I could smell the lingering scent she no longer had of her mother's.

"I needed you to believe in me in the field. Sight unseen. It's called faith. And just like my brother, you don't have any in me. " She whirled to leave, and I caught her wrist again. She broke my hold easily and delivered a backhanded blow that caught me straight across the cheek. "Don't touch me."

She didn't even slam the door when she strolled out. Just left it wide open, the chill of the night air whipping in. I knew she wouldn't forgive me.

You can't blame her.

I knew there was no fixing that level of betrayal.

———

Saffron

I COULD HEAR the rustle of plastic as someone shoved something underneath my door.

I was back in my childhood bedroom, and there was enough clearance under the door to get small bags through. Little tiny packets of gummy bears. Fucking Tabatha.

"I don't want to talk."

She said nothing. Just slid another sack of gummy bears underneath my door.

I'd been crying for well over two hours. I was raw and exhausted and wrung out. No one had any faith in me. It didn't matter what I did or what I accomplished, the people in my life that I loved the most didn't think I was capable. I hated this. What the hell was I supposed to do with this feeling? I felt rubbed raw as if someone had taken sand paper to the inside of my eyeballs.

I grabbed one of the bags that had been shoved under, snapped it open, and popped several gummies into my mouth.

Another bag slid under the door, which I took gratefully. Because even though I knew the truth, my body and my brain just kept rejecting it.

He'd said I mattered to him. But that wasn't love. He didn't believe in me. After everything, even knowing how much Gabe had hurt me. Did he really think I could forget that?

God, how stupid was I?

I chewed thoughtfully.

Tabs still hadn't said anything. But she knew when I got in these moods to let me vent.

Another bag appeared, and this time, there were some tissues. I snatched them up, swiping away the tears streaking down my face. "What am I supposed to do? I fucking loved him. And Gabe knew the whole time. What am I supposed to say? I did what he couldn't."

There were no tissues or gummy bears then. Maybe she was out. "I mean, how much does my own brother hate me? Our whole lives, all I've ever wanted was for Gabe to love me, and I thought he did, but now it seems like he hates me."

The voice on the other side of the door whispered. "I don't hate you."

I scrambled back, scowling, and then I reached for the door and yanked it open. Gabe tumbled into my room.

"What the fuck are you doing?"

"Look, I'm sorry. I knew you were upset and Tabs came to me and dropped the gummy bears on my desk and told me that I needed to fix it because it was my fault. I'm sorry you think I don't love you. All I'm trying to do is protect you. I'd give my whole life to fucking protect you."

"Fuck you, Gabe. Every conversation we have deteriorates, you know?"

"I try and talk to you, and you tell me to go fuck myself."

"That's because you need to be told to go and fuck yourself. I did something great Gabe. I caught the asshole who killed our parents."

"I'm sorry. I know that you're hurting, but Lock wasn't right for you anyway."

I shuffled my feet, gummy bear wrappers rustling around them. "For fuck's sake, Gabe, am I supposed to be alone for the rest of my life? You don't even let me experience anything, let alone love. I'm alone, Gabe. You won't talk to me. The brother that loved me is gone. My parents are gone. They left me, and then you left me. And now, I finally think that I love someone, and he has left me with no choice but to walk away. So don't you stand there and tell me you love me or you're protecting me. You're protecting your throne."

"No, I'm not. For fuck's sake, I'm not. Look, there are power plays happening in Rogues Division. Always. Jockeying for position. I've known about you and Lock for a while."

My stomach flipped, and bile threatened to jerk its way up my esophagus. "What?"

"I knew, okay? You're not that slick. Besides, even when you leave campus, I have someone watching you."

"Do you not see the problem with that?"

"Of course, I see the problem. I would rather not know about anything you do naked, okay? Because it's gross."

"Fuck you."

"I know you have a better vocabulary than that."

I flipped him the bird, and he smirked. That one expression made him look five years younger. He looked like my Gabe again.

"It's done. You got your way, or whatever."

"You think I want you to be alone? I don't, because I know one day I'm going to the field and I'm not coming back. For the last two years I have held myself apart from you because I didn't want you getting even more attached in case something happened to me. When our parents died, it put everything in disarray. There are always people jockeying for power. I'm trying to protect your legacy."

"It's too late for that because my heart is already broken."

Gabe took my hands. "All I've ever wanted to do is keep you safe. You were ready for the field six months after Mum and Dad died. You were so focused. Single-minded. You knew exactly what you wanted."

I frowned at that. "I'm not so sure. In retrospect, I don't think I was. It was harder than I expected knowing everyone was dependent on me."

"I'll let you in on a little secret. No one is ever ready."

I chewed on my bottom lip. "So this whole time, you've known about Lock?"

Gabe shrugged. "He made you smile. Not in a fake, blank way that you give to strangers on the streets, but that real one I remember in all the home videos where we'd both peek out and your eyes crinkled and you were truly happy. You think you two are slick? I could see it every time you smiled at him, every time he smiled at you. It was really gross, just so you know."

"Why did you let it continue? You must have known where it was going. You must have known that I was going to fall for him."

He shrugged. "You'd already lost so much. I couldn't stand to take it away from you. Look, for the record, I just tried to do the right thing. He cares for you."

"Don't give me that bullshit."

"He does. He gave you something that I couldn't give you. More than a sense of normalcy. He gave you room to breathe. I know I've held on a little tight since Mum and Dad died."

"A little?"

"Okay, a lot. But that was my job. I was supposed to hold on tight. I held on tight so you could have some freedom. But Lock gave you more than that."

"What bullshit. If he cared, he would have trusted me."

Gabe ran his hands through his hair. "Fucking hell, you don't give an inch, do you?"

"Should I?"

"No, you shouldn't. I have been overbearing and overprotective. I have undermined your friendships, your relationships, your joining the agency. This is all my fault."

"This doesn't change anything. I still made the choice in the field that nearly got everyone killed because I went after Graciella. All you're doing now is telling me that it wasn't worth it. The joke was on me all along. So yeah, I'm not really interested."

"I understand you should know the truth. He *does* love you. And if you have someone like him, I wouldn't worry so much about when something happens to me. He won't leave you alone. I know that's your biggest fear. When they died, you tried to stopped needing anyone. Hell, you wouldn't even let me come and get you. You packed up your shit and left Pittsburgh and made it all the way back here on your own. I know that was a trauma response, or whatever Madeline and the rest of the shrinks would call it, but you wouldn't even let me help. You're so fucking independent it's scary. You have every right to be angry. I'm just saying cut Lock some slack. And cut yourself some too, Saff. The only problem I ever had with Mum and Dad was the amount of pressure they put on you. They didn't even know they were doing it. Mum would always say things like, 'Ah, that's my Saff, just like her mama.' And it was building you up to want so much to be like them that you put all this pressure on yourself to be perfect. I know that you deal with things that I don't deal with. I'm a white man in espionage. My ticket is written. I know yours isn't. I'm not a fool. You carry around so much, and I wanted to take some of the burden off. But it was the wrong call. Lock made a wrong call in the Winston Isles too, but it made me give him another chance. Because everything he did, he did because he loves you."

The image of Lock attempting to paint my toenails was not one I needed. The image of Lock holding my hand and traipsing me through the old town market was not one I needed. The image of Lock holding on tight, and whispering my name as we talked about his brother and my parents and things we missed in the hushed hours of daylight... I didn't need those. Not at all. I didn't want them.

I knew the truth. He didn't love me. Not enough anyway.

36

LACHLAN

THREE DAYS. It had been three days since I had seen Saff. She hadn't been on the Rogues campus. At least not as far as I had seen, and she hadn't answered any of my phone calls either. Not that I expected her to. But still.

After the third day of getting nothing, I went by Tabatha's place, and I was surprised when she opened the door even after checking the security panel. "I know what you want," she said by way of a greeting.

I tried to glance past her. "I just want to talk to her."

"She doesn't want to talk to you, Lachlan. I don't blame her."

"I fucked up, okay? I just.. I can't sleep. I can't eat. I need to see her."

"No, you don't. She's trying to get her head on straight. Between you and Gabe, she really hasn't had a chance to do that. Just leave her be if you love her."

"What the fuck kind of answer is that?"

"It's an answer. You said you care about her. If you love her, leave her be. You and Gabe both think you did the right thing.

Trying to save her and rescue her, but you're forgetting she's a total badass who doesn't need saving. She doesn't need you to ride in. She needs you to *see* her. And I thought you were that guy, but you're just an imposter like the rest. And Gabe, I know what his problem is. A little boy who was desperate for love and finally found someone to love him, and then they died, so he paid them back by loving his sister too much. It's fucked up. But I understand why he did it. You... All you had to do was tell her, believe in her."

"You think I don't know that? I never meant to hurt her."

"Wanting to do something and actually doing it are completely different things."

"I just want to explain."

"You've explained enough. Go home. Move on."

I frowned down at her. "Are you kidding me? I just told you I'm in love with your best friend."

"Yes, you used your words. You have told me you're in love with my best friend. You haven't *shown* me, and until you can do that, or even better, *show her*, I don't have anything for you. Besides, you think you're the first fit guy to be sniffing around Saff? You're not. She's fucking gorgeous. Basically model good looks and a sweetheart and a killer right hook. That's not something you find just anywhere, and you fucked it up."

She started to close the door, and I stopped her with my hand. "Can you just tell her I love her?"

She laughed. *In my face.* Actually fucking laughed. "Lachlan, I am not your errand girl. I will not be passing messages back and forth between you and Saff, hoping that you two get back together. I thought you were fun. Someone to tease her into smiling and enjoying herself more. But you're a fuckboi. I know the type. The only way a fuckboi graduates is to actually do something worthwhile. You had that chance at Rogues. I can't respect you now."

"I was terrified for her, Tabatha."

"I know, but you still hurt my best friend. So yeah, congratulations, you're a man. Do the right thing by her, and you and I can talk again. And maybe, just maybe, I'll take off the voodoo curse I put on your dick. But until then, you better get moving fast. You can expect it to fall off in about three days."

"If it means I can talk to her and explain, it's fine. I don't need it any way."

My dick practically whimpered at the thought.

"Honestly, Tabs, I don't know what to do. I can't get her to talk to me."

"If you want her back, Lachlan, you'll think of something. Why the fuck you're here on my doorstep begging for my help is beyond me. Do you love her or don't you? If you love her, figure it out. If you don't, continue moping and whining and being a ballsack. It's up to you."

She slammed the door then, and I leaned my forehead against it.

She was right. What the fuck? I hadn't actually done anything to show Saff that I was sorry. I hadn't proven that I was the kind of man she deserved.

So start proving it.

I stood for a long moment, staring at the door. And then it clicked. Yes, I'd been dreaming of Saff. Yes, I was desperate to get my hands on her. But this wasn't about that. The one thing she'd asked me not to do, I'd done. Two things, actually. She'd begged me not to lie to her, and I had done that. I'd broken her heart. And so I had to mend that. And the other thing Tabs said about my fuckboi image... She was right. My whole life, I'd gotten by because Charlie had been there to do all the right things. I had very little practice at being a good guy. Very little practice at being the kind of man she deserved, so I just assumed I was bad at it.

But what if I wasn't? What if I could be someone different? What if I had the chance to be?

As I turned to walk away, I knew what I had to do. And the outcome didn't matter. All I needed was for her to smile again. To pull that off, I was going to need some help, and I was going to need to grow the fuck up.

———

Saffron

I NEVER EXPECTED to see him or talk to him again. What I'd expected to happen was to have Webster locked in a very deep, dark black site with the rest of the scum of the earth. But watching him walk into the briefing room uncuffed and unencumbered made something snap inside me.

I couldn't say exactly what the sensation was. I just knew it felt like cold steel crawling all over my skin, encasing every follicle, every nerve ending, until I was blisteringly numb. When I walked in the room, my brother stood. "Saff, I think it's important that—"

I didn't hear him. I just marched straight toward Webster. Saint stepped forward, trying to stop me. I sidestepped him easily, putting my foot behind his and dropping him.

Jason was next. "Saff, don't."

I gave him an open palm, using the full force of my hips and my arms. I could hear Gabe clamoring over their bodies, trying to get to me before I could get to Webster. But Webster didn't move. His gaze was steely and strong, but he didn't put up his hands to defend himself. He just stood there.

I launched myself at him, nonetheless, not caring about what was going to happen to me. At least I didn't have a full audience, but Hector and Jason were surely going to tell someone what had happened.

My elbow connected with Webster's cheek, and that moved him several inches. He still didn't put his hands up to cover his face. I delivered a punch. My flat throat jab had him coughing and bending over, and then I delivered a knee strike.

Behind me, Gabe wrapped his arms around me and tugged me back. "Stand down, Saffron."

"Fuck you, Gabe."

"Saffron…"

Webster, still wheezing, pushed to his feet. "It's not enough. Let her go."

"You hear that?" I said to Gabe. "He wants more."

Gabe just stared at me.

Webster said, "I deserve it. All of it. Just let her do it. I deserve everything."

I stared at my brother.

"Saff, there are things at play here that you don't understand."

"I hate you."

"I know. But this is important. We're working with him. He's our ally."

I was shaking my head before I realized I was moving it. This had to be some kind of joke. "How can you even look at him? He killed Mum and Dad."

Gabe sighed. "Saff—"

"No, don't *Saff* me. You're willing to negotiate with him? We don't negotiate with terrorists. Correct me if I'm wrong, but he is the very definition of a terrorist."

Webster spoke. "What you don't understand, Agent Abott, is that your brother needs me. I have more intel on Antonio Igno's company and the inner workings of his arms deals than anyone in the world. So I've been giving him that information. We can arrange for you to come and hit me some other time."

"Somebody is going to put a bullet in you, and it won't be me. I'm not turning into you."

I stalked out, ignoring my brother's pleas.

Jason was pushing to his feet.

Saint too as he said, "Saff, fucking hell."

They were my teammates, and I'd just put them down in hopes of destroying Drake Webster.

You didn't have it in your heart to kill him.

As much as I hated him, as much pain as he'd caused me, I wasn't going to just stand there and shoot an unarmed man. I wasn't capable of that. I shoved aside the pain that surfaced. That was the important thing.

Push it down. Do not feel this.

I felt like I could blow up at anyone who dared speak to me or look at me, and the idea that I might run into Gabe made me ill, just like it had five minutes ago.

I took the winding path to the main lodge as rage simmered just under my flesh.

I went to the private residences, completely ignoring the whispers of the workers in the other half of the manor. I just didn't have the energy for it. When I finally made it to my room, I closed the door, expecting the familiar surroundings to calm me, but they didn't. Instead, it made me even more restless.

As I passed my desk, I caught a whiff of something familiar and frowned. There was a note on the top drawer. *I owe you, and I'm sorry. I hope this begins my repayment.*

There was a trail of arrows pointing toward my bathroom. When I opened the door and walked in, there was a plain, nondescript bottle about eight ounces in size sitting on my vanity.

As I approached, the scent alone told me what it was, and I

froze. There was no fucking way. No way he could have done this. But as I leaned forward, too afraid to touch the bottle lest it shatter or disappear, I could smell it. It was my mother's perfume.

"What have you done?" I whispered.

Holy shit, he'd found my mum's perfume. After all this time, he had found a way to recreate it. He'd gotten me the one thing that I couldn't get myself. And he wasn't even here so I could say thank you and also punch him and tell him I hated him.

The question was, could I forget everything about how he'd hurt me?

37

SAFFRON

AFTER FINDING the perfume in my room, I used the atomizer to fill the little vial I continued to wear around my neck.

I'd looked for him to say thank you, but he was scarce.

I went by his cottage, knocked, and waited for him. But he didn't answer, even though I could sense that he was in there. He was doing what I'd asked and giving me space. But he had done this huge thing, and while we couldn't be together, at least I could say thank you. Right?

Who are you kidding, you want that man.

Want him or not, it wasn't going to happen.

That Friday, as I was heading down to the training center to evaluate my new recruit, I decided to take the elevator from the main office after meeting with my brother. The elevator doors opened and I smiled blandly at the three people in there until my head lifted and I saw that Lock was one of them.

His gaze stayed trained on me. The corner of his lips lifted in a barely imperceptible smile. But still, I kept my bland, neutral face on with a good morning for everyone then turned my back.

The doors opened again and the other two passengers

stepped out, excusing themselves on the gym floor, leaving Lock and I alone in the elevator heading down.

It was a short trip down to training. But that final floor required clearance. All agents and operatives had it. If you were working in the main house your pass let you past the first door but to get past the antechamber, you still had to tap in your key code on the off chance that someone who did not belong in the house was snooping where they shouldn't be.

I reached for the keypad, but Lock's fingers on my hips stopped me. The heat of his skin as he stroked my hip bone seared me. "You smell good," he said.

I wasn't sure why, but tears welled in my eyes. All I could do was nod and croak out, "Thank you."

"It was the least I could do."

I expected him to say more, but he was silent. Instead he leaned down and put his lips and nose by the shell of my ear. "You smell good enough to eat, Saff. And just so you know, I've been giving that a lot of thought. I miss you."

My pussy, traitor that she was, clenched.

Who said that? Who said that to someone? I miss you. What the fuck was that bullshit?

But before I could ask him to explain himself, or to keep touching me, he released me. And his heat was gone.

As he pressed himself up against the wall in the elevator. I whipped around to glower at him, and he was smirking at me as he said, "I prefer this Saff to the other one. This version of you has fire. The other version just looks sad."

"Maybe I *am* fucking sad, Lock."

He nodded once then reached around me and tapped in the code.

The doors opened, and he leaned to the side to let me pass.

Too shaken, I walked around him, my body on high alert just being in his proximity. Once I rounded the corner and was certain he couldn't see me, I booked it down to the training facility lockers, certain I'd just avoided a fucking disaster... literally.

"Fuck. Fuckity fuck."

"I know you used to kiss Mum with that mouth."

I stuttered to a halt when I noticed my brother coming out of one of the training rooms.

"What's got your knickers in a knot?" he asked.

"Nothing. I'm fine. Perfectly fine."

And then Gabe did the unthinkable. He grinned. My brother smiled at me. "It's good to see you more like your old self again. Feeling better?"

"Why do people keep asking me that?"

Gabe chuckled low. "Well, in general, you're tough. A ball buster who is not to be crossed. In the last couple weeks, you've been not yourself."

"Sorry that my mood couldn't be elevated for everyone."

His fingers grazed my elbow. "That's not what I meant, Saff." He sighed and tried again not to do that Gabe thing that he always did when he shut me out and shut me down. "What I mean is you're the life of this place. Your energy fills it. The agents, the staff, everyone, they love you for it. That's all. So when you're not like that, we notice. Everybody notices. You feel what you feel, and you should. You've been too locked away for too long. No one expects you to be happy all the time. No one wants that. It would be weird. But the fact that we see you smiling and laughing again, up to no good... It's good to see. It means you're alive."

I gave him a harsh nod. "Can I go now before you start analyzing the choice of color I'm wearing today?"

"Yep. The recruits are almost done up in polygraph."

"Anyone really good at beating the machine?"

"Yeah. There's one. I wish I could explain it, but he's cool as ice. One second he's actually pretty easy to read. The next he has ice water for veins. He's unsettling."

"You must love him."

My brother just laughed. "He's all right."

"Sounds like he'll make a good agent."

"Guess we'll see."

We parted ways at the hall on the way to the pool, and I turned into the women's locker room. Automatically I tapped in my code for my locker and then undressed without giving much thought putting on the uniform. When I pulled out my change of clothes, I frowned when I saw the wrapping at the bottom of my locker. I reached down and pulled it out, frowning at the purple tissue paper wrapped in a knot. It was my favorite color. Wrapped so neatly and tightly. It was carefully done.

My heart started beating faster as I glanced around the locker room, even knowing I was alone. My skin prickled and my breathing became shallow.

You know what this is.

There was no fucking way.

He couldn't have. There was absolutely no way that he could have.

And there, standing in my joggers and a sports bra, I ripped into the wrapping paper. My heart squeezed as I saw the inscription on the outside of the diary. I laughed at the fact that it wasn't at all profound, it wasn't even that witty or clever, but it was my mother's. *Life is short, you might as well eat chocolate.* And before I knew what I was doing, I sank down to the floor holding the diary against my chest, letting those tears that had pricked in my eyes earlier finally spill over. All that time I'd been holding myself together, trying to keep it together, I finally broke.

Lachlan King had broken me.

———

Lachlan

Touching her was admittedly a mistake. Okay, sniffing her had been the mistake.

Giving no fucks about decorum or what was proper or what I had promised her that I would do, I'd inhaled her scent and touched that soft patch of skin right at her hip bone. God, I'd been hard ever since. And edgy. I couldn't fucking think straight.

There'd been a few briefs about a new terrorist group we were trying to place an agent in. So I'd been doing a lot of research on that, but by and large, I'd been able to stay the hell away from her until today.

"Mate, you are having one hell of a day. You need to go hit the showers or the pool or get a workout in because you are edgy as fuck."

I snapped to attention and growled over the computer monitor at Saint. "What the fuck did you say?"

"Case in point."

"What are you on about?"

"I'm not sure you're aware, but we are trying to track down Remy O'Clare. We're doing research into past crimes, blah, blah, boring. And you are sitting there with your teeth clenched so tight I can see every fucking muscle in that carved Adonis jaw of yours. Mate, relax or something. Because Christ you are going to crack a fucking molar."

I forced my jaw to relax. "So now you care about my dental hygiene."

"It's not really about the hygiene I don't want one of your chipped teeth to come flying out of that ugly mug of yours."

"Please, I'm prettier than you."

Saint sat back and stroked his stubble. "Oh, you only wish you were. What is wrong with you?"

"Nothing."

He sat straddling his chair. "Okay, you say nothing, but I'll guess this has to do with a certain Agent Abott."

"Mate, leave it alone."

"I won't leave it alone. For two fucking weeks you've been moping."

"I don't fucking mope," I snapped.

"Sure you don't. You have been in a terrible mood, which is fine. I get it. It's plain how you feel about her. But do something about it. Take the edge off with someone, somehow, fuck, I don't know. But that level of tension you are feeling is about to pop. I can see it."

I glanced down at my hand, and even while holding the mouse I was vibrating slightly. Okay, he had a solid point. I was shaking. "I'm going to go get a workout in."

"You do that. I'll meet you back at the flat."

I didn't realize how late it was until I left the library. When I saw the pitch black outside, I checked my watch. Fucking ten p.m. Jesus.

Dinner had already come and gone, and most agents had already headed back home or closed down for the night. I planned to get in a quick workout, blow off some steam, and try and forget about Saff.

My dick twitched as if to say, *I am never forgetting about her. Matter of fact, let's revisit that favorite dream from last night. The one where she bent down looked at me and then moaned. That's my favorite.*

I cleared my throat I could feel the blood rushing to the tip of my erection, and I cursed. My movements were forced as I changed in the locker room.

This was bullshit. I knew why she was mad at me. I knew I'd

fucked up. I knew she wasn't going to forgive me easily, and I didn't expect her to. Hell, I didn't think she ever would.

I'd thought after a couple weeks it would get a little bit better. But it wasn't better exactly, just a little dulled. As long as I could just tune everything out and focus on work, I was okay. But the nights were torture. All I could do was dream of her. And no amount of jacking off was going to replace the memories of her.

The way her cunt would squeeze me tight. Or the way she looked when she was riding on me, her hips moving forward and backward, her tits bouncing in my face. When I closed my eyes, I could see the top muscles of her stomach. Her hands running through her braids as their long length cascaded down her back. I cleared my throat and reached my hand in my boxers, adjusting myself. Motherfucker. Last thing I fucking needed.

Then I realized I could hear someone else working out. "Hello?"

No one answered, but I could still hear them. I walked down the hall and turned right into the gym. Then I froze, my feet rooted to the spot. My dick, however, rose to full attention.

She wore biker shorts that hugged her ass like she was naked. Every dip and curve was molded and they were bunched right in her crack. Jesus Christ, I wanted to palm her ass, make her get on her knees, spread her cheeks, and dive in, licking her from clit to asshole and back again. Going to town. I wanted to feast on her.

The blood in my veins roared. Fucking hell. My cock was of no help, because even in my boxer briefs where he was supposed to be contained, he had zero intention of lying down and taking this quietly.

When she turned around, she squealed and jumped when she saw me.

I put my hands up and then tapped my ears, indicating her earbuds.

She removed them. "Fuck, you scared me."

"Well, I didn't want to approach because obviously you couldn't hear me."

"I guess I'm done. I'll leave."

"Stop. I don't want you to leave."

She said. "Do you want me to stay?"

My dick said, *Fuck, yes. And since you're going to stay, then get on your knees. Do we have lube? I can get into every hole. I'm going to fuck her every way that I can.*

Nope. I was not going to say any of that. No, uh-uh, negative.

"You don't have to leave. I'll go."

"No," she said. "You just got here for a workout. We can coexist."

How in the world did she think we're going to coexist when all my dick could think about was fucking her ass raw?

I cleared my throat. "Right. I'll just use the heavy bag."

"Right, sure. It's over there."

I cocked my head and muttered to myself, "Of course. I know where it is. Fuck. God, why is this so awkward?"

"What did you say?"

I shook my head and almost didn't reply. Then I turned around. "This is awkward, isn't it?"

"But I offered to leave."

"Fuck, Saff, I don't want you to leave."

My gaze stared down her body. She was wearing a perfectly plain, serviceable sports bra, but her nipples were hard.

I licked my bottom lip, and her eyes traced the path of my tongue.

"Please stop looking at me like that. You have to stop. You can't keep doing this."

"Me?" I took a step toward her. "I'm not doing anything. It's you, your smell."

"*You* gave me the perfume."

"Did you like it?" I asked her, my voice hoarse.

"Of course I fucking liked it. It is the most beautiful, thoughtful thing anyone's ever done for me, and I don't even know how you found it. I mean—"

"Fine. I'm glad you fucking loved it. All I wanted was for you to be happy."

"What the fuck is wrong with you? Why are you shouting at me?"

"Fuck," I muttered as I ran my hands through my hair. I had to get this churning need under control. I was operating on a short fuse, and I didn't want to be this way.

"I'm sorry."

"Fuck, I know this is awkward and tense." She rubbed her temples. "I just need time."

"You really think time's going to make this easier?"

"You don't?"

I stared at her. When had she gotten so close?

I shook my head. "No, I don't think it's going to get better."

"If we just stay away from each other, we can forget it. We can forget all of these feelings."

"I can't forget it. There's a part of me that is desperate to remind myself what you taste like. And there are other parts of you I want to taste, and none of them are appropriate."

"Other parts?" she squeaked.

"You don't want to know."

My dick, however, was making it very apparent.

Her gaze slid down and locked on my hips. And then she licked her bottom lip.

"Saff. Fucking stop looking at me like that."

"I can't fucking help it," she moaned. "You interrupted my

workout, and you're looking like that, with your tight shirt and your gym shorts."

"This is what people work out in."

"Well put on some fucking gray sweatpants or something."

My brow lifted. "How the fuck are gray sweatpants going to help?"

The corner of her lips twitched. "Well, at least you wouldn't be wearing boxers with those, so I could get a show."

I blinked at her once. Then again. And the laugh that burst out was sharp and quick, and the tension eased between us. "Fucking hell, Saff."

She swallowed hard. "Lock."

"I miss you," I growled, barely able to get the words out.

She bit her lip and turned from me. I turned around I started working on the bag, trying to think through all the things she and Gabe had been riding me about.

After about five minutes, she came over and tapped me on the shoulder. "Here, let me show you. You're still not engaging your hips enough. I want that motion to be fluid when you burst forward. A fluid motion and a quick retreat back with a spin. Make sure you're watching your back."

I frowned, trying to do what she said and realizing her way was easier. My body wanted to do it that way, but all the automatic movements from before were tripping me up.

"That's it exactly," she said. "And then you move your hips here." Her fingertips traced over my hip bones, and my dick was done for. Full-blown erection. My breath lodged in my throat as I tried to force my lungs to work.

It's okay, you put up a valiant fight, mate.

Desperation. I could almost feel the pre-cum leaking out of the tip.

Fuck, fuck, fuck, fuck, fuck.

She was barely touching me, and certainly wasn't touching me sexually, and I was so close to fucking coming.

She must have realized we were touching because she abruptly released me.

"I miss how you feel," I whispered, my voice sounding like it was borne out of cement. "May I assume you're in here because you needed to hit things too?"

Her dark gaze flickered to mine. "I needed a tension reliever."

Fuck me. I would give her one hell of a tension reliever.

"Want to get the pads out? I'll hold for you, and you hold for me."

She nodded. "Fair enough."

I held first, and Saff did not hold back. Christ, she was fiery and angry and in full warrior mode, her frustration evident in every strike.

My dick wanted to crow, *Don't talk to me about frustrated.*

My next reset wasn't fast enough, making her knuckles glid past the pad, nearly giving me a love tap. She stopped her motion just in time by adjusting her hips. "Shit sorry."

"I know you want to hit me," I teased.

"I don't want to hit you, Lock."

"I'm sure you want to hit me a little," I goaded her. "Go on. I deserve it."

"If I thought it would do any good, I would. But it wouldn't help." She started to take off her gloves, and I rushed to stop her. If she took off the gloves, this was over. She would go back to hating me. And it felt good to have a truce.

"Want to see what I've learned in the last couple weeks?" I rushed to say.

She laughed. "Lock, we're both tired."

I tossed her the pads. "Go on. I can take it. You've taught me well."

She lifted a brow. "You recognize having the pads is for your benefit, right?"

"Are you scared?"

"I'm not scared, Lock." She pressed her lips firmly together, and I could see when she decided. "Fine. If you can put me down, you get the gym. How's that?"

"And if I can't?"

"You go find somewhere else to take out your frustrations."

This was going to end badly. I could feel it.

She bounced around me a little. That was one thing she always did when she was fighting someone bigger than herself. Whenever she fought someone more her size, there was a lot less dancing. When she got one of us larger men, she always danced a little. As if forcing herself to be springy and light and quick on her feet. She faked to the right.

A move I was well acquainted with. As she did so, I hooked my foot behind hers and pulled forward, making her lose her balance. She was headed for a fall down onto the padded mats, but I wrapped my arms around her to hold her steady. "It's no fun if you're not trying."

She shoved my shoulders. "I *am* trying."

"Try harder, Saff."

She smiled at me and lunged. She came at me quick with kicks and a flying knee jump.

I caught her knee easily and tossed her on the ground.

When I reached for her, she easily rolled out of the way and flipped out a kick, catching me in the shin just below the knee. I stumbled but didn't fall.

Before I could even right myself she was on her feet, and using my leg as a ladder, she launched herself up, hooking the other leg around my back and her arm around my neck.

From behind, her legs wrapped around my waist. In my ear, her breath was warm and her voice was soft. I could feel every pant. I could feel her heart rate against my back as well as her breasts. In my ear, she whispered, "Come on, give up."

She wasn't squeezing hard enough, and she knew it. If she'd wanted to, she could have had me out in seconds just by holding the chokehold a little tighter.

"Never." I dropped my other knee, rolled her on her back, and delivered an elbow that forced her to release me. I rolled on top of her, grabbing her by the wrists and putting my whole weight on her torso. "Stop fucking moving, or you will hurt yourself."

"Fuck you, Lock."

"I know you're missing it too."

She tried to buck me up with her hips. But at that angle, all she was doing was bringing her hips in contact with my dick.

The more she did it, the more I clenched my jaw to stop a moan from escaping.

Her eyes went wide when she realized that I was growing. Thickening. She lifted her hips again. This time her motion was more of a hip roll, and a little moan escaped her lips. "Fuck," she whispered.

I knew I should release her. I was playing with fire. But I just couldn't find the fucks to give.

I leaned forward, close to her lips. "Yield."

She lifted at her chin, even though she was at a disadvantage. "Never."

And this time when she lifted her hips, she deliberately undulated along the length of my dick.

I dropped my forehead to hers. "Fuck me."

My lips crashing on hers wasn't planned. But goddamn it to hell, I couldn't stop. She was my kryptonite, and I was going to die if I didn't have her. Maybe this one last time. I rubbed my dick against her heat, and instead of squirming to be released, she moaned again. My tongue dipped into her mouth, and she shuddered. When I pulled back, my gaze locked on hers.

All she did was whisper, "Lock, please."

And that was all I needed to hear. In less than five seconds, I had her leggings dragged down, my shorts off and I was filling her slick, tight pussy in one brutal thrust.

There was no finesse. No love words, no tender caresses. We were desperate and short on time and could be discovered at any moment. All I could do was bury my face in her neck, slid a hand under her shirt, fight with her sports bra, and pump her full of my cock.

I was lost to the sensations as her hands dug in my hair, holding me in position. Her hips lifting to meet mine with every harsh thrust. And the constant murmur of my name on her tongue.

When she started to get louder, with her, 'Oh God, yes there,' And her, 'Please please please,' I bit her on the shoulder.

"Hush, or I'll be forced to make you come with an audience. There's no way I'm stopping."

I felt her quiver around my cock. I knew what was coming. The maelstrom that was headed for us. I wanted to take longer. To draw it out. But I couldn't. Because then she actively squeezed me from the inside and all I could do was throw my head back and grunt as I filled her with cum.

Her nails on my back were going to leave marks for days. I could feel the blood welling to the surface as she clawed at me trying to drag me deeper.

I don't know how long we lay there, on the mats, her quivering around me with aftershocks, my cock refusing to go down. But I managed to drag my head up to meet her gaze.

I was lost. We both were.

———

Saffron

I COULD FEEL his eyes on me. The heat of them, the way he watched me.

All I could think about was how he'd bit my shoulder and told me to be quiet or he would make me come with somebody watching.

Christ in heaven. I squeezed my thighs together, trying not to think about it. Trying not to think of him and the way his hands gripped my hips. His snarl of dissatisfaction when he couldn't get to me quickly enough. The way his big hands had wrapped around my ankles and dragged me to him when I tried to squirm away because it was too intense, too much.

My fingertips played across my lips, and in my peripheral vision, I could feel him. The smugness came off him in waves. He knew what I was thinking about.

Unfortunately, I got the distinct impression Tabatha did too. Because she looked over and lifted her brow as she assessed me.

I deliberately looked away.

When Gabe came in, he gave each of us a nod. "All right, the gang is all here. I recognize there were some ruffled feathers over our association with Mr. Webster, but he has yielded actionable intel."

I immediately sat forward. "What?"

Gabe nodded. "Yep. We have Graciella. We need an agile team, small and flexible. You won't have much support."

I couldn't help it. I immediately glanced over to Lock. That was us. "No support from other divisions?"

He shook his head. "The way Oversite sees this, it's our mistake to correct. We might get supplies if needed, but nothing else. So we have to move quickly. We don't know what she's doing back in New York or how long she'll be there. We can assume it has to do with Antonio."

I cursed under my breath. "Why would she go back? What did she leave behind?"

"That's what we need to find out. We have a capture order on her. Bring her back."

Lock's voice was low when he asked, "Is that a dead or alive order, or *distinctly* alive?"

Gabe sighed. "The request is alive unless absolutely necessary."

Graciela Natanya owed us blood. But we were Rogues, not the kind of people who killed people in cold blood.

"It'll be a small team. Saff, Lock, that's you, pick two others. All your initial com setups are still there, so you will have the equipment when you get there. She's headed to her favorite spa. You'll go in as staff."

"Security?" I asked.

Gabe shrugged. "I don't know anything about it, and neither does Webster. Be ready for anything."

"Anyone have any idea of her target?" I asked. "After slipping through our fingers, there is no way she'd turn back up in New York without an urgent reason."

"I've told you all we've got. You leave in two hours."

We all shuffled out, and Lock headed straight for his cottage.

I headed upstairs. I stepped in the elevator alone, but as the doors closed, a tiny delicate hand slipped through. "Oh no, you don't. You've got that *I've been shagged face*. Spill."

I swallowed hard and shook my head. "Nope. I do not have that face. Distinctly unshagged."

Tabatha laughed. "Bullshit. The way Lock was staring at you, he was practically salivating. He would do this thing where he looked at you, licked his lips, looked you up and down, and licked his lips again. Has he been eating out?"

I choked a laugh. "Oh my God, Tabs."

"Inquiring minds. And when was this?"

"I don't know what you're talking about, Tabs."

The elevator deposited us on the main floor, and as we strolled through the offices she kept the conversation to the new dating show on TV. But the moment we were in the residence, she growled at me. "Spill, woman. I need all the details."

"There are no details."

Except the problem was when I said that, I choked it out. A telltale sign I was lying. There were details. I wasn't going to tell her that though because she would judge me. She was my best friend, but she had a resting judgment face that was lethal.

"You have to tell me. It's been a while."

"Wait, what happened to that plumber guy? The one from the club you met three months ago?"

She shuddered. "Ugh, he kept insisting on seeing me outside of the arrangement where we just meet up for sex."

"That's probably because he liked you, Tabs."

"See, I didn't ask for any of that. I wanted regular sex on tap without any emotional entanglements. Why is that so hard?"

"You know, one of these days we are going to talk about just how fucked up we all are, but maybe not today."

"Yeah, not today because today we're talking about what you have been up to, little miss."

We marched to the living room, and I grabbed us a couple of sparkling waters. She frowned at hers. "I don't want this. I want wine."

"There will be no wine. I leave in two hours."

She groaned. "Tell me something before you get on that plane. Anything. I will take anything at this point. I am desperate."

I laughed. "Okay, fine. We shagged in the sparring room. Happy?"

"That's it?" She very dramatically threw herself back on the couch and rolled around. "Come on. I need more than that. Give me something. Mouth? Fingers? Where did he put his dick? Did you blow him? The way he was looking at you it was obvious he ate you out. But where was it? Are there surfaces in there I need to avoid?"

I pinched the bridge of my nose. "I need to pack a bag and get ready."

"You're not leaving until you tell me."

So I did tell her. And as I recounted the details for her, first her lips parted, then her jaw unhinged ever so slightly, and finally she was catching flies. "Holy shit, that is the hottest thing I have ever heard."

"Well, it can't be. Because *we* can't be. And we're about to go on a mission together, and he hurt me, and we don't work. I'm finally getting my dream, and he's supposed to quit. That was our only shot at maybe being together. But he didn't quit. So now what?"

Tabatha chewed on that one. "It was his one foot in-one foot out situation that was a problem. But he made a decision. He decided to be a Rogue. And now his rules are clear and defined. His loyalties are not in question. So he fixed the loyalty issue. And there's the perfume, the diary... Jesus, he is so fucking in love with you."

"Well, I don't know what I'm supposed to do with that."

"Hey, he's chosen not to be without you. He could have been out. But being out meant leaving you. So he stayed. But that means it's complicated."

"I don't know." I slouched into the couch instead of getting up to pack like I needed to.

"What do you want, Saff?"

"I want a boyfriend I can actually be with. I want someone who loves me, someone I can trust to have my back."

She just gave me a soft smile. "What you need is someone who sees you. Actually sees you clear to your soul, deep down to what you need. Which apparently is dirty talk and fucking on the gym floor."

I scoffed. "That sounds like judgment."

"I do an excellent judgment face. And this one is active, not resting."

I laughed. "I don't know, Tabs. We have a mission now, and we need to put all of that aside and do the job. Maybe when we get home we can figure it out."

"I hear you. But in the meantime, you'll be on a plane for several hours. So please bring lube."

I grabbed a pillow to hit her, but she was surprisingly fast. She was scooting out of the living room and heading back to the offices before I could fling it at her.

In two hours, I was getting a chance to prove myself again. Which meant I had to try and focus and put Lock out of my mind. It didn't matter how I felt about him, how much I wanted him, or how much I needed his touch. We had a mission, and that took precedence. My brain tried to push out what we'd done last night as I went to pack, but I kept thinking about what he'd said.

You are mine. And I am yours. No Rogue or villain or space or time is going to keep us apart. The sooner you realize I love you, the easier this will be.

The only question was, could I let myself be loved?

38

SAFFRON

As we disembarked from the plane, Lock said the one thing that all of us were thinking. "So we're just going to trust the villain that were not walking into a trap?"

I swallowed hard. Because he was right; I did not trust Drake Webster. And the fact that my brother did was a problem. That man had killed my parents. But for some reason, Oversight was leaning on Gabe, and Gabe was folding.

So now we were in New York, a major holding for Antonio Igno, and we were going to walk into one of his hotels and steal Graciella. Because according to Drake Webster, she wasn't just the hapless fiancée of his son Massimo. Father and son liked to share, and Graciella was heavily involved in the business. There wasn't anything Antonio didn't tell her.

"We don't get to pick the mission. We have to look alive, and get it done."

Tabs rolled her eyes. "Don't give us the party line. I can tell this pisses you off, and it should."

It did piss me off. But we were going to get her. And when we got her, we were going to get Antonio. One step at a time.

And if Webster was lying, if she wasn't here or it was a trap, I knew Gabe would kill him. And despite the orders from Oversight, he wouldn't hesitate.

"All right, let's get to the safe house and get ready."

Lachlan was watching me carefully. We hadn't talked about anything that had happened in the gym. My moment of weakness. I knew what he wanted. Problem was I didn't know what I wanted.

You know what you want. You want him to have faith in you, but you can't force that.

Fine. Yes. I was scared to death of ever reliving that moment. It was one thing to have open discourse as an agent. Lives were at stake after all. But he let feelings cloud his judgment, and that hurt. And I wasn't sure if I would ever be able to forget that. The way he'd talked to me made me feel so small, made me question everything I said and did. That was hard to shake.

The safe house was just down the street from the Bliss Experience Spa. The plan was hopefully simple enough. Graciella was scheduled for a facial, a massage, and sauna. I booked Tabatha in for spa treatments since Graciella didn't know what she looked like. If Tabs was able to corner her in the sauna, she would dose her with the same compound Lock had been given during his bag and tag, and we'd carry her out as quietly as possible.

Saint was our comms and demolitions expert as well as our backup covering the exits. Lachlan and I were going in as staff.

If the sauna plan failed, our next solution was for Lock to get her. Of course he would be very hands on with her, which I didn't love, but there was nothing I could do about it.

We had been warned that she would be with armed guards. But since she didn't have a guard with her in the Winston Isles, they likely wouldn't know me. So when she went into private areas for her treatments, I would be the one dealing with the bodyguards.

At the safe house, we all changed into our gear, and I grabbed my braids and tied them into a high ponytail. I caught Lachlan looking at me with a sappy smile on his face. "You look like a kid with your hair pulled back."

"I promise you, I'm grown."

"Don't I know it." He licked his lips. "You've got this, Saff."

"I had better. We're only going to get this one shot."

When the three of us were dressed, Saint marched out to set up the van we'd procured. Once we were in back of the spa, we did our comms check then our contact inside the spa let us in through the back door. She smiled at me. "I assume you're Saff?"

"Yes, I am."

"I'm Margo. Right through here."

She led me, Tabs, and Lock to the employee locker room and slipped me the schedule and said, "The bookings are for Jessica."

I gave her a confused look. "Who's Jessica?"

She laughed. "Ugh, a lot of stars will use pseudonyms. You know, to protect their privacy."

I checked the schedule. "This is wrong, I think. She's supposed to have her sauna first."

The young woman shook her head. "She changed it. She's not going to do the sauna at all now. She'll be starting with massage."

I glanced at Lock. "You're up."

He nodded. "Got it."

The three of us were shown to the massage area. Tabs and I waited in what was essentially a green room for the massage therapists. Lock went in and activated his comm unit.

I was shocked when he easily switched into an American

accent, asking her if the temperature was right and if she was comfortable. While he went through that rigamarole, Tabs and I stepped out, ready and waiting. But I was surprised to find only one bodyguard. There were supposed to be two.

Tabatha wasn't even phased. She walked up to him and asked if he would like some water. He declined but clearly checked her out as he did so. I pretended to try and tug her along and gave him an apologetic smile on her behalf. He studied me closely and then frowned as if he knew me. Oh shit.

He called after me. "Hey, do I know you?"

I shook my head. "No. I've just got one of those faces."

But he started walking toward me, and it felt like a tank was chasing me down. But suddenly, he stopped and sank to his knees then slumped forward.

I glanced up at Tabs, and she shrugged. "We were going to end up here anyway. This just expedited things. Let's get him in the room."

He had certainly looked enormous, and even with the two of us working on him, it was hard to drag him back to the green room. We had to use a two-man carry to get him out of the way.

While we wrestled him into a cupboard, I pressed my comm unit again. Lock was quiet. Too quiet. "Lock come in. Speak to us if you can hear us."

When he didn't say a word in response, my heart squeezed. *No, no, no.* We secured the guard and ran to the door, only to find the massage room open and no Graciella in sight. In the far corner, Lock groaned.

He was coming around and rubbing the back of his head.

"What happened to you?" I searched him over, looking for any bruises, cuts, punctures, anything to indicate he was really hurt. Other than the bump developing on the back of his head, he seemed fine.

"It seems Graciella didn't buy the American accent. When I

turned to get the oils and prep the syringe, she hit me with the fire extinguisher over there."

I cursed under my breath. Tabs was muttering a string of curses out loud, and on the comms, Saint was frantically searching for our target. He said, "She didn't come out any of the exits. We at least have eyes on them with the cameras. She has to still be inside."

Tabs looked at me. "What formation do you want to run?"

I forced my brain to think through the options. We had done this before and lost her. How had she escaped?

My gaze flickered to Tabs. "Let's say you know your boyfriend—or in this case, *boyfriends*—is notoriously security conscious. He even sends you to the spa with a security guard. Not to mention he rarely shows his face in public. But every now and again we get a reported sighting. How does it happen?"

Tabs shook her head. "Mate, I don't know. It's not like she's Houdini."

I glanced at Lock. "Unless she is. Lock, remember at the hotel when we ran that grid and were surprised because there was no way she should have been able to move past us unless she had a predetermined escape route. What if she had one here too? She frequents these places. She's publicly been Massimo's girlfriend for at least six months now. But what if he's just the public face? What if she's been privately seeing Antonio for years? Someone as beautiful as her wouldn't want to stay away from the spotlight. Somebody like her would *need* the spotlight. Need to be seen. So Massimo was excellent for that because he's not publicly tied to his father's interests."

Lock's eyes went wide. "So when she wants to do something like this, she uses public avenues but keeps her private access in case of emergency."

"Exactly. Tabs, get Margo back in here. See if we can get a map. Blueprint would be better."

In our comms, Saint laughed. "I'm faster. I've already put them on your tablet. But she's got a head start."

"Hopefully it won't matter. I'm looking for where she's going to end up. I don't want to follow her. I want to beat her there."

Tabs whistled low. "Holy hell."

I frowned staring at my tablet. This was a long shot, and I could feel the doubt trying to creep in. *What if you're wrong? What if you fail... again? What if this time you do lose a team member?*

I gnashed my teeth together, zoomed in on the map, and encircled the spot. "Can you guys see that? What is that? Where is it?"

This time it was Tabs who had the answer. "That looks like a commercial building with some live-work properties. If this is accurate, it'll drop her right out onto the main street. She can walk into those commercial properties and vanish. There's also a tube station near there."

I glanced at Lock, and he nodded. "Tell us what you want us to do." His words were clear and direct, and he was willing to follow me. Wherever I was leading he was willing to go.

"My money says she's going here. And if we lose her, we're not going to see her for a very long time. So let's go."

The three of us wasted no time running to the van, and Saint already had it warmed up and ready to go. And he drove like the devil himself was chasing him through the streets of Manhattan until we made it to the office building. He parked illegally, and all four of us strapped on our Kevlar and grabbed our guns, though it would be best not to get into a shootout in the middle of Manhattan. That would end poorly.

We clambered out, and I sent Saint and Tabs to the subway

entrance just in case. Then I went with Lock to the primary entrance that would take her into the commercial building.

Unfortunately, there wasn't much else for me to do except pace and worry and freak out that I'd made the wrong call. What if this wasn't right? What if she had simply walked out of an exit we didn't know about?

My gut said this was the way, though. But could it be trusted?

Lachlan's voice was low when he spoke. "This is the right decision, Saff. My opinion obviously doesn't matter, and it shouldn't. But I can see you second-guessing yourself. You're right about this. Trust your instincts."

I swallowed hard and lifted my gaze to meet his. "Since I was a kid, I've always hated making mistakes. I know mistakes in the field mean dire consequences. I just feel the added pressure, that's all."

He swallowed hard as he paced back and forth with me. To the rest of the world we probably looked like two employees on a smoke break. "I'm sorry. I know I've said I'm sorry before, but I don't think I fully understood. I should never have questioned your field decisions. I have the benefit of not being the one in charge. The benefit of not having my head roll if I make a bad call. You have to think of not just yourself but the whole bloody team. Trying not to get any of us killed, trying to catch the bad guy, trying to improvise the plan. I didn't account for any of those things in your decision-making, and honestly, it wasn't my place. I was just terrified for you, and I acted exactly like Gabe. Not because of your ability, so don't ever think that. I know I haven't been around very long, but I'm getting the impression you are one hundred percent a badass."

My eyes stung, and I blinked away the rushing flood of emotions. He was right, I didn't need him to have an opinion. I didn't need for his apology to sink in. But having him acknowledge that my decisions carried a certain weight and risk helped a lot. "I appreciate that." All I could do was nod as I try to shove aside the emotions. I didn't have time for them. But it did mean a lot knowing that he saw. He might not fully understand, but he could see a sliver of what I was dealing with.

The look he gave me was full of understanding and love. It was the second part I didn't want to see. Because our situation was still impossible. And just as I was going to say something, to beg him to stop looking at me like his world began and ended with me, the side door to the garage opened. And a woman with dark hair, wearing a spa uniform and flip flops stepped out.

"Graciella, I'm so glad you could join us. You have given us a merry chase, but God, will it be satisfying to bring you in."

She tried to dart back toward the door, but Lock blocked her path and shook his head. "Oh no, you don't. It was very rude of you to hit me on the back of the head. You should apologize."

She turned to face me with a glower. "So you caught me. You can't hold me. Although, I am surprised to see the two of you together. You weren't fooling anyone in the Winston Isles. The way you looked at each other was too passionate. A long-term couple doesn't look at each other like that or fuck like that. But you did give me a hell of a show."

I grinned at her. "Honey, if you're jealous, just say that. Now, let's get you back to London so you can share everything you have on your multiple boyfriends."

39

LACHLAN

I WASN'T EVEN nervous when I walked into Gabe's office.

He glanced up with a scowl that smoothed out when he saw it was me. "King, did we have an appointment?"

I shook my head. "No. But this is urgent and pressing."

He sat back at his desk, his brows furrowed and hands steepled. "What is it?"

Right to it then. "A while ago, you offered me something. A chance to be more. You were right. My life lacked meaning. Direction. And much to my chagrin, my grandfather was right. I was aimless. Hearing about Charlie, that I wasn't responsible, changed everything for me."

"Oh, yeah? How's that?"

"Part of me felt like I deserved my families disdain. That I needed to lean into that bullshit stereotype. And you were right about something else. I have been an island all on my own. But the Rogues Division has taught me about teamwork. The value in trusting one another."

He watched me intently but said nothing.

"In addition, Saff taught me how to open up again." Here

went nothing. "I understand the rules of Rogues Division. No fraternization. But consider that she's the actual heir, and she brought in the man responsible for the death of two agents. And she also brought in Graciella Natanya, so now you have a path to get to Antonio Igno."

Gabe pressed his lips together. "We're not changing the rules just for Saff. I love my sister, but we're not making special concessions."

And there it was. I wasn't usually a gambling man. But there were some moments in time when you had the perfect hand.

"I understand. Obviously, you want to know what you get out of it. And the answer is me. Even if I'm not allowed to date her officially, you have to know I intend to break that rule as often as possible. I will bide my time until my year is over and then I'll walk away from Rogues and she'll be mine. Or..." I continued, knowing I had his attention now, "I stay. Complete my training, and when I graduate, I'll become the billionaire Rogue you've been looking for. Call sign The King. I think it has a nice ring to it."

Gabe lifted a brow and watched me like a hawk. "You would give up what you call your freedom for my sister?"

"Every single day. Without question, without hesitation. I fell in love with her before I knew this place existed."

Gabe sat forward then and shoved a slip of paper toward me. "It's already done, but something tells me you're going to need a whole hell of a lot more than a slip of paper to ride off into the sunset with my sister."

I frowned at him. What the hell was he talking about? Curious, I picked up the slip of paper from his desk. It was a communique from Oversight. I scanned the document quickly, and then my gaze flickered up to stare at him over the paper. "Were you ever going to tell us?"

"Did you deserve to be told if you couldn't sack up and fight for my bloody sister?"

The sheet of paper outlined that Oversight was going to lift the restrictions on fraternization between agents, as studies had now shown that close interpersonal relationships led to healthier agents.

Now all I had to do was convince Saff to take a chance on me again.

Still, easier said than done.

Gabe's eyes met mine and he chuckled. "It seems you still have your work cut out for you."

———

Saffron

THERE WAS a knock at Tabatha's door while she was in the shower. When she got out, we were going to order food, and she was going to indulge my need for grease and wine and bad movies. One rule, no romcoms.

When I checked the security monitor, I frowned. How the hell did Gabe know where Tabatha lived?

He's ops lead. He knows everything.

I tugged open the door with an attitude and was surprised to find my brother with bags of groceries.

"Do you have plans on ruining my off time too?"

He ignored me and pushed past, heading straight into the kitchen as if he owned the place. "You know this place better than I do. Show me where her wok is."

"Your first mistake is assuming that she owns one."

His brows lifted. "Honestly, what grown adult doesn't have a wok?"

"Stop it, Gabe. What are you doing here? I promise you,

Tabatha doesn't want to see you. And I certainly don't want to see you. And why did you bring groceries?"

"Because I intend to cook for my sister. And her... friend. If she can be called that."

"Don't let her catch you insulting her in her own kitchen. It won't end well for you."

My brother sighed and leaned against the counter. "I can use a regular frying pan, but I intend to still cook for you."

I stared at him, unable to believe that this was my brother. "Are you sick or something?"

He shook his head. "No, but I probably have been acting that way for far too long. I know it's not much, but I would like us to start repairing our relationship. I've made a lot of mistakes. None that can be fixed with a simple dinner, but it's a start. It's something I can do. A small part of something that I can use to say I'm sorry for how I've treated you."

I couldn't believe the words that were coming out of his mouth. "What brought this on?"

"Someone reminded me that when you love someone, even if it doesn't get you what you want, you still do the best thing for them. And while I did think I was doing that, I was smothering you. You, little sister, are one hell of a field agent. And I owe you for catching Webster. Something I had been unable to do on my own." He rubbed at the back of his neck. "And instead of saying thank you, I berated you. You are 100% correct. I am not your father. I'm your big brother who loves you, but I need to give you space."

This was all I had wanted to hear the for last two years of my life, but now that I was finally getting it, it felt surreal. I didn't even realize I was crying until a hot tear hit my hand when I swiped at my nose.

"I don't know what to say, Gabe."

He shrugged as he pulled open several doors until he found

what he was looking for. As it turned out, Tabatha did in fact have a wok. He found the oil and then made quick work of putting on rice and cutting up vegetables and chicken. "I have something else for you too. The envelope in the bag, pull it out."

I did so and pulled out the contents. "What am I looking at here?"

"Just read it."

My eyes quickly scanned the document, and as I read, the bottom fell out of my belly. The fraternization restriction had been lifted. And when I looked at the date stamp, I noticed it was four weeks ago. "What did you do, Gabe?"

"When I saw how happy he made you, how much confidence he gave you, I realized I needed to give you some freedom and control. So, I put in the petition. I know it's only a small part of an apology, but it's a start."

Right at that moment, Tabs came around the corner and stopped short. "What in the home cooked meal is happening here?"

I smiled at my brother. "He came to cook us dinner. Oh, and agents can date now, so you and I no longer have to hide our affair."

Tab whooped and gave me a squeeze. "Finally. Are you ok that I still desperately crave the devil's eggplant though?"

I snorted a laugh as a reply. "Alas, me too. Two smart women like us, you would think we would make better choices."

When she released me, I hesitated as I approached Gabe. He was sautéing vegetables in the wok. I didn't want to burn myself or interrupt, but if we were going to get back to where we'd been before, it had to start somewhere. So for the first time in over a year, I hugged my brother. Just wrapped my arms around him and held on tight.

40

LACHLAN

I HAD NEVER BEEN OVER HERE BEFORE. I mean, yes, I had been in the offices, but the residence, no. My hands were sweating, and my heart was beating too fast. Thanks to Tabatha and Gabe, I knew where her room was. I just had no idea what to say.

Saint had done his best to give me advice. I wasn't sure if I should take that advice or not. It always seemed slightly dubious. As if in fact there was a booby trap waiting around the corner.

Tabatha had offered me some words, but they were mostly of the *hurt her again and I will castrate you* variety. Gabe was even less helpful. Surprisingly, now that he'd warmed to the idea that I made Saff happy, he tried smiling at me more.

Unfortunately for him, that often looked like a grimace or a baring of teeth. I was never sure. Once I contacted him to ask about trying to talk to her and grand gesture it up, he had told me where her room was and then chuckled to himself as he said good luck. And then, that's when it happened... His grimace sort of looked like a smile. Who knew?

I knocked on the door, and when she yanked it open in a

huff, she didn't look like Saff. She looked, well, like bad girl Saff with her leather leggings and sparkly top that looked barely bigger than a handkerchief and was held together by an intricate pattern of strings. "Lock, what are you doing here?"

All I could do was stare. And something told me I knew bad girl Saff. "Where are you off to?"

She shifted uncomfortably on her feet. "Nowhere."

She was coming to see us.

I knew that outfit now. In my mind, I'd seen it littered on the floor of my flat. This was what she'd worn on the night we met. She *had* been coming to see me.

Well, fuck that. I was not about to be out grand-gestured.

You're being ridiculous.

Maybe I was, but with the joint elation of knowing that she was also coming for me, it didn't really matter. But I wanted her to know.

"Well, I'm mostly here to tell you that I love you. I love your smile and the way you chuckle a little right before you kick my ass. It's so freaking hot. I love how you automatically think outside of the box, even if your ideas are outlandish. I love that you're always looking at another solution. I love that you always want to do the right thing. I love your dedication, not just to your family and friends but to keeping the world safe. I love that you're an amazing teacher."

"Lock..."

"I love the way you keep your mother's memory alive. I love that you tell stories of both of your parents. I love that you have not let the grief and pain of their loss consume you. I love that when you have a goal in mind you will keep pushing toward it. I love everything about you, Saff. I know I don't remember everything about our first time, but we get the chance to actually be together now. I'd like the opportunity to start fresh. To take you on a date. It'll be nice and safe. At my flat. I'll cook, and then at the time of your curfew I will return you back to campus."

Her lips twitched then. "In case you missed it, I'm twenty-two. I no longer have a curfew."

I made my eyes comically wide. "But what will people think about my virtue?"

"When I'm done with you, you won't even miss it."

I handed her the flowers I'd brought. Tulips. She took them with a smile and then placed them in a vase on the desk right by the door. I reached for her and she came willingly into my arms. My fingers teased the exposed expanse of bare skin. And goddamn, I wanted to hold tight and never let go.

She tilted her head back and met my gaze. "I love you, Lachlan."

My heart squeezed, wanting to bust out of its confines at the joy of hearing her say she loved me. At the same time, my gut knotted tight as I waited for the *but*. One didn't come, though.

"Saff, I have loved you long before I even knew why. I might not fully remember the day we met, but the echoes of you are still there. So strong that I *knew* I knew you. You are clearly dressed to go out, so come to London with me. We'll order food and dance in my living room and I'll feed you cake. I'd like to redo your birthday night."

She blinked rapidly. "This was not how this was supposed to go. I was supposed to turn up at your loft and seduce you. Instead, you've come here and made my heart so full."

"That's not a bad thing is it?"

She shook her head. "Not a bad thing at all."

EPILOGUE
LACHLAN

I PULLED my Tesla over directly in front of the house on Lancaster Road, completely surprised that I found a parking spot.

It was late afternoon, and the market had already closed for the day. Saff leaned back, her sunglasses on and a wide smile on her face.

The rare day off. Well, a rare day for Saffron. Gabe was finally training her, and I was back in the King Media fold, at least as far as the rest of the world was concerned. I still worked at King Media, but I was and always would be a Rogue. My job was to be undercover in the real world. I usually went in once a week and occasionally on the odd mission. But even on days I wasn't on mission, I was always on campus just to see her.

If she couldn't get off campus, I was there. I'd already established I was completely unwilling to sleep apart from her unless she was out on a mission. It wasn't necessary, but I'd made it a rule.

"What are we doing here?" she asked. We'd already spent the day tooling around the South Bank and then Soho. Had lunch at one of the London Lords restaurants. It was a perfect day. "I think we've missed most of the market."

I wrapped my hand over her knee, gently inching up the edge of her skirt. Saff just lifted a brow when I said, "We're not here for the market."

"Oh? Are we going to make out in the car like a couple of teenagers? I never got to do that. This would be a first for me. Are you going to make it fun?"

I leaned back and watched her as my hand navigated the rest of the way up her skirt. "I think we can arrange that. It's almost sunset. The windows are mostly tinted. We can make this all sorts of fun."

"On Lancaster Road? Shouldn't we be on Primrose Hill or something?"

I shook my head. "Nope. This place is special."

"All right, I'll bite. Why is this place special?"

I swallowed hard. I didn't want to rush the moment. I wanted to savor everything about her expression. I was also terrified because what if she hated this? What if she hated the whole idea of it? I loved her. I knew she loved me. And yes, I had proposed.

But what if this idea seemed too big, too grand, too much?

She squirmed under my fingers that had halted right before they skimmed her knickers. "Don't tease me."

I gave her a wicked grin. "Well, I'm not trying to tease you. I'm trying to work up the courage to tell you something."

Her eyes went gravely serious. "No changing your mind, King. You're stuck with me."

I blinked at her, taking a moment to let her words set in. "Woman, are you mad?" I leaned forward, sliding my hand around her neck and tugging her forward. "I'm absolutely bonkers about you. I have big plans for putting many babies in that flawless figure of yours. I look forward to you training our children into badass agents. I want it *all* with you. Why would you think I had changed my mind?"

"Something has been on your mind, and you don't want to talk about it. Every time I even broach the subject that something might be wrong, you change the topic. What am I supposed to think?"

"All day you've been thinking I was trying to back out?"

She shrugged. "I don't know. You were taking the long way around something."

Very deliberately, I slid her panties to the side and stroked over her clit. "So this morning in the shower, that was me not communicating?"

She ducked her head, giving me a shy smile. My cock immediately hardened at the memory of sliding into her arse. The way she begged me to come inside her, panting my name, asking me for everything that I had.

"Well, my arse is quite delectable."

I leaned forward, brushing my lips over hers. "On that you will get zero argument from me. Matter of fact, I want to rain kisses on it later. But we're not done with this topic of conversation. What exactly did you think was happening this afternoon when we had lunch and strolled around the Victoria and Albert? And every two minutes I kept kissing you and telling you how much I love you?"

"My mind has been going wild trying to think of all the possibilities. You've just been laying on the romance thick and making me nervous."

I stroked my thumb over her clit again, and she dragged in a shuddering gasp.

"Is this romance?"

She bit her bottom lip. "This is you making me crazy."

I kissed her nose then. "It's both. Can't I show the love of my life what the perfect day off looks like?"

"You can. I can just tell that something is on your mind. And I wish you would tell me so I can worry about it with you."

I sighed. "I don't want you to ruin my surprise."

"What surprise?"

I shook my head as I stroked her again. "I'm going to demand an orgasm first."

Her hips lifted off the seat. "I know it's been a little crazy with my schedule. But in my defense, I thought you were acting strange. Tell me what's going on."

I kept my word and told her nothing until I slid two fingers inside her, her heat wrapping around me. A quick flick of my thumb over her clit made her place a hand on the dashboard and throw her head back, moaning my name.

When she started to come down, I withdrew my fingers and smoothed down her skirt as I put my fingers to my lips and licked them clean, my eyes on hers the whole time. "Okay, now that we've gotten you a little bit more relaxed, look up."

Saff glanced up at the skyline that was now growing dusky. "I don't get it."

"No. That way up." I pointed at the window.

She glanced up at the bright pink house then the *For Sale* sign. She turned back to me.

"You didn't."

I gave her a sheepish grin and a shrug. "No, I wanted you to see it first. But I'm ready to pull the trigger if you are."

"But we have your place already."

"No. That was my place with Charlie. And you obviously have a whole manor house."

She shook her head. "No, that's Rogues Division. That has nothing to do with Saffron Abbot, soon-to-be King."

I nodded. "I know. I wanted something that was ours. And I saw this house was on the market. It's got five bedrooms, so lots of room for us to grow into It. It's been remodeled, so it's contemporary style, but the exterior is Victorian. It's got a terrace and a roof garden. Enormous bay windows. A spa bathroom that you will probably vanish into."

She glanced up at the house in awe. "Lachlan King, you surprise me."

"I hope I keep surprising you. Come on, let's go take a look at it."

I went around to her side of the car, opened her door for her, and took her hand to help her out. As we jogged up the steps, I kept her hand in mine, letting her warmth seep into me. And for once, I felt like I had a home. A real one. She saw me for exactly who I was.

When we reached the top step, I pressed the code the realtor had given me and we stepped inside.

The foyer was brightly lit with contemporary art on the walls. And Saff was already grinning ear to ear. She belonged here. This was home. Room by room we went, holding hands, planning what pieces of furniture we could put where, what we would need to buy. The fantasy was taking us over.

When we stepped into the master bathroom, both of our phones rang with an audible notification. That special ringtone that we knew all too well.

Our notifications were promptly followed by a ring to my phone. I answered immediately and put it on speaker. It was Gabe, my soon-to-be brother-in-law. "What's up, Gabe? What's the matter?"

Gabe's voice was unusually grave. "It's Saint. He's been hit by a car bomb."

To be continued in The Saint...

Click here to get your exclusive bonus epilogue for The King!

———

THANK you for reading *THE KING*, book 1 in the Gentlemen Rogues Series. I hope you're ready for a wild ride, the Rogues just get sexier from here!

How DID I end up on the auction block at this charity event you ask? I made a deal with the devil that's how. But you d what you gotta do.

And if this little auction will help me find my mother, then I'll do it.

But when the door opens and I meet the man who's won me, It's not who I expect and the devil has come to collect his due.

READ about Kaya and Saint in ———>THE SAINT!

WHILE YOU WAIT, dive in to Ariel and Tristan's story with **The Prince Duet:**

I've been a prince in exile, but I'm finally going home, tarnished crown and all. This time, I won't let anyone keep me away...Not Ariel, the woman I left behind. Not the killer on my tail. Hell, not even my cousin—the king—can stop me...

➜ Yes, you can pick up **Return of the Prince** and **To Love a Prince** now!

"...a dramatic, suspenseful and amazing read
that you just can't put down. I loved it!"
———**Goodreads Reviewer**

Can't get enough royals? Meet a cocky, billionaire prince that goes undercover in **Cheeky Royal**!

He's a prince with a secret to protect. The last distraction he can afford is his gorgeous as sin new neighbor.

His secrets could get them killed, but still, he can't stay away...
Read Cheeky Royal Now!

Turn the page for an excerpt from Cheeky Royal...

UPCOMING BOOKS

THE SAINT
THE ROOK
THE SPY
THE VILLAIN

ALSO FROM NANA MALONE
CHEEKY ROYAL

"You make a really good model. I'm sure dozens of artists have volunteered to paint you before."
He shook his head. "Not that I can recall. Why? Are you offering?"

*I grinned. "I usually do nudes." Why did I say that? It wasn't true.
Because you're hoping he'll volunteer as tribute.*

*He shrugged then reached behind his back and pulled his shirt up,
tugged it free, and tossed it aside. "How is this for nude?"*

*Fuck. Me. I stared for a moment, mouth open and looking like an
idiot. Then, well, I snapped a picture. Okay fine, I snapped several.
"Uh, that's a start."*

*He ran a hand through his hair and tussled it, so I snapped several of
that. These were romance-cover gold. Getting into it, he started
posing for me, making silly faces. I got closer to him, snapping more
close-ups of his face. That incredible face.*

Then suddenly he went deadly serious again, the intensity in his eyes going harder somehow, sharper. Like a razor. "You look nervous. I thought you said you were used to nudes."

I swallowed around the lump in my throat. "Yeah, at school whenever we had a model, they were always nude. I got used to it."

He narrowed his gaze. "Are you sure about that?"
Shit. He could tell. "Yeah, I am. It's just a human form. Male. Female. No big deal."

His lopsided grin flashed, and my stomach flipped. Stupid traitorous body...and damn him for being so damn good looking. I tried to keep the lens centered on his face, but I had to get several of his abs, for you know...research.
But when his hand rubbed over his stomach and then slid to the button on his jeans, I gasped, "What are you doing?"
"Well, you said you were used doing nudes. Will that make you more comfortable as a photographer?"

I swallowed again, unable to answer, wanting to know what he was doing, how far he would go. And how far would I go?

The button popped, and I swallowed the sawdust in my mouth. I snapped a picture of his hands.

Well yeah, and his abs. So sue me. He popped another button, giving me a hint of the forbidden thing I couldn't have. I kept snapping away. We were locked in this odd, intimate game of chicken. I swung the lens up to capture his face. His gaze was slightly hooded. His lips parted...turned on. I stepped back a step to capture all of him. His jeans loose, his feet bare. Sitting on the stool, leaning back slightly and giving me the sex face, because that's what it was—God's honest truth—the sex face. And I was a total goner.

"You're not taking pictures, Len." His voice was barely above a whisper.

"Oh, sorry." I snapped several in succession. Full body shots, face shots, torso shots. There were several torso shots. I wanted to fully capture what was happening.

He unbuttoned another button, taunting me, tantalizing me. Then he reached into his jeans, and my gaze snapped to meet his. I wanted to say something. Intervene in some way…help maybe…ask him what he was doing. But I couldn't. We were locked in a game that I couldn't break free from. Now I wanted more. I wanted to know just how far he would go.

Would he go nude? Or would he stay in this half-undressed state, teasing me, tempting me to do the thing that I shouldn't do?

I snapped more photos, but this time I was close. I was looking down on him with the camera, angling so I could see his perfectly sculpted abs as they flexed. His hand was inside his jeans. From the bulge, I knew he was touching himself. And then I snapped my gaze up to his face.

Sebastian licked his lip, and I captured the moment that tongue met flesh.

Heat flooded my body, and I pressed my thighs together to abate the ache. At that point, I was just snapping photos, completely in the zone, wanting to see what he might do next.

"Len…"

"Sebastian." My voice was so breathy I could barely get it past my lips.

"Do you want to come closer?"

"I--I think maybe I'm close enough?"

His teeth grazed his bottom lip. "Are you sure about that? I have another question for you."

I snapped several more images, ranging from face shots to shoulders, to torso. Yeah, I also went back to the hand-around-his-dick thing because...wow. "Yeah? Go ahead."
"Why didn't you tell me about your boyfriend 'til now?"
Oh shit. "I—I'm not sure. I didn't think it mattered. It sort of feels like we're supposed to be friends." Lies all lies.
He stood, his big body crowding me. "Yeah, friends..."
I swallowed hard. I couldn't bloody think with him so close. His scent assaulted me, sandalwood and something that was pure Sebastian wrapped around me, making me weak. Making me tingle as I inhaled his scent. Heat throbbed between my thighs, even as my knees went weak. "Sebastian, wh—what are you doing?"
"

Proving to you that we're not friends. Will you let me?"
He was asking my permission. I knew what I wanted to say. I understood what was at stake. But then he raised his hand and traced his knuckles over my cheek, and a whimper escaped.

His voice went softer, so low when he spoke, his words were more like a rumble than anything intelligible. "Is that you telling me to stop?"

Seriously, there were supposed to be words. There were. But somehow I couldn't manage them, so like an idiot I shook my head.

His hand slid into my curls as he gently angled my head. When he leaned down, his lips a whisper from mine, he whispered, "This is all I've been thinking about."
Read Cheeky Royal now!